Peter Watt has spent time as a soldier, articled clerk, prawn trawler deckhand, builder's labourer, pipe layer, real estate salesman, private investigator, police sergeant, surveyor's chainman and advisor to the Royal Papua New Guinea Constabulary. He speaks, reads and writes Vietnamese and Pidgin. He now lives at Maclean on the Clarence River in northern New South Wales. He has volunteered with the Volunteer Rescue Association, Queensland Ambulance Service and currently with the Rural Fire Service. Fishing, fighting fires, and the vast open spaces of outback Queensland are his main interests in life.

Peter Watt can be contacted at www.peterwatt.com.

Author Photo: Shawn Peene

Also by Peter Watt

The Duffy/Macintosh Series
Cry of the Curlew
Shadow of the Osprey
Flight of the Eagle
To Chase the Storm
To Touch the Clouds
To Ride the Wind
Beyond the Horizon
War Clouds Gather
And Fire Falls
Beneath a Rising Sun
While the Moon Burns
From the Stars Above

The Papua Series
Papua
Eden
The Pacific

The Silent Frontier
The Stone Dragon
The Frozen Circle

The Colonial Series
The Queen's Colonial
The Queen's Tiger

Excerpts from emails sent to Peter Watt

Praise for *The Queen's Colonial* and *The Queen's Tiger*

'Truly, you've done it again – kept me spellbound from start to finish with this great adventure . . . You keep on exceeding all our expectations, every new book is better than the last, and I am now faced with the prospect of a year-long wait to read what you have in store for Ian Steele, and for your devoted readers. Well done, and we all await your 21st book with bated breath . . .'

'I found *The Queen's Colonial* absolutely riveting. Couldn't wait to finish it and then was sorry I had. It's going on the re-read shelf.'

'Just finished reading *The Queen's Tiger*. As usual an excellent read. The manner in which you involve all your characters in the main plot and subplots is excellent. And when it all looks like failing, you can rely on a good old-fashioned Aussie King Brown to save the day!'

'I have just finished reading your latest book and you have captured my imagination for adventure again. Cannot wait for the next instalment.'

'Wow! Peter, you just get better and better. Great theme, and outstanding description makes me "see" the environment the characters are in. Thank you for a most wonderful experience every time I read one of your books.'

'I've just read your novel *The Queen's Colonial* . . . this is a ripping yarn.'

'Once again, the first book of your trilogy was brilliant.'

'Finished the book at 3.45 am . . . When are you going to learn NOT to write such compelling stories?? I really enjoyed this!'

'I have just read this book and wish I had discovered this author earlier!'

'Congratulations on *The Queen's Colonial*. I found the book superbly written and it enticed me to read late into the evening. Sadly it is finished and now I look forward to the next escapades of Captain Forbes.'

'*The Queen's Colonial* was riveting. Busting to read the next adventure!'

The Queen's CAPTAIN

PETER WATT

MACMILLAN
Pan Macmillan Australia

First published 2020 in Macmillan by Pan Macmillan Australia Pty Ltd
1 Market Street, Sydney, New South Wales, Australia, 2000

A catalogue record for this book is available from the National Library of Australia

Typeset in Bembo by Post Pre-press Group
Printed by IVE

Image of map on page viii courtesy of the Auckland War Memorial Museum, PH-CNEG-C13442.

MIX
Paper from responsible sources
FSC® C018183

For my beloved wife, Naomi.

MAP OF THE COUNTRY BETWEEN AUCKLAND AND THE RIVER WAIKATO, NEW ZEALAND, ILLUSTRATING THE WAR WITH THE NATIVES.

PROLOGUE

Umbeyla Pass
North West Indian Frontier

October, 1863

The wounded boy would not stop screaming for his mother.

Captain Ian Steele had so often heard that primeval cry. From the battlefields of the Crimean Peninsula almost a decade earlier, through the campaigns of Persia and India, young men desperate for unobtainable salvation all sounded the same.

He lay on his stomach in the dirt of a flat space little bigger than a tennis court with other red-coated soldiers, all gripping their Enfield rifled muskets as they awaited the next wave of rebellious Pashtun warriors to scramble up the slope, shouting *Allah Akbar!* in their Jihad against the force of six thousand British troops on their tribal lands.

These sounds and smells were so familiar in Ian's life. The sickly sweet stench of decomposing human flesh, the constant itch caused by microscopic lice and the stink of human waste were ever-present. Thirst and hunger were constant for the men isolated high amongst the rocks of the slope.

The plan had been simple. Following the quelling of the Indian mutiny, many soldiers had fled and joined the rebel tribesmen of the mountains to the north. The British administration in India chose to destroy the rebellious tribesmen, who they referred to as Hindustani fanatics, and a force of six thousand battle-hardened troops, consisting of Gurkhas and red-coated English soldiers, made up a column that was to quickly enter two mountain passes, the Umbeyla and Chamla, and then push the rebel tribesmen onto a British force waiting at the Indus.

But things had gone wrong from the start. The logistics train had not kept up with the advancing troops, and the rocky ground had taken its toll on the men and animals moving into the high passes. They were not aware that a well-armed force of fifteen thousand Pashtun tribesmen was waiting for them and instead of withdrawing, the commanding general decided to set up a defensive position either side of the Umbeyla Pass.

Ian Steele was known to his companions as Samuel Forbes – the identity of the British aristocrat he had swapped roles with so long ago. Ian was now in his late thirties and had not lost the hardness of his body forged by his early years as a blacksmith. He was not classically handsome but did have the face of a man women could trust, with its combination of gentleness and strength. A pact between the young colonial blacksmith and English aristocrat had realised Ian's dreams of serving the Queen as a commissioned officer, leading a company of infantry. But now – as he had often thought – his youthful dreams had been long shattered by the realities of war. His only consolation was that he was very good at leading men in combat, and his luck had held, despite the scars he bore of wounds from battles fought over the years in Queen Victoria's army.

'Three dead in the last attack. Five wounded,' Sergeant Major Conan Curry said wearily, settling beside his commanding officer in the dust of the defended area now known as the Crag Picquet on the eastern side of the Umbeyla Pass. The company sergeant major was the same age as Ian and sported a thick, black bushy beard streaked with grey. A recipient of the Victoria Cross, he too wore the physical scars of past battles.

On the opposite side of the valley below in the hilly terrain covered in thick scrub was the defensive position known as the Eagle's Nest, also manned by a brigade of British troops. But it had been the position that Ian and his company held that had taken the brunt of the fifteen thousand Pashtun tribesmen.

The expedition, commanded by Brigadier General Sir Neville Chamberlain, had gone badly from the first day they had reached the pass in pursuit of the Hindustani bandits. The terrain had been so rugged that only the elephants of the baggage train had been able to cope with it, and the two brigades had been forced to halt for forty-eight hours in an attempt to bring up mountain artillery guns and other supplies. The delay had been enough time for the British to lose the element of surprise, essential in this section of the Indian frontier with its long tradition of resisting all invaders. The delay in penetrating the pass had allowed a one-time bandit to declare a Jihad and assemble a formidable force, armed in many cases with locally manufactured rifled muskets equal to those of the British army.

'We need a bloody relief force soon, or the butcher's bill will be filled,' Ian muttered through dry lips. His face was blackened from the gunpowder discharges of both his

Enfield rifle and six-shot cap and ball Colt revolver, and only his grey eyes stood out on his face. So it was also for Conan, his best friend and subordinate and a colonial-born man of Irish blood. Ian was also a native of the British colony of New South Wales. Although his men did not know about his colonial birth, he had long earned the title of the Colonial Captain. It was said that Captain Samuel Forbes had commenced his career serving in the colony of New Zealand and New South Wales and had acquired some colonial notions of egalitarianism. The real Samuel Forbes had served in the British army in the colony of New Zealand as a young lieutenant and, at the skirmish against Maori warriors at Puketutu, decided he was not born to be a soldier.

Conan nodded his agreement. The big sergeant major had followed Ian through all their military campaigns and was due to complete his term of enlistment. Conan had a loving Welsh lass to return to in London, Molly, who owned a successful confectionery business, catering to the toffs of the world's greatest city. But under the current circumstances, Conan felt that he would not get off the hillside alive. It seemed his and Ian's luck had finally run out, like that of so many past comrades in arms.

'Wish there was something we could do about that lad,' Conan said, staring down the slope at the masses of dead bodies, most already black and bloated and under clouds of flies. The stench of decomposition was overpowering from the two weeks of constant attacks with no time to bury the dead. The Crag had been overrun and counterattacks with fixed bayonets had been ordered to retake their strategically vital defensive position on the hillside. Neither Ian nor Conan could count the number of Pashtun warriors they had killed with bullet and bayonet in the last two weeks.

'It is hard to even see where he is amongst the bodies,' Ian said as he listened to the pitiful voice of the young man slowly tapering away until it mercifully ceased. Neither man made a comment on the young soldier's probable death on the slope amongst so many others wearing the red coats of their friends and the flowing clothing of their enemy.

'At least the weather is holding.' Conan sighed. 'Not as bad as the bloody snow and cold we suffered in the Crimea.'

'It is known that the hills around here can get snowfalls,' Ian said, now cleaning the chambers of his revolver and reloading each cylinder with gunpowder and ball. 'Do you realise that Christmas is only about ten weeks away?'

Ian thought about the time of peace and goodwill to all men and smiled grimly. How ironic life was when, back in the vaults of London banks, he had accumulated a small fortune from treasures he and Conan had looted and been given during their fighting for the Queen in far-flung lands. He had no need to continue his dangerous life on the frontiers of the British Empire other than a promise to the real Samuel Forbes that he would satisfy the conditions of Samuel's grandfather's will, which specified that he serve at least ten years as an officer in his grandfather's old regiment. A sworn oath was an oath and, if Ian survived, he would also benefit financially.

'We should be back in London at the barracks,' Conan said, gazing down the slope as the sun began to disappear behind the scrub-covered hills surrounding them and the chill of a winter's night started to set in. Conan shivered, not so much from the approaching cold but the thought of what had occurred in the bloody afternoon's assault on the hill. Not to mention what was probably to come when the sun rose once again in the rocky hills occupied by the vast numbers of tough Pashtun tribesmen.

Ian laid his big Colt revolver by his hand and brought the Enfield forward, its bayonet stained dark with blood, ready for action. The rifled musket's greater range would be of more use before he took up his close-range revolver. Ian thought again about Christmas and gathering with family and loved ones. Conan had Molly waiting for him, but Ian had no one to return to in England; the woman he loved was now married to another man.

'Movement!' Conan growled and Ian could also see the figures of the enemy darting between the outcrops of rocks. What scrub covering originally existed on the slope to their front was long burned away and provided a stark canvas for the rotting bodies of friend and foe.

'Look to your front!' Ian bawled to his weary men, and rifles clattered into place. 'Do not waste powder and ball!' His men looked down the iron sights at the approaching Pashtuns bearing ancient muskets, more modern rifled muskets and swords. As they watched through fear-clouded eyes, the small numbers of enemy suddenly swelled to a vast oncoming wave rolling towards them, and they brought their arms to bear.

'Fire!'

Ian's order was instantly followed by a rolling volley of Enfields spitting out their lethal .577 calibre Minie rounds. Death was coming again as the sun set in the valley below.

London, England

Same Time

Ella Kasatkin stepped from her elegant carriage onto the cobbled street in front of the tenement house she so often visited. It was bitterly cold and the gaslights that illuminated the deserted narrow street seemed to shiver. Ella tucked her hands into the fur muff and walked towards the narrow door of the two-storey house. She did not need to knock as the door opened and a burly man stood filling the frame.

'Ella, my little dove. Come in before you catch your death,' he said.

'Good evening, Bert,' Ella said, looking past him to a little boy standing at the end of the hallway. Her pretty face lit up and the boy walked towards her.

'Aunt Ella,' he said formally, extending his hand as he had been tutored.

'Josiah,' Ella said, kneeling and embracing him in a tight hug. 'Have you been a good boy?'

Josiah did not see the tears streaking Ella's face as she continued to hold him to her. Josiah did not know that his aunt was in fact his mother. He had been put in the care of Egbert and his wife Meg just after he was born, to hide the shame of a child born out of wedlock. Ella had been informed by her father, Ikey Solomon, that the child had died, but she had not believed him. In a short time, Ella had traced the whereabouts of her infant son, and visited him under the nose of both her husband and father for years. Meg had died the year before from consumption, and Bert was now caring for the little boy on his own. The secret was kept between the employee of her father and herself, but only Ella knew who her son's father really was.

'Josiah, you have studies to complete,' Bert said, but not sternly. There was love in his tone and the boy disengaged himself to return upstairs and complete the book he had been given to read.

'I will make us some tea,' Bert said and his scarred face, the legacy of his life as an enforcer for Ella's father, was filled with pain. Ella removed her muff and followed the big man she had known since she was a mere child growing up in her father's palatial home in one of London's better suburbs.

Bert poured rewarmed tea from a pot into two chipped cups and placed them on the wooden table at the centre of the cramped kitchen.

'Are you in much pain?' Ella asked gently, observing the furrows in his face.

'It comes and goes.' Bert shrugged. 'The doctor says I might not be around much longer.'

Ella reached out and placed her hand over his big hand. Although a tough and, to some, a dangerous man, he had always treated Ella as a father would a beloved daughter. Ella had ensured that money continued towards the welfare of her son while at the same time, ironically, her father was also paying for the boy's care.

'I fear for the future of the boy when I go,' Bert said. Ella could see tears welling in his eyes. 'Your father has told me that if I am asked, I am to say that Josiah is a waif Meg and I adopted.'

Withdrawing her hand, Ella took a sip of the hot tea and was aware of the murmurs of laughter and cooking smells in the tenement. It was in one of the better working-class neighbourhoods, but she still wished Bert had allowed her to arrange for better accommodations for him and Josiah. Bert had insisted he wanted to be with his own class of people. Ella had to admit, both he and Josiah had always seemed happy here.

'You know I will take care of my son when your time has come,' Ella said.

'He needs the love of a mother,' Bert said. 'I have heard the stories on the street about your husband, my little dove. How he beats you and spends all your money on prostitutes, gambling and drink. If he was not your husband, I would have long ago removed him from this world – even without Ikey's permission.'

Ella was startled by Bert's declaration but could see the love for her in his tear-filled eyes. She looked away in her shame for the years of abuse she had suffered in her marriage to the handsome and dashing Russian émigré aristocrat. With the looming probability of the former tough man employed by her father dying, it would mean Josiah being sent to an orphanage. She knew her father was a hard man and would not interfere in case someone discovered the truth and halted his current rise in polite society, and she knew no one she could trust with her secrets. Ella faced a terrible decision. To declare Josiah her son would mean confronting both her father and her husband. But to not do so would mean seeing Josiah placed in one of the terrible orphanages reputed to be racked by cruelty and suffering for the children unfortunate to be locked behind those walls.

Ella had once loved a man, but he was not of her Jewish faith. She still loved him and her secret of the existence of that man's son was held from even Captain Ian Steele – Josiah's father.

Part One

The North West
Frontier, India
and
The Battle of Missionary
Ridge, Tennessee

1863

ONE

Lieutenant Samuel Forbes of the 3rd New York Volunteers stood on the bank of the Tennessee River, gazing at the high hills named on his map as Lookout Mountain and Cameron Hill. He had the niggling feeling that they would become significant in his life in the near future. Maybe it was because in his youth he had been a British officer on active service in the British colony of New Zealand and still had the suppressed instincts of military experience. It had been his youthful experience of combat that had originally forced him to face his opposition to violence and he had thereafter intrigued to avoid it as a soldier.

Now here he was, wearing the blue uniform of the army of Abraham Lincoln, serving as a commissioned officer in a war that was not really his own. Samuel could have been a twin to Captain Ian Steele, but he was in fact slightly narrower in the shoulders as his aristocratic heritage had not required him to labour in his youth as Ian had. But both men had a passion for poetry and shared a love for reading. Samuel had always desired to be known as a great poet in his own right and detested all things military after his traumatic experiences in New Zealand.

Only one thing could have forced Samuel to return to war, and that was love.

A forbidden love of one man for another.

For the moment, he shuddered, recalling the terrible carnage inflicted on the Union army at the battle of Chickamauga. He had led his men as bravely as he could, becoming known to them as the Limey Officer. Under a hot sun and cloudless skies, Samuel had felt helpless as he watched his men being cut down by volleys of Confederate musketry amongst the tall trees and in the open farm fields. What was supposed to have been a crushing blow to the Confederate army of General Bragg turned into a rout for the Union army and now they found themselves besieged in the southern town of Chattanooga. The critical element of any army was its logistics and the besieged force was threatened with having their supply line cut off.

'Samuel, you appear somewhat pensive.' The quiet voice of Major James Thorpe came from behind Samuel, who turned to the man who was the reason why he was once again a soldier.

'My limited experience tells me that we will have to break out sooner rather than later,' Samuel replied.

'That is being planned,' James replied, tempted to step forward and embrace the man he loved. 'I am racked with guilt that you are in this infernal place when you should be back at our home in New York.'

Samuel shook his head. 'You know that we were destined to be together for the remaining years of our lives.

How could I remain safely at home when every day and night I would worry about your welfare? No, I would rather die here – preferably in your arms.'

'That will not happen,' James said. 'We will both survive and return home. You knew that my convictions as an abolitionist left me no choice but to fight for the emancipation of our Negro brothers. I could not have sat around while good men were dying to achieve our desire to end slavery.'

'I know.' Samuel sighed, returning his gaze to across the river where a small paddle-steamer lay at anchor not far from the riverbank. 'You know, I only have another year before I can claim my inheritance. The last letter I received from Ian stated that he was being sent back to India with the regiment. I pray that he remains safe as we both will benefit when the ten-year period expires.'

James shook his head. 'I don't know how you have got away with your ruse for so long, considering that your brother apparently does not believe Ian is actually you.'

'Charles may have his suspicions, but he is unable to prove them,' Samuel said. 'I admit that we have had one or two close calls, but either the devil or God is on our side so far.'

'You must know that you cannot return to England to make your claim on the Forbes estate,' James said.

'I do not intend to,' Samuel replied. 'I will have lawyers on both sides of the Atlantic settle the matter. Ian will be the key to making sure that eventuates. After that, his fate will be in his own hands. But I think he will probably resign his commission and return to New South Wales. Or he may continue serving the Queen as an officer with the regiment. There always seems to be another war.'

'Let us hope that *this* damned war finishes soon,' James said.

Samuel wished that he could agree but from his experiences in the last six months of campaigning, he did not see any hope of that happening. The Southerners simply refused to accept that they were beaten. Starving, outgunned and outnumbered, they continued to resist – and not only resist, but win in clashes against the mighty northern juggernaut.

*

The large room smelled of polish and a clock beat a comforting rhythm. The wood-panelled walls were adorned with the portraits of former illustrious bankers, while the long timber table and its chairs were of the finest workmanship. Warmth from a nearby hearth kept the chill of the London early winter from the two men who sat at the end of the table. The pungent scent of cigar smoke lingered in the room, emptied now of its meeting of financiers.

'The opportunities in the New Zealand colony are boundless for land acquisitions for men with capital, Charles.' The man who had made the statement to Charles Forbes was a former school friend, John Chatsworth. He and Charles had attended one of England's most prestigious public schools many years earlier. Charles Forbes was in his early forties and his hair was beginning to thin. He still had the handsome, aristocratic looks of a man used to fine living, but he had many vices, justifying them as the due of a man born to his high station in society.

'I have read that the natives, the Maori, are still in rebellion against British rule,' Charles said, gazing at the map of the two islands of the New Zealand colony.

'They are no match against the might of the British Empire,' Chatsworth said dismissively. 'We will crush them with our army and navy posted there.'

Charles looked up at his old school comrade, who had

provided wise counsel in the past when it came to financial investments. 'From what I have read in the papers, it seems that the Maori have given us a bloody nose from time to time. I am sure they are in no hurry to give their land to us. As a matter of fact, I have a brother who fought them back in '45 and his regiment were soundly thrashed by the natives.'

Chatsworth pushed his chair away from the table, stood and walked to stir the glowing embers in the hearth with a fire poker. 'I have it on good intelligence from our friends in the foreign office that we are succeeding in bringing some of the tribes on board to counter their ferocious brothers in the field. Divide and conquer, as they say. God continues to create more people but has stopped making more land. I say, old chap, this is a golden opportunity to acquire land in a colony with rich potential towards rural production. I have been there and, in many ways, New Zealand reminds me of England when you clear away the forests. It has a wild beauty, such as can also be found in Canada.'

Charles leaned back in his chair, pondering the offer. Chatsworth had already acquired tracts of land, taken at gunpoint from its Maori owners under the weak excuse of war acquisition. Charles did not have a problem with how the land was being transferred into British hands – just that New Zealand was on the other side of the world, far from the British Isles and his personal oversight.

'I will give your offer much thought,' Charles said, rising from the table in the bank boardroom. 'I have an appointment at my club this afternoon but will contact you tomorrow with my decision.'

Chatsworth extended his hand. 'The land on offer is at a low price now but that will most probably rise in the near future when the savages have been brought to heel. You would do well to purchase immediately.'

Charles took the handshake. 'You will get my answer before the sun sets tomorrow,' he said, walking to the large oak door. He knew he would accept but before doing so, he would feign indifference. After all, he had his own intelligence and knew his old school colleague had gambled away much of his family fortune and was now desperate to liquidate real estate into cash. Charles also knew that Chatsworth's offer to other friends had already been declined. So, for now, he would leave Chatsworth to spend a sleepless night, then make him a lower offer.

★

Ella waited patiently for her husband in the drawing room of their expensive home in London. He was rarely home in the evenings, so she did not know when he would return. She had stood the servants down for the evening and was now experiencing both fear and doubt. Fear at her husband's reaction to what she was about to tell him, and doubt that she should do so.

She couldn't be sure why her marriage had gone so badly off track. Maybe because it had been more or less arranged by her father for traditional reasons. In his eyes, a Jewish Russian count had been preferable to a gentile British officer. Ella now recognised that there had never been love – Nikolai needed money, Ikey needed respectability and Ella needed to please her father after all her mistakes – but there had been friendliness, even affection in the beginning. When had that disappeared? Nikolai could still be charming, but now he saved it for the society matrons and men of influence. Ella sighed. She had tried to be a good wife, was still trying to hold their marriage together, which was more than could be said of Nikolai. It was whispered just within her hearing that he found love in the arms of other women between bouts of gambling and drinking. Nikolai often said he had given up so much when he'd defected to England after his personal rebellion against the Tsar, whose persecution of Jewish citizens had become intolerable, that he deserved his little vices. Ella and he often argued about it.

Her father had tried to help. He'd employed Nikolai Kasatkin in the legitimate businesses he owned after the marriage. But Ikey had noticed that his son-in-law had little financial talent – except for embezzlement, which Ikey ignored because Nikolai was also adept at keeping Ella from her father when the mood suited him. On the rare occasions Ikey was able to see his beloved daughter, she always insisted that she and Nikolai were happy, even if she knew her father could read the evasive sadness in her face.

Ella was careful to hide the bruising inflicted during her husband's vicious, drunken bashings from her father and her friends. Nikolai was usually sorry in the sober light of day. And he always took pains to remind her that she shouldn't provoke him with her nagging. In the past, she had dared to question Nikolai on his nocturnal life and had paid in pain for the question. Now, she was going to tell him something that she guessed would result in a severe thrashing.

Ella heard the clop-clop of a Hansom cab on the street outside the house and knew Nikolai had returned, as she could hear a woman's raucous laughter and Nikolai bidding her a good night. The door opened and Nikolai staggered inside.

'Nikolai, I wish to speak to you,' Ella said calmly even as her emotions were in turmoil.

The former army officer turned to the drawing room and saw his wife sitting with her hands clasped in her lap. He stumbled into the room and flopped into an empty chair.

'What is it?' he asked irritably. 'I have to get some sleep so that I can go to work for your damned father in the morning.'

Ella took a calming breath. 'I wish to tell you a secret, and pray that you understand why it has been a secret.'

Nikolai attempted to sit up straight, his attention drawn by the word 'secret'.

'What is it, woman?' he asked.

'I have a five-year-old son,' Ella said quietly.

Nikolai heard the words, blinked in disbelief and was silent for a brief moment. Then he struggled to his feet and lurched towards Ella, towering over her with obvious menace. Ella cringed away from the blows she expected for her revelation.

'Who, what . . .?' Nikolai slurred. The news had stunned him.

'It was before I met you,' Ella said in almost a whisper. 'My father attempted to lie that my son was stillborn and had him adopted by one of his trusted employees. I have taken opportunities to visit my son over the years, and the pain of watching him grow without knowing that I am his real mother has almost destroyed me.'

'Who is the father?' Nikolai questioned with anger rising in his tone. 'Is he someone I know?'

'It matters not who Josiah's father is,' Ella replied. 'It all happened before we met.'

Nikolai reeled away, shaking his head in drunken rage before he turned, swinging a punch at Ella's face that sent her flying from the chair. When she attempted to rise to her feet, she could feel blood trickling from her nose. She was fortunate that her husband was so drunk that when he attempted to kick her in the stomach, he lost his balance and crashed heavily into the wall. By the time Ella had regained her feet, her husband was crumpled against the wall of the drawing room, moaning. Ella left the drawing room to go to their bedroom. She locked the door against Nikolai, knowing from past experience that he would sleep off his drunkenness where he had fallen.

Ella did not sleep that night, and the swelling of her left eye from the blow was apparent by morning. Her husband's reaction to her secret had had its expected consequence. But now she had to face her father and inform him that she had known for the last five years about her son being reared by Bert.

All that mattered was that Josiah be returned to Ella, no matter what her husband and father did to stop her.

TWO

Weeks had passed since the force of British and Indian troops had occupied the hills above the Umbeyla Pass. The fighting was bloody and intense and even Brigadier General Chamberlain had been seriously wounded. Reinforcements had been sent for from other British regiments stationed in India, but no answer had yet reached the pass. Lines of picquets protected the supply lines for water, rations and ammunition, and the British mountain artillery provided devastating fire support to the soldiers under attack by the waves of Pashtun warriors.

Ian had received orders from his regimental colonel, Neil Thompson, that he was to relieve one of the picquet posts closer to the valley floor with a platoon-sized unit of men from his company. During a strange lull in the fighting during the day, Ian took his company sergeant major and twenty of his men into the picquet defence, an area of rocks piled to form a stone wall with firing holes. All were pleased to leave the Crag further up the hill, as it had taken the brunt of the assaults. It was now early November and the first task Ian set his men was to strengthen the picquet post with more rocks. Days earlier, the enemy had set up a battery of nine-pounder guns in the gorge but were immediately attacked by a force of Gurkhas who slew all the gunners and chased down the survivors. The Pashtun artillery had ceased to exist.

Ian still drove his men to ensure their fortified post would be able to withstand any possible future artillery bombardment. At night, he would gaze up at the brilliance of the star-filled night, puffing on his pipe, reflecting on what lay beyond the killing in these foreign hills. There were many times when his thoughts were clouded with memories of Ella. He had met the beautiful Jewish woman after the mysterious disappearance of his first love, Jane Wilberforce. Ian had come so close to happiness in Ella's arms but his occupation as an army officer, coupled with the secret of his real identity, had forced him to turn himself away from her love for him. Now she was married to the aristocrat, Nikolai Kasatkin, a fine soldier who Ian had met as an enemy in Crimea and an ally in India. Ian had to accept that. None of his secret fortune seemed important when he thought about Ella; he would have given it all to be with her.

'The lads are settled in for the night and sentries posted,' the voice of Sergeant Major Conan Curry said quietly as he produced his own pipe and began stacking the bowl with the precious tobacco.

'Good show,' Ian replied. 'I have received a dispatch that we will be moving out in a couple of days to another position when the road is finished. We have been tasked with manning the breastwork guarding the northern section of the new camp. All our forces will then fall back to the new camp.'

'We will be a bit exposed when we do that,' Conan replied, lighting his pipe and puffing the smoke into a curling cloud that settled around his head in the cold, still air. 'We have lost a lot of lads in the last few weeks.'

'But not from our company,' Ian countered. 'All we have to do is pray that reinforcements arrive, and we get out of here.'

'The boys still place their faith in you as the lucky Queen's Colonial,' Conan said with a grin. 'Every new recruit is told by the old hands of how you have a knack of keeping those under your command alive through the worst of the fighting.'

'Nothing more than bloody luck,' Ian said.

'Our luck has held out for a long time now,' Conan reflected. 'I think it will continue.'

But Conan was wrong.

When they departed the picquet post for their new position on the northern breastwork, the enemy had watched the British forces falling back, interpreting their movements as a retreat.

Under a clear blue sky in the early afternoon, the Pashtuns rallied every man available, launching a mass attack against the northern fortifications occupied by Ian's men. Ian and his company of riflemen fired as rapidly as they could until the enemy were upon them, and the rifled muskets became spears with their long bayonets attached. The desperate fight had come down to the most primitive of mankind's warfare, where soldiers killed each other on an individual basis, smelling the opponent's body and breath, and joining in his last seconds on earth as British bayonet clashed with Pashtun sword.

Ian roared encouragement to his men along the wall of stone, Colt pistol swinging at his side and sword in the other hand. Then they came over the wall, screaming hatred for the infidel, slashing at the faces of the young and old soldiers alike.

Ian fired at every Pashtun that he saw around him until he'd emptied the revolver, then resorted to his sword. He no longer felt the fear of death, but was simply driven by instinct to kill and survive. The red haze was back, and he roared his defiance whilst the screams of the terrified and dying were little more than a muffled sound in his consciousness.

A Pashtun warrior loomed before Ian, his sword raised. Ian stepped closer to him, using the hilt of his own sword to smash the face of his opponent. The man reeled back, blood gushing from his broken nose, but then lurched forward, screaming something Ian did not understand. Ian twisted his wrist, stepped back on his heel and thrust straight for the man's throat. His aim was true and the Pashtun warrior crumpled, dropping his own blade as he reached up desperately to grip the blade of Ian's infantry sword. Ian yanked his weapon to release it from the warrior's throat, and as it came away, the man fell at his feet, his body thrashing in his death throes.

Panting, Ian swung around to ensure there was not a threat from behind, seeing the Irish colonial, Conan Curry, swinging the butt of his rifled musket like a club at two enemies, with one attempting to distract him so the other could step inside Conan's guard to deliver a deadly slash of his sword. Ian immediately stepped forward to support his CSM. But he was too late: the warrior caught Conan with a wild slash across his broad chest. Conan staggered back from the impact, and Ian could already see the blood begin to soak Conan's uniform. In his rage, Ian rushed at the two Pashtuns, smashing into the one who had slashed Conan and knocking him down. Ian still held his sword but could not bring it up to use it effectively. Instead, he bit at the bearded face of his opponent, feeling his teeth rip through the enemy warrior's nose, tearing it away. The man screamed in pain as Ian spat the nose aside and attempted to bite at the man's throat. He was oblivious to the second Pashtun warrior preparing to slash at the exposed neck of the infidel. A bayonet thrust from one of the older soldier's in Ian's company froze the Pashtun warrior, causing him to drop his sword as the long British bayonet came out of his chest.

Ian realised that the man he was grappling with in the dust was forcing him on his back, desperate to get away from the British madman who fought like a dangerous animal. Then a rifle butt came smashing into the opponent's face. When Ian glanced up, he saw Conan standing over them both with his Enfield. Blood soaking the front of his uniform, Conan's face was a deathly grey.

Ian struggled to his feet, ensuring his sword was still in his hand. Around both men, the desperate struggle continued. Ian was quick to take in the situation. He glanced at Conan, who was still on his feet and, despite his wound, Ian issued his command for Conan to reach his troops in the company being held a hundred yards back with the regiment's reserve force.

'Get the rest of the lads up here,' Ian said loudly to be heard over the battle raging around him. Conan nodded and staggered rearwards as Ian stepped into the fray, sword seeking targets. He was stepping over the many dead and dying, fighting the desperate battle for the breastwork. A whisper coursed through his thoughts that his luck may have finally run out.

★

Ella's hands trembled and her heart pounded. She was standing before her father at his elegantly established home. As a former Jewish refugee from Russia, he had grown up on the mean back streets of London, big for his age and with above average intelligence and even better streetwise wisdom. He had found himself the leader of a gang of gentiles who accepted his leadership and over the years, he had accumulated a small fortune from his criminal activities. Ikey Solomon was smart enough to keep out of prison but was well known to the police, many of whom were now on his payroll. As the years passed, he had been able to establish himself as a respected businessman, generous with donations to local charities, and able to live comfortably in his later years. But he still continued to retain his fearsome reputation as a man not to be crossed.

Ella knew she was the only person who did not fear his wrath, but she was still nervous as she had come to confront him on a subject so delicate, she feared it could cause her to lose her father's love.

Ikey's long beard was grey with the years but his eyes were still bright with his perceptiveness on the ways of the world. 'You do not visit your poor old father enough,' he said, standing with his back to the warming coal fire in his large study. 'Nor have I seen you at the synagogue lately.'

'I am sorry, Father,' Ella replied, staring at a portrait of a young Queen Victoria. 'My mind has been distracted by other matters.'

Ikey gazed at his daughter with an expression of love and concern. 'I have heard rumours that Nikolai does not treat you well,' he said in a soft but probing voice as he observed the faint outline of the bruising to Ella's face, barely concealed by the powdered makeup.

Ella moved her gaze to her father. He'd never before

spoken so directly about her marriage problems. 'I am not here because of my husband,' Ella said, attempting to keep her voice from cracking. 'I am here because of my son – your grandson.' Ikey's expression crumpled at her words, but he did not respond, so Ella added, 'I have known of his existence for the five years past and have watched him grow.'

Ikey seemed to lose his strength, stumbling to a chair and sitting. 'I always suspected that you would one day learn your baby was still alive,' he said, shaking his head. 'That is the trouble for a father who reared a smart daughter. Bert has always denied that you knew he had adopted the boy. It seems that his loyalty is more with you than me.'

'Please, Father, do not blame Bert,' Ella pleaded. 'He didn't tell me. I guessed where you would place the child and found him myself, and asked Bert not to tell you. It was also me who named him Josiah.'

'I was always curious as to why a gentile like Bert would give your son a Jewish name,' Ikey said with a short laugh, causing Ella to relax a little. 'If you have known for so long, why are you telling me now?'

'Meg had passed, and Bert is dying from a sickness. I fear that my son – your grandson – might be sent to an orphanage and lost to our bloodline forever. I want your blessing to take Josiah under my roof, to be raised as my own.'

'How do you think Nikolai will feel about your decision?' Ikey asked, his eyebrows raised. 'I presume he is not aware that you even have a child.'

'I have already informed my husband that I have a son,' Ella said.

'So that is how you received your bruises,' her father said in a low voice. He paused before continuing. 'Your marriage to Nikolai is important to my legacy. He brings respectability to our family name in a city that despises Jews. His aristocratic blood is opening doors for us. Already, the upper circles of society are giving a grudging acceptance of my fortune, and our place in their world. I have been both mother and father to you since your mother died. All I have ever wanted was for you to be able to enjoy the respectability I can never really have. A baby before you were married would have been an obstacle to you achieving your future happiness.'

'My happiness is seeing my son grow as a fine young man,' Ella replied. 'I am a mother, as you are a father. You must understand that bond that can never be broken?'

'A mother's love is a powerful thing,' Ikey agreed. 'And a father's . . . I have a strong suspicion that your son's father is Captain Forbes,' Ikey said.

Ella simply nodded. 'Josiah was born out of an act of love,' she said, chin raised.

'Does he know?'

'No. I have not as yet told him of our son's existence.'

'I thought not,' Ikey replied. 'From my acquaintance with Captain Forbes over the years, I believe my grandson has good blood – even if it is not of our faith.' Ikey sighed but all Ella heard was her father refer to Josiah as his grandson.

'Bert has told me that Josiah is very smart and already writes and reads. He is strong in body and mind and Bert has been a good influence in caring for your grandson,' Ella prompted, watching her father's face. She could see a kind of acceptance and her emotions soared.

'If Nikolai is prepared to accept the boy under your roof, you will not have any complaint from me,' Ikey said. 'We do this now, so Bert can see the boy settled. It will bring him peace.'

'Yes, of course. We can tell all those we know that he is a waif that we have adopted,' Ella said. 'Or even that a distant relative has died and left her son to my care.'

'Are you able to live with Josiah growing up never really knowing that you are truly his mother?' Ikey countered quietly. Ella felt the terrible stab of pain in her body at her father's question. Tears welled in her eyes before she answered.

'Yes. At least I will be able to give him all the love and care in the world he deserves,' she answered. 'He will be a little confused, but Bert has always told Josiah that he is his father. It will remain our secret. Josiah has an understanding already that Bert may die, even if he does not understand death.' Ella bit her lip. 'I am afraid that Bert has brought him up in his own Christian faith.'

Ikey gave another sigh. 'The boy is Jewish, as his mother is,' he said. Ikey knew he had made the best decision at the time of Josiah's birth to adopt him out, to protect his daughter against the stigma of having a bastard child. Unknown to Ella, Ikey had also secretly visited Bert's residence over the years to view Josiah's development. Bert had done a wonderful job looking after Josiah. The boy had impressed Ikey with his intelligence and good manners.

Ah, if only Ian Steele had been of the Jewish faith! Things would have been different. As far as he knew his daughter did not know the real identity of her son's father, that Samuel Forbes, while a good man, was in fact an imposter. Life was complicated, but Ikey was a pragmatist.

The most important person in his life was his daughter, but, maybe now, he could open his heart to this boy who carried his bloodline. His grandson.

THREE

Charles Forbes made his offer on the confiscated land in New Zealand. A clock ticked, breaking the silence in the offices of Charles' solicitors, and the musty smell of leather and paper mixed with the pungent aroma of a cigar Charles puffed on. John Chatsworth grimaced at the offer.

'Take it or leave it,' Charles said. 'My offer is your last chance to make enough money to settle your scores of gambling debts.'

'We've known each other for years,' Chatsworth said in an almost pleading tone. 'It is less than I originally paid.'

'Business is business,' Charles replied. 'Sign over the deeds to me, and you will leave this office with some money, which is better than none.'

Chatsworth's shoulders slumped and he picked up the pen. Charles watched with satisfaction as his former friend signed the contract of sale. Charles had known he would, and already had the bank cheque prepared. He slipped it from his pocket and handed it over. 'Thank you for telling me about how the land is rich country that can be farmed with a good return,' Charles said. 'I am sure that my future investors will be happy to hear it.'

Chatsworth glanced at the figure on the cheque. 'You are an absolutely unscrupulous cad, Forbes, and nothing like your brothers. Samuel and Herbert brought glory to your family name.'

Charles frowned as Chatsworth stormed out. It was an open sore that he could not prove the man posing as his brother was an imposter. His real brother may or may not be dead, but if the imposter served out his ten years in the family regiment, he would be entitled to almost half the family's considerable wealth. His sister, Alice, was married to a Canadian army surgeon, Dr Peter Campbell, and by the terms of his grandfather's will, she would inherit very little. Not that it appeared Alice cared, living in Canada with her husband and two children, with another on the way. Her eldest had been conceived amidst the horrors of the Indian mutiny, where Alice had gained fame as the Queen's Tiger for her courage and service to the wounded. Her life-threatening brush with an actual tiger had helped the story along, too.

So only the man posing as his brother was a real threat to Charles' sole inheritance of the vast financial empire of the Forbes estate. From what Charles knew, his 'brother' was currently serving on the northern frontier of India, where he hoped he would be killed or die of some exotic illness.

Charles was still haunted by the attempted assassination years earlier; the gunshot fired at him had almost taken his life and he could not help but consider that the man behind the attempted assassination was his supposed brother.

The weapon used had been identified as an Enfield rifled musket, and the only persons in possession of those were members of the British armed forces.

He retrieved a flattened piece of cylindrical soft metal from his pocket, a lethal Minie round that had missed him by inches. He shuddered slightly, remembering that whoever had attempted to kill him may not have finished their mission. Many people would like to see him dead, from his estranged wife to the twin sister of the beautiful young woman he had murdered years earlier. Fortunately, the body of Jane Wilberforce had never been located in the haunting ancient Druid circle of stones where he had buried her. With no body, there was no official murder. The second murder he'd committed, that of a young stableboy, hardly counted as he'd been of no importance, though the memory of both killings always caused a surge of euphoria when he reflected on them.

Charles stubbed out his cigar as his solicitor entered the room, and replaced his talisman in his pocket. He passed the papers to the man who would witness them, smiling to himself as he reflected on the killings. The power he'd held when he'd witnessed the fear in their eyes, the rush of adrenaline as he'd slain them . . . those were highs like he'd never felt before or since.

★

There was no silence after beating off the Pashtun attack around the stone breastwork. Men cried out from their terrible wounds while others moaned in the last minutes of their lives. The thick copper-like smell of blood, gunpowder and even urine permeated the still air as the sun began to set.

Ian's hands were trembling uncontrollably and he could not reload his revolver with cap and ball. Conan was gone from the battlefield. He had stumbled back to the surgeon's tent only when Ian had ordered him to do so to be treated for his chest wound. Ian marvelled that he himself had not been wounded this time as in past conflicts. His luck had held but when he gazed at the tangle of bodies all around him, he knew the same was not true for many of his men. One of his company sergeants would temporarily take Conan's position and mark the company roll of dead and wounded.

For a moment, Ian was alone in his thoughts but knew he must lift the morale of the company. At least now he no longer served under the command of the despised and cowardly Colonel Jenkins, who had resigned his commission to pursue a career in politics. Jenkins was married to Lady Rebecca Montegue, the sister of Ian's first love, Jane Wilberforce. One of those ironies in life, Ian reflected bitterly. At least now his new regimental commander was a competent soldier and fair officer.

Ian rose to his feet to appraise the scene of the bodies of both enemy and red-coated soldiers entangled in death. His newly appointed company sergeant major would take care of the routine of supervising the survivors, ensuring the wounded received treatment at the surgeon's tent, resupply ammunition, and arrange food and water for the company.

Satisfied all was under control, Ian made his way to the rear to visit the surgeon's tent, arriving in time to see the big Irishman being sewn up. The sword had opened a long horizontal cut across Conan's chest, but had not broken his ribs open. Conan sat with his jacket off, blood covering his chest. He grimaced with each needle point penetrating his skin, refusing to cry out in his pain. Ian was overwhelmed with happiness to see that his close friend and subordinate was not about to die.

'You don't get another recommendation for the Queen's Victoria Cross, Sarn't Major,' Ian said with a grin as the army surgeon continued to sew. He was in his late forties with a bald head and spectacles, and he paused in his work. 'Does this man hold the Victoria Cross, Captain?' he asked in surprise.

'Crimea,' Ian answered. 'We have served together ever since.'

'You will be pleased to know that when I have finished here, he will be able to return to duty after a day of rest,' the surgeon continued.

'I will return with you after the good doctor finishes,' Conan said through gritted teeth as the needle once again penetrated his flesh.

'But only on light duties,' Ian replied. They both left the tent when the surgeon had finished with his patient. They passed by many wounded red-coated British and Indian soldiers waiting on litters outside, suffering from the terrible wounds inflicted by musket ball and blade. To one side was the inevitable pile of amputated limbs, and the moans of the wounded followed both men as they returned to the stone breastwork to await another possible attack on their lines. Luck was still on their side, but Ian also felt that luck could only be stretched so far, and they were still waiting for reinforcements to arrive before winter truly set in.

Night had fallen and Ian's men gathered around small campfires to reflect on their good fortune at being alive for one more day. Ian could hear the muted conversations around him as he sat with Conan, sharing a flask of brandy. Ian was finally able to control the trembling in his hands, allowing him to reload his Colt revolver, and the two men said little, as they both knew that when the sun rose in the morning, they would once again face death together.

*

Nikolai Kasatkin glared at the young boy standing self-consciously in the drawing room of his home.

'So, this is the little bastard,' he snarled. 'Why should I accept him under my roof?'

Ella placed her hand protectively on Josiah's shoulder. 'Because he is my flesh and blood,' she answered simply. 'I beg that you accept his presence here for my sake.'

Nikolai shook his head and stormed from the room. It was a humiliation too much to bear. He had no place for his wife's illegitimate child and wondered why his father-in-law had sided with his daughter on the matter. After all, if the child's parentage was known, it would besmirch his own family honour. When Ikey had summoned Nikolai to meet him, he had explained that Ella would not reveal the boy was in fact her son, but continue a story that the boy was the orphan of a distant relative, found and adopted from a workhouse. As the generous money Nikolai drew from his father-in-law's considerable fortune depended on his supporting the story, Nikolai grudgingly accepted.

That did not mean he had to accept the bastard-born five-year-old boy under his roof when he was not even aware who the boy's father was. He'd long suspected another man held Ella's heart, and here was the proof.

Nikolai had the coachman deliver him to a place for gentlemen, where the ladies were young and pretty. It cost money, but the French champagne was good. Here, he knew, was carnal pleasure without the restrictive bonds of marriage.

*

Nikolai lay in the arms of his favourite prostitute in the expensive gentlemen's club. The rowdy laughter of the well-heeled patrons fuelled by champagne in the rooms below drifted up to the double bed.

Nikolai had spent himself and lay back, staring at the canopy. The bed was warm and the body of the naked girl beside him equally so.

'What are you thinking, my dear?' she asked. She was in her late teens and had been schooled to speak with an educated accent, in line with what some of the patrons desired to hear. The girl was intelligent, and this had helped her with the aristocratic men she took to her bed. Over the pillow, they would confide confidential information and the girl would be able to respond with insightful perspectives. Not all wanted conversation when they had satisfied their carnal desires, but Nikolai enjoyed hearing an educated voice that came with a quick mind and desirable body.

'My wife has introduced her bastard son under my roof,' Nikolai replied as he leaned over the bed to retrieve a good Cuban cigar. 'I need to rid myself of him.'

The girl sat up, the sheet falling away from her breasts. 'You cannot kill him!' she exclaimed. 'For that, you would be discovered, and swing on the gallows.'

'What other options do I have?' Nikolai asked as he lit his cigar, filling the space between them with thick smoke.

The girl frowned and remained silent for a moment, deep in thought, before she suddenly broke into a wide smile. 'I have a friend,' the girl said, and Nikolai knew she really meant one of her customers. 'He is a learned man with a witch for a wife, but he is kind and gentle. For the right price, I could contact him for you.'

Nikolai wondered how many services above and beyond selling her body for the brothel the girl provided. 'Why would your learned friend be interested in my problem?' he asked.

'He and his witch wife are leaving England very soon. Sour old bat must be barren, and the professor has often spoken about how he would like to adopt a little boy. For the extra money you pay me, I can make you both happy and solve both your problems. Do you wish me to speak to him?'

Nikolai pondered her proposal. At least if a deal came off, he would not have the blood of an innocent boy on his hands, or the shame of an illegitimate child in his house. Nikolai had killed many men in battle, but he did not want the death of a child on his conscience.

'I will pay,' he said. 'But it must be done quickly.'

'I will be as quick as most of the gentlemen I take to my bed.' She smiled and Nikolai took a long puff of the cigar. The girl was wasted in the brothel, he mused. But what other choice did a young woman from the slums of London have?

FOUR

It was one of those chilly, serene evenings when every star in the heavens twinkled in the night sky.

Lieutenant Samuel Forbes sat at his small table, poring over a map he had been able to obtain from his beloved, Major James Thorpe, attached to Major General George Thomas' staff of the Chattanooga district. The lantern flickered briefly, and Samuel was reminded that it needed more fuel.

From his British military training, he could see that they would eventually have to take the high ground to their east, currently entrenched by the Confederate army. His finger traced a path across two railway tracks and a small pinnacle of land marked Orchard Knob, to higher ground marked Missionary Ridge, approximately three miles away. A mere three miles was very little distance when travelling a road as a civilian, but to a soldier under fire from high ground, it might as well be three thousand miles. Samuel knew the hills he had viewed from the bank of the Tennessee River may as well be on the other side of the moon.

He leaned back from the map and sighed. He had marched with General Grant's army since April, when he was signed on for his commission with an infantry regiment. All because his beloved James had a position on the general staff, and this meant that they could see each other on a regular basis.

But the past months had taken their toll as Samuel led his men in bloody battles to work their way to where they were now, located on the banks of the Tennessee River. He and James should not be here, Samuel thought. They should be back in New York, attending the theatre and dining in the best restaurants the sprawling and busy city offered. But James' burning desire to serve in the cause of abolition of slavery in the southern states had driven him to enlist in this madness. Samuel had attempted to warn him that war was a horrific experience, but this did not dissuade his lover.

'Samuel, I have just come from the sutler's camp! I have a gift for you.'

Samuel glanced up at the man standing at the entrance of his tent.

'James, it is good to see you,' Samuel said with weary happiness. 'What do I spy in your hands?'

James stepped inside the small tent and placed two cans on Samuel's desk. 'Condensed milk and preserved peaches,' James said. Samuel knew they would have cost at least a dollar each – a high price to pay the civilian suppliers of luxury goods. It was a far cry from the hard tack biscuits, referred to as worm castles by the soldiers, and tinned meat, disparagingly called embalmed meat. At least their coffee ration was not made from ground peanuts, as was the fare of the Confederate soldiers in the hills around them.

James opened the cans with a knife and passed the peaches to Samuel who used a spoon to ladle them into his mouth, followed by sipping the sweet condensed milk.

'It feels like the last meal of a condemned man,' Samuel said, wiping his mouth with the back of his sleeve as James lit a cigar, savouring its smoke while sitting on a camp stool opposite Samuel. 'I was examining the map and from my calculations, we will need to take the high ground.'

'You are right,' James said gloomily. 'I have just come from a meeting at headquarters and tomorrow, Thomas has been ordered to attack Orchard Knob to secure it. Your regiment will be in the vanguard of the assault.'

Samuel paused his spoon mid-air. 'Then, this *is* the meal of a condemned man,' he said.

James leaned forward, placing his hand on his lover's shoulder. 'You will not die. We have so much life to share after this is all over. No, we will persevere and win, and you will still be alive to share that with me.'

Samuel looked deeply into James' eyes, forcing back tears as he did so. 'You and I have lived through the hell of the last months, and know our time is measured in nothing more than luck. But luck eventually runs out, and I fear we will never realise our dream to be together for life. This is a foolish venture. As foolish as the time you and I travelled to London.'

James dropped his hand and his gaze. 'I have heard the talk around the tents that your men respect you for your courage in the face of the Johnny Rebs,' he said eventually. 'They look to you for leadership.'

'You sound more like my superior officer than my friend,' Samuel said, setting aside the can of peaches. 'Do you know that before we advance, I have this terrible desire to soil my trousers. My body trembles and I just want to run away. I am not courageous – I am a coward.'

'You are not a coward, my love,' James said fiercely, clutching Samuel's hand in a vice-like grip. 'Courage is knowing how to mask fear, and you are able to do that very well. Your men are inspired by your composure in the face of death.'

'Maybe I should have pursued a life on the stage.' Samuel laughed bitterly. 'I must be a good actor.'

'There is not a moment when the Minie balls are flying that I do not feel the pain in my heart for your safety,' James said quietly. 'I am racked with guilt that you joined President Lincoln's crusade to free the Negros. I know if I had not been forced by my conscience, you would never have had to return to the life you so detested. I can only hold desperately to the belief that you and I will survive.'

Samuel quickly wiped away the tears in his eyes. 'Cannot let my men see me crying,' he said.

'I have to return to HQ,' James said sadly. 'I will see you at first light.'

The men rose, both hit by an almost overwhelming urge to hold each other. But that was not possible, as there were too many eyes in the camp and theirs was a forbidden love.

★

Josiah was confused. He did not like Aunt Ella's husband, and knew the man did not like him. But the Count's voice had held the sweetness of honey when he'd invited Josiah to go on a carriage ride to a friend's house. Aunt Ella had gone out, so she was not accompanying them.

The Count had paid Josiah little attention in the weeks he'd passed under the roof of his big new residence, which had so many people in it and smelled of flowers and polish. It was a far cry from the house he had shared with Bert, who had been so kind to him. He had always known Bert was not his real father, but he couldn't remember ever knowing who his real parents were; it was all a bit muddled in his mind.

'Well, child,' Nikolai said with a beaming smile as the carriage set off. 'You are going to have a new home. Your Aunt Ella feels that you should stay with my friends instead of with us.'

Now Josiah was even more confused. His loving aunt had said they would be together forever. He did not reply and Nikolai ordered the coachman to proceed to the docks of the Thames.

Nikolai was far from happy. He'd spent a torturous few weeks pretending to come around to tolerating the boy whose very existence was a slur against his good name. He'd known he had to be patient to rid himself of the boy and had played the long game. He'd gradually convinced Ella that he would accept the boy under their roof as one would a son. Ella had been overjoyed and agreed to his proposal that they delay announcing his presence until they hired a suitable nanny. Nikolai smiled darkly to himself. Ella had been easy to fool, so much so that she had left Josiah with him when she went to visit a friend. This had left Nikolai a couple of hours to carry out his plan. He had made an agreement with his contacts and paid a generous amount of money to have them take the boy into their own family. Nikolai felt no guilt over what he was about to do. After all, this was a better option than organising an unfortunate accident to rid himself of the boy. The child was a living embarrassment. Nikolai didn't need to give the chattering crowds another reason to gossip. They always thought he couldn't hear them at those high-society gatherings, but if their disparaging whispers hadn't given it away, their barely civil attitudes made it clear. A count was welcome; a Russian Jewish count would be tolerated at best.

The carriage came to the docks where Josiah gazed with awe at the sea of masts of the great ships lined along the wharves. Bells clanged and people milled with an air of excitement.

'We are here, boy,' Nikolai said, dismounting from the carriage and helping Josiah down. He handed Josiah a Gladstone bag he had packed earlier, and stood watching passengers boarding the ship of sail and steam.

'Count Kasatkin!' A voice called from the crowd of people on the wharf waving to departing passengers. 'Over here!'

Nikolai spotted the man waving to him, then took Josiah's hand and dragged him into the crowd.

'Ah, so this is the little orphan,' the man said. He was short and bald, with a paunchy stomach. He wore spectacles and behind him stood a slightly taller, stern-looking woman in a bonnet and long skirt. The man leaned forward to Josiah, who shrank away, totally confused. 'I am told your name is Josiah,' the man said in a kindly voice. 'You will be going on a big adventure with Mrs Shortland and myself. It is time for us to board. We don't want to be late.'

Nikolai let go of Josiah's hand, and pushed him towards the short man and tall woman. He turned around, but the Count was already walking away. 'Come along, Josiah,' the short man said, gripping the reluctant boy's hand. 'It is time to start our journey.'

Nikolai watched from the carriage as Josiah disappeared into the crowd pouring aboard the migrant ship. He did not bother to wait for it to sail. The money he had paid had been generous and the couple respectable. As his carriage trundled away from the docks, Nikolai knew that he had done the right thing by the boy. Now, all he had to do was feign grief to Ella that Josiah had run away, and weather the storm of recriminations for his failure to protect her son. As if it mattered?

He shrugged. He supposed it was time to do his duty and give her a child of legitimate birth. That would take her mind off the little lost bastard.

★

Samuel Forbes had never personally killed anyone before. His role in the last few weeks of campaigning with Grant's Army of Cumberland had been as a leader who inspired his men by exposing himself to the withering volleys of small arms fire and artillery shells exploding all around them. Now, he carried his sword in one hand and revolver in the other as they charged fortified Confederate positions.

They were advancing on the feature marked as Orchard Knob and Samuel felt his men's burning determination to avenge their defeat at the battle of Chickamauga. They charged forward with bayonets fixed, up the scrubby, rocky slope through a withering fire of small arms. Samuel had almost forgotten his fear when, near the summit, a young Confederate soldier rose up on his knees from a pit with his rifle. He was only a few paces from Samuel, and the former British soldier could see absolute fear in the boy's face. Beneath his ragged clothes that hardly constituted a uniform, the rebel soldier couldn't have been more than fourteen.

Samuel brought up his pistol, levelled it at the terrified boy and screamed, 'Surrender!' but the boy responded by bringing the butt of his Springfield rifled musket to his shoulder. Samuel realised in that split-second his life was in dire peril. He hardly remembered pulling the trigger of his own revolver – just that the boy slumped forward, obviously dead from the bullet that had shattered his face. Samuel felt momentarily sick at what he had done but also realised he could hear someone amongst his men whooping, 'The Johnny Rebs are runnin'!'

Samuel quickly surveyed the heights above him and could see that the enemy were deserting their positions on the Knob, fleeing down the hill and climbing the higher, rugged ridges beyond. The Knob had not been as well defended as Samuel had feared, but when he looked over his shoulder, he saw the many dead and wounded of his own regiment lying where they fell. They had paid the butcher's bill, but he was still alive without any wounds. Then he saw the soldier carrying their colours stumble and fall as a musket ball took him down only feet in front of Samuel. A long-forgotten instinct reminded Samuel that it was vital the regimental colours must not be left on the bloody earth.

Samuel stepped forward, snatched up the colours and strode forward as the remaining Confederate soldiers desperately tried to shoot him down. Samuel was hardly aware that he was shouting to his men to follow the colours to the top of the hill. He hardly remembered planting the flag in the ground, or standing by it as the rest of the regiment of blue-coated soldiers poured into the deserted posts of their enemy, searching for souvenirs. Samuel could feel his body shake. Nausea overwhelmed him when he remembered the young Confederate soldier's fear-filled face before Samuel had killed him.

Samuel had finally killed a man, and he bent over to vomit.

★

It was late afternoon when the Federal troops surged off Orchard Knob and pursued the rebel forces onto the feature known as Missionary Ridge. It was not an attack sanctioned by General Grant, and he watched helplessly from his position as the waves of blue-coated infantry whooped and yelled as they scrambled amongst the rocks, trees and ditches on the slope of the ridge entrenched by Confederate forces. Musket and Minie balls tore into the blue-coated ranks and the horror of grape shot and canister from artillery guns added to the slaughter.

Lieutenant Samuel Forbes was swept up in the surge of his men and for a moment he felt no fear but considered how important it was to instil courage in these Yankee soldiers he was responsible for. He still carried the regimental colours so that his men could see the point of the attack and rally to him. Samuel did not want to kill another human and knew his main role as the Limey Officer was to inspire those he led. At the back of his mind, he had the satisfaction of knowing the man he loved above all was relatively safe on the general staff, behind the main line of combat.

'We got 'em!' a soldier cheered as he stopped to reload his Springfield, a close copy to the British Enfield.

Samuel instinctively glanced around for a ditch for cover from the horrific fire pouring down on them but realised he still held the colours and knew his men were depending on his display of courage for them to overwhelm the enemy defences above. Samuel forgot about seeking cover and joined his detachment as they struggled up the slope, using the trees, rocks and ditches they crossed for cover.

Samuel felt his throat dry from the exhausting effort and the thick gunpowder smoke filling the air. He took a quick swallow of the water from his canteen and glanced around to see a couple of soldiers cowering nearby. It was obvious that their bravado had left them, and Samuel felt a touch of pity.

'C'mon boys, up and at 'em!' he yelled and saw the two men look to him with terrified expressions. Samuel levelled his pistol menacingly at them and they rose to their feet, stumbling forward with bayonets fixed.

Samuel followed, crying out words of encouragement, rallying his men to the charge. For Samuel, it felt as if a stranger had taken over his body and he surged forward ahead of his troops, waving the colours, oblivious to the unseen projectiles rending the air around him. His luck was holding, and he noted they were only about ten yards from the summit. Already he could see the heads of rebel soldiers raised to aim and fire at the wave of blue coming at them with unwavering determination. The defenders rained down rocks when the rebels did not have a chance to reload their muskets and, as if suddenly a great wind was behind the attacking Union forces, they hurled themselves forward onto the summit to witness the rebel artillerymen limbering up their guns in their retreat from the high ground.

Samuel stood at the summit, once again holding the regimental colours aloft, looking down the rear slope at the retreating Confederate forces and, as his adrenaline seeped away, realised that he and his regiment had taken the ridge.

Exhausted soldiers collapsed around him, gulping in fresh air as the winds blew away the smoke of war. Some reloaded their rifled muskets, but most knew there would not be an immediate counterattack as they stood in the rock and timber reinforced trenches of the departed enemy.

Samuel's luck had held, he realised when he examined his torn sleeve where a bullet had passed through without injuring him. He sheathed his sword, knowing it was time for him to find his sergeant and take account of dead, wounded and missing men of his small command.

Samuel had taken a step towards a trench behind him when he felt the Minie ball slam into him, tossing him on his face on the earth of Missionary Ridge. As the excruciating pain hit, he had a final vague thought that this should not happen now. His luck had come to an end and so, too, his dreams for the future.

★

Ella was distraught.

She hardly heard her husband's words of sympathy for Josiah probably running away. All she knew was that somehow, her husband was responsible for the boy's disappearance and no matter what, she would find her son and bring him back. Ella knew that she must go to her father and beg his assistance in finding Josiah.

'I know that you have somehow orchestrated my son's disappearance,' Ella said in a low and controlled tone of anger as she advanced on her husband. 'If you have harmed him in any way, I will kill you.'

Nikolai was not surprised by his wife's fury, and took a step back as she came towards him, her face a mask of hatred.

'I swear on my soul that I do not know what has happened to the boy,' he lied, and felt the sting of Ella's hand on his cheek. He reacted by smashing her in the face with his fist, and Ella reeled away, crashing into a wall and crumpling to the floor, blood trickling from her nose. Ella wiped the blood with the back of her hand, struggled to her feet and once again faced Nikolai.

'If you ever strike me again, I will kill you,' Ella swore.

Nikolai was taken aback by the threat, but strongly suspected his wife meant it. She had always been strong-willed, even when they'd first been married. What a mistake it had been to think she could ever be coaxed or charmed into obedience. For a moment, he thought he could see a little of her ruthless father take hold of his wife. Nikolai wisely backed off. At least the migrant ship was well off the coast of England now, and on her voyage to a very distant land. It was time to celebrate with a drink and a compliant woman.

FIVE

'We'll get you out of here, sir.'

A voice drifted to him through his haze of pain. The bullet had caught him just below his knee, shattering the bone. Samuel felt that he could not endure any more pain and was vaguely aware that he was being lifted from the ground by strong hands. Then merciful darkness came, and the jolting journey back to the rear became a blur. Sometimes he heard himself scream in agony and other times the blackness returned, until he finally opened his eyes to see the pale light of a lantern inside a tent. Maybe he was dead, he thought as the nausea welled up. A hand was gripping his own and when he heard the voice, he felt a little better.

'How are you, Samuel?'

Samuel winced when he tried to answer. His throat felt dry so he turned his head towards James instead. James anticipated his beloved friend's need and dribbled water into his mouth. Samuel tried to smile his gratitude, clinging to James' hand with as much strength as he could muster against the agonising throbbing of his shattered leg.

'My leg,' he croaked.

James looked away. 'They amputated from below the knee while you were on the operating table,' he replied, squeezing Samuel's hand. 'Thank God for chloroform.'

Samuel had a vague memory of a cloth being placed over his face and a liquid dropped on it. He also remembered a sawing sound and the face of an army surgeon hovering over his own. Although he was in a state of semi-awareness, he had not felt any pain, and with a shudder realised that the sawing sound had to be his bone being severed.

Tears trickled down Samuel's cheeks. He had lost his leg. Nothing could ever be the same again.

'We are sending you on a hospital train to get better treatment,' James said gently. 'Before you know it, you will be back in New York and attending *Uncle Tom's Cabin* at the theatre we always loved. They will give you a new leg, and you will be as good as a new man.'

'Could you still love a one-legged man?' Samuel whispered.

James gave a sad smile. 'It makes no difference to me, dear Samuel,' he answered. 'I was so frightened when they brought you down, and I am just happy you're alive. I swear I will love you until the day I die.'

Samuel returned the smile and wished that he could embrace James, but he was hardly able to move on the army cot in his tent.

'The reports that came back to General Grant himself related by your men said how you fearlessly led them onto the top of the ridge and into the Reb's trenches. They said you were the first man on top of Missionary Ridge.'

'I don't remember.' Samuel sighed. 'I don't even know what came over me, except that I did not want to die a coward in front of my boys.'

'Well, you didn't die and you're not a coward,' James said wryly. He retrieved a damp cloth and placed it on Samuel's forehead. Samuel closed his eyes under his dear friend's touch. It was obvious to James that Samuel needed some rest before the army transferred him to a hospital train travelling north to a general hospital.

'I have to return to the staff,' James said, rising. 'You need to rest. An orderly is just outside to keep an eye on you and I expect to see you at our residence when I get leave. We will have such a grand time together.'

Samuel nodded and James bent down to kiss him on the forehead. Then Samuel was left alone with his pain.

★

Josiah gripped the railing of the migrant ship now wallowing in the English Channel in heavy seas. He'd hoped to see the land they were leaving, but there was no view through the sleet that lashed his face, and he shivered with the cold.

'Come below, Josiah,' Professor Shortland called. 'You will catch your death of cold up here.'

Josiah obeyed the summons and went below into the cramped first-class quarters the mysterious man and his wife had paid for. Josiah was soaked to the skin, and both confused and frightened. The man seemed to be kind, but his wife hardly spoke a word to him. She looked at him sternly so Josiah shrank away from her as Professor Shortland rubbed him down with a towel.

'There,' he said. 'You should change, and we will take supper.'

Josiah nodded as the whirlwind of feelings tightened his throat. Where was his Aunt Ella, who had always been so loving to him over the vague time he could remember? The scent of her perfume still lingered in his memory. The Count had said she'd wanted to send him away. What had he done to displease his dear aunt? Josiah let out a sob.

Professor Adam Shortland noticed the boy crying and knelt in front of him. 'Young man, don't cry. Before you know it, we will be in a new land where I will take up my tenure. You are now part of my family, and we promise to look after you forever.' Shortland glanced at his wife, who reluctantly nodded. 'The Count has told us of your misfortune in the slums and the workhouse and has generously paid us to ensure your welfare in the new land.'

Josiah could hear the words, but didn't understand what they meant. However, Professor Shortland was kind to him, and even the sea voyage was a new and somewhat exciting adventure. He'd only ever viewed the stinking sewer people called the Thames River, and was surprised to see that it drained out to an endless body of water with a salty smell in the spray.

'Count Kasatkin said that you have a rudimentary grasp of reading and writing, which is extraordinary for one of your tender years,' Shortland said. 'I find that a gift from God considering your impoverished background. I have many books and pray that with time, you will be able to grasp their meaning.'

Josiah could hear the gentleness in the man's voice and swallowed hard. He could accept his fate, for the moment. Later, he went to sleep in a small bunk in their cabin, dreaming of the beautiful face of his Aunt Ella. He knew that one day she would find him, and once again he would smell that perfume as she held him to her breast.

During the night, the ship plunged and wallowed in the troughs of the storm but continued its voyage south.

★

December had arrived and the battle-weary troops at the Umbeyla Pass finally received reinforcements.

Ian and his men had fought many counterattacks and the bodies on both sides piled up, but there were signs that their enemy was losing heart. Now with the reinforcements, Ian's regiment was tasked with attacking a large Pashtun force at the village of Lalu. Before Lalu could be assaulted, though, there was a need to take the high ground on Conical Hill.

'The lads are ready,' Sergeant Major Conan Curry said as Ian sat on a rock, toying with a twig and staring out at the rocky, scrub-covered hill they were about to advance on. Two columns of British commanded infantry were assembled, and Ian's company lounged nearby, smoking pipes. Ian could hear the murmur of his men as they tried to make light of what they were about to do.

'How do we do this every day?' Ian asked.

Conan shrugged. 'No other choice,' he replied. 'We are the Queen's men.'

Ian rose to his feet, lifting his rifle with the bayonet attached. On one side, he wore his sword and on the other, his revolver. Both men were bearded and their uniforms filthy from the weeks of being under constant fire. Their bodies were raw from scratching at the lice with dirty fingernails and dark stains on their uniforms were reminders of the men they had killed at close range.

'Very well, Sarn't Major. Assemble the men for the advance.'

'Sah,' Conan answered. Both men were now numb to

the consequences such a simple statement would bring to all in the next minutes and hours. The soldiers Ian led looked to him for their ability to stay alive. After all, it was always the other man whose luck ran out.

When Ian was ready, a runner from regimental HQ came to him.

'Are you ready to advance, sir?' the corporal asked, and Ian replied that he was.

A bugle sounded a few minutes later and Ian, in front of his company, roared out one word. 'Advance!'

The red-coated soldiers, with rifles fixed with bayonets, moved as one towards the conical-shaped hill. They had gone a couple of hundred yards through the rocks and scrub when withering fire poured down into the ranks of the two advancing columns of British and Indian infantry.

Chips of stone and puffs of dirt kicked up around Ian. Unlike most of his men, Ian had lost all hope of luck keeping him safe from the deadly lead balls in the air. Ian looked up to see the clouds of smoke from the fired muskets, and occasionally the head of a Pashtun warrior behind a rock. He knew they must close on the defenders of the hill as quickly as possible before the men firing at them could reload their cumbersome weapons.

Ian raised his rifle above his head and yelled as loud as he could above the ear-shattering sound of Enfields being fired from his men.

'Charge!'

The company broke into a stumbling, clawing scramble up the hill. Ian was first into the enemy's defensive position. Without conscious thought, he fired at point-blank range at a Pashtun warrior who'd risen from behind a slab of rock with a sword. The warrior fell when the Minie bullet took him, and Ian stepped over the dead man to engage another warrior, also armed with a sword. Ian thrust with the long bayonet, and his deft move caught the Pashtun in the chest.

He was vaguely aware that his men were similarly caught up in hand-to-hand fighting all around him. Men on both sides screamed in their last seconds of life, others cursed and a few grunted as they grappled with their foe.

Ian noticed that the Pashtun were retreating down the hill and knew his company had taken their objective. His concern now was to rally his company, ensuring a counter-attack did not dislodge them from their hard-fought gain. He looked around for Conan and saw him dressing down a young soldier for losing his rifle. Ian tried to grin but felt physically and mentally exhausted. His hands trembled uncontrollably as his mind attempted to block out the last few minutes.

'Sarn't Major,' Ian called loudly. 'Take count for our roll call and ensure platoon commanders deploy their men to defensive positions.' A few hundred yards away, Ian could see that the second column had also swept the hill clear of Pashtun warriors.

Ian now had to return to regimental HQ to be briefed by his colonel. Colonel Thompson kept the briefing with his company commanders short.

'Gentlemen, I have been advised that we are to pursue the enemy immediately,' he said to the weary officers standing around him. 'We have the Pashtun on the run, and we will not allow him time to gather his wits. Our next objective is Lalu. Are there any questions?' No questions were asked, and the officers dispersed to their companies to issue the colonel's order.

Once again, Ian stood in front of what was left of his company and gave the order to advance. But as he marched, his thoughts drifted. Utmost among them was that he only had a year of service before he could claim his reward from the pact he had made with the real Samuel Forbes, who was no doubt tucked up in his luxurious home in New York, watching as the Americans killed each other in their bloody civil war. All Ian had to do was survive, and then he could go home to the colony of New South Wales with his gathered fortune.

★

Ikey Solomon stared at his daughter's bruised face and his dark expression was one that terrified those who knew him. Ella stood in his living room, trembling, and he walked over to his princess and took her in his arms.

'Did Nikolai do this to you?' he asked with the growl of a bear.

'Yes. It is not the first time, and I'm sure it won't be the last,' Ella said, tucking her head against her father's broad chest. 'Papa, Josiah is missing. And I know Nikolai is responsible.'

'What do you mean by missing?' Ikey queried with a frown.

'I thought that my husband had accepted Josiah living under his roof and I let my guard down. I was away for a couple of hours and when I returned, Nikolai said that Josiah had run away. Our maid was on an errand and is not able to tell me what actually happened. I just know that something terrible has happened to my son – your grandson.'

Ella's reminder of the relationship Josiah had with Ikey caused him to still. He stepped back, producing a clean handkerchief for Ella to wipe the tears from her eyes.

'Are you absolutely sure that Nikolai is responsible for Josiah's disappearance?' Ikey asked.

Ella exhaled a heavy breath. 'I am sure, Papa.'

'Then your husband will have to answer to me.' Ikey's fury at the irrefutable evidence that Nikolai was beating his daughter was carefully controlled. It was bad enough that the man he called his son-in-law embezzled from the companies Ikey had put him in control of, but he was now blatantly abusing Ikey's cherished princess and had taken away the person she loved most in the world. 'My little princess, I swear to you that your husband will never again hurt you. I promise I will do everything in my power to find my grandson. I know a man who can help me.'

Ella burst into tears, clinging to her father, relief and hope rising in her. Her father always kept his word – it was how he'd long maintained the most fearsome reputation in the underworld of London criminals. No sane man crossed Ikey Solomon and expected to live.

★

Bert was summoned to Ikey's office and the two men met as friends rather than employee and employer. Bert had been retired from the services of Ikey a couple of years earlier and Ikey was genuinely distressed to see the poor physical appearance of the man who had been one of his chief enforcers. The flesh had melted away from Bert's body and the ravages of the illness were obvious in the once tough man's eyes.

Ikey poured a tumbler of scotch for Bert as he sat down at Ikey's desk.

'L'chaim,' Ikey said, raising his glass.

Bert picked up his glass and took a long swig. 'I know why I am here, Mr Solomon,' he said, placing his empty glass on the desk. 'I have heard that Josiah is missing. I feel that lowlife husband of my little dove has something to do with it. How can I help?'

Ikey sat back in his chair, pouring more scotch into Bert's empty glass. 'I think we need to meet with Inspector Field and pay for his services,' Ikey said.

Bert looked startled. 'Mr Field has always been our enemy. He almost discovered the secret of Captain Steele and Mr Forbes a few years back,' he said with a note of surprise. 'Why would you employ him?'

'For that reason,' Ikey replied. 'He is very good at finding people. He almost had you and I before a judge when we were young and foolish and he was a detective with the Metropolitan. Now that he is a private detective, he has no interest in what we were then. There are rumours he is considering retirement from his private practice and I can promise him a good bonus before he finally retires from chasing villains.'

Bert nodded. What Ikey said made sense. Someone once said you fight fire with fire, and Charles Frederick Field was famous in London circles for the cases he had taken on, both as a serving police officer and later as a private detective, although his continued use of the term 'inspector' did not sit well with his former colleagues.

The private investigator was bemused to see who his client was when Bert and Ikey attended his offices. The portly man with large, moist eyes and a husky voice was approaching his sixties and nothing much surprised him anymore. He leaned back in his chair and smiled. 'Mr Solomon, how strange you should consider employing me to assist with your problems,' Field said, enjoying the moment. He'd sought to nab Ikey Solomon for years and now here he was, asking for his help. 'How can I assist you?'

Ikey leaned forward and explained the situation. Field nodded, but said, 'You know the boy might already be dead?'

'I am aware, Inspector. But I would like to know all the same,' Ikey replied, producing a leather purse and sliding it along the desk. 'I think that should cover your costs, with a generous amount to inspire your professional instincts.'

Field agreed.

SIX

The lantern flickered in the chilly night air atop the small hill amongst the copse of ancient trees. The man had chosen the night as very few – if any – travellers would be on the lane below to witness his actions.

The man, in his thirties, was the new schoolteacher to the nearby Kentish village. He knew he was not authorised to undertake his dig on top of this hill, with its small ring of stones. No local villager would dare dig here, as it was superstitiously known as a place where the Druids had practised their bloody rites before the Roman legions came to hunt the religious men down. Many locals swore they had seen ghostly figures of the ancient ones on moonless nights, capering and chanting atop the tree-covered hill. For centuries, the place had been avoided, as no sane person would dare intrude on the home of dark spirits.

Cecil Smith came from London where he had studied

the classics and had a particular interest in the Roman occupation of England. He had heard from his young students about the hill and its mysterious circle of stones. In the back of his mind, he had mulled over the possibility that there may be Celtic ornaments buried in the earth of the hill, imagining there might even be gold amulets worth more than his annual salary as a schoolteacher in this backwater. The discovery of such artefacts might even bring him fame, and a better teaching position at a prestigious school back in London.

An owl hooted and Cecil shivered, attempting to prevent the villagers' superstition from affecting him as he bent and took the first shovel of earth from the mossy ground at the centre of the stone circle. The lantern flickered and the starry night sky began to fill with dark clouds. No matter how much he silently tried to convince himself that the hill was just a hill, he still felt his skin crawl.

But Cecil Smith shook off the creeping fear to continue removing earth in search of his hoped-for treasure. He had gone down about two feet when his shovel bit into something firm. It was not a rock, but something the shovel would not easily penetrate. Drawing the lantern close to its edge, Cecil placed his shovel aside and bent down to the small trench he had excavated. He used his hands to clear away the loose earth from the mysterious object and saw it was a rotting piece of material as a musty, unpleasant smell assailed him. Puzzled, Cecil scraped away more soil until his hand touched something hard. Maybe a hidden artefact, he thought, and was spurred on. But he recoiled in horror when he exposed a human skull with part of its hair attached to mummified flesh. In shock, Cecil stumbled back from what he deduced was actually a grave. Even to an educated schoolteacher without forensic training, he recognised from the clothing that this was not some Celtic princess buried at the centre of the stones.

Cecil sat down as the air became even colder and thought about what he had unearthed. He had a feeling that it was the recently buried body of a female, but for how long it had lain there exactly, he had no clue. If he reported the matter to the local constabulary, they would know he had been digging on the hill without the authority of the local councilmen. Cecil Smith was not about to continue his archaeological excavation, so he retrieved his lantern and shovel and trudged down the hill to the laneway that led to the village. He had to work out another way of communicating his find to the local police. He would draft an anonymous letter to them about his grisly find on Druid Hill.

★

English society lapped up the grisly murder case. The investigating police released the probable identity of the body they'd unearthed as a missing local woman, Jane Wilberforce, from the clothing and jewellery discovered on the partially mummified corpse. It was rumoured that the beautiful young woman had been a practising witch, and many in the village said that she was the victim of a shadowy group of followers of the old dark religion, who had sacrificed her. Police were investigating what they had determined was a stabbing murder and did not comment on local rumour, but the speculation satisfied the hunger for sensationalism for the newspaper readers.

One who read the account in the morning paper was a woman surrounded by wealth in her luxurious London house, who was both satisfied that her sister had been found at last, and almost overwhelmed by grief. Very few of her

closest acquaintances in the highest circles of British aristocratic society were aware that the body was that of her twin
sister.

Lady Rebecca Montegue-Jenkins had been separated
from her twin at birth. Rebecca had been raised under the
roof of a powerful English aristocrat while her sister had
grown up in poverty in a simple Kentish village. It was only
in the last couple of months of Jane's life that the two sisters
had secretly reunited. Their time together had been short
as Jane had suddenly disappeared, and Rebecca knew deep
in her soul that she had been murdered by Charles Forbes,
the man who had kept her as his mistress until she had met
Captain Ian Steele.

Rebecca's own husband was supposed to have destroyed
Charles as her wedding gift but had proved a weak man
without the stomach to carry out the task. Men were so disap-
pointing. Clive was a former army regimental commander
who now sat in the House of Commons, where he was
making a name for himself as an up-and-coming politician
thanks to Rebecca's fortunate connections. Whereas he'd
once been content to simply wait for his father's death and
take his seat in the Lords, with Rebecca at his side, Clive
now had loftier ambitions.

Rebecca rose from the divan, laying the lurid account
of her sister's death down, and walked to a polished teak
cabinet that held volumes of first edition books. She
touched a catch to slip open a hidden rack where an Enfield
rifled musket, normally issued to the army, was secured.
Beneath it was powder and bullets. She touched the rifle
and reflected on the last time the Enfield had been fired,
an ambush on the man she knew had murdered her sister
but one which had failed to kill him. If only she had the
marksmanship skills of Jane's lover, Captain Ian Steele,

then Charles Forbes would be dead. The discovery of Jane buried on the Druid Hill had confirmed that she had been murdered by Charles Forbes as there was no other person who had the means and motive to kill her twin sister. It was only a matter of time and opportunity before Charles Forbes would pay with his life for the brutal murder of Jane. Until then, Rebecca would continue to keep close tabs on the Forbes family. The gardener was on her solicitor's payroll and fed back all the rumours and goings-on in the manor. Rebecca was always prepared.

Rebecca took the rifle from the rack and held it in her hands. With her considerable wealth and power, she knew revenge was her right. Men so often underestimated women in the world she belonged to. But it would be so wonderful to see Charles Forbes humiliated in public in a trial for murder, and then know his life would be ended by the hangman's noose.

Rebecca decided if she could bring him disgrace before his downfall, she could wait a little longer for vengeance. Clive would use his influence to ensure only the best of the Metropolitan police were assigned to investigate the killing of her sister. He'd failed her once in regards to Charles Forbes; he would not fail her again.

★

The migrant ship rolled in gentle seas off the West African coast and Josiah stood at the railing gazing out at the distant, arid shoreline. He was old enough to understand that this journey was taking him far from the warmth of his Aunt Ella's love, but he was still confused as to why she would send him away.

Professor Shortland spent his spare time in Josiah's company, explaining things about nature and the night sky to him. 'All the stars in God's heaven will be different when we enter the southern hemisphere,' he had once said to Josiah as they had stood on the deck staring at the ever slowly moving stars above. Not that the information meant much to the young boy. If nothing else, Josiah was surprised at how pretty the stars were. The London smog and crowded tenements of his life with Bert and his wife had blocked them from his view at night.

Josiah surprised Adam Shortland too. The Count had told of how he'd discovered Josiah begging on the mean streets of the great city and felt sorry for him. But if the boy had been a street urchin, how had he learned to read and write? Education was not something the street children of London had access to. When he'd asked Josiah, the lad had simply said that Bert and his Aunt Ella had taught him. Shortland felt uneasy about this disclosure but preferred to remember the generous purse of money he had accepted from the Count. After all, they would be on the other side of the earth when their ship finally docked. Even if there was someone looking for the boy, there was little chance they would be able to find him.

★

Charles Forbes was at the family country estate in Kent when word of Jane's body being discovered reached him. He stood before the open fireplace in the billiard room with a tumbler of brandy in his hand, staring at the flickering flames, and tried to convince himself that her confirmed murder could not be traced back to him. His dark memories were interrupted when he was joined by his father, Sir Archibald Forbes. He was a man showing his age, and he had lost most of his hair. He walked with the aid of a stick and was in constant pain from the gout that racked his body.

'So, that is where you buried that girl. On the Druid Hill,' he said to his son.

'I always felt that no local person would ever dare interfere with the hill,' Charles said bitterly. 'But someone must have. Not that it matters anymore.'

Sir Archibald slumped down in a chair before the hearth and rubbed his hands. 'It's a damned cold winter this year.' The murder was merely a subject like the weather, easily passed along for the next discussion. Charles poured his father a tumbler of brandy.

'You may have unwanted attention from the police, now that the girl's body has turned up,' Archibald cautioned. 'It was widely known in the village that she was your mistress.'

'The police are imbeciles, and our parish constable has no means of implicating me in her slaying,' Charles replied, passing his father the glass. 'I doubt that he would even dare visit me to ask any questions.'

'You may be right,' Archibald mused, sipping the brandy and enjoying the warmth from the log fire at his feet. 'But one should have a plan. I was informed that you purchased land in New Zealand.'

'Yes, I got it for a song from a fool,' Charles said. 'I saw it as a way of establishing a base in the Antipodes for future expansion of our overseas investments. Our North American estates in the South have been badly affected by the Yankees' civil war.'

'Indeed. Perhaps in the eventuality of things coming a little too close to home, you might find a need to travel to New Zealand to inspect our property there.'

Charles nodded. 'It is very unlikely to happen, but perhaps you are right. Or a visit to India, as the Khan has invited me to invest funds in his mines,' Charles said. 'But

I doubt there is the slightest evidence any investigation could find to link me to Jane's death.'

A log shifted in the fireplace, causing a slight shower of glowing embers.

'I remember that Indian prince,' Archibald said. 'Did you not meet him at a tea party some time ago?'

'Yes,' Charles replied. 'He was in the company of Lady Montegue at Lord Cunningham's country estate. We seemed to have recognised a common interest in investing in his enterprises. Lady Montegue introduced us.' Charles didn't think to tell his father that by bizarre coincidence, Lady Montegue bore an uncanny resemblance to the dead girl.

'Well, if the misfortune of any police investigation leads to the doors of the manor, you have ample excuses to leave the country until all dies down,' Archibald said, sipping his drink. 'But, like you, I do not believe the police have any man capable of discovering the truth. They recruit from the working classes and we know those are men of little intelligence.'

However, on nearly all counts, both men were wrong.

★

They came in waves against the British left flank, across the rock-strewn sloping ground and through the thick scrub. Ian rallied his company and in disciplined volleys they fired into the ranks of fanatical Pashtuns. A cloud of smoke lay in the still air while the men quickly fired, reloaded and fired again.

'Fix bayonets!' Ian cried out to be heard above the crashing of rifled musket fire. The word swept through the ranks of his company. The British soldiers paused to lock the long knives onto the ends of their weapons.

Ian quickly surveyed the enemy only a hundred paces from them and realised his company was outnumbered. How many times in the last few years had he ordered the fixing of bayonets? He had long forgotten. Raising his sword in one hand and gripping his pistol in the other, Ian roared his next order.

'Advance!'

Grim-faced, the many frightened soldiers broke into a stumbling dash towards the ranks of screaming Pashtun warriors chanting their war cry of *Allah Akbar*. Each and every soldier in the company ranks knew that in the next few seconds, they would have to plunge the long bayonets into the flesh of their enemy and smell his breath on their faces. Many others tried to dismiss thoughts that they would be the ones to die or be mutilated by the enemy swords waving at them.

Ian could see in the corner of his eye Conan keeping close to him as he had always done in such engagements. Since the Crimean war, a tacit agreement existed between them that they would watch each other's backs.

Ian felt the knotting in his stomach as he had so many times before, expecting that his luck would eventually run out, and this is how his life would be ended – on some godforsaken piece of the earth that people in England hardly knew about. For a moment, Charles Forbes flashed through his mind, and the joy with which he would welcome his supposed brother's death. Ian gritted his teeth as he came up against the enemy ranks. He fired his revolver into the chest of a warrior attempting to swing his sword. The man fell back, only to be replaced by another, leaping over his fallen comrade's body. Ian's fury was at its height now and he screamed unintelligible words, determined that Charles would not be rewarded with his death.

Ian tripped on the body of a dead Pashtun soldier and felt himself falling. He crashed into the hard ground and above him he could see through the red haze a huge, bearded Pashtun warrior preparing to slash down at his exposed head. Ian tried desperately to bring his revolver into play but when he pulled the trigger nothing happened. He had a misfire, and from the fleeting expression he could see on the face of the man standing over him, he also realised that Ian was helpless. So, his luck had finally run out. Charles had won. For a split-second, Ian hoped his death would be quick as the enemy sword sliced through his body. Then he saw Ella's sad face in his mind and realised his final thought would be of absolute regret for things that might have been.

SEVEN

It was a blur.

Captain Ian Steele watched as the sword descended and he felt a glancing blow on his arm. Then the assailant collapsed on him.

'No time to take a nap, sah,' the familiar voice of Sergeant Major Conan Curry said, reaching down to grip Ian by the elbow and haul him to his feet. Ian rose groggily and felt the pain in his arm but could not see any blood as the sword had not penetrated the thick jacket. All he would experience was severe bruising to his arm.

The battle raged around them but even now, Ian could see that the shock attack from the outnumbered redcoats had caused the enemy to reel back in confusion. He could see that their bold counterattack had succeeded, and a similar scene was being enacted on their flank by other British units who had followed Ian's example of not waiting for the

Pashtun warriors to overwhelm them. He could hear the 'Hurrahs' being shouted from far and wide, along with scattered rifle fire as the attack on their flank from the Pashtuns had been foiled.

But the sound of celebration was marred by the groans and agonised cries of the wounded Pashtuns and British soldiers scattered all around. Ian could see that it was mid-afternoon and was hardly on his feet when a runner came from regimental HQ to inform him that they would bivouac on this ground for the night. Stretcher bearers moved amongst the wounded, taking away only British soldiers whilst the wounded Pashtuns were left to their fate, dispatched with a bayonet thrust to put them out of their pain. The less seriously wounded Pashtuns were also killed so they might not be able to threaten the British around them. The British and allied Indian wounded were carried back to the surgical knives and saws of the army surgeons.

Ian wiped the sweat from his brow with the back of his blood-stained sleeve. This campaign was far from over. He well knew they would have to pursue the Pashtun warriors until they were totally defeated. While Conan attended to the needs of the company, Ian sought regimental HQ for his orders.

★

At 4 Whitehall Place, Detective Sergeant Robert Mansfield of the Metropolitan Police read the unusual note he had received from the commissioner's clerk. He was to report to the commissioner in person at 10 o'clock that day.

Robert Mansfield was both confused and a little frightened. Why would the commissioner wish to speak with him? There was a push to remove drunken police officers from the force, but the detective knew he was not guilty of lacking sobriety. He glanced around the large room crowded with uniformed and civilian-dressed police conversing, swapping notes and tips on the horse races at Ascot. It was a normal day in the police headquarters for the Metropolitan Police.

Robert Mansfield was an extremely intelligent man in his mid-thirties with a reputation in the Detective Branch for his effectiveness at solving crimes. Although he did not have any higher-level education, he had a passion for books – particularly those of a scientific nature – which he used to improve on his lack of formal education. He was married and the father of three children, and though it was a struggle to support his family, his extraordinary history of solving crimes had brought him rewards from grateful citizens, especially those whose property was returned when Robert apprehended the criminals involved.

Robert had an intense dislike of the ruling class, who he viewed as parasites on humanity, but his work was mostly amongst desperate middle-class citizens, the poverty-stricken working class and the unemployed.

None of which explained why the commissioner wished to meet with him.

Detective Sergeant Mansfield found out when he sat in the commissioner's office at 10 o'clock on a cold and damp Tuesday morning. A coal burner provided warmth in the corner of the room, but condensation caused a sheen of moisture on the walls.

'I have a job for you, Sergeant,' the commissioner said, sipping a cup of tea. 'A member of parliament has made a special request for you to go to Kent and investigate what appears to be the murder of a young woman there.'

'Sir, Kent is not in our jurisdiction,' Robert said. 'Why would their own detective branch not investigate?'

The commissioner set his cup in its saucer on his desk and frowned. 'I do not question why this matter should be of importance to the state of England and nor should you. For whatever reason, those with power have decided it is. So, you will pack a suitcase and take the train to this Kentish village with written approval from my office on behalf of parliament. I have a copy of a file for you to read that has been compiled on the murder. If there are no further questions, my clerk will issue you with the relevant travel documents and allowance for boarding with the local constable.'

Robert accepted a folder passed to him by the commissioner and left the office to return to his section of the building. He sat down on a very battered chair and flipped open the report. From what he could ascertain from the doctor in charge of the autopsy, the decomposed body was believed to be that of a youngish female and still retained traces of penetrating wounds to the body. From the long tufts of hair remaining, clothing and sparse jewellery, local villagers felt that it was the body of a Miss Jane Wilberforce, who had mysteriously disappeared almost a decade earlier. There was little else except that she had been unearthed on a small hill known to the locals as Druid Hill. Robert was bemused to read that the local people of the district said she was a witch. Robert was a man of science and scoffed at that observation.

The police detective would go to Kent as ordered, and close the case before Christmas Day, so he could come home and share the day with his family in their modest tenement house.

★

News of the Metropolitan policeman's imminent arrival spread quickly through the Kentish town's population.

The discovery of the witch's body on Druid Hill had been all that the local people could gossip about from tavern to church. Many of the rumours were outlandish, concerning sacrificial rites, but the parish constable listened whenever he was accosted in the streets of the small town.

Parish constable Michael Covell was annoyed that he had been ordered by his superiors to provide all assistance to the police detective from London with an investigation into the obvious murder of the young woman. Michael had not been appointed to the village when she disappeared, but the policeman in his mid-thirties had established a rapport with the local people and knew the story well. He stood at six foot and had thick curling hair. He was broad in the shoulder and respected for being able to handle the unrulier elements in town.

There was a knock on the door of the parish constable's house just after dark as a cold, wet wind howled through the deserted streets. Michael's wife Agnes answered the door, revealing a tough-looking man of medium height, his overcoat pulled tight.

'Mrs Covell?' he asked.

'Inspector! Do come in. It's terribly cold out there,' she said with a warm smile.

Michael stepped forward, moving his pipe to his left hand so he could offer the inspector his other. 'I see that you found us well enough,' he said. 'The missus has prepared your room and you're in time to join us for supper.'

Robert thanked his hosts for their hospitality, though hers had been far more welcoming than his. It was to be expected, he supposed. Robert paused to watch a couple of well-kept toddlers playing on the floor of the kitchen for a moment. The stone house was small but warm, and the aroma of roasting lamb wafted in the air.

'This way, Inspector,' Covell said gruffly, and led him to a tiny room with a single bed and one chair. Robert placed his suitcase on the bed and shucked his raincoat. He took the opportunity to freshen up before returning to the kitchen, where he shared in a delicious roast leg of lamb served with baked potatoes, peas and pan gravy.

Idle chitchat across the supper table filled in the time until Covell's wife, Agnes, cleared away the remains and left the two men to their conversation as she put the children to bed.

Covell produced a bottle of stout, pouring two glasses. It was time to get down to business. 'I am not sure why London should send you here on a local matter,' Covell said. 'We have our own detective branch.'

Robert shrugged as he sipped his stout. 'I am not sure why I should be here either. I was directed by the commissioner by request of a member of parliament. Someone important wanted me down here.'

'I have heard from the lads in the police here that you have a reputation for solving cases,' Covell said. 'What makes you think that you can do any better than our own investigators?'

'I suppose I am not as easily influenced by the village as your people might be,' Robert replied. 'I mean no offence to you, but I come here without any preconceptions.'

'The girl disappeared almost ten years ago,' Michael said.

'Can you tell me the precise time she disappeared?' Robert countered and an expression of annoyance crossed Covell's face. He did not reply but stood to retrieve a folder on a kitchen bench. He passed it to Robert, who opened the file to peruse a scant amount of information noted within the papers, written in a neat copperplate style. The precise hand-written notes, presumably transcribed from Covell's predecessor's account, told Robert that the constable sitting opposite him had a relatively good education. This was encouraging.

'I see that a well-born man, Charles Forbes, is mentioned as having been romantically involved with the deceased,' Robert said. 'Have you spoken with him as yet?'

Michael took a swallow of his drink. 'It is not necessary,' he said. 'Mr Forbes is the son of Sir Archibald Forbes, who has a seat in the House of Lords. Mr Forbes is beyond reproach and hardly capable of murder. Besides, there is another who was involved with Jane Wilberforce. His brother, Samuel. But he is off somewhere with the army in India, so I am unable to speak with him. Neither would have a motive to kill the girl.'

The village constable's observations were influenced by the innate subservience to the upper classes that dogged the working class, Robert thought, but he said nothing on that point of view.

'It is my experience that a three-way romantic entanglement is a good enough motive for murder,' Robert said, closing the file. 'I also notice from the doctor's report at the autopsy that he found the remains of a child within the deceased. That may also be another good reason for murder. A highborn man of the manor may not wish to have it known that his mistress was with child, especially as she was said to be the village witch? Not good for either man's reputation.'

Covell frowned. 'I suppose that your observation has merit,' he finally, grudgingly, answered. 'But the Forbes family have powerful connections in this borough and beyond.'

Robert shook his head. In his work in the streets of London, he well knew the effective interference in the legal system by those in powerful positions. Robert had a hatred of those same people as he knew well the misery of the slums from where he had originally come. His policeman's natural instinct for criminals made him feel that the man he was after was either Charles Forbes or his brother, Samuel. Robert suspected strongly he was dealing with a love triangle, strengthened by the medical observation that the deceased woman carried the fragments of a foetus.

The first person he and the parish constable would speak with was Charles Forbes. It was as good a place to start as any, but Robert also had to admit to himself that, with the time that had passed since the murder, his chances of bringing anyone to justice were slim to none.

EIGHT

Detective Sergeant Robert Mansfield was impressed by the carriage ride along the avenue of tall trees to the stately mansion at the end of the drive. Sitting alongside Constable Michael Covell, who was wearing his uniform, the two men alighted and were met by a stableboy who sauntered over to them.

'What brings you here, Constable Covell?' he asked.

'We came to pay our respects to Sir Archibald, and speak with Master Charles,' Michael replied.

'The master and Sir Archibald are in today. I will speak with their manservant,' the stableboy said. He was in his late teens and had come to the parish constable's attention once before when stolen property had been reported by a shopkeeper in the village. However, Michael had been able to clear him in his investigation, and the stableboy was grateful.

Both police officers waited at the entrance and a stern man came to the doorway.

'I am Sir Archibald's valet. May I inquire as to the reason for your uninvited visit?'

Robert stepped forward, passing the servant his visiting card. 'You can inform Sir Archibald that I wish to speak with his son. I have been assigned to the matter from the London Metropolitan Police,' Robert answered in a chilly tone. 'This is an official matter requiring Master Charles' cooperation.'

The dignified servant raised one eyebrow as he examined the calling card, turned and went back inside.

Charles himself eventually came to the entrance.

'I do not see that you were invited here,' Charles said haughtily. 'However, I will extend you the courtesy of asking why you are here?'

'It is about the murder of a village girl, a Miss Jane Wilberforce,' Robert said bluntly. 'We would like to ask a few questions.' Robert was sure he saw the aristocrat blanch. He had dealt with so many criminals before, and his gut told him that the man's reaction to his statement was little different from those of criminals he had interrogated in the past when confronted with their misdeeds.

'I am sorry that I cannot help you, Constable,' Charles replied, still holding the calling card.

'It is detective sergeant,' Robert replied irritably. 'Not constable.'

Charles let the card fall to the stone entrance. 'If you wish to question me, you may do so through my solicitors in London,' Charles replied. 'If that is all . . . Sergeant. I am a busy man and bid you a good morning.'

With his parting statement Charles turned his back on the two police officers and retreated inside the manor.

'That was a waste of time,' Michael said as he turned to walk back to their one-horse gig.

'Not in my opinion,' Mansfield said under his breath. 'A toffy bastard always has something to hide when he chooses to run to his solicitors.'

Michael glanced at his companion and could see a set, grim smile on his face. 'That is what the rich do,' he agreed.

'My instincts tell me he knows something,' Mansfield said. 'All we need is evidence.'

Michael shook his head as they alighted the gig. As far as he was concerned, only a miracle could help them if the London policeman was right. Even in his limited policing career, Michael knew there was a separate law for the rich and powerful.

★

'Who was that?' Sir Archibald asked as his eldest son joined him in the sumptuous billiard room.

'A detective sergeant from London,' Charles replied, taking a decanter of top-shelf scotch from a cabinet and pouring himself a large drink into a crystal glass. 'Why would a London policeman be interested in investigating the death of that girl?'

'You appeared disturbed by his visit,' Sir Archibald said, observing his son's unsettled demeanour.

'There is something about the man's attitude. He does not know his place,' Charles said, taking a long swallow of the fine liquor. 'Does he not know who we are?'

Sir Archibald frowned. Why would such an insignificant murder in Kent attract the attention of London? Even he felt some concern. 'Do you have any high-placed enemies in London, Charles?'

Charles stood staring at an expensive painting on the wall

opposite him. It was a landscape by a renowned Dutch artist and reminded him of that time long ago when someone had attempted to shoot him. Who, he did not know. 'I have made many enemies in our financial dealings. None that I know of would have the power to control this investigation,' he answered.

That night, Charles did not sleep well. He tossed and turned in the great bed into the early hours of the morning, his mind racing. Someone was out to get him.

It was as if the ghost of Jane Wilberforce had been sleeping in her grave and, when dug from the earth, her spirit had been released and come back to haunt him. Was it possible that by burying her body in the sacred site of the ancient ones, he had caused this curse on himself? Charles could not get that thought out of his mind.

*

After treatment in a general hospital in New York, Samuel was declared fortunate as no infection had set into his leg, which had been amputated at the knee. After a month, he was fitted with an artificial leg and released. Samuel took up residence in the townhouse he and James shared overlooking the vast new park being constructed. He took an opiate medicine to dull the pain and most days just sat reading magazines and newspapers, avidly following the news about General Grant's army.

The most important time of the day was when a servant brought up the mail delivery. Most times, a letter would arrive from James, who was advancing with Grant's Army of Cumberland. James wrote that the fighting had tapered off as both armies assessed their casualties, tactics and logistics before engaging again. Samuel smiled when he read that his beloved James was still relatively safe.

One afternoon Samuel was composing a letter to James at his desk in a top room with a view of the snow falling outside. His personal servant, an old man who had once been a disposed farmer in England and emigrated to the United States, knocked discreetly at the door to Samuel's attic study.

'Sir, there is a colonel here to see you,' he said.

'Please show him in,' Samuel said, and he grabbed his crutches to be standing when the officer of superior rank arrived, as he had not been officially discharged from the army. He struggled to keep his balance as the servant brought in a man with a bushy beard and sideburns. His uniform was immaculate, something Samuel was not used to seeing on most senior officers he encountered.

'Sir, I find it difficult to salute in my present condition,' Samuel apologised to the senior officer and a smile crossed the face of the colonel.

'There is no need to salute, Lieutenant Forbes. I am Colonel Briggs, and I have come from Washington to see you in person.'

For a second Samuel wondered if he had in some way infracted military rules. 'Is something wrong?' Samuel said. Was it that James had been killed in action and the colonel had come to inform him of his death? The horrifying thought entered Samuel's mind, almost causing him to fall.

'From what I can see of your injury, I feel that you should sit, Samuel,' the colonel said kindly, and Samuel did so, wondering if the use of his Christian name by the superior officer was an attempt to soften the bad news he was about to deliver. Grey-faced, Samuel awaited the crushing blow, not knowing how he would react.

'It is with great pleasure that I bring news that Congress has awarded you the Medal of Honor for your heroic actions

84

at Missionary Ridge. The president personally read the account where the men and officers stated you had led them with exceptional bravery through shot and shell to be the first on the ridge, carrying the regimental colours. You will personally be presented with the award in Washington at a date to be transmitted to you in the near future. Not a bad Christmas present, if I may say so myself.'

Stunned, Samuel blinked, still trying to comprehend what he had heard. He did not consider what he had done that day to be exceptional. He'd only led the charge because he was too frightened to let down the men he'd led into the hell of flying lead and canister shot.

'May I shake the hand of a true hero?' the colonel asked, stepping forward with his hand extended. Samuel took it, hardly noticing the other man's firm grip. 'I find it rather ironic that a former British officer should win the medal, considering we were at war with you a half-century ago, and you Limeys burned down the presidential house in Washington.'

'I believe in the cause to free your slaves, sir,' Samuel replied, releasing his hand. 'We Limeys abolished slavery long ago.'

The colonel smiled at the mild rebuke and stepped back. 'I have left my calling card with your manservant,' he said. 'You may contact me at any time if you have any questions. I should leave you to recover in peace. I hope we meet again in Washington, when you may have the opportunity of meeting with President Lincoln. Good day, sir,' he said and left Samuel alone with his swirling thoughts.

For a long time, he stared out the window at the feathery snow falling below. He knew that his Christmas would be spent alone, but it would be in a warm house with servants and a fine Christmas dinner of goose and fresh vegetables.

It would not be so for the hundreds of thousands of soldiers somewhere south of New York, awaiting yet another bloody battle. The Southerners were a formidable fighting force; outnumbered, lacking supplies and even shoes for their troops, they continued to resist incursion into their lands.

Samuel returned his attention to the blank sheet of paper on his desk and began to write to James about the prestigious award and the chance he might meet the American president. For a man who detested war, Samuel had strangely proved to be an able commander. Had he been with the British army, the equivalent award to the Congressional Medal of Honor was the newly instituted Victoria Cross.

★

Ikey Solomon found a temporary peace of spirit in his rare visits to his local synagogue, but he was pleased to be able to return to his comfortable house in the great city of London. Snow was falling and it was a special time of year, with the approach of Christmas for the gentiles and Hanukkah for the Jews. His visit to the synagogue had caused a revelation as he'd experienced a strange and disturbing dread about what lay ahead for no explicable reason. Ikey knew age was upon him and his mortality was under threat. It was as if the voice was telling him to make recompense for the bad things he had done in his life. He knew that God had given him the time and opportunity to make amends. He would start with his precious daughter, and as such, had summoned a man to his home.

His heavy and expensive overcoat was removed by his butler when Ikey entered the warm residence. 'Mr Sharon is waiting for you in the dining room, sir,' the butler said.

Ikey thanked him and walked to the dining room, where a man in his thirties stood with his hands clasped behind his back by a display cabinet of fine liquors. David Sharon was a tall man of thin build and wore spectacles. He had the look of a bookish academic, but his fine suit denoted a man of means.

'David, a good evening to you,' Ikey said, removing his mittens and rubbing his hands. 'May I offer you a drink?'

'Mr Solomon, I came as soon as I received your message,' David said. 'Is all well?'

'I just needed to brief you on a few matters,' Ikey replied, walking to the cabinet and removing a decanter of sherry and two glasses from the shelf. 'Take a seat.'

Both men sat down, nursing their crystal glasses of the golden liquid. 'I need to clarify your position with the company if anything should happen to me,' Ikey said eventually. David's eyes widened but Ikey waved off his concern. 'I am not troubled by any specific threat,' he continued. 'But if anything should happen to me, I want you to guide my daughter in all matters pertaining to my business enterprises – legal, and less-than-legal.'

'But what about Bert?' David asked.

'Sadly, my old friend may not be with us much longer, with the disease that takes his life each day,' Ikey said sadly. 'David, your mother was a great friend of my wife before she passed, and I swore to provide you with the best education a boy could receive. Now look at you. A big-shot lawyer in London. I am proud of you and grateful for all your work assisting me in the past.'

David bowed his head. He well knew how Ikey had supported his widowed mother, as well as providing the money for David's education. Without that help, David might have remained in the slums and eventually run with a gang not unlike the one Ikey had put together years earlier. That would have led eventually to a violent death – or dreaded incarceration in one of Her Majesty's prisons. Instead, David now had his own successful private practice representing the wealthy in matters pertaining to finance. But though he now travelled in the best circles of London, he never forgot where he came from and also worked for Ikey off the books. He was not shocked to be exposed to the original means of Ikey's vast income.

'You know there is nothing I would not do for you, Mr Solomon,' David said.

'There have been very few people in my life I could truly trust,' Ikey said. 'One of those I trust is a Miss Molly Williams, who once worked for me. Another is a man who is an imposter but the most honourable man I know, Captain Ian Steele. Naturally, also Bert, and not least, you.'

'I am honoured that you feel that way about me,' David said. 'Now, what can I do to show my gratitude for all that you have done for my mother and myself?'

Ikey produced a sheet of paper and handed it to the solicitor, who read it quickly before looking up at Ikey with eyes wide. 'I am a little confused at your request,' he said, taking off his glasses and wiping them with a clean handkerchief. 'What you propose will probably require some underhanded efforts – and money. Bribery is an offence under the law.'

'Whatever you need, just ask me,' Ikey said. 'I don't have to tell you that no one outside this room will ever know.'

David nodded his head, folding the sheet of paper and placing it in his coat pocket. He was absolutely confused, but knew a request was actually an order from the man who had given him his golden chance in life. The Jewish solicitor left Ikey's company that night, knowing that what he had in his coat pocket was explosive.

NINE

Captain Ian Steele stared without seeing into the small campfire burning in the frigid air of the clear night. He rubbed his hands and reached for the enamel mug of tea that was already cold.

'Would you be looking for some company, sir?' the familiar voice of Sergeant Major Conan Curry asked quietly in the dark.

'Join me, Sarn't Major,' Ian answered. 'I can heat us another brew.'

Conan sat on the hard earth on one side of the fire and also scrubbed his hands over the flickering flames. From the dark, both men could hear the routine sounds of the company at rest. Muted conversations and the occasional cursing of the country and its climate could be heard, but otherwise all was normal.

'I heard that the Bunner and Chamla tribes are talking

about a truce, and maybe even the Bunnerwals,' Conan said. 'Any truth in the rumours?'

'There is,' Ian replied. 'From the little a company commander gets told, it appears that if they agree to chase the Hindustani fanatics out of Malka, we will all be able to go back to India – and possibly back to our barracks in London.'

'Ah, wouldn't that be grand?' Conan said. 'Once again to sit with Molly by a warm fire and drink ale until I fall down drunk.'

'I would think your thoughts might be of a soft bed and a warm body in the form of Molly.' Ian grinned with a tired expression.

Conan returned the smile. 'I never thought that I would ever think of London as home.'

'Home is where your heart is and your heart is with Molly,' Ian replied.

'How about your heart?' Conan asked after a swig of the overproof rum now warming his body.

Ian paused. His heart too had been in England, but now . . . 'I envy you, Conan.'

'A rich and courageous officer such as yourself would have no trouble finding a suitable young lady of good breeding,' Conan countered. 'At least our service has made us both rich with what is in the London banks.'

'I have to live long enough to enjoy the fruits of our ill-gotten gains,' Ian sighed.

'You aren't entertaining dark thoughts, Ian, my lad,' Conan chided. 'The boys look to you to be there in the thick of it when the blood starts running.'

'Lately, all I dream about is going home and resigning my commission,' Ian confided. 'My old dad never really talked about his war with Napoleon. He never talked about the feelings you have before a battle, or what it was like to survive and survey the carnage after.'

'Ah, but your old dad fought Christians,' Conan said. 'We fight godless heathens for Queen and country.'

'England is no longer home. I want to go back to our little colony of New South Wales, where I can smell the eucalyptus and hear the butcher bird's sweet song in the morning. Maybe I will go north to the colony of Queensland and buy property there. I heard that the weather is better in the Queensland colony.'

Conan did not comment. Molly Williams was his universe and the success of her confectionary shops in London – along with the looted treasures that he had converted to cash – assured a comfortable retirement. Years had passed since he and her two brothers had enlisted rather than face the law for robbery, and now he was the only one left alive of the trio. He had also earned the Victoria Cross and found his place as an Irish senior non-commissioned officer in the army of his traditional enemy. But it was the unbreakable bond he had formed with Ian that kept him in when he had been granted the opportunity to be discharged after serving his term of enlistment. If Ian left, so would he. Conan held to the unshakeable belief that they would both survive the military campaigns they fought together for the Queen and her empire.

A bugle sounded its mournful but haunting tune of 'The Last Post' and Conan rose to his feet. 'Time to see that my boys are all getting their sleep,' he said. 'I will be seeing you at "Reveille".'

Ian acknowledged Conan's good night and continued to stare at the last of his campfire as it turned to glowing embers. He knew that when he returned to his little conical tent, he would not sleep very well. The killing and pain would return to haunt him in the night hours and his body trembled uncontrollably from the fresh memories of slaughter.

Just occasionally, amid the terrible dreams of war, a gentle and pretty face would drift from the smoke of battle, and Ella would smile at him. Oh, but that he could turn back time and be with her forever.

★

The sun shone in Josiah's face as it rose above the rolling green seas. The weather was mild and Josiah wondered how this could be when only weeks earlier it had been so cold in London. Professor Shortland stood beside the little boy gazing across the bow at the rising sun.

'We are going east from Cape Town now,' he said.

Towns and directions did not mean much to Josiah. He hoped that he would see the little girl who had befriended him on the voyage. Her name was Eliza and she was travelling with her father. Eliza's father said her mother was now in heaven, and that they were going to start a new life on the other side of the world. Distances did not mean much to Eliza either. A friendship had developed between the four-year-old girl and five-year-old boy, and they met whenever the weather permitted them to go on the deck of the migrant ship. Indeed, Eliza appeared with her father now and Josiah felt a surge of happiness when he saw the little girl with ringlets of hair the colour of the sun and eyes the blue of clear skies. She was holding her father's hand, a giant with a ramrod, well-dressed manner.

Professor Shortland greeted the impressive man when they joined him and Josiah at the ship's railing.

'Ah, Major Crichton, a good morning to you,' he said. 'And a good morning to you, Miss Crichton.'

'A fine day, Professor Shortland,' Major Colin Crichton responded. 'With good winds and good weather, our journey may prove to be a comfortable and speedy one when we reach the Roaring Forties. I presume you are eager to take up your tenure in the colonies?'

'I am, Major, and you your liaison duties with the army there?'

'Alas, I will not have long in Sydney Town, as my duties will be taking myself and my daughter to New Zealand. The Maori are still causing us problems, and past experience has taught some of our wiser generals that they are a formidable foe. We have had fewer problems subduing the savage tribes in Africa.'

'The life of a soldier,' Shortland reflected. 'Always crisscrossing the Queen's Empire to bring civilisation to the ignorant and the true faith to the heathen.'

Crichton did not make a comment on the learned man's opinion. He had seen enough death and destruction to wonder if there really was a benevolent God following the British army into foreign lands.

'I believe that you will be lecturing at the University of Sydney,' Crichton said. 'Your son will be proud of you in the years to come.'

'Josiah is not really our son,' Shortland said. 'He was put into our care by a very philanthropic gentleman who rescued him from the slums. He knew of my journey to take up my post and donated a generous sum to have us take the boy into our care. As my old classmate at Cambridge, Mr William Wentworth, once said, he imagined "the opportunity for the child of every class to become great and useful in the destinies of this country", and Josiah, who has proved to be a very intelligent young man, will be our shining example of how even a boy born of the slums will one day rise in society because of education and manners taught. We have hopes of formally adopting him when we reach New South Wales.'

The British major glanced down at Josiah standing beside his daughter. 'So, the boy is a bastard?'

'That he may be by the laws of the land, but I feel all men are created equal and Josiah's possible rise to fame one day will dispel that stigma,' Shortland countered defensively.

'Sadly, it is my experience that one has to have the right blood to be a leader. One has to be born of the upper class,' Crichton said. 'But you may one day prove me to be wrong, Professor.'

Josiah and Eliza took no notice of the adult conversation but were happy in each other's company on the deck of the ship rolling gently in the southern seas. A pod of dolphins broke the surface off the bow of the ship, attracting the attention of the two children, who leaned over the railing to catch the sight. It was fascinating to watch the dolphins rise above the surface with such a fluid motion and then disappear only to reappear again. However one word he had heard used stuck in Josiah's mind. *Bastard*. He'd heard the word before, and he knew that it was not a nice word. Why did it refer to him? Then Eliza unobtrusively took his hand as they continued to watch the dolphin pod escort the ship towards the east, and the thought drifted from his mind.

★

Count Nikolai Kasatkin stepped from the gentlemen's club into the snow-covered London street, shadowed by the dim light of a gas lamp. It was virtually deserted, but his personal carriage was waiting. The driver sat at the front on a high seat, swathed in a heavy coat against the cold. Nikolai knew it would be a chilly trip home, but was fortified by wine and spirits and smelling of the expensive prostitutes he had bedded that night.

He opened the door of his carriage compartment and it was only when he was halfway in that he noticed the dark figure of a man waiting for him on the coach seat. Even in the darkness, Nikolai recognised his father-in-law, Ikey Solomon. Surprised, Nikolai asked, 'What are you doing here?'

'I could ask you why you have just left that abomination of a house,' Ikey replied. 'But I know it is your second home. Get in.'

Nikolai obeyed but felt uneasy. Ikey had rarely taken much interest in his private affairs. Why should he suddenly appear this night on the eve of the Christian celebration of Christmas?

'Bert,' Ikey called once Nikolai was settled. 'Drive on.'

The coach clattered into a forward motion, the sound of the single horse's hooves partly muffled by the snow.

Now Nikolai was very uneasy; his usual coachman had been replaced by Ikey's feared enforcer. 'What do you want?' Nikolai blurted as calmly as he could.

'I want the absolute truth from you, or this journey will end at the Thames, where I have some friends waiting to take a boat trip.'

Nikolai knew exactly what Ikey meant and, although he had faced many situations on the battlefields of Europe, he also knew this was one time he was not able to manoeuvre out of peril. He was unarmed and Ikey would not be unarmed. 'What truth do you speak of?' Nikolai asked.

'Where is Josiah?' Ikey asked in a conversational tone. From past experience, Nikolai knew just how much danger he was in.

'I doubt that you would harm the husband of your daughter,' Nikolai countered in his desperation. 'How could you explain if I went missing from her life?'

'A drunk man falls into the Thames and drowns. Such a tragedy. My daughter would become a widow and grieve for her departed husband, but fortunately, she is still young and beautiful. I am sure she would not be wearing black for long,' Ikey said blandly. 'Where is Josiah?'

'No harm has come to him,' Nikolai said urgently. 'He is with good people on a migrant ship bound for the colony of New South Wales. I made the decision that it would be a social embarrassment for your family if it was ever revealed he is Ella's illegitimate son. Such a revelation would cause a scandal when you are attempting to appear as a respectable businessman. I did the right thing by all of us. He is with a good man and his wife. In fact, the man is a professor on his way to take up a tenure with the University of Sydney, and I have paid him well to support Josiah.' Nikolai then disclosed the ship's name and departure date. He hoped his father-in-law would see the sense in his decision to remove the boy as far from England as possible, and continued to spill the grandiose plans the professor had for Josiah's bright future.

Ikey listened in silence. 'Bert, stop the carriage,' he called and it came to a stop just as a light flurry of snow-flakes drifted down. Ikey turned to Nikolai. 'Thank you, Nikolai. There is one more thing. If you *ever* lay a hand on my daughter again, I will kill you,' he growled. Nikolai blanched as Ikey continued. 'I don't care that you visit your painted jezebels, but I do know that you are stealing from me to pay for them. That will also stop. I will forget the money you owe to me. From now on, I want to hear only that you are treating my daughter like the queen she is.

If I hear otherwise, you will have an unfortunate accident. Now, get out of my sight.'

Nikolai stumbled from the coach into the cold of the unfamiliar street. The coach clattered away, leaving him half sober from his terrifying brush with death. He was shaking uncontrollably and not only because of the cold air. He tried to prevent the thoughts of the big carriage wheels crushing his bones.

Ikey sat back in his seat and thought about all his son-in-law had chosen to confess. Ikey knew from a long history of interrogating men that Nikolai was telling the truth. At least he now knew his grandson's destination, and who he was with. He could go to Ella and tell her that Josiah was safe. Then again, much of what Nikolai had said about Josiah's existence proving to be a scandalous blot on their reputation for respectability in English society was true. And he now had the comfort of knowing the boy was probably with a well-educated husband and wife in a place as far from London as the moon was from the earth. Why disturb the hand fate had dealt them?

All he had to do now was to bring Ella around to his way of thinking and hope that she would reconcile herself to never seeing her son again. With any luck, the Russian count would yet provide a legitimate heir for his family dynasty.

TEN

Captain Ian Steele felt the flurry of light snowflakes against his face. Campfires burned and illuminated pockets of soldiers outside their conical tents huddled around their warmth. It was Christmas Eve and the enemy had finally been defeated, but so many red-coated British soldiers had not lived to celebrate this holy day in the Christian calendar.

'Happy Christmas, Ian,' Conan said, squatting down to warm his hands over Ian's small campfire. Ian produced a small bottle of rum, poured a generous share into a spare enamel mug and passed it to Conan. 'Not like we knew back in the colony.'

Ian sighed and raised his own mug. 'To those we have left behind – here, England and home.'

Conan returned the toast and the two men gazed into the dancing flames resisting the assault of the small snowflakes, now whipped into a flurry by a rising wind.

'Has anything been said about what we do when we withdraw from here?' Conan asked.

'From what I have been able to glean from Colonel Thompson, we may be transferred back to India. From there, who knows? But, just possibly, perhaps back to our barracks in England.'

'Ah, to be back in London.' Conan sighed.

A shooting star of some size briefly flashed across the sky between the scudding clouds. Both men glanced up at it. 'For a moment I thought it might be the trail of an artillery shell,' Ian said, returning his focus to the fire. 'War has a way of changing a man's perception of the world around him. I think a decade of my life is about to end.'

'But you have to admit that our time has been far from dull,' Conan said, seeing that his friend and superior officer was in a melancholy state. It was hard to comprehend that the man on the opposite side of the fire was capable of walking away from being the legend he had become amongst the young and old soldiers of his regiment. When Conan stared into Ian's face, he could see the expression of a man who had carried too much responsibility for other people's lives. Conan was worried. What became of men who were once warriors when they put aside their uniform and weapons?

'Sir, Captain Forbes?' The voice caused both men to peer into the dark shadows.

'Yes?' Ian replied. A young officer emerged, wrapped in his heavy overcoat.

'The colonel has invited all officers to join him in the officers' mess tent to celebrate our victory over the heathen Pashtun, and to toast the Queen this Christmas Eve.'

'I will be in attendance,' Ian said, rising to his feet and shaking off the light covering of snow.

'I should get back to the lads,' Conan said, also rising from beside the small fire. 'A jolly Christmas, sir,' he added, saluting.

'Merry Christmas, Sarn't Major.'

Ian stumbled to the well-lit tent where he saw his fellow officers gathered. He was greeted warmly by them and gave his respects to both the colonel and president of the mess committee. The regiment's best silver was laid out on trestle tables covered with the whitest of linen tablecloths. Tradition demanded that war should not interfere with the finer aspects of civilised behaviour, and Ian found a place at the table as servants produced roast goose and baked potatoes for dinner. Bottles of fine red wine also appeared at the table along with cigars, and later, port wine for the toasts. Ian reflected on how nights such as these would no longer be a part of his life when he resigned his commission. He looked down the table, listening to the laughter of his fellow officers and knew with a pain in his heart that he would miss the fellowship of men who, like himself, put their lives on the line to assist in spreading the mighty British Empire.

When dinner was over, toasts made to the sovereign and the regiment, they sat, sipping port while puffing on cigars. The colonel rose and made a speech. He finished to a rousing cheer and the officers banging their fists on the table. As if he had forgotten something, he rose again and the officers of the regiment fell silent.

It was then that he announced that orders had come down instructing the brigade to return to England. His announcement received a roar of approval and many hands thumped the table in appreciation of what the men considered the best Christmas present they could receive at the edge of the Empire.

Ian hardly cared; England was not home. England was the place he had made the greatest mistake of his life by not declaring his undying love for Ella Solomon.

★

Nikolai Kasatkin was in a foul mood.

He had been humiliated by his father-in-law and was shamed by his quickness to confess to sending Ella's bastard son away. He had humanely placed Josiah in the care of a good couple and given them the financial means to raise him. Where was the gratitude? He could have easily sent the boy to one of the dreaded workhouses, where he would most likely have died of neglect.

How dare Ella seek the assistance of her father? he thought. He climbed the stairs to his luxurious London townhouse . . . but that was not true, was it? The house had been gifted to him and Ella as a wedding present. Nikolai had no illusions about his marriage. It had been a marriage of convenience, but they had been on friendly terms until the Russian had sensed that their lives were haunted by the memory of Ella's first love, who must have been the father of her bastard. She refused to discuss it, but also refused to let go. How could Nikolai compete with a ghost?

Snow fell in the near-deserted streets as Nikolai entered his residence. The servants were asleep, but the house was still warm from the heat of the hearth.

He made his way to the study where he had a stock of fine liquors. There, he lit a lamp and poured himself an expensive cognac. It was then that he heard the footsteps. Ella was dressed in a neck-to-ankle nightgown and had a shawl over her shoulders.

'You have decided to return home,' Ella said in a tone as icy as the streets outside. 'Did my father speak with you tonight?'

Nikolai turned to face his wife. 'So, you set your father on me as the hunt master sets his hounds on the fox,' he said, glaring at Ella standing in the doorway. 'You and your father can both go to hell.'

'Did you tell my father what he wanted to know?' Ella asked, pulling her shawl tighter around her shoulders.

'I did,' Nikolai grudgingly replied. 'You can ask him my answer.'

'I am asking you,' Ella said. 'Where is my son?'

'He is safe,' said Nikolai, taking a swig of the cognac and enjoying its mild burning feeling in his throat. 'If you wish to know anything else, ask your damned father.'

Ella took steps into the room to confront her husband. 'Where is Josiah? I demand an answer now.'

'If you wish to know now, you must first tell me who the boy's father is,' Nikolai demanded.

Ella remained silent for a short space of time, obviously pondering her reply to the question. 'Captain Samuel Forbes,' she replied finally.

Nikolai felt the blood drain from his face. He was speechless. He had fought alongside the British officer in India years earlier, when they had rescued an Indian prince who had been valuable to the Empire. Ikey had revealed the officer's true identity as a colonial from New South Wales. This was the ultimate betrayal, his wife having a child with a man he had fought beside. It didn't matter that it had been before he had met Ella; it only mattered that she should pay for it.

Nikolai exploded in a black rage, backhanding Ella across the face. She went reeling into the wall and then slid to the floor. Tears of rage welled in her eyes as she placed her hand against the cut on her cheek. 'You will pay for this,' she said, slumping against the wall.

Ikey's words echoed in Nikolai's memory and his stomach dropped. He took a step towards her. 'I did not mean that to happen,' he said, offering his hand. She shrank away from it, so he pulled back. 'Please forgive me.'

Ella struggled to her feet by herself. 'You have promised time and again that the beatings would stop, and yet they always continue,' she said, holding her hand to the bleeding cut on her cheek.

'What now, are you going to run to your precious father?' he asked angrily, the feigned concern evaporating. 'Do you think I am afraid of your father?'

'You should be,' Ella spat, blood leaking through the fingers clutched to her face. Nikolai glanced at his own hand and saw blood on his ring.

Ella turned and stumbled away, leaving Nikolai with the tumbler of cognac in his hand, trying to convince himself that the feared Jewish underworld leader wouldn't dare harm him. Despite disagreements, he was still family.

Nikolai emptied the crystal tumbler of its contents and felt the burning effect reach his stomach. Would she tell her father? He shuddered and poured himself another cognac.

★

Detective Sergeant Robert Mansfield completed his written report to his commissioner. He had returned to London just before Christmas with a feeling of frustration. He looked around the large, noisy room he shared with his fellow police officers, hearing the raised voices of a group of uniformed police questioning a suspect in one corner of the cluttered room of desks, chairs and filing cabinets. The room stank of stale tobacco smoke, urine and vomit. It was a long way from the neat, tiny police station in the Kentish countryside where he had sat to write his police diary, breathing in the scent of fresh air, flowers and roasting meat from the attached residence. The hospitality extended by Constable Covell and his family had been warm, and the two men had developed a mutual respect for each other.

Robert was aware of a slight lull in the noise around him and looked up from his desk to see a very attractive and obviously wealthy woman approaching him. Robert placed his pen by the inkwell and stood when she asked, 'Are you Detective Sergeant Mansfield?'

'I am, madam,' he replied, impressed by her beauty and her aura of power. He had no liking for the aristocratic class, but this woman had a hint of a gentle smile at the corner of her eyes. 'May I inquire as to your identity?'

'I am Lady Montegue-Jenkins,' she replied. 'May I sit?'

Robert quickly found a chair, noticing that all eyes seemed to be on him, or rather, on his esteemed visitor. She sat opposite him, brushing down her long dress as she did so.

'How can I be of assistance, Lady Montegue-Jenkins?' he asked, slightly nervous about her presence in the dingy police room.

'I have learned from your commissioner that you have recently returned from Kent with a suspect in your investigation into the murder of a young woman there who was found buried on Druid Hill,' the lady said. 'The commissioner has informed me you suspect Charles Forbes, son of Sir Archibald Forbes.'

'He is just one suspect, Lady Montegue-Jenkins,' Robert replied cautiously. Now he knew who had been powerful enough to have had him sent to Kent. Robert had read the name of a Mr Clive Jenkins in the papers, and also knew that he was a prominent member of parliament who may one day become the prime minister of Great Britain.

'Who else do you suspect?' she asked quietly so that those around them could not hear the conversation.

Robert knew it would be career suicide to conceal any information from the woman sitting opposite him. Power and wealth had an influence on justice, as he well knew.

'I have yet to speak with his brother, Samuel Forbes,' Robert said. 'I feel both brothers had a motive in the unfortunate woman's cruel demise.'

'Sergeant Mansfield, I can assure you that Samuel Forbes had nothing to do with . . . with Miss Wilberforce's death. You can dismiss him as a suspect.'

Robert frowned. How would this upper-class lady be so assured? 'With all respect, Lady Montegue-Jenkins, my experience tells me that no one can be dismissed as a suspect until I question them.'

'Captain Forbes is currently serving Her Majesty in India,' the lady said as a table and chair were scattered at the end of the room when a drunken man decided that he was not about to be thrown into the cells. Both ignored the ruckus. 'Charles Forbes is the man who committed the murder.'

Robert stared at the woman. How could she know that? But he couldn't ask her that. Instead, he leaned forward on his desk, asking, 'If I may ask, why do you have such an interest in the fate of a poor village girl in Kent, who many said was a witch?'

'I have my reasons, Detective Sergeant,' Lady Montegue-Jenkins replied.

'I think I would like to know those reasons, my lady.'

She gave him a smile that didn't quite reach her beautiful eyes. 'I think that you will be summoned by the commissioner to return to the village and continue your investigation,' she said. 'I think you will vigorously pursue Mr Charles Forbes. I also think that you will find the evidence to have Mr Forbes pay for his crime on the gallows.' She paused, letting her statements sink in, before continuing, 'To assist you, I have the name of someone you should speak with when you return to Kent.' Lady Montegue-Jenkins produced a slip of paper and pushed it across the desk. Robert picked it up and read the name.

'Who is this person?' he asked.

'All will be revealed when you speak to her,' the lady said with a nod. 'Trust me, the young woman has information you will find very interesting. I will bid you a good morning, Detective Sergeant Mansfield, and pray that you are successful in bringing to justice the man who killed Miss Wilberforce.'

With that, Lady Montegue-Jenkins departed the police station, leaving Robert staring at the name he had been given. His police instincts told him there had to be a strong link between Lady Montegue-Jenkins and the dead girl, and he was not a bit surprised when he was once again summoned to the commissioner's office with instructions to return to Kent after Christmas.

ELEVEN

'Where is Josiah?' Ella demanded.

Ikey stared at his daughter's face, seeing the cut cheek and swelling of her eye. They stood in the living room of Ikey's London residence as the sleet replaced the snow on the streets of the city. It was early morning and the servants were going about their chores of cleaning, cooking and restacking the fireplaces of the double-storey house.

'When did Nikolai do this to you?' Ikey asked in a dangerous tone.

'When I asked him about Josiah last night,' Ella replied. 'He told me that he gave you the answer.'

Ikey stood and walked to the window with his hands behind his back. 'Your son is well, and that is all I will tell you for the moment, princess.'

'Why?' Ella beseeched. 'You are a father and I am a mother. You must know that the most important thing in my life is my child. Please, Papa, tell me what Nikolai has told you about Josiah. I beg you.'

Ikey turned to his daughter as a horse cart clattered by on the cobblestones of the street. 'I can promise you that Josiah is not in a workhouse but in the care of a fine man and woman who I feel will take good care of him. It is better that he starts a new life, as you should.'

'You *feel* he will be taken care of?' Ella echoed, her frustration at the circuitous conversation coming out. 'How can you be certain that is true?'

Ikey slumped into a big leather chair by the fireplace. 'You may be right, my little princess. I do not really know what these people who have taken Josiah into their care will do to him. But it is too late. Josiah may be on the other side of the world by now, beyond our reach.'

Ella knelt by her father's knees, tears streaming from her eyes. 'I implore you, Father. Where is my Josiah?'

Ikey sighed. 'He has been taken by a man and woman to the colonies.'

'Which colonies?' Ella countered.

'The colony of New South Wales,' he replied.

Ella stood up, wiping the tears from her cheeks with a dainty handkerchief. 'Then I must go to the colonies to fetch my son back,' she said firmly. 'I am sure that Nikolai told you who these people are who have my son.'

'He did,' Ikey said. 'A Professor Shortland and his wife. The professor is taking a tenure lecturing at Sydney University.'

'Thank you, Papa,' Ella said with a warm smile. 'I love you and forgive you for taking my son at birth. But I am glad that I had the opportunity to see him grow in Bert's care.'

'I am sorry now that I didn't tell you what I had done,' Ikey admitted. 'It was wrong of me. I am glad you worked it out. I, too, visited my grandson and it warmed my heart to see him grow into a fine and intelligent young boy, and broke it that he could not be with us. I see you and his father in him already.'

Ella could see her father's eyes glisten and knew that Josiah had won a part of the old man's heart. He was, after all, of his own blood. He had often regretted that he had discouraged his only daughter's love for the gentile soldier, Ian Steele. The man was ten times the worth of his son-in-law, aristocrat or not. But time could not be turned back, and Captain Ian Steele was rarely in England. From what Ikey had learned, there was an irony that his grandson should be emigrating to the colony of his father's birth.

When Ella had departed, Ikey summoned a servant to him and gave him one order.

'Fetch Bert to me.'

★

Entrenched poverty and strutting colourful peacocks.

Captain Ian Steele and his regiment had been transferred back to India and a life away from the horrors of the North West frontier. The town of Yeddo reminded the Scottish soldiers in Ian's company of home, with its pleasant climate and rugged hills and valleys covered in forests of tall trees. The town had been seized by the English after subduing a rebellion by the local people and was designated as a civil administration area. Ian's regiment was temporarily garrisoned in the town to recover from the vicious battles at the pass. For Ian, his schedule included dining in the officers' mess at night, attendance at tea parties hosted by senior civil servants in the luxurious gardens surrounding their mansions, an attempt to hold on to British customs, albeit with dark-skinned servants dressed in fine uniforms serving the guests.

It was while attending one such afternoon tea party under the colourful marquees that Ian saw a familiar face. It was that of the Indian prince whose life and family Ian had saved during the Indian mutiny years earlier. The Khan held court with a couple of senior British civil servants dressed in suits and top hats. Ian was wearing his red-coated dress uniform with the many medals he had earned for his campaigns from the Crimea to the Indian mutiny. The prince glanced in his direction as Ian balanced a dainty cup of tea in his hand and the Khan broke into a beaming smile of recognition. He said something to the civil servants to excuse himself and walked over to Ian.

'Captain Forbes, Allah has granted my wish that we should once again meet in this world,' he said in his perfect English.

'Your Majesty, it is good to meet under better conditions than when we were together last,' Ian replied. Neither man offered their hand as it would be a breach of protocol.

'Terrible conditions. And yet I will be always grateful to have met you then.'

'I think you expressed that gratitude on the ship steaming home,' Ian said, remembering the small fortune in precious stones the Khan had presented to him and Conan for their service to the family being protected in the interests of the Empire.

'I have regained my kingdom, thanks to the British army,' the Khan said. 'I profit with my contract to have lead mined for the Queen. Life has resumed normality since the rebellion was put down. The only difference is that now the East India Company has been replaced by the British government. Are you here as a part of the Indian British army or as one of the regiments from England?'

'My regiment has its home in our London barracks, and

I hope we will be returning there very soon,' Ian said as a servant took away his empty teacup.

'But you must accept my earlier invitation to stay with me at my home before you depart,' the Khan said with sincerity. 'At twelve years of age, my son has grown to a man and my wife thanks Allah every day for our salvation. Do you know of the Russian count's life after India?'

Ian frowned. 'Last I heard, he is living in London and married a beautiful young lady of means. I think he is well.'

'Ah, it is good to hear that the count has found a meaningful life,' the Khan said. 'I will consult with your colonel and inform him that I require your services until you depart,' he continued. Ian knew that request would be granted, as his life in the regiment was simply a round of social engagements. Even his company, still under the watchful eye of its sergeant major, Conan Curry, was bored with barracks life. Leave for them tended to end with brawls and drunkenness rising in the ranks. Punishment parades were held too often, and it was one duty Ian did not relish as he sat in judgement on the men who had only weeks earlier faced the terrifying battles with the fierce and courageous Pashtun warriors.

'I will look forward to accepting your generous invitation and I am sure my commanding officer will be pleased to grant my leave,' Ian said.

'We may be able to accommodate a tiger hunt in your honour, Captain Forbes,' the Khan said. 'Your sister, Mrs Alice Campbell, bagged one of the biggest Bengal tigers in my district when she was here. How are Dr Campbell and Mrs Campbell, if I may ask?'

'The last I heard, they are both in Canada where the doctor practises surgery,' Ian answered. It had been almost a year since he'd had any mail from them, and he missed their company very much.

'Your time with my family will not all be, as you say, a picnic,' the Khan said. 'My son wishes to learn how to use one of your Enfield rifled muskets so that he may be able to hunt big game one day. I have been informed that you are very familiar with the weapon. My sources have told me you often carry one into battle instead of waving your sword and pistol.'

'I long learned that enemy marksmen single out men waving swords and pistols, so it makes me harder to identify if I am waving a rifle around instead,' Ian said with a hint of a smile.

'Your courage is legendary, Captain Forbes,' the Khan said. 'My sources are everywhere and I have followed your campaigns with great interest. It appears that Her Majesty's army and navy are everywhere. The Queen has a vast empire, as did my Moghul ancestors.'

'We wish to bring civilisation to the ignorant heathens,' Ian said with an almost sarcastic tone. He had long dismissed this idea. He was simply a pawn in fighting for new sources of markets and materials for wealthy aristocrats and the growing middle class in England. But zealot missionaries followed in the wake of the army, spreading Christianity to the natives conquered. Ian accepted that he was a professional soldier and his role was to obey the decrees of the Queen's senior civil servants and army commanders. But he didn't have to like them.

*

Permission was granted for Ian to take leave with the Khan's family, and Ian transferred command to his company second in command, Lieutenant Ross. Ian had faith in the junior officer from his previous service alongside Ian over the years.

Conan cornered Ian in his office, the sound of marching men and orders bawled by non-commissioned officers floating in from outside.

'Morning, sah,' Conan greeted with a salute and his swagger stick tucked under his arm. 'I heard that you will be taking a little leave with the Khan.'

Ian glanced up from signing off a report and grinned. 'Conan, if only the lads back in our colonial village could see you right now in your smart British uniform, they might die of shock. I vaguely remember a private soldier who cursed the British and swore he would desert the moment he had the chance. And here you are now, wearing all your medals for your service to the Queen, including the Victoria Cross.'

Conan relaxed; it had been a long time since he had seen the easy smile on his friend's face and heard him gently teasing him. 'Ah, but this is here and now, not then and there,' Conan replied. 'What's this about going to live in a royal palace?'

'Only for a week or two,' Ian replied, blotting his signature with paper to absorb the excess ink. 'His son is requesting rifle practice with the Enfield and it is not the Khan's palace. He has quarters in one of the better houses in the town.'

'I am a better shot than you,' Conan said with a pained expression. 'Maybe he should have requested my services.'

'I can assure you that I am only carrying out the orders of the colonel to assist with good relations,' Ian said. 'I will be with you all when we sail for England in a couple of weeks, and I will be there to witness your reunion with your beloved Molly at the wharf.'

Conan broke into a broad smile under his bushy beard. 'I was just a bit concerned that the prince might reward you handsomely with some more of those sparkling stones,' he said.

'If he does, Sarn't Major, be also assured, I will share it with you, as is our custom,' Ian said. 'One day, what we have earned over the wars we have fought will be our retirement fund.'

'You also have the reward Mr Forbes promised when you made the pact with him,' Conan reminded. 'It is what you deserve for risking your life so many times for the boys of the company.'

Ian paused, reflecting on Conan's statement. Ian had followed the civil war in North America and was able to reassure himself that Samuel would no doubt be safely ensconced in New York with his friend, James. With a little under a year to pass on the ten-year obligation to serve with his grandfather's regiment, they would have to once again meet and exchange roles. Samuel would return to England to claim his inheritance, and Ian would no longer be a British officer. It would not matter that Charles would attempt to denounce him. Ian knew that Samuel was prepared for any confrontation. If required, and it surely would be, Samuel could demonstrate that he was the real Samuel Forbes, something Ian doubted he himself could manage under intense interrogation. Any attempt by Charles to discredit him would be met with scepticism from those around him. It would be seen as a well-known ruthless and avaricious man in London circles trying to snatch all the family fortune for himself with a twisted and outrageous story of impersonation. It would be viewed as a plot only the popular novelist Charles Dickens could contrive.

But what would Ian do when he took off the red coat and became a civilian again? He only knew that he would return to his real home in the colony of New South Wales, where he would no longer be a blacksmith. He now had enough money to set himself up as a colonial gentleman of means.

Ian stood away from his desk and accompanied Conan outside to the parade ground to review his company of riflemen. It would be hard to give up these men who came from the slums of English cities, some on the run from the law, and others simply seeking excitement in their lives. They were his family.

★

It was still cold in New York City but Samuel Forbes was warm in the house. Despite the two servants who pottered around the two-storeyed building, Samuel felt alone as he surveyed what would be Central Park. It would be a grand area of several hundred acres and Samuel was looking forward to exploring the section already completed in company with James when the spring came to the city. Samuel had received a letter from the front that James was to be posted to Washington in spring, and they would be able to spend time together before he took up his duties in the country's capital. There would be fine dining and attendance at theatres; a time to try to put behind them what they had experienced on the bloody battlefields of the war.

Samuel was counting the days and weeks until they were once again together, keen to show James the medal President Lincoln had personally presented to him in Washington. Samuel had been in awe of meeting the president, the man who had bravely made the proclamation to free all slaves on the North American continent and at the same time fought to keep his country as one nation.

The president had known of Samuel's previous service as a British officer, and smiled when he commented that a half-century before, he might have been one of the invading

British soldiers who had burned down his house in the war of 1812. Samuel mumbled something in reply before being passed on to the secretary of war, who introduced him to an Irishman who had served as an officer with a New York regiment, and had also been awarded the Congressional Medal of Honor. The two men had stood in an anteroom, drinking coffee and eating small cakes. The Irishman had been born of a good family in Ireland but had chosen to travel to the gold fields of California in the late fifties. His luck in finding gold had not been with him, but as an enterprising and educated young man, he had made his fortune in New York. When the war broke out, he'd enlisted in a New York regiment almost wholly composed of emigrant Irishmen straight off the ships, arriving from a country devastated by the shadows of poverty brought on by the potato famine and English ownership of their traditional lands. His courage in leading his men had earned him the North's highest award.

'I met a captured Reb officer who lamented that the North had more Irishmen in their army than they had in the South,' the Irish officer said with a grin. 'He feels because of that, the North will probably win this war.'

Samuel remembered how strange it was that he found himself in a tavern with the Irishman as they raised repeated toasts to President Lincoln and their respective regiments. The fact that the Irish officer was a Papist mattered little to Samuel, as they had witnessed and experienced the hell of war.

Samuel read over James' letter again. They were seeing little action as the Confederate Army retreated to consolidate somewhere. Although not beaten, the Johnny Rebs were suffering from a lack of men and supplies. Samuel was reassured by his words and smiled. Not long now.

'Sir?'

Samuel pocketed the letter before turning to see his valet standing in the doorway. 'What is it, Grimes?' he asked, just a little annoyed at being disturbed from his pleasant thoughts.

'There is an officer who wishes to speak with you.'

'Please bid him come in out of the cold, Grimes,' Samuel said, feeling the discomfort of his artificial wooden leg. He leaned on a walking stick and guessed that the officer who had come to visit him had an answer to Samuel's request to continue serving in a staff position.

The officer appeared behind Grimes, who ushered him into the room before leaving.

'I am Samuel Forbes,' Samuel said, extending his hand to the man whose rank was that of a captain.

'Captain Avery,' the tall young man said without smiling. 'I must congratulate you on the award from President Lincoln, sir.'

The polite deference of the term 'sir' caused Samuel a twinge of suspicion. The captain outranked him. Was it that his request to resume his military duties had been rejected because of his injury? Samuel knew of other disabled officers who were still able to serve.

'I presume that you have come about my request to continue serving,' Samuel said, releasing the other man's hand.

'No, sir,' the captain said with a frown. 'It is my sad duty to notify you that your friend, Major James Thorpe, was killed in action two weeks ago while he was on a reconnaissance mission for General Grant south of Chattanooga. His party were ambushed by Reb irregulars, but his body was recovered and he has been buried. I am sorry to have to deliver the news to you.'

Samuel could feel the weight of his body on the walking stick and fought to remain standing. He had just lost his reason for living.

TWELVE

Detective Sergeant Robert Mansfield arrived in the village and was warmly welcomed by Constable Covell.

'I was informed that you would be returning to us,' Michael said, ushering the London detective into his small police station. 'Have there been any further developments in your case?'

Robert shook off the cold air of the Kent countryside beside a coal-burning fireplace and produced the slip of paper, handing it to the uniformed policeman. 'Do you know this girl?' he asked.

Michael stared for a moment and his expression changed. 'Bridie. She was working at the Forbes manor before being dismissed a couple of months ago. A bit of a scandal around here. The girl got herself pregnant and is living with her stepfather at the far end of the village, in a farmhouse.' Michael looked up at the detective. 'What does she have to do with our murder case?'

Robert removed his heavy overcoat, hanging it on a hook on the wall. 'Does anyone know who the father of the girl's child is?' he asked, removing his pipe and plugging it with tobacco from a small pouch.

'Could be anyone.' Michael shrugged. 'You know what it is like with young girls. The stableboy, one of the servants . . .'

'Or possibly the master of the house,' Robert said, tamping down the tobacco before striking a match. 'A good way to get rid of the problem is to dismiss her services at the Forbes manor.'

Michael placed a kettle on a hook inside the hearth, preparing hot water for a pot of tea. 'That is a possibility,' he said. 'But it's not illegal. How does that help with your suspicions concerning Charles Forbes?'

'Our young Bridie must be a tad bitter about being dismissed from service because the master has gone and got her with child,' Robert replied. 'There's an expression that a woman scorned can be a very vindictive creature. I think that we should speak with her after a welcome cup of tea.'

★

The two police officers found the rundown shack on the edge of the village. It was apparent from the weeds growing in the small field and repairs required to the roof that Bridie's stepfather was not capable of farming.

They were met at the low-set door by a man who was gaunt and rheumy-eyed. His breath smelled of alcohol and it was obvious from his demeanour he did not welcome visitors.

'What do you want, Constable Covell?' he asked, standing in the doorway.

'I just wish to speak with Bridie, George,' Michael replied.

'What sort of trouble is the girl in?' George countered.

'No trouble,' Michael replied. 'Just a few friendly words.'

The sickly man barring the doorway reluctantly stepped aside, allowing Robert and Michael to enter. The interior of the house was dank, damp and filthy. It stank of rotting food and urine. From a corner of what could be considered little better than a hovel, a woman in her late teens appeared from behind a dirty sheet that served as a wall. She looked pale and exhausted, and both police officers could see that she was showing her pregnancy. George shuffled into the room behind the policemen, coughing as he did.

Michael introduced Robert to Bridie as a detective from London. 'Detective Sergeant Mansfield just has a couple of questions,' Michael said as Bridie stared at them through listless eyes.

'Who is the father of the child you carry?' Robert asked bluntly, and Bridie cocked her head at his question.

'What is it to you whose bastard I carry?' she countered defiantly. 'I heard in the village that you went to the Forbes house to ask them about that witch who was killed.'

'We did,' Robert said. 'Nobody seemed to know anything.'

'Maybe I know something, something that you might be interested in.'

'But it will cost,' Bridie's stepfather interjected with a sniffle. 'Us poor folks need help. You can see my stepdaughter needs help if she isn't going to end up in a poorhouse with her bastard.'

Robert turned to the sickly man behind him. 'It will depend on whether Bridie can be of assistance in solving the mystery of the slain girl's demise,' he said. 'She has to tell me something before I can consider finding payment, then we can call it a reward.'

Bridie smiled grimly. 'I can give you more than you would have ever dreamed of,' she said. 'But first, me and me dad need to see money. I can even tell you about a second murder you don't even know about. A stableboy who was slain for knowing too much. If I tell you who the man is, my life will be in danger, and I'll need money to get away from the village.'

Robert was taken by surprise when Bridie revealed the second murder but did not allow himself to show his ignorance. 'I will need time, but if you tell me the name of the stableboy, I will be in contact with you again.'

'You'll get that when me and me dad see the money,' the girl answered shrilly.

On this note, Robert and Michael departed the ramshackle property and returned to the police station. Robert turned to the village constable. 'Do you know what the woman was referring to?'

'A few years ago, there was a fire in the Forbes' stables, and a young man was found with severe burns. From the report of my predecessor, it appears he had been trapped by the fire and died. The report said he died of misadventure.'

'Was the boy buried in the village cemetery?' Robert asked.

'I believe he was,' Michael replied. 'He had no living relatives, and I suspect that his grave is not marked.'

'Well, we have to find his grave and dig him up,' Robert said, causing the constable to glance at his colleague with shock. But all he saw in return was absolute determination.

Robert knew that he must contact Lady Montegue and convince her to put aside a 'reward'. He would also have to contact his commissioner and have the best medical coroner travel from London to conduct an autopsy. No doubt Lady Montegue would fund such a request.

But first, they had to find the grave and exhume the dead stableboy.

★

Ian Steele was impressed by the opulent interior of the Khan's temporary residence, a mansion with lush gardens enclosed by the high walls. Ian was warmly welcomed and shown to his quarters, which was a spacious room that opened onto a patio overlooking a cool and green corner of the garden with a water fountain. The Khan's residence was a welcome respite from the austerity of barracks life. Ian wished Conan could have enjoyed such luxury, but his sergeant major was tasked with supervising the company back at its garrison barracks.

At dinner that night, Ian met the Khan's son, a handsome young boy with olive skin wearing a jewelled turban similar to that worn by his father. The boy was reserved upon meeting Ian, and his pretty mother stood a short distance away with a shy smile of welcome.

'You are the officer who accompanied my family during our escape from India,' the boy said stiffly. 'I am Sanjay. I am pleased to meet you, Captain.' The boy formally held out his hand and Ian accepted the introduction. From his little knowledge, Ian knew that Sanjay was a Hindu name and was surprised that the Moslem prince had named his son by that religion.

As if reading his thoughts, the Khan spoke. 'We named our son to show my Hindu subjects that we are one of them,' he said with a smile. 'It means, in their faith, "triumphant".'

Ian nodded his understanding, letting go of the boy's surprisingly strong grip. 'A noble thought,' Ian said. 'I look forward to teaching you the use of the Enfield rifled musket, Prince Sanjay.'

'I have promised my father that I will soon shoot and kill one of the fierce tigers of the forest with an Enfield,' the boy said. 'I feel that it has the potential to do that.'

'Your English is excellent,' Ian complimented him. 'I am sure you will demonstrate the power of the Enfield in the future hunt.'

The boy looked pleased and turned to his mother, speaking to her in his native language. The two departed, leaving Ian alone with the Khan. 'I think that it would be a fine time to show you the gardens of the palace,' the Khan said. 'We shall sit by my fountain and observe the sun go down and the heat of the day follow it into the dark hours.'

Ian allowed himself to be guided into the sprawling gardens, where the servants had retired from their manual work maintaining the lawns and shrubs. The Khan plucked a ripe mango from a tree and passed it to Ian.

'The fruit given to us by Allah, may His name be blessed,' the Khan said, and Ian had to agree. Of all the fruit he had partaken of in his journeys to foreign lands, the mango had proved to be his favourite. They strolled to a fountain whose waters trickled with a soothing sound in the garden.

The Indian prince gestured to a stone bench for them to sit. 'There is another reason why I requested your presence here, Captain Steele,' the Khan said, and Ian was startled to hear his real name used. His false identity must be the worst-kept secret in the world, he groaned to himself.

'How did you learn my name?' Ian asked quietly.

'We have a mutual friend,' the Khan said. 'While I and my family were temporarily exiled in England, I was fortunate to be feted by your merchants and even the royal court. It was while I was at an afternoon tea party that I was approached by a beautiful woman of high birth. Her name was Lady Rebecca Montegue, and she was engaged to your former commanding officer, Colonel Jenkins. She had heard how you and your company of soldiers had rescued my family and was very interested in learning more about our adventure. Later, I was invited to her manor to attend a private dinner and we became good friends. It was the first of many visits, and Lady Montegue revealed your real identity to me. She did so only to assure me that I had been rescued by the finest officer in the British army – even though he was really a colonial from New South Wales. Rebecca informed me of her link to you through her murdered twin sister, and said that she was sure her sister was murdered by your so-called brother, Charles Forbes.'

Ian sensed that the friendship between the Indian prince and the English aristocrat was more intimate than he spoke of. What had probably occurred was pillow talk. Her marriage to the despised Clive Jenkins was no more than a convenience. Rebecca had her heart set on becoming the wife of the most powerful man in Great Britain – the prime minister. With her powerful connections and influence, she might just achieve her ambition.

'What do I have to do with any of this?' Ian asked.

'Lady Montegue told me that you also strongly suspect Charles Forbes killed her sister, Jane, and that you seek justice for her death. Lady Montegue was able to have me conveniently meet with Charles Forbes while I was in London to speak about investing in my lead mines. He showed some interest, and I felt that it might lure him here, where justice could be served by our thugees.'

Ian knew about the fearsome reputation of the thugees, a cult of killers who worshipped the Hindu goddess, Kali. They would infiltrate parties of travellers and use a method of strangulation on their victims before they robbed them. The British administration in India was currently attempting to hunt them and bring them to the gallows.

'If that worked, you can be sure that Charles would die at their hands,' Ian said. 'Aren't you afraid the plot may be traced back to you?'

'I am a Moslem and do not have any official contact with this Hindu organisation,' the Khan said with a broad smile. Ian knew his contact must be unofficial. 'But that is one plan, and relies on Charles Forbes' greed. Perhaps you can offer some insight?'

'Oh, he's greedy enough,' Ian replied with a fleeting image of the detested man's body kicking and struggling as a thugee tightened the noose around his neck, vengeance for Jane's terrible death at his hands. 'It is a good plan, save that Charles is not one to stray far from the pleasures of London.'

'I can but try,' the Khan said. 'If you think of another way, please do let me know. For now, you should enjoy the pleasures my Yeddo palace provides. I know my son is eager to learn from a British warrior as much as he can about your ways of soldiering.'

They rose and walked back to the palace just as the sun set. Ian thought about the plot to have Charles killed and felt no guilt. It would also assist the real Samuel Forbes to claim his inheritance, free of Charles' interference. Ian had long suppressed any ideals concerning life and death; he had witnessed too many soldiers die in the cause of expanding the Empire who had deserved to live. Charles Forbes had forfeited his right to live.

★

Sir Archibald Forbes rarely left his manor in Kent. Age and gout had forced him into a sedentary life, and receiving his copy of *The Times* newspaper had become a highlight of his day. It helped while away the hours and also allowed him to review the events of the world. Sir Archibald took pride in forecasting financial impacts of foreign strife. He had predicted that the civil war in America would impact the cotton factories of England and had proved to be right. He was annoyed that the British government did not side with the rebellious Confederate states to break the blockade of southern cotton exports. Britain had come close to intervening on the side of Jefferson Davis and his Confederacy, but at the last moment chose to remain neutral when they considered that Lincoln's overpowering number of soldiers and the industrial strength of the northern armies might eventually defeat the south.

The servants had stoked the open fires of the sprawling house and Sir Archibald sat in his favourite leather chair with his feet on a soft stool, warming his slipper-clad feet as he sipped sweet sherry from a small crystal glass.

He picked up his copy of the paper and began to scan the news. When he flicked to the second page, his eye caught a small article concerning the war raging in America. There was an etching portrait of a Northern American army officer, and a story of how a former British officer, Lieutenant Samuel Forbes, had been awarded the North's highest military honour for bravery, equivalent to Britain's Victoria Cross.

Sir Archibald was stunned. The likeness and name were no doubt that of his son, although Sir Archibald knew the man was actually the son of his despised brother, Sir George Forbes, who resided in the colony of New South Wales.

How could this be? Sir Archibald asked himself as he stared at the article. Samuel was currently serving with the British army in India. Then Sir Archibald remembered the constant warnings from his eldest son, Charles, that the man Sir Archibald was convinced was Samuel was in fact an imposter. He swallowed the remaining sherry and placed the glass and paper on a small teak table beside his leather armchair.

Sir Archibald rang the bell beside his chair, summoning his valet. Charles had to know about his discovery.

Sir Archibald was overwhelmed by the fact that Charles had always been right about the imposter in the family, but he was also stunned to read how Samuel had actually been recognised as a war hero across the Atlantic, albeit by the Americans.

THIRTEEN

It was the perfect night for an ambush in London's back-streets. The fog was so thick that it limited vision, and even muffled sound.

Bert stood in the shadows of a doorway on the narrow, deserted street where even the lamplight had little illumination. He waited patiently, ignoring the pain that came and went through his body. The illness that afflicted him was nearing its end, and Bert knew that he had little time left.

Ikey had summoned him for this mission, knowing his faithful henchman was near the end of his life, but Bert had accepted his orders without question because of his beloved dove, Ella. He had watched over her from the day she was born, had seen her grow into a beautiful and compassionate young woman. Too often he had seen the marks of brutality on her face when she visited her son in secret. He knew the perpetrator of the violence was her husband, but Ikey had protected him, even when he discovered his aristocratic son-in-law was embezzling money from the company Ikey had set up to import valuable furs from Russia. It had been convenient to have Nikolai manage the company as he spoke Russian and had contacts in the land of his birth.

Now, things were different. Ikey had issued warnings and Nikolai had foolishly ignored them. No one was given a second chance by the ruthless Jewish gangster, even if his public face was now that of a respectable and wealthy businessman.

Bert had carried out his surveillance a week earlier, learning of his target's movements through the week. This night, Bert had learned Nikolai took a Hansom cab to a specific address in the less salubrious district of London City. It was not one of the slum areas but a district of clerks and civil servants. Bert was opposite the tenement house whose door he knew Nikolai would enter in the late hours of the night. It was an opium den.

Bert also knew that Nikolai usually left in the early hours of the morning to walk along the street to a more used road, where he would be picked up by the same Hansom cab driver.

Bert shrank back into the shadows of the doorway as the Hansom cab arrived on time and Nikolai alighted. It was obvious from the brief conversation Bert could hear that Nikolai paid the driver generously to return at a specified time, taking him home to the comfortable townhouse he shared with Ella.

Bert felt the razor-sharp knife resting in his hand. It was a pity he had at least two hours to wait before Nikolai reappeared in the street, but Bert shrugged off his pain and discomfort. This was something he had wanted to do for a long time. There was only one small detail that might ruin his plan; the cab driver might arrive before Nikolai exited the house. Bert knew that he would deal with that situation if it arose. After all, he had nothing to lose anymore.

★

Samuel Forbes sat in a chair in the small office that smelled of cigar smoke. The wallpaper was new and influenced by European fashion. The bald man with impressive side whiskers sitting on the opposite side of the expensive mahogany wood table droned on in the legalese concerning last wills and testaments. He glanced up from his perusal of the document in front of him.

'Major Thorpe must have had a high regard for you, Lieutenant Forbes,' he said. 'He has left you all his assets and money. I can assure you that by doing so, you are now a man of considerable wealth and influence.'

When Samuel asked James' net worth, he was stunned. It was even more vast than that of the Forbes estates in England and abroad. Samuel knew that James' estranged family had been very wealthy, but not to this extent. As the only child, James had inherited their wealth and his advisors had expanded it.

The lawyer's revelation had changed everything in Samuel's present state and even the future. He did not need to return to England and claim his inheritance for himself. Ian could have it all, and if his ten-year commission had been anything like Samuel's time at war, he deserved every penny.

But Samuel knew he would have given away his new fortune for just one more day with James, to see his slow smile and hear his voice. Samuel grieved but there was some conflict in his feelings. So many fine young men around him on the battlefield had been ripped and torn by shrapnel and bullets. His feelings had hardened, and he knew why he had not been able to weep for James' sudden demise. Samuel felt the pain but the war had frozen his ability to express his deepest feelings.

★

Nikolai stepped outside the tenement house onto the street, and Bert was pleased to see that he was waiting for his cab to arrive. In the distance, Bert could hear the distinctive clop-clop of a horse approaching. Nikolai was a good fifty paces away and Bert stepped from the shadows to walk quickly towards his target, knife swinging at his side.

Bert was only ten paces away when Nikolai turned to see him approaching with his head down. Startled, Nikolai stepped back, his hand thrust into the pocket of his coat.

Bert raised the knife, preparing to deliver a slashing cut across the Russian aristocrat's throat, and did not see the small derringer pistol pointed at him. The first barrel discharged a shot that took Bert in the chest, and the bullet from the second barrel caught him in the forehead. Bert fell to the street, the knife clattering away. Bert's pain from the terrible cancer was gone, as was his life.

The Hansom cab appeared out of the fog as Nikolai stood over Bert, the derringer in his hand. He quickly pocketed it as the cab driver drew his horse to a stop, looking curiously down at the figure sprawled in the gutter.

'Is everything orright, master?' the cab driver asked. 'I thought I 'eard a couple of gunshots.'

'Everything is good,' Nikolai said, scrambling into the cab. 'The man you see is drunk and tried to accost me. He was so drunk that he fell over, and I fear that he may have hit his head.'

'What about the noise I 'eard?' the cab driver asked with a frown.

'You heard nothing,' Nikolai retorted. 'I am sure that a significant payment will ensure your deafness in this fog.'

The driver shrugged. This customer was generous, and he suddenly did not remember hearing anything as he approached. He spurred his horse forward and did not look back at the body in the street.

Nikolai felt his heart pounding and noticed that his hands were shaking. He knew who the man was that had attempted to take his life, and he knew why, and he knew what would happen next. Bert's death would be reported to the police, and the two bullet wounds would ensure an investigation. Although Nikolai had acted in self-defence, he had no witnesses to corroborate that fact, and the inquiry would eventually lead back to Ikey. Nikolai knew that when that occurred, Ikey's wrath would be beyond control, and he would plot a slow and painful death for Nikolai. But he'd have to catch him first. Nikolai decided immediately that he would be on a ship out of England before Ikey discovered the failure of his man's mission to kill him.

Fortunately, he had been able to stash away a considerable fund of money for a rainy day, and now was the time to cash in and depart England. He could not return to Russia, as the Tsar's secret police would arrest him for treason. His best option was to return to India, where he knew he could establish a comfortable life with the capital he had embezzled from Ikey Solomon.

The carriage halted outside his house and Nikolai kept his promise to the driver with a hefty tip for his silence. The cab disappeared into the fog and Nikolai went inside to recover the well-hidden chest that held the means of his escape, knowing he would be gone before Ella awoke that morning.

★

When the village constable and the London detective approached the village priest about burials, they were pleasantly surprised to find that the stableboy had been given a marked grave by Sir Archibald Forbes as a tribute to him saving the valuable horses he'd been able to release before the fire took hold at the Forbes Manor that terrible night. The priest led them to the grave, simply marked by the boy's name, date of birth and death.

'We will need to exhume the boy's body, Reverend,' Robert said as the three men stood at the foot of the neglected gravesite.

'It is not a good thing to disturb those sleeping in the arms of the Lord,' the priest said.

'From our enquiries, the boy had no living relatives and the exhumation has been approved in London for a medical examination.'

'But the Forbes family doctor ruled his death as misadventure,' the priest protested. 'I cannot see how your exhumation will do any good to the living or dead.'

'That will be seen when our doctor from London carries out an independent review,' Robert replied. 'Once that is done, the boy will be returned to the arms of the Lord.'

The priest frowned but realised the detective was not going to be swayed. 'Very well. I will arrange our gravediggers to assist you.' He walked away and Michael glanced at Robert. 'What do you expect to find?' he asked.

'I don't know, but it is worth undertaking a more thorough examination of the body,' Robert replied, digging in his pocket for his tobacco pipe. 'The man coming from London is legendary amongst the Met police. If death is by any other means than misadventure, he'll find it. If what Bridie has alluded to is true, it can't be mere coincidence that the boy died at the Forbes estate when my prime suspect for Jane Wilberforce's death is Charles Forbes. Call it a copper's instinct. All we have to do is find the evidence, and my suspicion is it will point its accusing finger at Master Charles Forbes.'

Robert plugged his pipe and lit it. Smoke curled around his head as a gentle breeze rustled the weeds growing on the mound where an innocent boy lay forever under the earth.

★

The almost mummified body of the dead stableboy lay on the table at the police station. It barely had any flesh remaining, and the effects of intense heat were evident. The London doctor who worked for the police stood over it as Robert and Michael observed beside him. The doctor's keen eye saw the two barely discernible marks on the dead boy's chest. He took a scalpel and cut a section beside one of them. Putting the scalpel aside, he used his fingers to open up the flesh as the two observing police leaned forward to watch what was revealed by the incision.

'Puncture wounds,' he grunted, holding apart the dried flesh. 'This young man may have died from two deep, penetrating wounds.' The doctor then opened the body up and removed a lung and the heart. He examined the heart and held it up to show the London detective. 'Another puncture wound to the heart,' he said. 'I daresay that I will not find any soot in the lungs, Sergeant.' And the doctor was right.

Smoke from Robert's pipe filled the room as the doctor went to a sideboard, where he recorded his findings while the two policemen waited patiently.

The doctor finally turned away from his writing.

'What is your medical conclusion, Doctor?' Robert asked.

'This cadaver exhibits two deep puncture wounds to the

chest, one piercing the heart, and it appears, in my professional opinion, that they were sustained before the fire
consumed the body.'

'Not death by misadventure?' Robert queried.

The doctor began gathering the tools of his trade into
a small bag. 'No, Sergeant,' he replied. 'I will be issuing a
certificate to say that death was the result of the fatal injury
sustained by a penetrating object which I as yet cannot
identify. But whatever it was, it would have been used with
great force, and most probably inflicted by a person, or
persons, to the body before us on the table.'

'Murder,' Robert said softly. Bridie had been right in her
statement, and it was time to learn what else she knew. But
that would require money, and he was waiting to hear back
from Lady Montegue-Jenkins. Justice would be served,
Robert thought to himself. It was a difficult case to prove,
but little pieces were slowly coming together.

FOURTEEN

Egbert Johnson – better known as Bert to those he trusted – was laid to rest beside his wife, Meg, with no family members in attendance. The very small crowd gathered around the grave consisted mostly of just a few old criminals who had either come to pay their respects or to reassure themselves the dreaded enforcer was truly dead and about to be buried.

Ella stood beside her father under an umbrella unfurled against the steady rain. Ikey had always made sure his employees were not buried in unmarked graves. The big Jewish man had an understanding of Christian funeral rites and had also made sure a minister attended to say the ritual words over the coffin as it was lowered into the muddy earth of the cemetery.

Ella did not hold back her tears for Bert. She had genuinely loved the man who had been her protector as she had grown up, and then had raised her son in the first years of his life. Now, both Bert and Josiah were gone, and Ella wept for both losses.

The mourners dispersed when the simple coffin was lowered into the grave. Ella watched as her father placed a large round pebble on the gravestone before turning to their carriage. Ella followed, wondering again if her husband knew something about Bert's death. It did not seem possible that it was only a coincidence that Nikolai had disappeared from London the morning after Bert's death. A considerable amount of cash and jewellery were missing from the safe Nikolai had thought was his secret. But Ella was a Solomon and there were no secrets in that house for her. She'd found it months before and had even spied on her husband depositing cash one night, getting a fleeting glimpse of the considerable amount of money.

Her father rubbed his jaw and held a hand over his chest. When Ella turned to look at Ikey she could see pain etched in his bearded face.

'Papa, are you unwell?' she asked, taking hold of his arm.

'It is nothing, little princess,' Ikey said. 'It will pass. Just a bit of pain in my chest and a bit in my jaw. I have had this before.'

Ella knew they were close to Ikey's opulent residence and that she must fetch a doctor, as her father appeared to be in more pain with each passing minute. Suddenly, his face went a deep purple colour and he fell back against the leather seats of the carriage.

'Coachman! Coachman!' Ella cried out in her despair, helplessly gripping her father's arm.

The coach clattered to a stop and the driver tumbled down to open the door to the coach. He stood in the rain and stared at Ikey. He had once been a soldier on the battlefields of the Crimea and knew death when he saw it. Ikey's eyes were half open as if trying to focus on a living world, and yet already viewing what lay beyond life.

The coachman shook his head slowly. 'I'm sorry, Countess Kasatkin, but I think your father is dead.' Ella continued to grip her father's arm as she broke into a deep sobbing.

The coach driver stood awkwardly in the rain, watching as the daughter of the feared underworld figure sobbed her heart out. Bert had been a good friend to him and he very much missed his old colleague. A superstitious thought passed through the coachman's mind; was it that Ikey had chosen to join Bert in death because of their many years of deep understanding and friendship? He shook his head. Ikey was not sentimental – except about his daughter, who now wept for him, and who was about to inherit a vast empire built on blood and violence.

★

Detective Robert Mansfield was back in the Kentish village, armed with money to pay the former servant girl of the Forbes manor. Lady Montegue–Jenkins had not hesitated in providing a fund to assist his gathering of evidence against Charles Forbes.

Now, he and Constable Michael Covell once again visited Bridie and her stepfather. Robert produced a small wad of English currency for them to see before he even asked his first question, then replaced the notes in his pocket.

'What can you tell me about Mr Charles Forbes?' he asked, and could see the young woman's eyes light up with wonder at what was a small fortune to her being held in the police detective's pocket only inches away.

'I think Master Forbes slew Harry the night the stables burned down,' she replied.

'Why do you think that?' Robert asked.

'Because Harry had proof that Master Forbes killed the witch girl. A bloody coat from the night she was killed,' she blurted out. Robert and Michael exchanged a glance as she ploughed on. 'Harry told me he'd hidden it in the stables, and I thought he was just fibbin' but . . .' She looked away, biting her lip. 'I wanted better for meself. I thought he was a good man, and if I could get him to notice me . . .'

A heavy silence fell. Robert waited for the girl to continue but she couldn't seem to find the words. 'So you told Charles Forbes that Harry could prove he was connected to Miss Wilberforce's murder.'

Bridie nodded, letting out a shuddering sob. 'He told me not to tell anyone or I'd be badly punished. I didn't know he'd hurt Harry, I swear!'

'And then what happened?'

'Not fifteen minutes later, the fire started in the stables. I know it was Master Forbes, I just know it!'

'If you knew it, why didn't you come forward?' Robert asked.

The girl looked shamefaced. 'Master Forbes, he . . . he's a bad enemy and a good friend. Well, at least until he's done with you,' she said bitterly, rubbing her hand over her swelling belly.

Robert had written down her words in his notebook as she spoke. He looked up at her. 'You swear that what you are telling me is the truth?' he asked.

'I swear,' Bridie said. 'I need the money to get me and my da away from here, or Master Forbes will kill me like he slew Harry if he finds out what I just told you.'

Robert pondered her statement. Without any real evidence, it was merely the word of a former servant girl with a grudge. But she had risked much to say what she had seen . . . He put his hand in his pocket to retrieve some pound notes. They were enough to get her to London to find lodgings. Bridie grasped the money with such tightness, it seemed the notes could adhere to her fingers.

'You will get more if you ensure you tell me where you are at all times. If you fail to do this, I will arrest you for assisting Master Forbes in slaying Harry,' Robert said sternly. 'You should have reported your suspicions to the police immediately and by not doing so you have possibly helped him get away with murder. Do you understand what I am saying?'

Bridie nodded and her stepfather added his agreement to keep the London detective sergeant informed of their movements. He had once languished in an English prison for theft, and did not want to return.

Robert and Michael left the property at the edge of the village in silence, each pondering what they had been told.

'I think it is time to visit the Forbes manor again,' Robert said. 'It may not be directly concerned with the death of Miss Jane Wilberforce, but it is a start if we unsettle him concerning the death of the stableboy – especially if we inform the man that a second opinion has indicated murder rather than misfortune in Harry's death.'

As they walked back to the small village police station, Michael could see the grim expression of determination on Detective Sergeant Mansfield's face. Michael was in awe of his colleague's doggedness in pursuing his chief suspect. It had commenced with little more than the London detective's hunch that he had reason to suspect a man born to power and riches guilty of murder. But Michael knew enough about the law that they would virtually require a confession to prosecute the case, and he did not think there was much hope of Charles Forbes ever admitting that he killed the stableboy and set the stables on fire to cover his heinous crime.

★

After the traditional week of mourning for her father's death, Ella received a visit from a man she vaguely remembered seeing in her father's presence. His calling card said his name was David Sharon and that he was a solicitor.

Ella had the man shown into what had been her father's study and he introduced himself as her father's legal representative. Ella asked the servant to bring coffee and seated herself at the desk.

'I suspect that my face may be familiar to you, Countess Kasatkin,' David said, sitting down in a chair with a leather briefcase in his lap.

'I confess that it is, Mr Sharon,' Ella said as a maidservant brought in a tray with a coffee pot and cups. 'I hope that you enjoy coffee. It is a beverage I came to enjoy on my rather short visit to America.'

'As a matter of fact, I do,' David said. 'But my visit is less social than I would like it to be. I have come to brief you on your father's enterprises. You are the sole heir to his rather large holdings in London and elsewhere.'

'I am pleased that someone actually knows what my dear departed father controlled,' Ella said with a sad smile. 'My father was very protective, and I was hardly aware of how he made his fortune for most of my life.'

'Before he branched out into more respectable businesses, your father had other forms of income, and some still exist today. I swore to Mr Solomon that you would never be privy to those existing forms of income for the sake of your respectability. However, I will be allowing certain persons to continue with that rather dark side of income to report to me. I can assure you that all monies collected will be issued to you.'

Ella had already given some thought to the matter. 'I would prefer that any money from what you call my father's dark enterprises be allocated to charities for the poor of London,' Ella said. 'I am practical enough to accept that if I stopped that side of my father's enterprise, I would cause men with families to be out of work.'

David Sharon nodded and looked at Ella with a new respect in his expression.

'I can assure you, Countess Kasatkin, that your father's investments in many areas have paid very well and you have a rather large income for life. Your father was a truly remarkable man.' He opened his briefcase and slipped a paper from it. 'There is something your father had me do before he passed,' David said. 'A rather unusual request.' David passed the paper to Ella, who read it and gasped. She looked to the solicitor.

'Is this a forgery?' she asked, her heart pounding in her breast.

'It is not,' David said. 'Let us say that the birth certificate you hold was just a little overdue to be registered. However, a friendly clerk in London was able to correct the oversight and the form is real.'

Ella stared at the details pertaining to the birth of a baby boy named Josiah and listed his father as one Ian Steele, captain in Her Majesty's army, and his mother a Miss Ella Solomon, fiancée. It may not have suited the mores of Victorian England, but it was an honest and legal document.

'I am afraid there has been a terrible clerical error,' Ella said. 'Josiah's father is Samuel Forbes.'

A mysterious smile crossed the legal man's face. 'Ikey instructed me to tell you that the man you have known as Samuel Forbes is actually a former blacksmith, born Ian Steele in the colony of New South Wales. He is an imposter but, according to your father, one of the finest men he had the pleasure of knowing.' David smiled softly. 'Your father was always aware of your undying love for the man and I think he had a premonition of his own death. In my last conversation with your father, he insinuated that there were things to be rectified in his life before he joined your beloved mother in the afterlife. It seemed a rather curious thing to do, as I know that you are married, but I also know your father eventually had no respect for your husband for all his crimes against you and Mr Solomon himself. And I have heard that the Count has disappeared from England.'

Ella could not take her eyes off the official sheet of paper with its impressive seals. 'That is correct, Mr Sharon. It seems that you know more about my father and I than one would expect.'

'It has been my task for many years,' David said. 'I have always owed your father more than you could ever know. Please consider me amongst those you hold closely. I am always at your service, whatever you may require in the future. The formal reading of the will is to be held next week, but I think you already know you are the sole benefi-ciary of all your father's estates and enterprises, both legal and less-than-legal. You have many people working for you in the daylight and in the shadows of the night.'

It was too much to think about now. Ella felt stunned from the lawyer's visit, and he seemed to sense it. 'I think you may have a lot on your mind right now so I will excuse myself from your presence and return to my practice,' he said. 'Thank you for the coffee, Countess Kasatkin.'

Ella belatedly noticed that the solicitor had not drunk any of the coffee poured for him. Nor had she partaken of her own cup. David made his own way out of the room, leaving Ella alone to take in the significance of the birth certificate of her son. It was the most precious piece of paper she had ever held and proved her claim to Josiah. She now had the financial means to search for him on the other side of the world. It was obvious that the man who had just departed the room was able to manage her father's enterprises in her absence.

As Ella sat at her father's desk in his study her mind reeled at the revelation about her son's father. An imposter, Mr Sharon had said. The enigma of the man she had always loved just whirled in space. Was this the real reason Samuel . . . no, *Ian* had kept her at arm's length? Why had he not trusted her to his real identity? Her father had known.

The day before, Ella had opened her father's bank security box so that she might learn more about him, but all the papers had revealed were details of stocks, shares and business ventures in England and abroad. The only thing to catch Ella's eye was a list of names of prominent people, with coded notes scribbled beside each entry. Ella had been surprised to see even Lady Rebecca Montegue-Jenkins had her name on her father's list. Ella still remembered fondly how Lady Montegue had kindly arranged for her and Ian to be at her ball, after which Josiah had been conceived. Why would her name be on Ikey's list? What did it all mean?

Then Ella had found a letter in her father's handwriting, addressed to *My Little Princess*. She'd read it carefully with tears in her eyes as Ikey laid out carefully considered plans to ensure his daughter's prosperity and, hopefully, happiness.

Ella stared at the framed photograph on her father's desk, a formal portrait of father and daughter from years before.

Her father had given her the means to find her son, and to protect Ian Steele in the times ahead.

'Thank you, Papa,' she whispered.

★

Captain Ian Steele was in his third week at the Khan's household. As much as he enjoyed the break from the routine of military life in the luxurious residence, he also missed the brotherhood of his regiment.

Ian would spend the evenings in the company of the Indian prince, sipping refreshing sherbet drinks after sumptuous feasts. They had become friends and discussed many subjects from politics and history to the Khan's troubles with local agitators. The Khan made a comment that Ian was far more knowledgeable than other British officers he had encountered from the old East India Company administration, and Ian admitted to his love of books.

'Ah, but I could have you transferred from the British army to train my bodyguards,' the Khan said one night as the two men strolled in the garden under the twinkling stars. 'My son has come to look up to you as his red-coated warrior. Your lessons in firearms cause him to babble to his mother and I that, one day, he will also be an officer in the British army. But we both know that cannot be.'

'He might be eligible for a commission with one of the Queen's Indian regiments when the time came,' Ian offered half-heartedly, as he knew even those positions were occupied by British-born officers.

The Khan looked away. 'To many of my countrymen both Hindu and Moslem, I am a traitor for siding with you British in the recent uprising,' he said. 'I have many enemies who wish to see me dead. I even strongly suspect that I may have traitors amongst my servants. I knew you could not stay, so I have hired another European to teach my men modern warfare tactics and weaponry. My contacts told me that Count Kasatkin is living in Paris, so I contacted him and he is available to fill that role.'

'Nikolai!' Ian exclaimed. 'From my knowledge of the count, I think your choice is wise. He has much military experience.'

'He demonstrated his personal courage during the rescue mission, and he also speaks an Indian language,' the Khan mused. 'He should arrive next week, when you are due to rejoin your regiment. I am sure that you and he will be pleased to meet once again.'

Ian did not comment. He respected the Russian count as a soldier, but he was also the husband of the woman he loved and that left a bitter taste in Ian's mouth. That he was living in Paris and returning to India was a puzzle, though. Nothing was mentioned of Ella accompanying him, and Ian thought it rude to inquire.

A week later, Ian returned to his regiment and his company of men. He left with some regrets as he had become very fond of the Khan's young son. Many times, as they sat together in the shade of a mango tree, Ian would reflect how wonderful it would be to have a son of his own to teach and share moments with.

As Ian once again entered the regimental barracks, Count Nikolai Kasatkin was arriving at the Yeddo residence of the Khan to take up his duties, training the Indian prince's small army of bodyguards.

FIFTEEN

Josiah had never dreamed of such a large body of water surrounded by land. It had taken three months to travel from England to the Australian colony of New South Wales, but to a five-year-old it felt like a lifetime.

He stood on the deck as the ship steamed through the great sandstone heads, gazing at the occasional wisps of smoke rising from chimneys of houses and cottages scattered along the shore on the heights. Eliza stood beside him, gazing in awe at the sight of so many ships anchored in the inlets of the harbour. They were steamships still with sails, and amongst the ocean-going giants were the smaller ferries and fishing boats.

'So, we have finally arrived,' a voice said behind Josiah. 'A new life in a new land.' Josiah knew it was Professor Shortland. He placed his hand on Josiah's shoulder. 'I have been informed that there are very good schools in the colony, and I am sure you will prove to be an excellent student.'

Josiah liked Professor Shortland. Even Eliza's father seemed to have respect for the short little man with the spectacles and round face. But the professor's wife was another matter. She had hardly spoken to him throughout the journey, except to occasionally chide him for minor infractions of the rules she imposed. She was a cold woman with a sour expression and sometimes Josiah heard her shrill voice raised in anger with the kindly man, complaining bitterly that they had gone to the farthest part of the world, leaving her family who she feared she would never see again in her lifetime. But the professor would admonish her that he had no choice other than to take up a generous teaching position at the new university in Sydney. In London, they'd barely been able to survive on his associate salary.

Josiah could feel warmth in the air as the ship now steamed towards the central part of the harbour. He'd been told that it was summer in the Australian colony, and though that made no sense, Josiah was more interested in what lay ahead when they landed. The professor had shown him pictures in a book of strange – almost mystical – animals that he said were native to the land. There was a strange creature called a platypus and another creature that hopped which he said was a kangaroo. Josiah was very much looking forward to seeing these exotic creatures.

The ship slid through the calm waters of the harbour and came to a wharf surrounded by tenement houses on high ground and tall buildings that overlooked streets bustling with traffic. Horse-drawn carts trundled along the thoroughfares and well-sprung coaches carried smartly dressed men and women to meet the arriving migrant ship.

They went below to gather their belongings before

returning to the deck as the gangplanks went down to the wharf.

Josiah led his new family onto the land that was to be his new home. He remembered hearing Mrs Shortland snort, 'At least we were not born colonial. We are proudly English, with nothing in common with these convicts.'

★

Ian was smoking a cigar and sipping sherry in the regimental officers' mess with his colleagues when he noticed a captain wearing the uniform of a cavalry officer.

'Campbell, old chap!' Ian said when he approached the rather dashing figure standing alone in the spacious room that spilled out to a well-ordered garden beyond with its exotic shrubs and flowers.

'Good God!' Scott Campbell said. 'Captain Forbes. How the devil are you?'

'I'm surprised to see you back here in the uniform of the British army,' Ian said, looking down quickly to see that Scott's missing hand had been replaced by a gloved artificial hand. 'I thought that after your experiences during the mutiny, you might have had enough of India.'

'I was able to get a commission with the army but, alas, only that of a captaincy. It was better than serving in some godforsaken place with the infantry. Besides, the army recognised my knowledge of the Indians, which made me of some value to them. At least I was able to gain a commission into a cavalry regiment, albeit it one of Sikh horsemen. Good cavalrymen, though.'

'I read how the East India army did not take very well to being disbanded,' Ian said. 'I should get you a drink. Scotch and soda?'

'You have an excellent memory, old chap,' Scott said.

Ian gestured to one of the Indian mess stewards and ordered a scotch and soda for the cavalryman, brother to one of Ian's best friends, Dr Peter Campbell, who was married to Alice, nee Forbes, Ian's supposed sister.

When the drink was delivered by the servant on a silver tray, Scott took the tumbler in his good hand and raised it in a toast. 'To meeting again unexpectedly with friends.'

Ian responded by raising his own glass. 'Tell me, old chap, do you hear from your brother in Canada?'

'Peter rarely writes, but Alice is the correspondent in the family. The dear lady keeps me abreast of their lives. We are uncles to a boy and a girl, with another nephew or niece on the way.'

Ian smiled. 'I had not heard they were expecting again. What excellent news.' He was pleased to hear the news of Peter's growing family. It was one of the few stable things in his life.

'I heard that your regiment was up on the frontier a few weeks back, and that we took a lot of casualties against the tribesmen.'

'It was bad,' Ian replied. 'A lot of good men remain in those hills and will never see home.'

They both fell silent out of respect for the dead. After the moment passed, Scott asked, 'Your sergeant major, Conan Curry, if I remember? Is he well?'

'Sergeant Major Curry is alive and well and whipping new recruits into shape as we stand here enjoying a drink together,' Ian answered. 'I have heard rumours that the regiment will be returning to our barracks in London for Christmas.'

'I do not envy you,' Scott said with a smile. 'Despite being born in Canada, I have come to dread the cold. I am more than happy to see out my service in India now that the mutiny is over. Maybe meet the widow of some rich English civil servant, and eventually settle down to the indolent life as a country squire.'

'Good luck with that.' Ian grinned. 'I am sure the foreign office will find another campaign, somewhere in the British Empire, for my regiment to serve. There is no shortage of places in Africa and the Far East where trouble is always on the boil. It is getting a bit tedious here.'

'Well, at least my regiment has something to do,' Scott said, draining his drink. 'The local Indian prince has trouble with a few malcontents left over from the mutiny. He has lead mines that have come under sporadic attacks by bandits. We have been sent out to search for the bandit gangs.'

'I know what you are referring to,' Ian said. 'I was fortunate to spend some time on a transfer to the Khan's palace. He mentioned that he had lost a payroll to an ambush a few weeks ago. He has since hired a former Russian officer, Count Kasatkin, to train his bodyguards.'

'Wise of him,' Scott said. 'I know the local administrators put a lot of stock in protecting the Khan because of his proven loyalty to the Queen and because he supplies lead to our coffers.'

'That may be,' Ian said. 'But the Khan is also a good man and deserves our protection.'

A bell sounded for supper and both men made their way to the dining room. Ian was pleased to reacquaint himself with the former Canadian. He was, after all, a fellow colonial in the service of Queen Victoria.

★

Captain Ian Steele did not realise that his chance meeting with Captain Scott Campbell would be the catalyst to breaking the boredom of barracks life. It was only a week later that he was summoned to parade before the regimental commanding officer, Colonel Neil Thompson, that Ian learned he was about to return to active service.

Ian stood to attention in the palatial room that served as the colonel's office. It was part of a mansion that had once belonged to a very wealthy Hindu businessman who had chosen the side of the mutineers and had since fled the country.

'Be at ease, Captain Forbes,' the colonel said. 'I have a mission very much suited to your colourful past exploits with the regiment. I am granting you leave to return to the service of the Khan to assist him with a small problem he has.'

Ian immediately guessed it had to do with the subject of the roaming bandit gangs preying on the wealth of the lead mines. 'Yes, sir,' Ian replied. 'Anything I can do for the regiment. If I may venture, has this something to do with the troubles the Khan is having with bandit gangs?'

The normally taciturn commanding officer smiled. 'I am unsurprised that you have your finger on the trigger,' he said. 'Yes, we are collaborating with an Indian cavalry regiment. My staff were approached by a Captain Campbell of that regiment, specifically requesting your assistance. Coupled with his request was that of the Khan himself. It seems that you are a very popular man, Captain Forbes.'

At least Ian knew the two men requesting his services and liked both of them. 'Sir, if I may, I would request to have Sergeant Major Curry join me in whatever enterprise lays ahead. I am sure that Colour Sergeant Leslie is more than capable of filling in as acting CSM while we are temporarily detached from the company.'

'I concur, and will add that you may nominate a section from your company of seven men to go with you on this

mission – whatever it may be. I presume that you will identify seven of your most reliable men.'

Ian was very pleased to be able to take some of his men
from the company and would rely on Conan's intimate
knowledge of the soldiers he would consider the best for the
mission. 'Thank you, sir,' Ian said. 'I am sure that whatever
we are to embark on will bring honour to the regiment.'

The colonel rose from behind his desk and walked over
to Ian. 'You have twelve hours to get your kit together,
and have your selected men paraded for me before you
report to the Khan's palace. Good luck, Captain Forbes.'
Unexpectedly the commanding officer held out his hand,
and Ian accepted the firm handshake. 'I know the Colonial
always succeeds – and brings his men back safely. Good
hunting.'

As Ian departed the commanding officer's headquarters,
Colonel Thompson shook his head and frowned. There
was much he would have liked to warn his best officer
about, but his lips had been sealed by the government civil
administrator. Damned politics overrode military common
sense and Colonel Thompson slumped down in his chair
at his desk. Poor, damned Captain Forbes may have little
chance of surviving his mission. If he had only known
the truth.

★

In the chaotic time after the reading of her father's will,
where Ella found herself in a strange world where the
criminal basis of businesses blurred with the socially accept-
able face of enterprise, she still found herself drawn to the
list of names she'd found in her father's papers. To have
been secured in that bank vault, it must have been valuable.
She sat at her father's desk and looked over the list again.

There were lawyers and bankers she had never heard of but who must have been familiar to her father. One or two of the names even appeared from time to time in the social columns of the papers. But what did it all mean?

'Countess, Lady Montegue-Jenkins is here,' Ikey's old valet said at the door of the office. 'I've told her you're not receiving but she wishes to speak with you.'

Ella was startled to hear the name of the woman for whom she had much respect. 'Thank you. Show Lady Montegue-Jenkins in immediately. I will meet with her in the drawing room. Please tell Cook to send tea.'

The valet disappeared and Ella secured the list in the desk drawer, locking it with a key. She brushed down her black dress, feeling just a little in awe that she should receive a visit from such a renowned woman. She was not dressed to receive the aristocratic wife of a prominent member of parliament. Taking a breath, Ella went downstairs to join the lady in the tastefully decorated drawing room.

Ella stepped inside and saw Lady Montegue-Jenkins admiring a painting. 'I can see this rather delightful painting is by the French artist, Edouard Manet,' she said, turning. 'I must congratulate your late father on his taste in art.'

'My father liked the idea of Monsieur Manet painting life as it is on the streets, Lady Montegue-Jenkins,' Ella replied. 'My father liked his bold brushstrokes.'

'How appropriate,' the lady replied. 'I am so sorry for your loss.'

'Thank you,' Ella replied stiffly. 'Would you care to sit? I have ordered tea.'

'Thank you, Countess Kasatkin. Or may I call you Ella? And I would be happy if you would call me Rebecca. I feel we have much in common,' Rebecca said as she gracefully perched on the divan.

'Very well then. Rebecca,' Ella said, seating herself as well. 'I am happy to be on familiar terms, but I cannot imagine that we have much in common,' Ella said.

Rebecca smiled with a disarming sweetness. 'I admired your father very much,' she replied. 'He forged a financial empire, snubbing his nose at the nobility. I wasn't sure if you knew, but I was one of his clients. He assisted my husband to win votes in his electorate.'

'I did not know,' Ella said, stunned to learn that the imperious lady had dealt with her father, though she was not surprised that her father had the means to influence an election.

Rebecca nodded. 'Your father was very discreet. He had a lot of influence amongst those who count in London, especially in the working districts. But now he has departed this world, I have been informed that you have taken over the role of managing his estates and enterprises. Many would say it is a task well beyond that of a mere female. But you and I know better. I have come today to ensure the smooth transition of my relationship from father to daughter.'

Ella nodded, appreciating the woman's directness and her vote of confidence in Ella's abilities. 'If my father had dealings with you, Rebecca, then I would be happy to continue that tradition.'

'I am pleased to hear that,' Rebecca said as the tea tray arrived. While the tea was poured, both women remained silent. Ella was quickly learning that some things needed to remain confidential – especially the contact her father had with one of England's richest and most influential ladies.

'You and I have a lot more in common than you appreciate,' Rebecca said, daintily sipping her tea from the fine china cup. 'With time, you will see just what I mean.'

Ella smiled at the lady's mysterious pronouncement. She liked the woman, but she could play this game too. 'If you mean the true identity of Captain Samuel Forbes, I already know it from papers my father has left me,' she said, causing Rebecca to raise her eyebrows in surprise.

'Then you will know why he could not be with you, even though I know he wanted to be,' Rebecca said gently. 'But, very soon, the pact he made with the real Samuel Forbes many years ago will be complete. Captain Steele is a very honourable man who would never allow any woman to mourn for him. I also know that your husband, Count Kasatkin, has left you. He is currently in India, working for an Indian prince who I personally know.'

Rebecca's statement startled Ella. Her intelligence was very good, and Ella was sure that Nikolai had more information concerning Josiah's whereabouts.

'Oh, I also know that you have a son, Josiah,' Rebecca added, which startled Ella. She wished she had not entered the arena with Lady Montegue-Jenkins. She was a formidable person, Ella reflected. Possibly even dangerous – to her enemies. Now, Ella had even more reason to court her as a friend.

'I do,' Ella replied. 'My husband had him sent away to the other side of the world. Once I have settled the matters of my father's estate, I intend to fetch him back.'

'I know you will succeed,' Rebecca said with respect in her expression. 'You are your father's daughter.'

SIXTEEN

For weeks, Samuel Forbes sat alone in the house overlooking Central Park, barely eating and hardly aware of the constant pain from the wound he had received on Missionary Ridge. Eventually, he accepted visitors, but his melancholy continued and a letter from the army informing him that he had been promoted to major was of little comfort. What was the point of this world if James was not in it?

Samuel often reflected on why life had come to this and remembered how passionate James had been about the freedom of all men. James had attended abolitionist meetings in New York before the war, and Samuel had accompanied him. When the war finally broke out, James had seen it as a crusade to crush the slave-owning states. The self-proclaimed Confederate States of America had to be defeated so that there was a chance the slaves could eventually be free men. He would often remind Samuel that Samuel's own country had outlawed slavery as far back as 1833, and now Lincoln had finally announced the abolition of slavery throughout America. At least James had lived long enough to see his dream come true, officially if not in actuality, but the terrible war dragged on with long lists of soldiers killed in action appearing every day in the papers on both sides of the Mason–Dixon line.

Samuel had an innate hatred for war but, at a critical moment, had been perceived as a fearless warrior by those he led. And as he sat staring blindly out his window, Samuel made an inexplicable decision that went against all he held sacred; he chose to return to the war and fight on. It was not an act of revenge for James' death, but a matter of seeing the great crusade reach an end – one way or the other – for all James had held sacred.

For Samuel, returning to the frontline was an act of love in the memory of the man he cherished beyond all others. So Major Samuel Forbes would accept the offer for a posting to the staff of General Ulysses S. Grant.

★

Detective Sergeant Robert Mansfield knew that he did not have enough evidence to obtain a conviction for murder against Charles Forbes without a confession – and he was realistic enough to know that would never happen.

However, the policeman knew he had enough to unsettle his prime suspect in the death of the stableboy. Sometimes, suspects confronted with substantial circumstantial evidence were rattled enough to start making mistakes. Robert had a policeman's instinct that this same prime suspect was probably a double murderer, and he was a man who had to be stopped, regardless of his high standing in English society.

This time, he would confront Charles Forbes alone, as he knew that his friend and colleague, Constable Michael Covell, was in a difficult position because of the influence of the Forbes family in the village.

Robert took the small gig out to the Forbes manor. He was grudgingly ushered inside by the butler through a back entrance, and Robert knew this was a deliberate insult to remind him that he was considered little more than a mere tradesman. Then Robert was shown to a billiard room, where he was met by Sir Archibald Forbes and his son, Charles.

'Constable,' Charles greeted Robert with a sneer.

'It's detective sergeant,' Robert corrected cheerfully, knowing that the greeting was meant to demean him. 'I would like to put some questions to you about the death of your stableboy, Harry. It happened some time ago, I understand.'

'A terrible accident,' Sir Archibald said. 'We paid for the funeral and the headstone for the unfortunate boy.'

'I have reason to believe that Harry did not die of the fire but was stabbed before the fire occurred,' Robert said, noticing that Charles suddenly paled. 'Twice.'

'How could you believe that?' Sir Archibald demanded.

'Because I had the body exhumed,' Robert replied. 'I saw with my own eyes the two wounds to his chest, and the medical examiner has confirmed it. The fire charred his body, but it didn't kill the boy,' Robert said, turning to Charles, who remained silent. 'Do you have any idea how that might have happened, Mr Forbes?'

'You will get out of my house this very moment,' Sir Archibald exploded. 'How dare you insinuate that my son has been involved in any nefarious deeds? Do you know who we are?'

'Oh, I know that you hold a seat in the House of Lords, Sir Archibald, and that you command much power,' Robert stated. 'But the people of England have placed upon my shoulders the responsibility of seeking justice for them.'

'Get out now!' Sir Archibald said in an enraged voice. 'I will be writing to your superior officers to complain about your unfounded accusations against my son. I will have you thrown out of the police force, mark my words! I will make it my mission in life to strip you of everything you possess so that you may learn to live on the streets where you belong.'

Robert turned to see himself out. But this time, he made his way to the front door with a grim smile. Charles had said nothing but his reaction to the news that he was being investigated for the death of the stableboy had taken him completely unawares. He had probably been expecting further questions concerning the death of Jane Wilberforce. The father's threat to have him dismissed from the Metropolitan police might have worked on lesser police, but Robert was unconcerned. He knew who was behind his posting to the little village in Kent, and Lady Rebecca Montegue-Jenkins was more than a match for the arrogant Forbes family. If he did his job correctly, Robert had a formidable force backing him.

Robert stepped outside the sprawling country manor house and looked up at the sky. A storm was rolling in, and he hoped that it was an omen in this part of the English countryside where they still held superstitious beliefs about the existence of witches. Right now, he had a fleeting thought that if Jane Wilberforce was a witch, she might still hold power over the living and lead him to substantial evidence which would one day see Charles Forbes led to the gallows.

Robert took the reins of his horse and drove the gig back to the police station just as the first explosive bolt of lightning hit the earth atop Druid Hill.

Robert shuddered, and not from the chill preceding the storm front.

★

'Did you kill that boy?' Sir Archibald asked angrily when the impertinent officer had departed the house.

'No, I did not kill Harry,' Charles lied. 'That damned policeman was bluffing. Our own doctor declared the boy died from the effects of the fire.'

'I know you killed that wretched village girl,' Sir Archibald said, slumping into a leather chair. 'Did it give you a taste for taking life?'

'No, Father. I had no reason to do harm to Harry.' Charles continued to lie but experienced a chill of fear. The mention of the two stab wounds had unsettled him. Charles was coming to accept the policeman was a lot more intelligent than the average man, despite not being of aristocratic blood. What else might he stumble on that could implicate Charles in both killings?

As if reading his thoughts, his father spoke. 'I feel that you might find this a good time to get as far away as you can from England, until this preposterous investigation dies out. If you are not here, the police cannot ask you any more questions. If by the slightest chance they do find something, you will also be out of reach of our law. I would be able to warn you by telegraph to remain in hiding.'

Charles carefully listened to his father's words and accepted that what he said made a lot of sense. A legitimate trip to another part of the world would not appear as if he was fleeing from legal jurisdiction. He could gamble that nothing would come of the investigation, but something warned him Detective Sergeant Mansfield was a dangerous man. As it was, Charles had been losing at the tables lately, and did not believe his luck was good. He had two options for travel, a visit to the Indian prince he had met in London concerning investing in lead mines in that country, or to travel to New Zealand to inspect the tracts of land he had purchased from his one-time old school friend. He knew he had little time to decide.

*

Sanjay, son of the Khan, was overjoyed to see Ian reappear at the palace, although he had been taught not to display boyish enthusiasm in public. He walked over to Ian, dressed in his red-coated uniform, and extended his hand. 'Captain Forbes, it is good to make your acquaintance again,' he said with as much formality as he could muster, and Ian saw the warmth that was in the boy's eyes.

'Have you been practising the skills I taught you?' Ian countered with mock seriousness, and the boy nodded vigorously.

'Captain Forbes, welcome once more to my house,' the Khan said, stepping from behind his son. Behind the Khan, a colourfully dressed man was staring blankly at Ian, and it took him a moment to recognise Count Nikolai Kasatkin.

'I have prepared a room for our discussions on why you are here,' the Indian prince said. 'Captain Campbell has already arrived. The men that you have brought with you will be billeted with my own bodyguard, and I am sure they will find their accommodation a little more pleasing than their barracks.'

Ian knew his seven men and Conan would be looked after and followed the Khan up the broad marble steps until he was a few paces from Nikolai. 'Count Kasatkin,' Ian said, extending his hand. 'I see that we are back together again.'

'I would expect nothing less than the Prince request the best man in the British army to assist us,' Nikolai replied formally, accepting Ian's gesture of goodwill with a firm grasp. When Ian looked into Nikolai's eyes, he could see neither malice nor warmth. Ian guessed that Nikolai had learned of Ian's previous contact with Ella, and decided to shrug off the man's coolness. After all, he had to respect that she was married to this man.

Nikolai led Ian to a vast room and Ian was impressed by a large table at the centre holding a model of the surrounding landscape. It had little hills, roads and rivers marked as well as villages and the mines.

The Khan was chatting to Scott when Nikolai and Ian approached the terrain model.

'Impressive,' Ian commented, and the Khan smiled.

'I had my craftsmen carve wood from the map I instructed them to use for their display. I feel that they have reproduced the land you will be operating in very accurately. Now I will reveal our mission, and your role, Captain Forbes.'

Ian was aware that Sanjay had followed him into the room. The Indian prince noticed Ian's concerned expression as to the presence of his son. 'My son must learn the operations of his future kingdom if he is to rule efficiently. I was Sanjay's age when I also was introduced to the business of politics and war.' The Khan walked across to another table and picked up a billiard cue before returning to the map table.

'I have been plagued by bandit gangs interrupting my supply lines to the city. One particular man with much military experience leads the bandit gangs.'

'If you can say that a former corporal has much military savvy,' Scott snorted derisively.

'Napoleon was once a corporal,' Ian retorted, raising a smile from both the Khan and the former Russian soldier. The humorous retort was lost on the cavalry officer.

'We should return to the matter of why you and Captain Campbell have been seconded to my mission,' the Khan said. 'I have a very special delivery to be made in a week from the area of my mines. It is not lead but a Moghul treasure discovered in a river not far from the mines. We thought the discovery was a well-kept secret, but my intelligence sources inform me that the so-named General Jakoby also knows. I suspect that he will plan to ambush and take the valuable treasure before it reaches here. We need a plan to defeat the bandits.'

'How many men does he have under his command?' Ian asked, eyeing the tortuous terrain between the mines and their present location.

'We have an estimate of possibly five hundred men under arms,' Nikolai replied quietly. 'Most are armed with Enfield rifled muskets, captured during the mutiny. Jakoby needs money to encourage more men to his cause. He pretends that the mutiny is not dead but that the Indian people will rise again. From what Captain Campbell has told me about the man, he is really just a simple thief who will desert his followers as soon as he has enough money to do so. Should he capture the shipment, that would be enough to pocket a substantial amount for himself, as well as pay off his closest followers. Our mission is simple: we stop that happening. If you are wondering, the civil administration is not tasking the British army with this, as it would be a political admission that they have failed to quell the mutiny. We know that what we are up against is not a political movement but simply banditry. The civil administration prefers to see the Khan settle the matter. I estimate that we have twelve hours to come up with a plan, and then march out to execute it. Are there any questions?'

Ian made a quick mathematical calculation in his head; he had eight men, besides himself, the Khan's bodyguard numbered about fifty men, and Scott had brought only five horsemen with him, who would no doubt act as a forward screen ahead of their march. But then, Ian considered, the Khan would probably leave half his bodyguard at the palace for protection of his family. Ian wished that a battery of field artillery had been included in the request for assistance from the British army, because they were looking at twenty-five to accompany their expedition, amounting to just under forty men to face off against five hundred.

SEVENTEEN

John Jakoby stood on a hill, surveying the terrain to the south of his position. He was a man in his thirties, tall and lean with an olive complexion. His appearance was the result of an English mother and African father.

John Jakoby had been born into the slums of Liverpool, where his mother worked as a prostitute to survive. The many sailors who sought her services came from every corner of the earth, and Jakoby grew up learning to survive with his wits and fists in the dockside slums. But Jakoby was also a man of extremely high intelligence, seeking to leave a life of abject poverty behind him by enlisting in the British army. He had a great capacity for learning languages, and had been able to master Bengali as well as other Indian dialects.

He had served as a cavalry corporal in the East India Company, and was amongst many British soldiers who had rebelled when the Company was disbanded. The rebellion of Company men had been put down harshly when the British army arrived, replacing the former mercenary force.

Jakoby had the knack of being able to steal while serving with the Company, and this had eventually brought him to the triangle where he was flogged. This had been authorised by one Major Scott Campbell, and the leader of a growing bandit force had never forgotten the humiliation. One day, he would show the mighty British Empire that there were still some who hated its arrogance. The former soldier had been able to gather sepoys who had rebelled in the mutiny into a well-disciplined force. They accepted Jakoby because he understood their cultures and spoke their languages. Besides, they recognised that he was not of pure European stock and was able to secure Enfield rifled muskets through a shadowy Russian agent who encouraged continuing resistance to the rule of the British. Jakoby also had to pay for the weapons and ammunition with hard currency, but it would all be worth it when he was able to establish his own little kingdom in the north of India. His spies in the city were closer to the ruling prince than the Khan knew. Intelligence gathered revealed the existence of the Moghul treasure of gold and precious stones to be transported from their source back to Yeddo. Jakoby knew that they would not be moved without a heavily armed escort.

Now, he swept his telescope across the horizon of hills covered in evergreen trees in an effort to locate where on the winding trails through deep valleys he would set up his ambush.

John Jakoby closed the telescope and turned to look down on his camp of tents. It was ironic that he had been able to fuse Moslem and Hindu into his small army, when the mutiny had divided the two great religions. He should have fought with the rebels instead of riding with Major Campbell's squadron of cavalry. If he had, he might have been able to unite the warring factions and would now have a real army.

★

As the sun rose over the palace, Ian stood with Conan in a tree-lined courtyard. Around them assembled the Indian bodyguard soldiers of the Khan, Scott's small contingent of Sikh cavalrymen and Ian's own select section of infantry marksmen. Horses snorted and neighed while oxcarts creaked as supplies were loaded for the mission.

'Are you happy about the plan drawn up by Captain Campbell?' Conan growled.

'Not completely.' Ian sighed. 'But the Khan has appointed him overall commander of our little adventure.'

'So, he composes the vanguard, using his cavalry of lancers to ride ahead on the trail north to act as reconnaissance, while we march with the oxcarts to the mines,' Conan continued. 'I expect the buggers we are likely to make contact with will see us coming for miles in the hills north of here.'

'I agree, Sarn't Major,' Ian replied. 'But I doubt that we will have any trouble until we have the merchandise and are on our way back. That is when I think this so-named General Jakoby will attempt to ambush us. If that happens, we are going to pray our riflemen can fire and reload in record time.'

When Ian surveyed his seven hand-picked riflemen, he was pleased to see that the Khan's tailors had managed to replace their red coats with green jackets. Ian knew that they would soon be in the deep gorges and green forests, and now his men would be less conspicuous. He had also convinced the Khan to pay for each man to be equipped with an American Colt Army model .44 calibre revolver. The men were deeply grateful to Ian for the additional weapons, and Ian also knew that he had considerably increased the firepower of his small force.

A bugle called, causing pigeons to set aloft in fright from the rooftops. It was the call to arms and the armed party set out, oxcarts trundling along in the rear. Ian's men shouldered arms on a barked order from Conan and smartly broke into a march through the streets of the city, to the curious stares of the inhabitants. Ian strode ahead of his men, pondering what lay ahead in the forest-covered hills. An inner fear whispered that death lay before them.

*

Ella's friendship with Rebecca Montegue grew with each visit. Rebecca seemed pleased to have a friend outside the stuffy circle she mixed with in the upper echelons of British society, while Ella was happy to have a female friend who believed in her ability to rule her new empire.

In the drawing room of Ella's grand home in London for afternoon tea, Ella poured tea under her friend's watchful eye.

'Do you know, from the moment I met you those many years ago, I sensed that you have a gentle and honest soul. It is hard to balance that when I know how your father's fortune was made,' Rebecca said. 'I know you have inherited a complex financial empire of dark and light. I have observed how you have been able to balance your morality as a great leader. I admire you for this.'

'Thank you. I truly value your esteem, Rebecca,' Ella said sincerely, passing Rebecca the bone-china cup and saucer.

Rebecca sipped the tea carefully. 'I confess, I envy you, too,' she said, placing the cup delicately back on its saucer. 'This society we live in does not consider us capable of leading vast enterprises. If I could, I would have dreamed of leading Britain as the prime minister myself, but the closest I will ever come in this man's world is to promote my husband and hopefully, he will one day be the prime minister, and I will guide policy towards the future through him. There is so much to reform, and the only way I can achieve that is to be the quiet voice in his ear.'

'You do not love him,' Ella stated bluntly.

'No,' Rebecca replied easily. 'But I am fond of him. Did you love your husband, the Russian count?'

Ella sipped her own tea as she reflected on the question. 'I thought I could, but I always lived with the ghost of the man I truly loved,' Ella answered. 'I think Nikolai sensed that, and the ghost haunted us both.'

'We all have our ghosts, Ella,' Rebecca said thoughtfully. 'Do you recall when we first met, I told you that we have a lot more in common than you know?'

'Of course,' Ella said with a slow smile. 'We are both women who control the lives of many men.'

'Even more than that, Ella,' Rebecca said. 'None of my friends know the woman they consider blue-blooded aristocracy is actually the daughter of a village woman who was forced to adopt her baby out to a rich and powerful aristocrat and his wife.' Rebecca released a deep breath, like she'd been holding it in for years. Then she added, 'I am not of noble birth – nor was my twin sister. Oh, if they only knew!'

Ella was stunned by the confession and hardly knew how to reply. 'Your secret is safe with me,' she said finally. 'Where is your sister now?' Ella noticed the sadness that immediately appeared in Rebecca's expression.

'She was murdered, many years ago.'

Ella's eyes widened. 'I am terribly sorry.'

'There is more,' Rebecca said, sipping her tea. 'It concerns our dear Captain Steele. He is a particularly close friend of mine.' Rebecca must have noticed the cloud pass over Ella's face. 'Oh, dear, Ian is nothing more than a friend. My lovers are numerous, but he has never been in that company. But, at one time, Captain Steele was a lover of my twin sister, Jane, who was killed by Charles Forbes, Ian's supposed older brother.'

Ella tried to conceal the shock she felt at these confessions, but nothing slipped by Rebecca. 'This was long before Captain Steele met you,' she said. 'I know Ian loves you with all his heart, but he had to keep his oath to the real Samuel Forbes to complete ten years of service with Samuel's regiment. That term will be complete in a very short time and my intuition tells me he will seek you out.'

Ella now understood why Ian had behaved the way he had over the years – and Ella's marriage to Nikolai had cemented the lack of contact with him. Oh, if only Ian had told her the truth from the moment they had met! Life might have had a different and happier outcome for them both. She felt tears well in her eyes. It was too late now – even if the whereabouts of her estranged husband was not known. She was still a married woman with a mission to find her son.

'Do not cry,' Rebecca said gently, leaning forward to pass Ella a dainty handkerchief. 'You are still a young woman of great beauty and wealth. I am sure you will find a way to be with Captain Steele in the future.'

Ella shook her head. 'Everything is so complicated,' she said bleakly, dabbing at her face. 'I don't even know how to begin.'

Rebecca squeezed her hand. 'I will help you.'

★

After the colourful convoy passed across a small plain, they came to the tree-covered hills to their north with a well-beaten track.

Captain Scott Campbell, as overall commander of the force, called a bivouac for the night and put out picquets to protect against any surprise attack. Ian had his men also join in sentry duties. Conan assumed the role of Ian's batman and prepared a small fire to cook their rations and prepare a pot of tea. They had hardly settled in when Conan and Ian were joined by Scott and Nikolai.

'I thought I should bring some medicine against the chill of the night,' Scott said, holding up a bottle of dark rum.

'A welcome addition to our tinned meat and peas,' Ian said as the two guests settled down beside Conan and Ian. 'Have you eaten?'

Nikolai and Scott said that they had. Ian glanced at Nikolai, whose expression was still blank. What did he expect? Ian thought. The man was the husband of the woman he had loved and that was it. Had loved? No, still loved, despite the impossibility they could ever be together. He remembered the oath he had sworn to Ikey Solomon to respect the union of Ella and Nikolai. It was simply time to move on with his life, as short as it might be under the current circumstance. He had a job to do and the lives of his men now came first.

The four men shared the bottle of rum and when it was empty, Conan and Scott drifted away to inspect the welfare of their men, leaving Nikolai and Ian alone by the campfire. A silence dropped between them as Nikolai poked at the small fire with a stick, stirring the glowing embers.

'I can sense that you are wondering about my wife,' Nikolai said, glancing up at Ian on the opposite side of the fire.

'It is none of my business,' Ian replied. 'Ella is your wife.'

'I had to leave London,' Nikolai said. 'My life was in danger from her father.'

'Ikey?' Ian said in surprise. 'Why would your life be in peril from Ella's father?'

'Because he discovered I was taking money that was not mine to take,' Nikolai answered. 'He sent one of his men after me and I had to kill him in my own defence. Given who Ikey is and what he is capable of, it seemed prudent that I make a hasty exit from England.'

Ian sat back on the log he was using as a seat, taking in what the Russian told him. Knowing Ikey's feared reputation, Ian could accept that if Nikolai had embezzled, then his life would have been in jeopardy.

'How has Ella reacted to your situation?' Ian asked.

'I did not tell her before I left,' Nikolai answered. 'It did not feel right that she should be placed in a situation between her father and her husband. I left with money I had stashed away and took a ship to France, where I was contacted by the Khan, seeking my services as a man who could assist with his personal protection. I accepted his offer and here I am.'

'Have you written to Ella since you fled England?' Ian asked.

'No. It is better that she does not have any further contact with me.' Nikolai sighed. 'I cannot return to England while Ikey lives.'

'It is very noble that you should choose to take the path you have taken to prevent any conflict of loyalties for Ella,' Ian grudgingly conceded. 'But it is possible that Ella would have sided with you, or could have reasoned with her father on your behalf.'

'I don't think so,' Nikolai said bitterly. 'I think it is time that I inspected the sentry posts before I retire.' He rose, throwing the stick into the fire, and strode off into the dark, leaving Ian to ponder his last remark. Why would Ella not welcome Nikolai's return? Or at least seek to be with him wherever he went?

Somewhere in the night, an animal growled. Ian knew he was in the territory of feared beasts of prey. But he also knew the most dangerous animals living in the forests were men armed with Enfield rifled muskets.

EIGHTEEN

Professor Shortland and his wife, Elizabeth, were able to secure a small house only a short carriage ride away from the new university in Sydney. The university administration had organised the accommodation and Josiah liked the little cottage with its garden out the back. As usual, Mrs Shortland mostly ignored his presence in the house, even when Josiah tried to please her.

One day, when the professor was at lectures and Mrs Shortland remained in bed with a cold, Josiah decided that he would go in search of his little friend, Eliza Crichton. He had a rough idea where she lived, as the professor had taken him to the Victoria military barracks to visit the British army major.

Josiah set off on his adventure, rationed with a couple of pieces of bread and a small slab of roast lamb wrapped in a handkerchief. Bullock wagons, drays, coaches and light sprung gigs trundled along the wide road whipped by a hot summer wind. Josiah kept walking, hunched against the wind, until he entered narrower streets that looked vaguely familiar. People pushed past him with hardly a look until he came to a place where drunken men spilled out onto the street. He did not know what a hotel was but could read the name over the door: *The Erin*. He stood for a moment, gathering his bearings, when a voice said behind him, 'Wotcha got, boy?'

Josiah turned to see three boys a few years older than him dressed in rough and dirty clothes. He sensed their menace and clutched his cloth-enclosed meal close. One of the bigger of the boys stepped forward, reaching for Josiah's lunch. Josiah snatched it away and suddenly found himself slammed into the ground. He heard the laughter, and this stung more than the fact he had been knocked down. Josiah struggled to his feet and was aware that the boy had taken his meal. He was already unwrapping the bread and meat when Josiah decided he was not going to let the bigger boy get away with the theft. Josiah charged with his head down, butting the boy who had assaulted him in the stomach. A hiss of air indicated that he had winded the boy, who punched Josiah in the face, causing him to reel back. The blow hurt but Josiah ignored his pain and readied himself for another attack.

'Get out of here or I vill call the traps!'

Josiah could see the three boys back away before scuttling off to a side road with his lunch. Before Josiah could pursue them in his rage, he felt the collar of his shirt being held.

'Settle down, boy,' the heavily accented voice boomed. 'You are a gutsy young fella for one so young.'

Josiah was panting and realised that he had no choice other than to obey. When he was released, he turned to see a broad-shouldered man with a broken nose and piecing grey eyes smiling down at him. 'Vot's your name, lad?' the man asked kindly.

'Josiah.'

'Vell, Josiah, do you have another name?' the man asked.

'I don't know,' Josiah replied. He instinctively liked this tough but gentle man.

'I am pleased to meet you, Master Josiah. My name is Max and I live here at the pub. I haven't seen you in this part of the town before. Vhere do you live?'

Josiah thought about the question and simply turned to point in the direction from whence he came.

Max frowned. 'I think you should be getting back to your ma and da. This part of town is not a good place for a young lad to go vandering alone unless he can fight. I have seen you stand up for yourself, but you lack the pugilistic skills necessary to defend yourself against the street urchins who prey on the weak around here. Maybe a few lessons vill set you straight.' Max paused and seemed to think for a moment.

'Come inside and I vill get you cleaned up before ve find out who you belong to,' Max said finally. Josiah followed him and was taken through the bar, where Max said to the man serving drinks to his working-class patrons, 'Got a guest, Mr Duffy. I'm going to take him out to Kate to see if she can help find the boy's home.'

Then Josiah was taken to a warm kitchen, where a pretty young woman sat at a table, shelling peas from the pod. Next to the woman was a man with broad shoulders.

'Who is this?' he asked.

'All I know is that he is Master Josiah, Mr O'Keefe, and as you can see, he has been set upon by that gang of ruffians from the street over. Master Josiah could do with some lessons from you in the future if he is going to vander our streets.'

'Or you could teach him, Max. After all, you trained Michael,' the man called O'Keefe said.

The pretty young woman identified as Kate rose from the table and walked across to Josiah. She knelt and examined the cut to his face. 'There's a little blood, and you're going to have a mighty fine bruise, Master Josiah,' she said with a smile.

'Ya, is alvight, Katie,' Max growled. 'We should get him something to eat and find out vhere he lives.'

Another person entered the close confines of the kitchen. She was an older lady with grey hair pulled back into a bun and wrinkled skin.

'Who is our guest?' she asked kindly. 'Frank said Max rescued the boy from in front of the pub.'

'The boy said his name is Josiah but does not know his family name, Bridget,' Max answered. 'He is a brave little lad to take on the three toughs from the next street.'

'Well, leave him with Katie and myself and we will work out where he comes from,' Bridget said, kneeling to inspect the boy's bruising. She spat on the corner of her apron and dabbed the boy's bruises with a gesture of maternal love. Josiah liked all the people around him as he sensed he was safe in this warm room with warm people. He knew from the way they talked that they must be those people Professor Shortland called Papists, as he already knew the Irish accent. Josiah had been told to avoid the Papists because they were not the chosen people of God, and doomed to the fires of hell. Josiah was confused because these people did not have horns and were kind to him. He was given a hot meal of beef stew with chunks of fresh bread and, eventually, Bridget and Katie were able to glean that he was living with a lecturer at the university by the name of Professor Shortland.

It was Max who escorted Josiah back to his home, to be met by a distraught professor. Josiah was reluctant to leave the company of the man who talked funny, but knew how he could find his way back to the Erin Hotel.

★

John Jakoby squatted by a campfire in the company of his second in command, a dangerous former Indian sepoy.

'They are sending a force up the valley track to the mines,' the man said, dipping his hand into a bowl of lentils. 'Our spies think that the force – as small as it is – is composed of professional soldiers from the British army. They will be formidable to attack when they return with the treasure.'

Jakoby clutched an Enfield rifled musket and a brace of Tranter revolvers in a cummerbund around his waist. For a moment, he remained silent, reflecting on the intelligence. 'Then we weaken them before they reach the mines,' he declared. 'They will not be expecting an attack on their way into the hills before they take possession of the treasure. Both times, we will be able to pick our ground.'

The former sepoy paused in his eating, glancing around at the bandits lounging under makeshift shelters, and shrugged. The general's plan had merit. They would chew away at the armed force until it was so decimated that taking their prize would be much easier.

★

Captain Scott Campbell's small force escorting the ox-pulled carts was well into the hills and, so far, the journey had been uneventful. At times, he was forced to remind Nikolai to keep his men alert. Scott could see that the Khan's men were not enthusiastic about the mission, and displayed a lack of discipline. At night, some of Nikolai's men would fall asleep on sentry duty and Scott made a promise that he would shoot any man guilty of military neglect in the future. This threat caused a rift between Scott and Nikolai and only Scott, Ian and Conan shared their campfire at night now.

On the fifth day of the trek, the column found themselves following a narrow trail bordered by a fast-flowing stream on one side and steep tree-covered hills on the other. Scott's cavalrymen were ahead of the advancing troops, while Ian's men took up the rear behind the ox wagons.

Ian scanned the terrain along the winding track. The bend ahead on the track had already caused Scott and his men to disappear from sight, and Ian was uneasy. All rationale said the bandits would not ambush them until they were in possession of their precious cargo, but Ian also considered that if he was the bandit commander, he might consider weakening their force in a place tactically favourable to them. Such a place lay ahead. Ian turned to see Conan following him.

'Sarn't Major, get the men to unsling their arms,' Ian said, and Conan passed on the order. The riflemen now clutched their Enfields, also scanning the steep slopes. They were the best and most experienced men in Ian's company, and already appeared edgy as they approached the bend in the track. Nikolai's men continued marching ahead of the wagons, but behind Scott's lancers. The Khan's select bodyguard marched with their Enfields slung over their shoulders.

Ian was about to call to Nikolai concerning his fear of an ambush when a fusillade of small arms fire tore into Nikolai's unprepared men. They fell without a chance to unsling their Enfields, and panicked confusion reigned in their ranks.

'Behind the wagons!' Ian shouted to his own men and they scrambled to take cover behind the stout timbers, returning fire at the unseen enemy. If nothing else, Ian knew the return fire might keep the ambushers' heads down. As it was, Ian noticed that the ambushers were concentrating their fire into the ranks of Nikolai's men.

'Sarn't Major,' Ian called out. 'Form a skirmish line up in the tree line! Advance towards the enemy.'

Conan immediately gathered the soldiers and they made a dash over the short distance to the edge of the steep slope. Ian joined them, and when he was satisfied that each man was in place, he gave the order to advance. The line of men moved forward cautiously with their barrels pointed forward. Ian had his revolver in one hand as he peered through the groves of tall trees. Suddenly, a rifle fired on his right, quickly followed by a couple more. The enemy had been sighted in the trees and Ian quickly ascertained they were probably on the flank of the ambushers, who had not expected those on the track to counterattack. More rifles fired from Ian's men as they rushed forward to keep their enemy unbalanced. Ian saw one of the bandits rise only feet away with a startled expression, and Ian emptied three shots into him. Ian's aim had been true, and the enemy crumpled into the mossy grasses of the forest. The determined counterattack by the outnumbered men under Ian's command worked, and they watched others appear amongst the forest, fleeing for their lives. Ian decided that to give chase might bring his small force into contact with a larger group of the bandits and ordered a halt. Expertly, his men had already reloaded, ready for any possible resistance or counterattack, but Ian could hear the firing fade away and guessed that the bandits had withdrawn.

'Fall back to the road,' Ian ordered and the men obeyed.

On the road, Ian and Conan took stock of the situation and saw Nikolai stumbling towards them. He appeared to have been wounded, with blood dripping from his scalp. Behind him, a few unwounded of his men followed in a state of shock.

When Nikolai reached Ian, he simply stared ahead. The wound to his head had been a grazing shot that had furrowed his scalp. Blood dripped down to his shoulder.

'We did not see them,' he said, touching his wound. Conan removed a clean cloth from inside his jacket and passed it to the Russian. 'If it was that bandit gang, then it makes no sense to attack us now,' Nikolai said.

'Surprise is one of the best weapons a soldier can have,' Ian answered. 'We were not expecting an attack at this stage of our journey, and this General Jakoby is no fool. We can probably expect the same again on our return, and I suspect with the numbers of well-armed men under his command he will finish the job. He is obviously a very smart commander and the British army – or should I say the East India Company – have taught him well. How many do you anticipate that you have lost of the Khan's bodyguard?'

Nikolai held the white cotton cloth to his head and it quickly turned red. 'Half,' he answered miserably. 'My wounded are in bad shape, and I will need the carts to transport them.' One of Nikolai's uninjured men came to him, and their short discussion caused the count to grow pale.

'What is it?' Ian asked anxiously, hearing the fear in the Indian soldier's voice.

'He says that he saw Captain Campbell's men being cut down, and that he also saw the bandits take the captain prisoner.'

Ian was shaken by the revelation. Scott had told him that the man leading the bandits was once one of his own, a light-fingered solider who Scott had ordered to be flogged. No doubt the former East India lancer would be pleased to see Scott in his hands. Ian shuddered. He had no illusions that revenge would be a slow and agonising death for Scott.

'Nikolai, have your wounded taken back down the track to the city in the carts. Use your able men to provide an armed escort,' Ian said.

'What about our mission to return with the Khan's treasure?' Nikolai countered.

'That mission is over,' Ian replied in a flat voice. 'You are free to join us in pursuit of the force that ambushed us. Captain Campbell is worth a lot more to me than all the gold and silver in India.'

He walked away from the bewildered Russian. A silence had descended on the towering forest of trees and night was coming to chill their bodies. Two could play at springing the unexpected, Ian thought as he surveyed his small complement of men. He who dared just might win.

NINETEEN

'It is suicide to attempt to rescue Captain Campbell!' Nikolai protested. 'We do not know where they have taken him, and we do know that they outnumber us. As far as we know, Captain Campbell may be dead by now.'

Ian ignored the Russian's protests and called Conan over. 'We will gather up the extra cartridge boxes from the dead and send the rifles back with the wounded. We will also take rations for three days, and all the water we can carry in spare canteens.'

'I have just the man to lead us,' Conan said. 'Private Bobbins was a poacher before he saw the light of redemption and enlisted. He has eyes like a hawk and will be able to find the path they took.'

'Good show,' Ian said. 'With each of our men armed with Tranter revolvers, we have multiplied our firepower. Go and brief him that we wish to follow the bandit gang.'

Conan nodded and walked over to the seven soldiers awaiting orders.

Nikolai was gazing at his senior Indian non-commissioned officer already organising the carts to return the wounded. 'I will send the rest of my men back as an escort for the wounded,' he said. 'But I will go with you in your foolish attempt to rescue Captain Campbell.'

Ian smiled. 'I remember the last time you made a similar offer, and we got out of a rather tight spot.'

'We were lucky,' Nikolai replied. 'Your company arrived on the beach when the mutineers' cavalry were on top of us.'

'I remember it well.'

Ian joined his tiny army. 'As Sarn't Major Curry has informed you, we will be following the bandits with the aim of rescuing Captain Campbell. However, I am not going to order you to accompany me, and if any man wishes to return to the city with the wounded, he can step forward now.'

None moved. 'Would I have to hand back me pistol if I do, sir?' one of the younger soldiers asked.

'Yes,' Ian replied.

'Then I'm with you, sir,' he said with a grin. 'I always wanted a Tranter.'

His reply raised a nervous chuckle from the other six.

'Sarn't Major Curry has issued you all with extra ammunition and rations, and time is not on our side. Private Bobbins will lead the way and remember, we move quickly and quietly. Time to go.'

With his final words, Ian's section moved into the forest. Nikolai fell in beside him and they watched as the former poacher searched for anything that might prove to be a main path for the withdrawing enemy force. He soon picked up signs and the rescue party followed in an extended vee formation. Soon, the sun would set in the hills and Ian knew that they would be in inky darkness. With any luck, the withdrawing bandit gang would never imagine the men they had ambushed would be hunting them and relax their guard to camp for the night. In the pitch black of the forest, any campfire would show. Where the bandits had surprised them in the ambush, they in turn would fall victim to their own tactics.

Darkness fell and Ian moved his men together so that they would not be separated. He did not stop for the night to form a bivouac but pushed on and was rewarded when Private Bobbins reported that he had spotted the glow of campfires ahead through the forest.

Ian called in Conan and Nikolai. 'We take up positions to surround what we can,' he said, not sure of the numbers they were up against. 'But, before we do that, I am going to take Private Bobbins and reconnoitre their camp. You will remain here in a defensive position. If we get into any trouble, I want you all to withdraw back to the road and then return to the town.'

Conan and Nikolai understood and agreed.

Ian slipped forward with his pistol drawn, following the British soldier who had once used his skills in the night to poach rabbits on his master's estate. With the greatest stealth, they soon found themselves at the edge of what appeared to be a large encampment of many cooking fires. Ian was not surprised to see that no sentries had been posted. After all, they had no fear of being pursued by the tiny force they had ambushed.

'How many do you think there are?' Ian whispered to Bobbins as they lay on the earth, watching the glow of the small campfires.

'Hard to say, sir,' Bobbins answered. 'Maybe twenty to thirty. I can see one tent.'

'Probably for their leader,' Ian said. 'Privilege of rank. Can you see Captain Campbell?'

'No, sir.'

Ian stared hard at the edges of the camp, but anything outside the glow of the fires lay in a blackness accentuated by the stands of tall trees. He hoped against hope that Scott was somewhere in there alive. It was possible the bandit leader might attempt to ransom him, but Ian knew he could not rely on that. 'Stay here and keep watch, Private Bobbins,' Ian said. 'I will return to the men.'

With that, Ian slithered to the rear, knowing that his men waited a couple of hundred yards away.

★

'Captain Campbell, it is grand to meet with you again,' Jakoby sneered. 'But you would probably not recognise the soldier you once had flogged.'

Blood had dried on Scott's face from the beating he had taken on the forced march with the retreating bandits. His hands were tied tightly behind his back and his uniform was ripped. 'I remember you, Private Jakoby,' Scott replied in a weary voice.

'It is General Jakoby to you, Captain, and you may address me as sir,' the bandit leader said, sitting beside his fire, surrounded by a small group of his followers.

'Generals don't make stupid tactical mistakes like that ambush,' Scott said. 'You overdid it, and now you've denied yourself the opportunity to take the treasure we were to bring back.'

Jakoby rose and walked over to Scott. 'I have the men and arms to attack the mines and take more than just the old treasure.' He smiled grimly. 'Destroying your column was a demonstration. *We* rule here, not some British-supported prince. And now my men will see how a British officer dies. I am not sure if I will have you flogged to death when the sun rises or find another way to draw out your death . . . your screams, your begging for mercy . . . it will be so entertaining.'

Scott felt a sickening fear of what lay ahead. He knew he would die an agonising death in this godforsaken place on the Indian frontier. His death would be nothing more than an inglorious forgotten bump in history and what remained of his body would be feasted on by the wild animals of the forest. But even with all hope of salvation gone, he was determined not to let his tormentor see fear in his face.

'You have no words, Captain Campbell?' Jakoby asked, staring into Scott's face.

Scott remained silent and Jakoby turned to a couple of his men, speaking in their dialect. They stepped forward and roughly took Scott by the shoulders, marching him to a nearby tree, where they secured him with stout ropes. Scott knew these would be his last hours on earth. He thought of his family in Canada, his dearest brother, Peter, and his beloved sister-in-law, Alice. They had shared so much during the Indian mutiny. How he truly envied his younger brother's good fortune in being married to the remarkable Englishwoman, and how he wished he might have found the same love in his lifetime.

After a couple of hours, when the camp appeared to be sleeping, Scott did something he had rarely done before; he prayed, imploring that a miracle might happen and free him of his growing terror. The only answer he received was the mournful hooting of an owl.

★

Ian found his men in the dark and called Conan and Nikolai in, briefing them on what lay ahead.

'We found their main camp and calculate their force to be about thirty strong. They feel secure enough not even to post picquets. They have lit campfires and I calculate that by early morning, most will be in a deep sleep around those fires. Our best plan of action is to approach as quietly as we can and take them by surprise. We have the advantage in firepower, even if they outnumber us. Our best chance is to bayonet as many as we can before we have to use our firearms. Every shot will have to count.'

'Are you sure that there are only about thirty in the camp?' Nikolai queried.

'Twenty to thirty,' Ian answered. 'Maybe a few more. Our best approach is to use a single column to attack into the heart of the camp. That way we concentrate our force.'

'I will brief the men,' Conan said. 'We will fix bayonets now.'

Conan quietly called in his six remaining men and briefed them of the plan. Then they moved cautiously forward to join Private Bobbins. It was just after midnight when they assembled in the forest at the edge of the enemy camp.

Weapons had been checked and Ian's men, grim-faced, readied themselves. They knew the plan and on Ian's order, they rose to move forward. So stealthy had been their approach that the bandits slept soundly beside the campfires that were now glowing embers.

When they reached the first three enemy sleeping at the perimeter, Ian's men expertly plunged their long bayonets through their throats, choking off any cries of alarm. The bayoneted men struggled against the long knives pinning them to the ground as they died. One of the bandits must have been a light sleeper, sitting up as the shadowy figures towered over him. He cried out and was promptly bayoneted in the chest.

Figures stirred by campfires and Ian knew that they had lost the element of absolute surprise. Now they would have to rely on the sudden and savage assault of an unprepared enemy.

'At them, boys!' he yelled and immediately fired his revolver into a couple of the enemy rising in front of him. They fell back and it was then that Ian noticed that the bandits had left their Enfields in the tradition of the British army, in small pyramid-like stacks. Only their self-proclaimed general could have taught them that.

Now his men were using their revolvers to deadly effect at close range. Voices screamed in a foreign language and the panic was obvious in their tone. Even now, many of the bandits were scattering for the safety of the forest without attempting to recover their weapons. Those who dared attempt to snatch their Enfields were mown down by pistol fire or bayoneted by Ian's men. Ian could see Nikolai firing his revolver until it was empty, and then resorting to using the sword he always carried.

'On me!' Ian roared above the din of the close-quarter fighting, and his small party instantly obeyed. 'Reload!'

Ian cast about for any sign of Scott, and his spirits soared when he heard a voice call from the darkness. 'Over here!' Ian rallied his men to follow him in the direction of Scott's voice. Private Bobbins had constructed a makeshift torch and its light flickered on a figure tied to a tree. At the same time, Ian also saw a figure in the shadows, flitting towards Scott with a curved sword.

'There!' Ian cried in alarm. Conan raised his Enfield with the swordsman only twenty paces away. Conan trusted his experience to snap off a shot through the dark.

The figure suddenly halted, and quickly disappeared into the darkness of the forest.

Ian was first to Scott and immediately cut his bonds.

'I never really believed in the power of prayer, old chap,' Scott said. 'But you are a goddamned miracle sent from heaven.'

'We'd better get out of here fast before the buggers get back their courage, and reform for a counterattack,' Ian said, handing his loaded revolver to the Canadian. Ian knew that he could use the multi-shot weapon to defend himself with his good hand. Ian had snatched up an Enfield captured from the bandits, along with its powder and ball.

Conan did a quick count and was overjoyed to see that none of his men had been killed or injured in the short but savage attack. Nikolai was wiping blood from his sword with grim satisfaction.

'I had my doubts, Captain Forbes,' he grudgingly admitted. 'But you pulled it off against all the odds.'

'We still have to get out of here and back to the Khan,' Ian answered. He organised his small column to withdraw into the silence and darkness of the great forest in the hills.

★

General Jakoby was in a seething rage as he stumbled on a few of his panicked men in the forest. How could he have been so stupid as to not post sentries? In underestimating his enemy, he had made one of the greatest mistakes of his military career. They had run against what Jakoby calculated to be a force his bandits outnumbered by at least three to one. It was time to eliminate any of the British soldiers before they could reach safety.

He would send a runner to his main camp a mile away and have a force of at least two hundred assemble and join him in the hunt for the men who had humiliated him so easily. He slashed at a tree with his curved sword, remembering how close the bullet from out of the dark had come to taking his head off. The damned officer who had once ordered him to be flogged had been rescued, an even greater humiliation.

General John Jakoby was not about to repeat the mistake of underestimating the man who had led the rescue party again. Next time, he would kill Captain Campbell on sight and, if he was lucky, capture the captain's rescuers and punish them with the most excruciating torture he could imagine. He would have them tied to a branch of a tree upside down and have a fire burn under them. They would scream for mercy as the flames caught their hair alight and the heat fried their brains. No mercy would be granted.

★

Gossip from the Kentish village always found its way to the Forbes manor via the servants' network. The most disturbing gossip originated from the tavern, and today's chatter centred on old George, who'd drunk too many ales and had boasted that his stepdaughter Bridie had come into a generous sum of money. They'd be off for greener pastures just as soon as Bridie's terrible sickness subsided, what with her being in a family way.

Most of the patrons dismissed his drunken ramblings but the boasts reached the ears of Charles Forbes. It appeared the old man had not given the reason for his boasting, but Charles had a good idea he was the subject of the sudden change of circumstances for the man and his stepdaughter and experienced a chill of fear. Charles was quickly learning not to underestimate the police detective from London, and sensed that someone of great influence was behind the detective's investigation into his role in the murder of Jane Wilberforce, and now that of the stableboy as well. Although he felt the police did not have enough evidence to arrest him, Charles could not take any chances. He had only one choice to avoid any scandal arising from his links to either Jane Wilberforce or the stableboy's suspicious deaths.

Charles stood in the freezing cold of the evening, waiting in the shadows just outside the village. He had ridden a rarely used winding track to the ramshackle cottage overgrown by weeds and shrubs. It was in the early hours of the morning on a cloudy night, and Charles knew that the villagers would be tucked away in their warm beds. Even the village dogs would have sought shelter from the sleeting rain.

Charles shivered against the night air as he watched the house until the lantern was dimmed, and then stealthily moved from the shadows to the front door, barely hanging on its hinges. The door creaked when he entered but Charles guessed correctly that Bridie and her stepfather were deep in their intoxicated sleep. He groped cautiously through the single room until his foot edged against a mattress. He could smell the stale body odour and hear the deep breathing. Charles withdrew the long blade from the walking stick he carried, kneeling beside the body on the mattress of straw. He felt in the dark for a form and slid his hand over the face of Bridie. She stirred, raising her hand to push away the annoying thing that disturbed her sleep and suddenly gasped, arching as she did so. The long blade ran through her breast in a fatal stab. Charles clapped his hand over her mouth until her body relaxed, slumping back on the pallet. Perhaps he should have felt something for the woman who had shared his bed, or for the babe within her, but all Charles experienced was a grim sense of satisfaction that the traitorous slut could no longer spill his secrets.

When he was certain she was dead, he groped his way back to the rickety table where he guessed he would find the unlit lantern. He found it and lit the lantern, its light flaring to reveal Bridie's stepfather waking and sitting up to blink his confusion. Charles took a couple of paces to thrust the sword into the man's throat, strangling any attempts at a scream.

Charles watched with satisfaction as the blood squirted from the dying man's neck. Bridie's stepfather feebly attempted to grasp the long blade, but Charles twisted it and the man was soon dead.

Charles withdrew the blade, picked up the lantern and threw it on the straw of Bridie's mattress. The straw quickly flared and flames licked at the wooden walls, rapidly climbing into the thatch of the roof. Charles was surprised at how fast the flames spread, and quickly sheathed his sword and exited the burning building.

He reached his horse tethered behind the cottage in a grove of trees and pulled himself into the saddle. When he glanced back at the cottage, he could see it fully alight and burning with the ferocity of a savage beast in its death throes.

Satisfied, Charles rode home to get some well-earned sleep.

★

Constable Michael Covell stood in the bleak rain, gazing at the shell of the house. What little that was left of Bridie and her stepfather was recovered and this time, the fire had destroyed most of the flesh. He shook his head and wondered how it was that one of the critical witnesses for Detective Sergeant Mansfield's case against Charles Forbes could die in such a manner. Was it purely coincidence, or a means of preventing Bridie from telling what she knew in a court?

The constable walked away, discounting the possibility of coincidence. Charles Forbes had to be involved and the village policeman knew there was little hope of proving that.

TWENTY

Detective Sergeant Robert Mansfield was not surprised to see Lady Montegue-Jenkins sitting in the commissioner's office when he entered. Robert had returned from the Kent village and submitted his report on his findings, which the commissioner had read. Robert greeted the lady with due deference and was invited by the commissioner to take a chair.

'Mansfield, I must congratulate you on your work in Kent,' the commissioner said, indicating Robert's report on his desk before him. 'It has come as something of a surprise to read that you believe Mr Forbes may be involved in another suspicious death, and that you feel with the witness you have located, we may have a better chance of summoning Sir Archibald's son to answer to the charge of murder.'

'May I ask if you have been able to obtain any evidence as to Charles Forbes' involvement in the death of Jane Wilberforce?' Lady Montegue-Jenkins asked.

Robert turned to her. 'I believe the two deaths are linked. It may be possible that the stableboy at the Forbes country estate may have known something he should not have concerning the village girl's death. But that is merely a presumption based on my policing experience, and I do not have legal evidence to support my theory.'

'Call it a woman's intuition, but I believe you, Detective Sergeant Mansfield,' she said quietly. 'Do you feel that you are in a position to arrest Charles Forbes?'

Robert glanced at the commissioner and could see who was controlling the interview. 'In the matter of the stableboy's death, the evidence is circumstantial, and would require the best prosecution lawyers we have to convince a jury. No doubt Forbes will retain the best defence in the British Isles.'

'Then I take your answer as yes to arresting Charles Forbes,' Lady Montegue-Jenkins said. 'Be assured that I will ensure the best prosecution in England will be at your disposal.'

Robert noticed that his commissioner had not said a word but simply nodded in concurrence with all Lady Montegue-Jenkins said. His only contribution to the discussion was to lean forward and say, 'I will ensure that an arrest warrant is drawn up today. You will carry it with you to Kent, Detective Sergeant Mansfield. I will have a couple of constables accompany you to make the arrest.'

'Sir, with due respect, Constable Covell is the local policeman. I think that he and I are capable of arresting Forbes. A man of Forbes' highborn position is not likely to make a scene when we come for him.'

The commissioner thought for a moment. 'Very well, Detective Sergeant, I concur with your choice. If there is nothing else to discuss, I know Lady Montegue-Jenkins has much to do.'

'Yes, sir. Thank you, sir,' Robert said. 'Your ladyship.'

'Detective Sergeant? Might you please escort me to my coach?' the lady asked, rising from her chair. 'Thank you, Commissioner,' she tossed over her shoulder as she walked out, clear in her expectation that Robert would follow. He followed her to the busy street below, where a grand coach drawn by two fine horses waited. The smartly dressed coachman stepped from his seat to open the coach door for the lady.

'I wanted to thank you, Detective Sergeant, for the fine work you have done on this case,' Lady Montegue-Jenkins said. 'I want you to know that regardless of the outcome, I am personally grateful for your efforts.'

'I thank you for your kind words, Lady Montegue-Jenkins,' Robert replied.

'If there is anything further you require to advance the case, please send word,' she said as she stepped into the coach.

'Just one thing, your ladyship,' Robert said. The lady regarded him with interest. 'Forgive a policeman's curiosity, but . . . who is this slain village girl to you? I know obsession where I see it.'

Lady Montegue-Jenkins paused, and for a moment, Robert feared he had offended the powerful woman. Finally, she replied, 'If the slain girl was your sister, would you not go to the ends of the world to find justice for her?' With that, the door to the coach snapped shut and the coachman resumed his place and drove off, leaving Robert pondering her answer. It was not possible for the dead girl discovered on Druid Hill to be related to a woman of such high standing. Was it? Robert shook his head and returned to the police headquarters.

★

The sun was rising when Ian and his party reached the trail back to the highland town. Ian breathed a sigh of relief when he saw that none of his small party had been lost in the inky darkness of the great forest. They were all exhausted, and Scott shivered from not having a jacket on. Ian located a spare green jacket from their supplies and Scott thanked him. 'I did not expect to see another day alive,' he said gratefully to Ian. 'You risked much to come for me when, for all you knew, I was already dead at the hands of Jakoby.'

'Your brother would never have forgiven me if we had not tried,' Ian answered simply, shrugging off Scott's gratitude. 'Alas, we will not be able to rest for long as I suspect that Jakoby has lost a bit of face in losing his prisoner. I only wish we still had your cavalry horses.'

'The bastard killed them all in the ambush,' Scott spat. 'But I agree, he will be hot on our heels. According to my calculations, we have probably six to twelve hours' lead on him.'

'Unless he has a party of his men between us and the Khan's palace,' Ian cautioned. 'His men appear to be the people of these hills and forests and if this is so, I suspect that he will have sent a runner to alert them to our escape, with orders to intercept our withdrawal.'

'I did not consider that,' Scott said. 'It appears that you are now in command, and not I. You know your men better than I.'

'Until we return to the Khan,' Ian said. The two officers shook hands on their pact. Ian provided a briefing to all assembled and issued his orders for the march. He was reluctant to use the track but knew it was the fastest way out of bandit country. He ensured that he had a scout leading the marching men placed well forward to warn them of anything suspicious ahead, hopefully avoiding any further ambush.

★

When Robert arrived in the Kentish village, he was immediately informed by Constable Michael Covell that the residence of their main witness had mysteriously been burned to the ground in the early hours of the morning days earlier, and the very charred remains of two people had been discovered in the ashes. They both knew it was most probably the only real witness they had in their case and Robert immediately suspected that, somehow, Charles Forbes had been alerted to Bridie's role as a police witness. Just another death attributed to the English nobleman. But he had no proof.

Regardless, Robert would execute the warrant, but he had a sinking feeling that they would have no evidence to present against Charles Forbes in court. If nothing else, it would cast a dark shadow on Charles Forbes' reputation. Fleet Street would revel in the news of one of Britain's leading aristocrats being brought before the courts on a charge of murder. What was the old saying? Where there is smoke, there is fire.

They arrived at the Forbes country estate in the afternoon as a drizzly rain chilled them. Both men went directly to the main door. They were not about to use the tradesman's entrance and were met by the valet who had a habit of looking down his nose on all unless they were recognised for their good pedigree.

Robert demanded that they be allowed inside the house in the Queen's name, waving the warrant in the startled face of the imperious valet. He stepped aside and the first person they saw standing at the bottom of the wide marble stairs was Sir Archibald, who demanded to know why they had burst uninvited into his home.

'I have a warrant to arrest your son, Charles Forbes, on the charge of murder,' Robert said. 'I demand in the Queen's name that he present himself to me immediately.' Robert added the reference to the Queen just to take the wind out of the English aristocrat's sails.

'My son is not present,' Sir Archibald replied, turning pale. 'He is currently abroad on business for the family.'

Robert was now the one to have the wind taken out of his sails. 'I require you to inform me where your son has travelled,' he said.

'That is none of your business,' Sir Archibald said haughtily. 'If you have any more questions, you can address them through our firm of solicitors in London. Now, I insist that you depart my home, or I will raise your uninvited intrusion with your superiors.'

Robert glared at the old man, who turned his back and shuffled away.

'What do we do?' Michael asked.

'Question the staff. Someone must know where he's gone.' But the servants of the Forbes household were of no help, and either tight-lipped or terrified; but Robert sensed none of them actually knew where Charles Forbes had fled to. Bitterly disappointed, the two policemen returned to the cold and wet day outside.

'What now?' Michael asked.

'We return and report the result of our attempt to execute the warrant,' Robert said. His mouth tasted like ashes. 'If Forbes has skipped the country, it will be up to others to find him.'

The detective sergeant felt cheated but believed in a word he had once heard a former East India man use: *karma*.

★

201

A cold wind whipped at the small column of men trudging along the winding trail in the tree-covered hills. Ian had ordered his men to march with their Enfields so that they did not have to waste time unslinging them from their shoulders. Ian's forward scout disappeared around a bend in the road bordered by high stony cliffs.

'How far do you estimate we are from the Yeddo?' Nikolai asked Ian.

'I calculate possibly a day to two days,' Ian replied and was about to signal a rest when shots rang out from behind the bend. Immediately, he yelled the order for his men to take up positions on the adjoining slope. The men scrambled into the cover of the trees with their rifles ready. Ian took up a position with them and had a sick feeling that his scout had been shot down. If so, his death may have saved that of his comrades.

'You appear to have been correct in your assessment. Somehow, Jakoby has got a message to his gang ahead of us,' Scott said, crouched beside Ian. 'The fool has learned nothing of tactics. If he had let our forward man pass, he would have caught the rest of us in his ambush.'

Ian silently agreed with Scott but had the sinking feeling that his small force was considerably outnumbered by the ambushers. Ian issued orders for his small party to form a rough circle for all-around defence in the forest above them. The remaining riflemen took up positions behind trees or lay on their stomachs in small rocky gullies.

A shot splattered rock fragments a few feet from Ian, followed by a volley fired down through the trees from above. The enemy held the high ground, pinning them down, and while Ian's men had relatively good cover, he already knew from the volume of fire they were sustaining that they were definitely outnumbered by the unseen force.

His only consolation was that Jakoby's men kept their distance, no doubt with the memory of how lethal Ian's small force was at close quarters.

'Sarn't Major, can you see where the fire is coming from?' Ian called to Conan, who was manning the higher point of the all-around defence.

'I have spotted one or two of the buggers flitting between the trees. They look like they are trying to close in on our position.'

A couple of Ian's own men returned fire and were rewarded with the sound of the enemy crying out as they were hit. Ian thanked the powers for allowing him to have his company drilled in the use of the Enfield as a marksman weapon.

'They'll think twice about getting too close,' Conan called down.

'Good show, Sarn't Major,' Ian replied, knowing that if his enemy had the numbers, they were likely to form up using the cover of the forest and, with their advantage of height, make a charge downhill to overwhelm his small force. The situation was grim and Ian's mind raced with any possible way to extricate his party from the situation. Ian needed a killing ground; a stretch of ground with no barrier to his riflemen to sight and kill the enemy. It was time for unconventional methods. Something he had read in military strategy was that the best defence was an offence. He turned to Scott and Nikolai crouching beside him. 'Our only hope is to sweep the hill above us. Form a skirmish line and advance to the summit.'

'We don't know Jakoby's numbers,' Scott said, gripping his pistol in his good hand.

'If we remain here pinned down, it will only be a matter of time before Jakoby is able to muster his force and swamp us with his numbers. We have little water and rations as it is.

Our ammunition will eventually run out even if we are able to keep the bastards at bay. I have no illusions of the fate that awaits us if Jakoby is able to take us as prisoners.'

Nikolai rubbed his chin, staring up the hill above them. He was leaning on his sword and frowning. 'I think Captain Forbes describes the only viable way we have to survive – maybe not all of us.'

'Agreed,' Scott said with a little reluctance. Ian passed Scott his revolver.

'As you will have difficulty reloading, I think you will need my pistol. I have my Enfield and a bayonet.' Ian slid the revolver into Scott's belt.

Scott accepted the gesture, knowing Ian had considered the extra firepower the spare revolver gave them.

'Time to brief the men on our plan to get to the top,' Ian said grimly, sliding the bayonet onto the barrel of his rifle. 'I am sure Sarn't Major Curry will love the idea.'

Ten men prepared to storm the slopes of the hill, sweeping away any resistance. It was the only hope they had, but Ian also knew he was bound to lose lives in their mad dash to the top. The enemy would be on their flanks as well as in front of them. Sheer guts and grit were all they had on their side.

Ian issued the order. 'Advance!' As one, ten men rose to their feet, rifles and revolvers extended, the long bayonets on the rifles glistening in the weak rays of sunlight breaking through the forest canopy. The wind made a frightening low moan in the chill of the day as the first shots rang out, targeting the fleeting visions of the green-coated, grim-faced men spread out in a skirmish line advancing towards the bandits, who were startled by the audacious sight before them. The first of Ian's men dropped when a musket ball slammed into his chest, but his men did not falter. After all, they would follow the Colonial into hell if he asked them.

TWENTY-ONE

The gunfire from the cover of the trees continued, but Ian thanked God and the Khan for the gift of the Tranter revolvers, which took a deadly toll on exposed bandits. Ian was racked with thirst and exhaustion as he scanned ahead. He saw the crest and was pleased to note that it did not appear to be occupied by his enemy, who had obviously been positioned on the lower slopes to assemble for an all-out assault on his tenuous defensive position just off the track.

Nikolai was scrambling up the slope beside Ian, occasionally snapping off a shot from his revolver, when he suddenly grunted and pitched forward. Ian halted, turning back to see Nikolai roll onto his back, his face creased with pain. Ian could see the blood spreading on his jacket and realised that the Russian had been shot in the gut.

'Leave me!' Nikolai gasped in his agony. Regardless, Ian stumbled to him. Just as he did, a bandit wielding a sword emerged from behind a tree, charging at the two men. Ian snatched up his bayonet-tipped Enfield and rose to meet the attack. The bandit swung too early and Ian deflected the sword with the barrel of his rifle, expertly countering with a twist of the weapon to thrust the long knife into the bandit's chest. At the same time, Ian heard a pistol shot behind him and glanced down at Nikolai, who had shot a bandit approaching from behind, killing him. The dead man lay only a couple of paces away.

'Leave me!' Nikolai groaned again. 'I am surely a dead man.'

Ian withdrew the bayonet from the dead bandit and could see Conan moving towards him. He had blood on his green jacket, and it was impossible to tell if it was his or an enemy Conan had killed.

'I'll help you get the count up on the top,' Conan said, and the two men dragged Nikolai into cover. The crest was like a small fortress with its rocky formation, and the remainder of the small party joined them. It was then that Ian felt his heart sink. Only four of his men settled into the new defensive position. One of the survivors was wounded, suffering a vicious slash to his shoulder. Conan took out his roll book and noted down the names of the men presumed killed and also noted the wounded.

Ian made Nikolai as comfortable as possible, gently removing the jacket to see that the Minie ball had entered the Russian's back and ripped out through his stomach. The exit wound was terrible, and Ian could see that the projectile had mashed the man's stomach and entrails before exiting. Ian knew there was no hope of Nikolai surviving his wound with even the best army surgeons on hand.

'You did a foolish thing, stopping to bring me up here.' Nikolai grimaced, fighting the overwhelming pain. 'You could have been killed.'

'You are Ella's husband, and I swore to Ikey many years ago I would look out for you,' Ian said, kneeling by the critically wounded man.

'That is rather funny when you consider Ikey tried to have me killed in London,' Nikolai said with a twisted smile. 'Now he and I are both dead.'

Ian knew it was senseless to contradict the Russian. They were both experienced soldiers who had witnessed such wounds on the battlefields of the Crimea. In many cases, gut-shot soldiers would beg to be shot, or carry out the act themselves to avoid the agonising and slow death.

'I will write to Ella and tell her you died a hero's death,' Ian said gently.

'I doubt that your words will bring any consolation to my wife,' Nikolai said sadly. 'I have not lived a good life these past years. I was never very kind to her. I sought comfort in the arms of many women because I knew my own wife did not love me. Her heart was with another and I now know it was you, Captain Forbes. Or should I say, Captain Steele.'

Ian was wordless in his shock from the dying man's revelation. He had despaired of ever seeing Ella again and now her husband was saying she had never stopped loving him.

'There is something else I think you should know before I leave this earth,' Nikolai continued. 'You have a son. A five-year-old boy.'

Ian now hardly believed his ears. 'A son . . . how could that be?' he asked.

'Ella gave birth before we were wed, and I was not informed. Ikey had the baby removed but Ella was able to find him. I was only recently made aware of the boy's – your son's – existence, when Ella chose to have him come and stay with us. In my jealousy, I had the boy smuggled out of England. I regret that. But it is all too late now.' The stress of talking was taking its toll but Ian had so many questions to ask and persisted.

'Does my son have a name?' Ian asked as Nikolai closed his eyes in an attempt to lock out the agonising pain surging through his body.

'Josiah,' Nikolai croaked. 'I sent him to the Australian colonies. To Sydney Town.' Suddenly, the count cried out in his agony. 'No more! Mercy! No more!' he yelled, and Ian knew that the critically wounded Russian was beyond rational conversation. He picked up Nikolai's pistol and held it to the critically wounded man's head. The single shot ended the Russian's pain forever.

For a moment, Ian cradled the shattered head, tears running rivulets through the gunpowder that blackened his face. Whatever had happened in his life in London, Count Nikolai Kasatkin had proved to be a brave soldier.

'Nothing else you could do,' Conan consoled him, seeing the pain in his friend's face. 'I would expect you to extend the same mercy to me if I am ever gut shot.'

Ian glanced up at Conan. 'We are in a hopeless situation,' he said.

'We've been in worse,' Conan lied.

'Do you have any idea of how we are going to get out this time?'

'The speed with which Jakoby was able to get into position to ambush us again tells me he knows these hills like the back of his hand,' Conan said.

Ian shook his head, staring down at the dead Russian. 'It's hopeless.'

Conan stared at his commanding officer, unfamiliar with his defeatist attitude. 'We could wait until night and attempt to break through his lines?' When Ian didn't reply, he prompted with a 'Sah?'

'I have a son. Josiah,' Ian said softly. 'We cannot die on this godforsaken hill.'

Conan did not reply but stared down the slope. He could see movement, and then stone splintered near his head from a random shot from amongst the trees below. One of the men reacted from only yards away and Conan heard the soldier's whoop of joy as he took out the bandit who had fired at them. Conan knew that surrender was not an option as the bandits would simply torture them to death for their amusement and revenge for the many comrades Ian's party of trained soldiers had extracted from their ranks.

Conan left Ian with the body of Nikolai and crawled carefully to each soldier manning the small perimeter. He attempted to encourage them with words of how they held the advantage of firepower and the natural fortress of the stony crest. But he would also grimly remind them to keep a last bullet in their Tranters for themselves if they were eventually overrun. When he reached Scott, he sat down with his back to a large rock.

'Captain Forbes is in a bad way,' Conan said wearily. 'He is not his confident old self. Something has changed in him. I have soldiered with him for many years and just now I could see the change.'

'Has he been wounded?' Scott asked.

'Not in the physical way, but he has just learned from the Russian that he has a son he never knew about, somewhere back home in New South Wales. He has not been himself. I think that you may have to take command, sir.'

'I will talk to Captain Forbes, Sarn't Major,' Scott said. 'Would you be a good chap and reload my revolvers? My good hand is a little shaky.'

Conan took the six-shot pistols and reloaded with cap and ball as Scott made his way to Ian, sitting by the body of Nikolai. The sun was setting on a chilly overcast day that was turning to a freezing cold night.

'How are you holding up, Sam?' Scott asked, settling down by the despondent infantry officer.

'Not well,' Ian answered, rubbing his forehead with his hand. 'I can't think of any way we can get out of this situation. Jakoby is obviously surrounding the hill, and it will only be a matter of time before they rush us with their superior numbers. Only a miracle can save us, and I'm all out of belief in miracles.'

'So was I until you rescued me,' Scott said. 'We are still alive and with sufficient ammunition to thwart a frontal assault.'

'I thought about attempting an escape in the dark,' Ian said. 'But we are so few and Jakoby would just pursue us until none were left alive.'

'I was told that you have just learned about having a son,' Scott said, extending his right hand.

'I don't know that learning I'm a father was such a good thing,' Ian replied, accepting the gesture of congratulations. 'I don't think my son will ever know I existed. It might have been better if I was killed not knowing.'

'We have to come up with some kind of plan. We owe it to your men,' Scott said, withdrawing a tobacco pipe, clenching it in his teeth and lighting it. The smoke from the bowl was swept away on the bitter wind.

'The only thing I can come up with is to send Private Bobbins down the hill on a reconnaissance mission to seek out any weakness in their siege lines. He was a poacher back in England and has a reputation in my company as a natural-born man of the night. It is the only thing I can think of.'

'It is better than just sitting here waiting for Jakoby's men to come for us,' Scott said, puffing on his pipe.

'I will summon Sarn't Major Curry and brief him on Bobbins' mission,' Ian said slowly. 'I will go with Private Bobbins and you can assume command.'

Scott cast about the handful of men in the rocks. He, a cavalry officer born in Canada and without a horse, was now a British infantry officer, he thought with grim humour. Scott clapped Ian on the shoulder. 'Good luck, old chap,' he said. 'It will be Christmas soon and I promise the fattest roast goose you've ever had when we get back to the garrison mess.'

Ian attempted a smile, but it came out as a grimace as he rose to seek out Conan and Private Bobbins. He located them and told them of his plan to use the night to probe the extent of the enemy lines between the crest of the hill and the road below. Ian ensured his revolver was primed and set out with the English soldier when the darkness was well and truly upon them.

The two men slithered out from amongst the rocks, working their way cautiously in the darkness through the trees. Ian kept his pistol pointed forward, ready to fire and beat a retreat back to the relative safety of the hill's summit. Private Bobbins led with his rifle and bayonet pointed forward in a crouch, ensuring he did not provide a silhouette of any kind for bandit eyes.

Ian counted his paces as well as he could and calculated that they had advanced at least a hundred yards, stopping occasionally to listen for any sounds. If there were so many men besieging them, how was it possible they remained so quiet? Nor were there any campfires, only the silence of the forest and moaning of the wind in the branches of the trees. It was eerie and Ian experienced more than the cold of the night creep over him. Bobbins was only inches away, his presence hardly noticeable.

'Sir, something is queer,' he whispered. 'My experience tells me that we are alone.'

'I get the same impression,' Ian whispered back. 'Or the bandits have not occupied this part of the hill.' For a moment Ian thought about his next move. 'We will see if we can reach the road.'

The two men crept closer to the base of the hill until they found themselves gazing down at the track leading back to the city. It was deserted, and Ian knew what they must do next.

Ian and Private Bobbins carefully clambered back up the hill until they could see the crest and its rocks against the night sky filled with twinkling stars.

'Captain Forbes and Private Bobbins coming in,' Ian called quietly. From the corner of his eye, he saw the barrel of an Enfield covering them. Both men entered the circle of rocks to be met by Scott and Conan.

'Damned if I know what is going on, but Private Bobbins and myself did not see any sign of Jakoby's bandits between us and the road,' Ian said, taking a swig of water from a canteen Conan passed to him. 'No sight or sound. No campfires – nothing. It is as if they have just vanished. I think we take the chance and make our way to the road tonight. We have a better chance of escaping that way than waiting for Jakoby to slaughter us up here. Sarn't Major, pass the word along to the lads that we leave now, while we still have the night on our side.'

Conan spread the word to the few remaining soldiers, and they left the hilltop in single file with pistols in hand, ready to deliver a withering fire if they were spotted by the enemy. They moved silently and cautiously and found themselves at the edge of the road before first light. By sunrise, they had marched at least two miles along the winding road until they came to a place where the valley widened onto a small grassy plain.

Ian and his men were stunned with what they saw in the early sunrise spread out before them on a meadow in the valley.

TWENTY-TWO

The scene before the handful of Ian's men reminded him of an English country fair. White conical tents, fluttering flags and red-coated soldiers dotted the military camp. Ian could also see a battery of artillery guns as a detachment of Sikh cavalrymen galloped towards Ian and his men.

'They are members of my squadron,' Scott commented, and Ian recognised the battle colours of his own regiment on a flagpole beside a larger tent.

The cavalrymen came to a halt and Scott recognised a young English lieutenant leading them.

'Sir, it is good to see you are safe,' the British officer said to Scott as he saluted. 'We feared that you may have been slain.'

'Mr Wren, I think we should report to whoever is in charge of the camp,' Scott replied.

'That would be Colonel Thompson,' the cavalry officer said. 'He is currently in his tent.'

Escorted by the cavalry detachment, Ian and the remainder of his men shouldered arms and marched through the ranks of the curious red-coated soldiers with heads high. Some of the onlookers called hoorahs, raising their caps.

Eventually, Scott and Ian came to the largest tent and Ian saw his regimental commander sitting on a camp stool in front of his HQ, sipping on a cup of tea at a small table set out with breakfast. He looked up at the dishevelled men in the green jackets as they approached. Ian stopped and saluted smartly. Conan brought the men to a halt.

'Ah, Captain Forbes, it is grand to see that you have survived and returned to the bosom of the regiment,' the colonel said, replacing his cup on the table spread with a white linen tablecloth. 'I presume that you are Captain Campbell,' he continued, addressing Scott.

'Yes, sir,' Scott replied, eyeing off the chapatis and jars of jam on the table. 'But I am afraid I have lost my command some days ago to the work of the bandits under Jakoby's leadership.'

'I am saddened to hear that, Captain Campbell. I am sure that they died bravely,' the colonel said, rising from his camp stool to walk over to Ian and his small party, where the colonel turned to his aide. 'Major, ensure that Captain Forbes' men are given a hot meal and a chance for some rest. Captain Campbell, Captain Forbes, follow me inside, if you please.'

Conan spoke with the regimental major and took the survivors away for a badly needed meal and change of uniform while Ian and Scott entered the tent. Inside was a table with a map displayed on it surrounded by three camp chairs, with a portrait of the Queen overlooking the setup from one of the canvas walls.

'I have no doubts that you are both wondering why the regiment is here,' the colonel said.

'We were pleasantly surprised to see you,' Ian replied.

'Our civil administrators decided that a show of force was required after all, to demonstrate to Jakoby's bandits that they are not welcome in this region.'

So that was why they had not encountered any resistance on the slope of the hill in their withdrawal, Ian thought. The bandits had got wind that a large force of well-armed British soldiers was advancing on them.

'I'm afraid that I must take responsibility for failing in our mission to retrieve the Khan's treasure,' Ian said with a note of bitterness, and was surprised to see a smile appear on his regimental commander's face.

'On the contrary, Captain Forbes,' he said. 'Everything went to plan. We had the treasure smuggled down a secret track to Yeddo while you distracted the bandits. It has since been divided between the Khan and our government. I am assured that it is worth a fortune and now fills the coffers of the Crown. I could not tell you at the time that you were intended to draw Jakoby's attention to your force, as the Khan had discovered a traitor in his household who was providing intelligence to Jakoby in the hills. We knew we could not possibly bring it to the town with the numbers of well-armed men he had in his command. The only mistake Jakoby made was choosing to ambush you and Captain Campbell's force on your way to the mines. The fact that you survived proves to me that he bit off more than he could chew, as I expected he would.'

Ian listened to the explanation in utter disbelief. They had been sent out on a near suicidal mission to fill the coffers of the British government, and to swell the Khan's personal fortune. He glanced at Scott, who looked pale but said nothing.

'I am sure that you both will require some good food and a rest before resuming your duties,' the colonel said. 'We will be withdrawing to our barracks in the morning, and I am pleased to say the regiment will be able to stand down for Christmas. If you have no questions, gentlemen, I suggest that you have breakfast and clean up. I have been instructed that you will not have to pay for your new uniforms – courtesy of the Khan.'

'That is very generous, sir,' Ian said, and the sarcasm was hard to hide.

'I know it is hard to lose men, Captain Forbes,' the colonel said with a note of sympathy. 'But they serve the interests of the Queen. We all do.'

Scott and Ian departed the tent and were met by Lieutenant Wren, who led them to a tent, sparsely furnished with a table, one camp chair and two low-slung beds. He returned with new British uniforms, and a private soldier brought them a meal of chapatis, jam and a pot of hot tea.

Ian was reluctant to give up his green jacket as he'd noticed how well it blended with the colours of the forest, giving them better concealment in the trees. But he was also pleased to be back in the uniform of his regiment.

The two men ate their meal in silence before changing, and Lieutenant Wren returned with a bottle of rum. 'Compliments of Colonel Thompson,' he said, saluted and left the Canadian and Australian with the bottle between them. Outside, they could hear the comforting sounds of the regiment in its bivouac; men laughed, NCOs bawled orders and there came the occasional sound of a bugle playing its reassuring notes to the soldiers, gunners and cavalrymen deployed in its defence. This was Ian's home, his family . . . except now he knew he had a son somewhere in his old home of New South Wales.

'My men died so that others could get richer,' Scott said bitterly as he poured the rum into two metal mugs.

Ian accepted the mug passed to him. 'My men trusted my leadership. I handpicked them for this mission, and now three lie dead, and for what? They did not die for honour or standing in line against the Queen's enemies. They died for nothing.'

Scott nodded and raised his mug. 'To those damned good men we left in the forest – and on the road,' he said. Ian raised his without comment and they took a deep swallow of the fiery liquid.

'I am finished with soldiering when my ten years is up,' Ian said, feeling the warmth of the alcohol begin to take hold of his body. 'I fear that all I know about life is carnage and misery. There must be more. When my time is done, I will go home and look for my son.'

'Where will you retire to?' Scott asked.

'Home for me is the colony of New South Wales, in a little village that lies at the foot of the Great Dividing Range,' Ian said.

Scott glanced at his friend with an expression of slight confusion. 'From what I know through my brother, your family home is in Kent,' he said with a frown.

'I will tell you a secret – although it is not much of a secret anymore – I am not the person you know as Samuel Forbes. My real name is Ian Steele and I am acting on behalf of the real Samuel Forbes.'

For a moment, Scott just stared at Ian as if seeing an alien creature. 'Good God, old chap. Is this true?'

Ian nodded and then went on to unfold the events that had

led him to this place and time on the Indian frontier. Scott listened, hardly drinking from his mug, until Ian finished.

'Do Peter and Alice know who you really are?' he asked.

'I doubt it,' Ian replied. 'I have been very good at concealing the truth from them. There were many times I wished I could have spoken with Peter and Alice as I am now confessing to you.'

'I can assure you that your secret is safe with me,' Scott said, once again raising his mug to Ian. 'I propose a toast to our colonies of Canada and New South Wales and to the Queen who rules over all in the Empire.'

Ian responded and a silence fell between the two men as the regiment went about its duties outside the canvas walls of their tent. They both crawled to their camp beds, craving sleep. When he woke, Ian knew he had to write the most important letter of his life.

So much had changed in the dark forest, he thought before his exhausted body gave into sleep.

*

Charles Forbes stood at the railing of his ship, gazing at the coast of Africa. He held a glass of excellent French champagne as he watched the low outline of the continent's coast on the horizon. It was a wonderful, calm day and his first-class cabin was well appointed. Charles mixed easily with the other wealthy passengers at meals and in the salon, playing cards and smoking fine Cuban cigars. The further the ship took him from England, the safer he felt from the clutches of Detective Sergeant Mansfield. He had underestimated the man born of the lower classes but had wisely taken his father's advice to flee until such time as the investigation died a natural death. Charles had deliberated over which of his two potential destinations would be better; either India, to visit the Khan, or New Zealand to inspect the vast land holdings he had purchased. Charles had balanced one choice against another, and finally booked himself on a ship. It would be inconvenient to be out of England, but it was only a temporary nuisance, and he would celebrate Christmas Day off the coast of Africa in grand style.

★

As promised, Scott ensured that a fat roast goose was served on Christmas Eve at his officers' mess in the town where they were garrisoned, and Ian would dine with him before returning to his own regimental mess to share the moment with his homesick fellow officers.

Scott and Ian shared a liberal amount of wine and rum as fellow officers sang Christmas songs and the Indian servants went about their duties amongst the raucous young men wearing their formal mess dress and medals. Many of the cavalry officers noted the number of campaign medals Ian wore, and their respect for the infantryman was evident in the drinks that flowed from the bar at no cost to Ian.

But towards the latter part of the evening, Ian excused himself and, to the shouts of the now drunken officers in the mess wishing him well, departed. But when the carriage sent to fetch him arrived at the gates of his regimental barracks, he was met by a Sikh sentry with a message that he was to report to Colonel Thompson at the regimental HQ.

Ian tried to clear his head as he was escorted by one of the Sikh sentries to the colonel's office where he was met by the adjutant, Captain Evans.

'Ah, I see that you have been fraternising with our allies in the cavalry, Samuel,' the captain greeted him with a broad smile. 'I am off to the mess to join the others. I pray that your meeting with the CO will not take up much of your time, and you must relate to your fellow officers how you survived your time chasing Jakoby and his bandits.'

Ian assured him that he would join the rest of the regimental officers as soon as he was done with his mysterious meeting with Colonel Thompson. That a meeting should be called on Christmas Eve baffled Ian. It was normally a time when the regiment stood down to celebrate the joyous marking of the birth of the Saviour.

Ian squared himself up and marched to the colonel's office, where he knocked and was told to enter. Ian walked in and saluted smartly. 'Reporting as ordered, sir,' he said to the commanding officer sitting behind his mahogany desk.

'I was informed that you were spending some time with those horse people in their mess,' the colonel said with a half-smile. 'I pray they did not do too much damage to you, Captain Forbes.'

'No, sir, they were very hospitable to a mere infantry captain,' Ian said with his own half-smile. The friendly rivalry between infantry and cavalry was a long tradition. It was said that the cavalry looked down on their poorer cousins slogging along the roads that the cavalry galloped along with panache.

'I do not wish to disturb your time tonight with the officers of the regiment but this afternoon I received news that we have a rather serious situation. The Khan's son and wife have been taken by Jakoby's bandits, and Jakoby is demanding a large ransom for their return.'

The news shocked Ian as he was very fond of the young boy. 'How could this happen?' Ian asked.

'From what I have been told, the boy was with his mother and escorted by members of the prince's bodyguard. We thought that we had uncovered the identity of the spy in the Khan's household but it appears there was more than one. Half the bodyguards turned on their companions during the journey and killed them. They left one man alive to carry the message to the Khan's residence for him to pay his half of the treasure we returned to Jakoby.'

'When did this happen, sir?' Ian asked, still trying to process the terrible situation.

'The taking of the boy and his mother happened this morning, but we have just learned of the event this afternoon,' the colonel replied. 'Our civil administration immediately brought it to my attention as the Khan is very important to them in this region. I expect I will be tasked with mounting a rescue expedition. Damned inconvenient, considering Christmas Day is tomorrow and the regiment deserves a rest from its duties. I have been informed that the prince has requested a meeting with you, Captain Forbes, immediately. If you do not wish to comply, I will under-stand why and tell the Khan to bugger off.'

Ian frowned. He no longer had any respect for the Indian prince who had put him and his men at serious risk just to make more money for himself, but the boy was a different matter. 'I will meet with the Khan tonight, sir,' Ian replied.

'Very well, Captain Forbes. I will arrange for a carriage to take you to him,' the colonel said. 'You must realise that whatever you and he arrange between yourselves, I will support as I have the full support of our civil masters here. I also have full confidence in your abilities to plan a mission for any rescue mission you may undertake.'

'Thank you, sir,' Ian said, grateful for his colonel's confi-dence in Ian's military experience. 'I will have to forgo my evening in the mess and travel to meet with the Khan,' Ian continued.

'Good show, Captain Forbes,' the colonel said, rising

from his desk. 'I will extend your apologies in the mess to the PMC.'

Ian saluted and hurried out.

★

The Khan's residence was in disarray when Ian's carriage arrived. Ian was recognised by one of the Indian guards and escorted to the Khan.

'Captain,' the Indian prince said, greeting Ian urgently in a large ornate room with marble floors. 'I am pleased that you accepted my invitation.'

Ian did not feel the same warmth he had for the Khan when he remembered how he and his men were almost wiped out so that the Khan and the British administrators could get their hands on the old Moghul treasure.

'I was informed by Colonel Thompson that Sanjay and your wife were abducted today by Jakoby and his men,' Ian said. 'I will offer my services if there is any hope of returning your family to you.'

The Khan could sense the hostility in Ian's offer. 'I cannot apologise for those men you lost on your mission, but I can reward you handsomely if you are able to bring my son to me safe and well.'

'And your wife?' Ian queried.

'My wife also,' the Khan answered, and Ian could see that it was his heir that counted most to the Indian prince.

Ian thought for a moment and explained how he wanted the payment distributed. The Khan raised his eyebrows in surprise. 'You are sure?' he asked, and Ian said he was. 'Very well. I give my word on the life of my son that your request will be fulfilled.'

'What can you tell me about the ambush?' Ian asked, getting down to business.

The Khan went through the same story that the colonel had told Ian, adding that from what his staff had heard in the marketplace, Jakoby's commanding position was tenuous now he had failed to secure the treasure. It was obvious that the next plan was to ransom the heir to the Khan's domain for his half of what had been recovered. A note had been sent back with the surviving loyal bodyguard, indicating where and when the Khan's share of the treasure would be sent. He passed the roughly drawn map to Ian, who studied it, attempting to fix its location in his mind from his knowledge of the terrain. Ian glanced up at the Indian prince.

'Jakoby has thought his plan out well. He has indicated a place easily covered by rifle fire in the event we should attempt to double-cross him. I can also see that he has likely routes designed for a withdrawal.'

The Khan looked at Ian. 'I did not see any marked on his map,' he frowned.

'There are none marked but I have some knowledge of the area,' Ian said. 'I know I would use the nearby ridges and gullies as my way of retreating if I was confronted by a larger, well-armed force.'

'What chance do we have?' the Khan pleaded.

Ian stood, reflecting on all he knew about Scott's former trooper, now a bandit chief. Ian did not underestimate the former East India Company cavalryman, and thought that he would need to confer with Scott. 'I need to speak with Captain Campbell before I make any plans to rescue your son and wife,' Ian said.

'I have been promised by Colonel Thompson that he will provide whatever you need in your mission,' the Khan said.

'The colonel also assured me of the same,' Ian replied. 'The first matter essential to returning your family is that you are prepared to sacrifice your share of the treasure.'

'If I had any confidence that was all that was required to bring back my son, I would do it,' the Khan said. 'I would give my very life, Captain Steele, if that could return my son safe and well.'

'I think that answers my question,' Ian said, reflecting on what his own reaction might be if it had been his son in the same position. 'Requesting your permission to take my leave,' Ian continued. 'I will meet with you in the morning.'

The Khan nodded and Ian was conveyed back to the British barracks. He knew he was about to spoil a few Christmas Day celebrations.

TWENTY-THREE

The candles flickered in the predawn from a breeze in the chilly night air as three men huddled around a table staring at the two maps on its surface. Two of the three men were suffering from the effects of consuming too much alcohol on Christmas Eve while the third man was just a touch hungover.

Captain Scott Campbell and Sergeant Major Curry had been fetched from their beds by the duty officer in the early morning hours to be taken to Captain Forbes' quarters and did so with grumbling protests. They were met with a pot of black tea, chapatis, chutney and Ian, who explained the urgency of meeting. Now, they attempted to focus on the two maps.

'Jakoby was once one of your men,' Ian said, leaning on the table with both hands and addressing Scott. 'What more can you tell us about his character?'

Scott rubbed his eyes. 'You know he has more intelligence than the average soldier I commanded,' he replied. 'You have seen how he is unpredictable in his manner of waging war. He fights like those Spanish irregular troops under Wellington's command in the Peninsular War. Guerrillas, they called them. A small force fighting against a larger force with sudden unexpected strikes on regular columns of troops. He used a larger force against us, but I suspect he has become a master of employing guerrilla tactics.'

Ian stared at the hand-drafted map beside the formal British map of the area. The British map was not as detailed as Ian would have liked but the terrain was also very rugged. However, the British map did show basic formations of hills and valleys. 'This is where we are supposed to deliver the Khan's share of the treasure,' Ian said, frowning and pointing to a location on the British map. 'But to get to the place Jakoby has nominated, we have to pass through these narrow valleys.'

Conan stepped forward, staring down at the map. 'Perfect place to ambush us.'

'Are you saying that Jakoby intends to ambush us before we reach the place he has ordered for the delivery?' Scott asked.

'I just have a feeling your man will not be able to concentrate his whole force near the town when he knows that we have a regiment with artillery and cavalry so close by. He appears smart enough not to put his so-called army into a clash with the regiment's artillery and cavalry. No, he would have brought with him a small force to take delivery under his conditions. He has no doubt worked out that we would muster all our arms to counter his attempt to retain the treasure. It seems that he has spies in town keeping him abreast of our movements. He no doubt feels we will follow his orders and only send a small force to escort the treasure in the exchange.'

'So we do what he does not expect.' Conan grinned. He had served alongside Ian for so long that he had become accustomed to his captain's train of thought in such matters.

'What do you mean?' Scott asked.

'We use his tactics against him,' Ian replied. 'It is a big gamble, but it is the only hope we have of out-thinking him. We have the Khan send his share of the treasure under the escort of his loyal bodyguards as Jakoby has instructed. But we have a small, well-armed and disciplined contingent of selected members from our company leave the town tonight under cover of darkness to advance along this ridge line,' Ian said, pointing to a row of steep hills overlooking the track leading to the rendezvous point. 'They will carry only extra ammunition, water and a day's rations. They have to be able to move quickly without being burdened by their normal accruements. They will also resort to wearing green jackets and be armed in the same manner as we were for the trek to the mines. I am sure that the Khan will be able to supply what we need.'

'If I am guessing right,' Scott said, indicating a point on the map, 'you are making an assumption that Jakoby is going to attempt to use the element of surprise and ambush the Khan's escort in this area. That he will use this narrow track to withdraw with his loot.'

'I know I am gambling, but I do not think Jakoby has any intention of handing over his hostages. By resorting to this tactic, he gets to seize the treasure and retreat while still in possession of the young prince and his mother. I suspect while he holds Sanjay and the Khan's wife, he knows that the Khan will be reluctant to take any offensive action against him in the future. By using the high ground, we should be able to move behind Jakoby, who will be forced to remain on the lower slopes if he is to carry out the plan that I strongly suspect he will. I also know if I am wrong, we will lose not only the treasure but probably also the Khan's family.'

For a moment, just as the sun was peeping above the crests of the towering hills, the three men remained silent, each going over Ian's plan in their heads, measuring its strengths and weaknesses.

'I think it is the only real hope we have,' Conan finally agreed.

Scott nodded. 'I could do with some sleep. I should also wish you both a happy and merry Christmas.' He held out his hand to Ian, and then to Conan.

'You will be able to do that, Captain Campbell,' Ian said. 'This is no mission for a cavalryman.'

'If you think that you are going without me, Captain Forbes, you are not as smart as I took you for,' Scott said. 'After all, Jakoby was once one of my troopers and has a lot to answer for. I still have vivid memories of facing my rather painful death at his hands.'

Ian frowned but nodded his agreement and the Canadian took his leave.

'I take it for granted that I will also be included,' Conan said, and Ian could hear a touch of pleading in his friend's voice.

'Naturally,' Ian said. 'We only have another forty-eight hours, so time is short. I am going to rely once again on you quietly selecting ten men from the company for this mission. I know the timing is not good as the men are stood down for Christmas, but I only want those ten men to be volunteers. Sadly, we may not get our full quota.'

Conan grinned. 'I think you will be pleasantly surprised. I know the feeling in the company is that the lads will follow the Colonial to hell and back.'

'For those who volunteer, you can tell them that they will be richly rewarded by the Khan if we are successful. But only inform those who volunteer willingly. They are not to relate the promise to any others in the barracks. Oh, and I made a deal that you are also to be rewarded.'

'What about you?' Conan asked.

'I told the Khan that I do not wish any monetary reward for what I am doing. I prefer to see that the families of those men we lost in the hills be compensated.'

'But it will be you who should be rewarded if we are successful,' Conan argued.

'No, it is the men who will give up Christmas and place themselves in dire danger,' Ian replied. 'It is time we commenced our preparations, Sarn't Major.'

Conan shook his head but went about his duty to recruit the best men he considered suitable for the highly dangerous task of turning the tables on the self-styled leader of the small, rebel army of bandits. Conan knew at least one soldier who would volunteer without question – Private Bobbins.

Ian was alone in his quarters pondering his plan. If he had out-guessed his enemy, then they had a good chance of rescuing the Khan's family. If he was wrong, they would fail and possibly some of his own men would pay with their lives. Ian had only his military instincts to rely on and hoped that his many years engaged in small but vital operations would prove to be his saviour.

*

Ella had accepted Rebecca's invitation to stay with her and her husband for Christmas. Although Ella did not celebrate

Christmas, she knew the time was special to all her non-Jewish friends and acquaintances.

Ella left her comfortable house on the western side of the sprawling city that was now considered the leading capital of Europe. Britain ruled a quarter of the world's population, and London was the hub of all administrative and commercial dealings with the rest of the world. Ella's carriage conveyed her to the sweeping Montegue estate, where she was met warmly by Rebecca. There was a festive air warming the bitter cold of winter that seemed to extend to even the army of servants manning the many jobs around the house and estate.

'My dear, it is so wonderful for you to be our guest at this time of year,' Rebecca said and turned to introduce a man Ella had heard about but had not met in person. Ella knew that Rebecca's husband had once been Ian's commanding officer, and Ella knew from Ian he had proved to be an incompetent and cowardly officer.

'Mr Jenkins,' Ella said. 'I have heard many stories about you.' Ella deliberately did not add that it was a pleasure to meet him.

'A pleasure to meet you, Countess Kasatkin,' Clive Jenkins said, sensing that the very pretty young woman disliked him for some reason. He made his apologies and hurried back to friends drinking in a large room decorated with fine works of art and sprigs of pine.

'I think my husband is a little frightened of you,' Rebecca said, guiding Ella by the elbow into another large and ornate room where the ladies dressed in their finest clothing were mixing. Many sported expensive jewellery and Ella felt a little self-conscious that she did not display the same wealth. She was clad in a dress that was obviously expensive but not too showy.

'I feel that I may be out of place with your friends,' Ella whispered to Rebecca as they entered the room, all eyes turning to her.

'They are mere housewives in fancy dress,' Rebecca whispered back with an arch smile. 'They do not have a fraction of the power you possess.'

Rebecca's words gave Ella confidence and Rebecca swept her forward to meet the first in a long line of guests to the Montegue manor. Later that evening after a sumptuous meal, Ella was aware that many of the men eyed her with desire while their wives gossiped about the Jewess in their midst. Neither distracted Ella as the women did not dare express their contempt for her to her face, and the men kept their distance. Rebecca was right; she was a woman of influence, ruling over her domain with the power of life and death.

Rebecca led Ella to a smaller room, away from the multitude of guests spending Christmas at the manor in a twenty-four-hour-long party. They were alone and Rebecca asked quietly, 'How go the plans to find your son?'

'They are progressing,' Ella answered. 'It's been complicated. I am currently transferring the management of my father's many enterprises into the hands of a trusted person while I am away, Mr David Sharon.'

'I know him. You have chosen wisely,' Rebecca said. She paused before saying slowly, 'There is something I think you should know, and I feel when I tell you, you may wish to sit down.'

Mystified, Ella took a seat on a fashionable divan with her gloved hands in her lap.

'I received a telegram from India yesterday from my friend, the Indian prince,' Rebecca said sadly. 'I am afraid that I have terrible news to tell you, Ella. Nikolai was killed in action in northern India in the service of the prince.

232

He sent me the telegram because he hoped I would pass on the sad news to you as a dear friend.'

'Oh!' Ella gasped, hands flying to her face. 'When did this happen?'

'I am afraid the telegram had little information, other than that Nikolai was killed in a clash with bandits,' Rebecca said, kneeling down beside Ella and taking her hands in her own. 'I am so terribly sorry to have to relay the news to you in this manner, but I felt that you should not be alone when you learned of your husband's death.'

Ella clutched her friend's hands, trying to reorient herself. 'I am saddened to hear of my husband's untimely demise, but I confess, we should never have married. Nikolai knew it too. I feel guilt that I was not a better wife, and yet happy to be free of the treatment he meted out to me in his drunken rages.' She paused, confused by the news and her emotions. 'I am truly free to be my own woman and seek what is most important to me in life,' she whispered finally.

'I would presume that besides finding your son, you might be also yearning to be with Captain Ian Steele?' Rebecca asked.

Ella turned to her friend with tears in her eyes. 'I can only pray for such a thing to happen,' she said. 'He has always been in my dreams from the first time my eyes fell on him. I cannot say why I should be so . . .' Ella struggled to find a word or phrase to describe what the colonial soldier meant to her. All she knew was that her life could not be complete until both her son and Josiah's father were by her side.

★

'Parade! Attenshun! Your parade, sir,' Conan said as the ten soldiers shouldered arms in the courtyard of the Khan's town residence.

Ian looked down the rank of soldiers, now dressed in the new green jackets quickly sewn together by the Khan's staff. They also carried the Tranter revolvers on their hips, and every man looked worse for wear from the copious Christmas ale and rum they had consumed the evening before.

'I wish to express my personal thank you to each and every soldier on this parade for volunteering for what could be a dangerous mission. I know that you have a lot of questions, but they will be answered when we clear the limits of the town when you will be briefed on our mission. It is my pleasure to inform you that, if we are successful, and we will be, the Khan will reward you handsomely.' Ian could see the weary expressions disappear at the mention of a reward from the Indian prince as he was known to be wealthy beyond all imagination. 'Should any of you fall in action, your reward will be distributed to your families in England.' Heads nodded at Ian's additional statement. 'Private Bobbins, step forward.' Startled, Private Bobbins stepped smartly from the ranks and marched up to Ian, halting and saluting by touching the stock of his rifle. Ian returned the salute.

'With the concurrence of the colonel you are now promoted to the rank of corporal. Congratulation, Corporal Bobbins,' Ian said with a smile, passing him a set of chevrons. 'I doubt that you will have time to sew these on before we leave but your section will now know who leads them.'

Corporal Bobbins could only mumble a thank you, step back and salute as he marched back to the rank, smiling at his success. Extra rank meant extra pay.

'In an hour, we will march out to commence the mission, so get some rest before we do so. Your parade, Sarn't Major,' Ian said.

'Yes, sah!' Conan replied, and marched forward to fall out the ten soldiers.

Ian walked back to the wide columned veranda where the Khan had been watching the small parade.

'I should be going with you, Captain Steele,' he said.

'As we discussed, sir, it is more important that you remain here while my men and I bring back your wife and son. My men are hardened soldiers who know their job.'

'I know that you are right and my prayers to Allah, blessed be His name, will be answered.' The Khan sighed. 'In the morning, the chests will be escorted to the location Jakoby nominated. I expect that you and your men will by then be in the hills.'

'All going well, we should be,' Ian said. 'By tomorrow evening, Sanjay will be nagging you to take him hunting.' Ian could see the pain in the Indian prince's eyes and was beginning to understand why. After all, he too was a father.

'I hope I'm not late.'

Ian knew the voice well and turned to see Scott approaching them. Ian could see that he had two big Colt revolvers in his sash and wore a blue coat that could blend in with the shadows of the forest. Besides the pistols, Scott also wore his cavalry sword.

'Bloody typical of the cavalry.' Ian grinned. 'Always late for the battle.' But behind the banter was always the thought that they might fail, and Ian's luck had finally run out.

Just after dark, the column of Ian's men moved quietly from the highland town, commencing their trek into the surrounding hills. They would have to march as far as possible in the night to reach their rendezvous with victory – or death.

TWENTY-FOUR

Progress at night through the forest on the ridge was slow. The volunteer soldiers had white patches sewn into the back of their jackets to help with keeping in contact with the man in front, and they moved in single file, quietly and cautiously.

By dawn, Ian was satisfied they had almost reached the location above an obvious choke point on the track below. A cold, wet mist lashed his party and clouds enveloped the ridge line, which may have given Ian's detachment concealment, but also hid anything ten paces away and Ian feared they may stumble on the enemy in the misty rain. Although they might find themselves outnumbered, the firepower they had compensated for that.

Behind Ian struggled Scott, while Conan led the rest of the men. At about eight in the morning, Ian called a halt and his men formed a defensive circle, squatting miserably, soaked to the skin and shivering with chattering teeth. Conan joined Scott and Ian, who attempted to keep his map dry by hunching over it.

'Where do you think we are?' Scott asked, peering over Ian's shoulder at the map.

'I calculate that we are around here,' Ian answered, pointing to a location on the map. 'I have verified this point from a couple of compass shots I took on those two hilltops we can see on the horizon. They should have given us a rough idea of where we are.'

Conan scanned the horizon, glancing down at the map. 'That seems right to me,' he agreed.

'Then we take the chance and start moving down the slope,' Scott said. 'With any luck, we might just take Jakoby's ambush in the rear.'

Ian folded the map and shoved it under his jacket. 'Conan, brief the men and give them a ten-minute break to eat their breakfast before we move. It is vital that we do so as quietly as we can. According to my calculations, the Khan's treasure escort should be passing below in about two hours.'

Conan moved back to the circle of British soldiers, briefing each one quickly, and the party settled in to eat what might be their last meal of hard tack biscuits, washed down with mouthfuls of water from their canteens. Each man also checked his ammunition to ensure that the powder cartridges were still dry.

★

General John Jakoby was very satisfied with his preparations for the ambush. No doubt that if the Indian prince had enlisted the assistance of the regiment garrisoned in the town, the British would have already left to patrol the route to the rendezvous point. But Jakoby's spies had reported that the British were still in their barracks. It appeared that the Khan valued the life of his son more than his share of the Moghul treasure.

Jakoby smiled. There would be no exchange as he knew the value of the local prince as his hostage for any future negotiations. The boy's mother had been the plaything of his men the day before as Jakoby forced her son to watch. When they had finished with her, Jakoby personally beheaded the princess in front of her son. Sanjay had screamed for her life to be spared, but in vain. Now, the boy sat a few feet away, with his hands and feet secured with rope, shivering more from despair than the misty rain of the low clouds surrounding the edge of the hill.

'Our sentries report that the Khan's party is not far away,' one of Jakoby's lieutenants whispered to him.

'How many?' Jakoby asked.

'Only twenty on horse, and a cart.'

'Good,' Jakoby grunted. He had forty well-armed men strung along the higher ground overlooking the track, and they were on strict orders to allow the horsemen to ride into the centre before he gave the order to open fire. The left-hand section of Jakoby's ambush would then envelop the rear while the right-hand section did the same at the front of the column of horsemen, completely cutting it off from advancing or retreating. It would be a slaughter and the chests of treasure would be his.

*

Ian had taken his time moving through the trees towards the track below. He would halt the detachment and send Corporal Bobbins slithering forward to assess whether it was safe to continue. At one stage, the British NCO reported that he had spotted two bandits just ahead, oblivious to his presence as they sat and smoked.

'That is a good sign,' Ian whispered to Scott and Conan who had joined he and Bobbins. 'It corroborates my feeling that Jakoby would attempt to use surprise and the tactical advantage he has in this part of the forest.'

'Sir, we cannot pass them,' Corporal Bobbins cautioned.

'We can if they are dead,' Conan said with a cold smile, sliding his wicked-looking, razor-sharp Bowie knife from a sheath on his belt.

'I will go with you, sir,' Bobbins shakily volunteered.

'No, Corporal Bobbins, I will go with the CSM,' Ian said. 'It is something that the CSM and I have done before.' Ian could see an expression of hardly concealed relief on the British soldier's face. 'Captain Campbell, you assume command if anything untoward should happen to the CSM and myself.'

Scott nodded. 'You will return with blood on your Bowies,' he said.

Leaving their Enfields and only armed with revolvers, Ian and Conan made their way through the mist until they came to the position where Bobbins had spotted the two bandits. Ian could feel his stomach gripped with fear but at the same time, his head filled with determination to eliminate the obstacle ahead.

It was the low sound of voices that alerted Ian and Conan to the exact position of the two bandits, blissfully unaware that they were being stalked, and Conan spotted their vague shapes in the mist. Both men were sitting and gazing down the slope with their backs to them. With a nod, Ian signalled the approach. They crawled on their bellies until they had the large trunks of the trees behind the unsuspecting bandits between them. The soft, thick debris from the leaves of many seasons deadened any sound, and when they were a mere ten paces away, Conan and Ian eased themselves to their feet, stretching cramped muscles for a second before leaping forward onto the two bandits. It took mere seconds to slice their throats, strangling any attempt to call out by holding their hands over their mouths, and lowering their dead bodies into the wet, leafy mat of the forest floor.

Conan glanced at Ian and could see that his green jacket was now mottled with blood, as was his own. The task complete, both men made their way back to the soldiers waiting for them. It was time to move further down the forested slope and take up positions behind Jakoby's ambush. The only real problem, Ian mused, was finding where exactly it was laid out, if he was to have the advantage of surprise and tactical deployment of his small force. Ian felt sick with fear. Had he calculated correctly where Jakoby would plan his ambush? In minutes, he would learn whether his gamble had paid off.

★

Professor Shortland was dead.

An out-of-control dray drawn by two big draught horses had run him down not far from the university, killing him instantly. Josiah did not fully comprehend the meaning of death, but he knew that the kindly man would not be coming home. Mrs Shortland hardly wept for the death of her husband and ignored Josiah altogether as she sat in the small living room with its drapes closed against the summer sun. When she did finally stir, she slapped Josiah across the head, cursing him with words he hardly knew in his childish confusion. Something about him being a millstone around her neck now that the stupid man she had married had got himself killed.

Josiah attempted to avoid the troubled woman and when he could not, she would hit him with a long stick in her bereaved rage. Josiah left the cottage, walking for miles, tears streaming down his face. His journey ended at the Erin Hotel, where the Duffy family took him in with soothing words of comfort when Josiah informed them that Professor Shortland was dead.

For two nights, Josiah was given bed and board at the hotel. During the day, he would help Max in the cellar and Max would tell him stories about Kate's brother, Michael, who had escaped to New Zealand after he had been falsely accused of murder. Max said that if Michael had the chance, he would have become the colony's best bare-knuckle fighter.

'Vee haf to return you to Mrs Shortland, boy,' Max said sadly. Josiah wanted to protest but was wise enough not to argue with adults. 'But there is no rush,' he added, making Josiah smile.

The day came when Frank Duffy, as head of the family, argued with his wife, Bridget, that the boy was the legal ward of Professor Shortland's wife, and must be legally returned to her. Max volunteered to take Josiah home and they walked together the two miles to where Max knew Josiah resided. Josiah found himself cringing when the tough German knocked on the door.

'She ain't here anymore,' a middle-aged woman said, popping her head around the front door to her cottage next door. 'Mrs Shortland has taken a ship back to England.'

'Ven?' Max asked, stunned that any woman could just leave a young boy alone without a word.

'I think 'er ship left the Quay yesterday. She'd be well on 'er way by now. Is that the lad Professor Shortland adopted?' the woman asked, staring at Josiah.

'*Nein*,' Max lied. 'He is vif me.'

'Sure looks like 'im,' the woman said with a suspicious expression.

'Come along, boy,' Max said, taking Josiah's hand and walking away. Max did not want Josiah to be placed in the hands of the police until they put him in an orphanage. There had to be a better option, and the German knew any discussion would be made around the kitchen table that night. The family would decide what was best for the little boy who clung to Max's hand as if to never let it go.

Josiah sensed that the tough German man was his protector but wondered what was to happen to him now. So many people had come and gone in his life that he did not really know who he was.

That evening, when the pub was closed and Josiah was in a narrow bed upstairs, he could hear the murmur of the now familiar voices drifting to him in the dark from the kitchen. He recognised Kate, Max, Bridget and Frank's voices.

'It seems that Josiah has been deserted by the professor's wife,' Bridget said after relating the events Max had revealed to her. 'That means in the eyes of the law, the poor child is as good as an orphan. And so far from his home in England without anyone he knows here.'

'He knows us,' Kate said. 'He has been polite and has good manners for one so young.'

'We don't even know his family name,' Frank said. 'And all we can do is turn him over to the police so that they can find somewhere for him to live.'

'One of those horrible government orphanages?' Bridget snorted in disgust. 'The little chap deserves better than that. He is a very unusual boy. Wise for his age.'

'So what do we do with him?' Frank asked in exasperation.

'Maybe he could stay vif us here and learn the trade in time,' Max offered.

'He has shown an unusually high level of learning, and I think that Josiah should be given the opportunity to attend school before he takes on an apprenticeship with us,' Kate said.

'I think that Josiah deserves to be with a good family,' Bridget said. 'In the meantime, he can stay with us until the matter is resolved.' Frank, Kate and Max nodded. Josiah was already asleep upstairs in the knowledge that this place felt like a home.

★

Ian had wormed his way into a small gully that also had a view of the bend in the road leading into the stretch of undulating track below them. He removed his small telescope and adjusted the focus to see down to the bend where he should at any moment view the approaching troop of the Khan's escort.

'There!' Conan hissed beside him. 'I can see a couple of Jakoby's men.'

Ian put down the telescope and scanned the area between the tall trees, seeing the movement of a couple of careless ambushers. Adjusting his vision, Ian swept from them to observe movement spread out along the edge of the track. His spirits soared; he had out-thought his enemy and placed his own men in an advantageous position. Ian hoped to see the boy and his mother but could not. Hopefully, they would still be with Jakoby, safe and well. 'Get the word back to the men that we are in the right place and tell them not to shoot. No one is to fire until I give the order.'

Conan slithered away and Scott joined Ian.

'Conan told me that you have Jakoby's party in sight,' he said quietly, withdrawing one of his revolvers. Ian pointed his arm in a sweeping motion. 'From there to there,' he said.

Just as he had uttered the words, he became aware of a sound breaking the silence of the forest. It was the distinct noise of a cart creaking along and the muffled sound of hoof beats. He raised his telescope and looked with shock as the first of the Khan's escort appeared around the bend in the track. Leading the escort was the Indian prince himself, riding a fine mount and wearing a sword at his waist.

'Damn him to hell!' Ian swore softly. 'He was supposed to stay back in town and let us do our job.'

'Who?' Scott asked.

'The Khan,' Ian answered, reaching for his Enfield beside him. Ian knew he must make a split-second decision and pulled the trigger of the rifled musket. The sound echoed in the hills, causing the Khan's mount to rear, throwing him heavily to the ground.

Ian's warning shot brought a scattered round of shots from below, and Jakoby's men rose so that they could better fire on the escort that had not fully exposed itself. Only the bandits at the extreme left had been able to pour in a relatively effective fusillade on the mounted guards, causing some of them to be toppled from their horses.

Immediately, shots rang out from Ian's men to his left and right at the bandits who had foolishly exposed themselves, and the deadly accurate Minie balls found easy targets. Survivors swung around in confusion to meet the completely unexpected ambush on them. But Ian's men continued to fire rapidly. Ian recognised that this was the moment and roared above the din of the battle. 'Fix bayonets!' The infantry captain knew they were close enough to close with the enemy before Jakoby's men could react with any real defence.

After a couple of seconds, Ian roared out his next order. 'Advance at the double.'

His men rose, yelling defiance at the confused bandits and charged between the trees into the position occupied by Jakoby's men. Bayonets found targets of bandits attempting to reload their rifled muskets, but the ferocity of the British troops swept them aside. Many dropped their weapons and fled in terror before the green-jacketed madmen.

Ian and Scott also followed the line of advancing troops. Ian had discarded his rifle and was now using his revolver, snapping off shots at any bandit who had not taken the opportunity to flee. At the same time, Ian cast around in his desperation to locate Sanjay and his mother.

The Khan's men had rallied and commenced a charge on foot up the hill, waving swords and engaging the ambushers on their flank. It was desperate hand-to-hand fighting and for a second, Ian saw the Khan wading into the battle. Ian had to admit the man was not just a soft Indian prince.

Then Scott yelled to Ian. 'I've found him!'

Ian glanced around to ensure no enemy were able to threaten him, rushing over to Scott standing near a tree with smoke wisping away from the barrel of his pistol. When Ian reached Scott, he saw the frightened boy sitting with his back to the tree, his hands and feet bound and a gag in his mouth. Ian quickly cut away the ropes and removed the gag. The boy gasped. 'He killed my mother,' Sanjay said and broke into a sob.

Ian realised that the firing continued and knew they were far from safe. Some had not fled, realising that they outnumbered the madmen who had attacked them from behind.

Ian hefted Sanjay to his feet. 'Guard him, Scott,' Ian said, leaving the two alone. Scott pulled the boy to the ground to avoid stray shots.

'Do you know how to load one of these?' he asked the young boy.

'Yes, Captain Campbell. Captain Forbes taught me,' Sanjay said, taking the empty revolver from Scott, who passed him the powder and ball while Scott scanned for any threats, armed with his other pistol. When Sanjay finished loading the pistol, he immediately scooped up an Enfield from a dead bandit nearby and commenced loading it as he had been taught by Ian.

★

General John Jakoby was furious. His men were fleeing and worse, he realised that he had been outmanoeuvred by his enemy. When he looked around him, he also knew that he might be killed or captured as the enemy who had struck from above were moving to the flanks, cutting off escape through the forest. From where he stood, Jakoby could see the son of the Khan had been freed, and beside him, Captain Scott Campbell, the man he most hated in the world.

Jakoby was armed with a Tranter revolver recovered after the first ambush he had carried out on what he now knew as a decoy column under the command of Captain Campbell. His only hope of survival was to recapture the Khan's son to then be used as a hostage. With any luck, he would also finally eliminate his hated former commanding officer. Jakoby moved forward. Captain Campbell was facing away from him as he approached, the continuing gunfire giving cover to his approach.

Scott's attention was fixed on two escaping bandits running blindly in their direction. They were only armed

246

with swords and Scott calmly raised his revolver, waiting until they were well within range before he fired. His shots were successful, but he had emptied his pistol. Sanjay immediately handed him his second loaded revolver, taking the empty one from Scott to reload.

'Major Campbell!' The call from the forest was unusual, as whoever had spoken used Scott's former rank when he was with the East India Company. A chill of dread coursed through Scott when he recognised the voice of his former trooper. Scott immediately raised his pistol in the direction of the hidden voice, but he was not quick enough. Four bullets tore into Scott's body and he fell beside Sanjay.

Jakoby stepped out from the cover of the tree and walked towards the terrified boy kneeling on the leaves of the forest, still reloading Scott's revolver.

'You are coming with me,' Jakoby snarled with his pistol levelled on Sanjay.

Wide-eyed, Sanjay could hardly move and then remembered the sword flashing as Jakoby sliced through his mother's neck and watching her headless body tumble to the ground. Fear was replaced with fury and Sanjay forgot everything – except that he would kill the man who had tortured his mother. Sanjay snatched for the loaded Enfield. He had already cocked it before Jakoby suddenly realised what was happening. Jakoby fired erratically, once, twice and on the third shot, the revolver hammer fell on an empty chamber. He watched as if time had suddenly slowed as Sanjay lifted the rifle to his shoulder and fired. The Minie bullet ripped into the bandit leader's chest. Jakoby hardly knew he was dead when he crumpled into the forest floor.

In his fury, Sanjay rose and, using the rifle butt as a club, rained down bone-crushing blows on the dead body, smashing Jakoby's skull open and into a pulp. It was only the weak call to him from Scott that caused his hatred and fury to abate. Sanjay turned to see the British officer attempting to prop himself against the trunk of a tree. Blood welled from a wound to his chest, face, shoulder and stomach.

'Captain Campbell!' Sanjay exclaimed, dropping the Enfield to go to the side of Scott. 'I will fetch help.'

'No use,' Scott said. 'I'm a dead man.'

Sanjay knelt beside Scott, feeling helpless. The gunfire was dying down and Scott attempted to pass his revolver to the young Indian prince. 'Take this.' Scott gasped as the pain from his many gunshot wounds racked his body. 'It is yours now.'

Sanjay took the pistol, ready to use it in the defence of the brave British officer and himself.

'Sanjay, my son!'

Sanjay turned to see his father scrambling up the hill towards him, followed closely by Conan Curry.

Sanjay then felt his father's arms wrapped around him.

'Oh, Sanjay, you are alive.'

When Sanjay glanced at Scott, he saw a painful smile and then, Scott closed his eyes for the last time.

Conan knelt down beside Scott, taking his hand, but could plainly see that the captain was dead. Ian arrived with Corporal Bobbins as Ian's men went through the clothing of the dead bandits in an attempt to recover any coins they might have on them. The bandits were defeated and the few survivors fleeing back to their base in the hills. Ian noticed the dead bandit leader lying a few feet away with the fatal wound to his chest.

Sanjay saw Ian's interest. 'That is General Jakoby,' he said. 'He killed my mother and Captain Campbell and I have killed him.'

Ian looked at the boy who looked more like a man, wondering if his time with Sanjay had helped bring the bandit's death about. Ian nodded his respect and turned to Conan. 'Sarn't Major, we need to assemble the men and take stock of any casualties.'

Conan carried out his task and returned to report that they had suffered no casualties.

'Just one,' Ian corrected, kneeling beside Scott. 'Captain Campbell.'

TWENTY-FIVE

The Khan had Jakoby's head removed to spike on a spear planted in the town's marketplace as proof that the leader of the bandits was dead. Word from the marketplace suggested that his remaining men had drifted away to pursue criminal activities in other districts.

With reverence, Ian had Scott's body returned with them to the town for burial. All the time, Ian knew that he must write to his dear friend, Dr Peter Campbell, in Canada to inform him of his brother's death.

Back at the town, Ian went through Scott's personal effects at his quarters in the cavalry barracks. There was very little, other than Scott's medals, some money and his uniforms. These would be posted to Peter.

'I have met with the Khan,' Conan said as Ian sorted the dead officer's gear. 'He has kept his promise to pay the lads and those family members of the men we lost in the first mission. It will be enough to keep the single men drunk for a year and the married ones with families financially well off for a couple of years. He also insisted that you and I accept these with his undying gratitude for saving his son.'

Conan opened his hand and Ian saw two shining, blood-red rubies. 'I did not ask for any financial payment for our mission to save Sanjay,' Ian said.

'The Khan said you'd say that, and that it is his equivalent of a medal for our services,' Conan replied. 'I think we would look a bit churlish if we did not accept his generous gift.'

Ian looked into his sergeant major's face and could see the unspoken desire to keep the valuable gemstones. 'You are probably right, Conan. We will accept his offer with our gratitude. We are not soldiers of fortune, but servants of the Queen who do our duty according to the whims of our political masters.'

'Do I detect a hint of sarcasm in your statement?' Conan said, gratefully wrapping his hand around the two very large gemstones.

Ian sat down on the edge of Scott's bed. 'I only have one ambition left in life now.' Ian sighed. 'All the money in the world is not worth a fraction of finding my son and seeing Ella. Our regiment seems to have only short periods of peace before we are sent to some godforsaken corner of the earth to fight wars to expand the Empire, like the Romans did. We dress it up in bringing civilisation and Christianity to ignorant savages. I only have a few months left of my pact with Samuel. After that, I am going home.'

'You read too many of those history books,' Conan said, making light of his friend's despair. 'I also mean to get out of the army when you do.'

'I hope that you will marry Molly,' Ian said. 'She has waited almost ten years for you.'

'Ah, but I am a fortunate man,' Conan agreed. 'We will sit by the fire and I will tell our children stories of the countries and people you and I have seen campaigning for the Queen. A pint of ale by my elbow and Molly in the kitchen roasting a haunch of beef.'

Ian envied the wonderful simplicity of his company sergeant major's dreams. For Ian, his life hadn't been normal from the day he had first met Samuel Forbes. He glanced down at his hands and could see they had that slight tremor that never went away – nor did the nightmares in the darkness of his quarters filled with death.

★

Ella had consolidated all her business interests with her chief advisor, David Sharon, who assured her he was well and truly able to keep all Ella's enterprises functioning. Ella's house on the western edge of London was closed down and she had packed for the long sea voyage to the other side of the world in search of her son. The ship was fitted out with luxurious quarters and Ella could easily afford the first-class fare.

Now, she stood at the end of the gangplank to board with Rebecca, who had travelled to wish her a bon voyage.

'It will be coming onto a change of season when you arrive in Sydney Town,' Rebecca said. 'I hope that you have packed for the colonies.'

Ella smiled at her friend as the other passengers climbed the gangplank to the tearful farewells by friends and relatives. A brass band played popular songs and were ending their bracket with the traditional Scottish tune of 'Auld Lang Syne'. The ship's steam horn hooted and Ella leaned forward to peck her aristocratic friend on the cheek. 'Thank you for your kind friendship,' Ella said. 'I will write as often as I can. It may be by the time I reach New South Wales your husband will be prime minister.'

'I pray so,' Rebecca answered with a wry smile. 'I have invested my best years to ensure that happens.'

Ella was assisted by one of the ship's officers to ascend the steps to the ship. When she reached the deck, she turned to look back at Rebecca below. She was smiling up at her and Ella remembered the time she had stood on the same dock, watching as Ian steamed to war. Ella remembered the pain of not knowing if he would come back alive, and for a moment felt the same emotions again. She had crossed the Atlantic to New York to pursue her dream of becoming a female surgeon, but that aspiration had never been fulfilled. Now she was travelling even further to a land hardly explored. A vast land of deserts, jungles and snow-covered hills when the winter came to the southern hemisphere. It still remained a land of mystery with its exotic and strange animals. But it was an outpost of the British Empire and Ella knew that was where she would find her son. Any dreams of ever seeing Ian again had long faded. For all she knew, he may be dead.

The great ship slid away from the wharf and Ella looked back at the city of London, wondering if she would ever return to the land of her birth.

That same afternoon, a letter arrived at her London residence from India.

★

After the mission to rescue the Khan's son, Ian had been summoned to his commanding officer's HQ, where he was congratulated on his success in not only retrieving the boy but also breaking up the rebel force commanded by the former British soldier, John Jakoby.

Back with his company, Ian's legend grew as other men under his command learned of the reward granted for volunteering for the dangerous mission. The word spread amongst the troops of how Captain Forbes had also ensured the families of those killed in the original decoy mission were sent money as compensation for the loss of their lives.

Life resumed normality in the garrison town; drilling, marching and time on the improvised musket range for the Enfield rifled musket. Ian was a guest of the Indian prince, who had moved back to his palace with his retinue of servants and bodyguards. On the visits, Sanjay was always in awe of the British warrior who had come to his rescue, and when Ian was in his company, his thoughts drifted to the whereabouts of his own son, somewhere in the colony of New South Wales. With only months left to serve, Ian planned on returning to Sydney Town in the hope of finding the son he only knew as Josiah.

One day, Ian had returned with his company from the firing range outside the town to be met by the regimental adjutant, Captain Andrew Paull.

'I say, old chap, the colonel wishes to speak with you,' the adjutant said.

'Do you know what about?' Ian asked suspiciously. Was there yet another dangerous mission to be undertaken?

Captain Paull shrugged. 'Something about you resigning your commission.'

Ian remembered the formal report that he had submitted to finish ten years of service to the regiment. He made his way to the office of the commanding officer where he was met by the duty officer, a young lieutenant who saluted Ian. 'The colonel is expecting you, sir. You may go in.'

Ian nodded and marched to the office, knocking on the door and hearing the colonel bid him enter. Ian stepped inside, saluted and stood to attention in front of Colonel Thompson's big desk.

'Ah, Captain Forbes, stand at ease, and you may wish to take a chair.'

Ian was reassured by this informality. 'Thank you, sir,' he said, sitting in front of the colonel, who was perusing a sheaf of papers on his desk.

'Permission for you to resign your commission has come from London, effective as of July this year, and I am going to be the first to say that I am losing one of the best damned officers in the British army.'

Ian was humbled by the compliment from the officer he had respected and admired. He thanked the colonel for his kind words and Colonel Thompson rose from his chair, clasping his hands behind his back.

'It is no secret in the officers' mess that you wish to retire to our colony of New South Wales where you were originally posted twenty years or so ago, Captain Forbes,' the commanding officer said, walking away from his desk. Ian did not comment because the man he was referring to was the *real* Samuel Forbes, not he.

'I have a dispatch from London seeking officers in the Indian regiments who have some experience in small-scale warfare, and your name immediately came to mind. I know you have such a record from under the command of the previous regimental colonel, Colonel Jenkins. It appears that in all cases of you leading small-scale forces, you have been able to achieve your missions.' As the colonel spoke, Ian was puzzled as to what was on his mind.

'Thank you, sir.'

'Don't thank me yet, Captain. It appears that the Maori

of New Zealand refuse to recognise that they are an occu-pied country and a couple of companies of Forest Rangers have been raised there to carry out missions not dissimilar to those you conducted in the past. I am in a position to have you and Sarn't Major Curry posted to New Zealand to conduct a report on the effectiveness of the newly raised ranger forces. It would place you close to New South Wales when your resignation becomes effective in July. That is, if you have no business at home in England.'

Ian was amazed to hear the offer. It was true that a posting to New Zealand would place him geographically close to his old home colony, with just the Tasman Sea separating New Zealand from the Australian mainland. Ian had already arranged to have much of his wealth transferred to banks in Sydney the last time he was in England, leaving just enough in London to live on until he could journey to Sydney Town after his discharge from the service of Her Majesty, Queen Victoria. The offer was very attractive as it would save him weeks of a sea voyage to and from England. Ian had not had a reply to the letter he'd sent to Ella and presumed that he was no longer a person of any concern in her life. After all, why should he be?

'Sir, the posting would certainly suit me,' Ian replied. 'I am going to miss the regiment and the men of my company.'

'There will always be a home for you in the regiment, Captain Forbes,' the colonel said warmly. 'I expect that you will wish to speak with your company sergeant major about him being posted with you. It is ironic that the men in the regiment refer to you as "the colonial" when you have chosen to settle in New South Wales.' Ian smiled to himself at the colonel's statement. If only he knew . . .

★

256

'Molly will not be very understanding,' Conan grumbled when Ian took him aside at the edge of the barracks parade ground.

'If you remain with the regiment, you might find yourself languishing here in India for another couple of months,' Ian said. 'The colonel has promised that after service in New Zealand, you will be sent back to our barracks in London. That has to be a better alternative than sitting out here at the end of the world waiting for your discharge.'

Conan stared across the parade ground to a section of soldiers cleaning their muskets. He craved a more settled and safe life away from the constant military campaigns the regiment had found itself fighting. So many friends and good men were gone in his life, buried in foreign fields and forgotten by the growing middle-class public of England, who read their papers over the breakfast table before going to their relatively safe jobs in a city being transformed by major engineering works into a modern metropolis that ruled the Empire.

'It makes sense,' Conan grudgingly replied. 'But I have met a few of those Maoris in Sydney and they are big and dangerous buggers.'

'From what I have read, there is little more than skirmishing with them. It will be an easy posting just observing the ranger companies work in the forests there,' Ian said.

Conan noticed a soldier with his hands in his pockets on the other side of the parade ground. 'Excuse me, sir,' he said, and Ian knew that his loyal friend and CSM was about to revert to what his life had been in the last decade. 'That man over there!' Conan bellowed. 'Get your hands out of your pockets or I will come over there and rip them off!'

Ian grinned. In spite of everything, he would miss all this.

Part Two

Waikato and
The Wilderness

1864

TWENTY-SIX

South of the North Island of New Zealand's major town of Auckland was the Waikato district, adjacent to the Bay of Plenty. There, a great Maori war chief, Rewi, would take a stand against the British military attempting to seize the lands of his people for distribution to European settlers, the *pakeha*. The British outnumbered and outgunned the warrior chief and his small force, but the well-known fighting spirit of the native people was well respected by the British army.

The Ngati Raukawa chief, Te Paerata, had selected a site to build a *pa*, as the Maori fortification near the village of Orakau was known. The fortifications were situated in a grove of peach trees and were well underway when intelligence from a land surveyor informed Brigadier-General Carey of their existence. The British general was under the impression that the concealed trenches, underground bunkers and wooden palisade walls were not able to withstand the British assault. In under two days, Carey had sent a force of fourteen hundred men – divided between Majors von Tempsky and Blyth – to assault the *pa*. Rewi had fewer than two hundred armed warriors with another one hundred women and children within his *pa*. The eventual clash would become a battle many would remember.

★

Charles Forbes sat at a table in one of Auckland's better hotels with a tumbler of whiskey. He had arrived weeks earlier and met with the Forbes enterprises agent who had travelled from Singapore.

'God-awful place,' the agent, a middle-aged, overweight man with spectacles said as he lifted his own tumbler to his mouth. His name was Phineas Smith and he was the manager for the Forbes enterprises east of India. Charles had always read his reports with some suspicion and wondered how much he was skimming from the profits of their exports from Asia. 'It reminds me of my days living in England with this weather of constant rain and cold.'

'It is possible that so many from the British Islands like to settle here,' Charles said, 'because it reminds them of home.'

'Well, your purchase of seized lands around the North Island will pay handsomely in the future,' Smith said, leaning back in his chair to glance around the large hotel dining room. Tables were occupied by men in various uniforms of scarlet and dark blue. It was hard to tell the difference between regular British officers and those of the local militias. The room was also occupied by women in long dresses and Charles suspected that they were not the wives of the officers who frequented the hotel.

'Some of the officers I have been able to make contact with during my stay here have informed me that the local natives south of here are in rebellion again. You wrote to me that there would soon be land in the Waikato district for purchase at reasonable prices. It does not seem so.'

'A native chief known as Rewi has little chance against the force sent by Carey to disperse his warriors.' Smith waved off Charles' concerns, looking around to catch the eye of a waiter. He needed another whiskey and hopefully Forbes would stand for a meal. 'I am curious as to why you should travel such a long way from London to inspect your property out here in the backblocks of civilisation,' he said, turning to Charles.

'Let us say it was an opportune time to see some of my family's real estate on the other side of the world,' Charles replied. 'I have noticed that Auckland is growing, although I am not impressed by its dirt-covered streets. I can see that it is being modelled on our way of life in England.'

'If you say so.' Smith shrugged. 'But I will be glad to get back to Singapore after we review the business opportunities here.'

They chatted for a while and Charles did not offer to pay for a meal, so Smith excused himself to return to his lodgings, leaving Charles to ponder his choice of locations to hide out. Maybe taking up the Indian prince's offer would have been better, but there were too many English administrators in India, and Charles felt that this did not put him far enough from the long arm of British justice. As uncouth as the large town of Auckland was, it was at least safe. Charles ordered another whiskey and a good cigar.

*

Ian and Conan's transport ship arrived in Auckland. As the ship steamed into the harbour, Ian and Conan were reminded very much of Sydney Harbour. There were many ships at anchor and on the wharves and Ian noted that there was also a wide variety of warships; ranging from the more impressive blue water naval ships to the smaller brown water armoured gunboats used for shelling shore installations along riverbanks. This was a country at war.

The ship docked and both men disembarked onto the wharf wearing their red-coated uniforms. Ian could see many variations of uniform amongst the soldiers loitering or working around the wharves, ranging from navy blue jackets to the traditional red coats of British regular soldiers. The colonial militia wore forage caps and the wharf was busy with men loading timbers onto outgoing merchant transports and unloading war supplies – as well as luxuries – from England.

As there was no one to meet them, Ian enquired as to the whereabouts of the army headquarters in the busy town and was directed to a location not far from the docks. He and Conan hired a carriage to convey them to a stone building of two storeys, where they were saluted at the front entrance by two red-coated soldiers.

Ian produced his papers and was led to an office manned by a captain from a regiment Ian knew from his time in London. The man looked just a little harassed when Ian entered the cluttered office. The captain glanced up at Ian, who introduced himself and passed his papers across the desk. Conan waited outside the office, eyeing the soldiers who scurried past him with some disdain for their obviously unregimental dress.

'Ah, Captain Forbes, we were not expecting you so soon,' the clerical officer said after scanning Ian's documents. 'We are in a little bit of a spot with the Maori down south of here at the moment. The ranger unit you have been attached to is currently on active service in the Waikato district. We do not have any idea how long their commander, Captain von Tempsky, will be away. As for your quarters, I am afraid that they have not been prepared for you and . . .' The captain glanced down at the paperwork, searching for Ian's travelling companion. 'Sergeant Major Curry VC.' The recognition of Conan's highest British decoration raised the eyebrows of the captain. There was just a small hint of respect for Ian now. 'If it is possible for you to seek private accommodation at your own expense, that would help us considerably until we can properly quarter you and the sergeant major.'

'That is not a problem for us,' Ian replied. They both had the money on hand to temporarily reside at the best hotel they could find in Auckland. 'I suspect that in your administrative position at HQ you could recommend your very best establishment for us?'

The captain scribbled down an address and a note to the publican that he was to endeavour to provide the best rooms he could to the distinguished soldiers from India. Ian guessed that Conan's Victoria Cross helped.

Ian left the office and met Conan in the corridor. 'The army needs time to sort out our quarters. We can be tourists for a day or two before we commence our posting.'

'Where will we stay?'

Ian held up the piece of paper. 'The best thing I ever did in my career was recommend you for the VC,' Ian said with a grin to a confused Conan.

★

Captain Gustavus Ferdinand von Tempsky moved his rangers to a site where he suspected that the Maori chief Rewi would reinforce his warriors from. Von Tempsky was a handsome, colourful and flamboyant man of charisma and great learning. A former Prussian army officer, he had

265

travelled the world and fought as a mercenary against the Spanish in Central America. His travels with his family had then brought him first to the Australian colonies and thence on to New Zealand where he met Captain William Jackson, the man who formed the new irregular unit of the Company of Forest Rangers. In time, the two men became friends and Jackson had the Von, as he was known to the rangers, command a second company of Forest Rangers.

Now, he lay on his belly surveying the undulating plain of ferns for any sign of the Maori warriors. The plain had once been a sea of tall trees, but the land was so rich they had been cleared and now crops competed with the ever-present ferns of New Zealand. He could see where the *pa* was located on a gentle slope but could not see the traditional wooden walls surrounding it. What the Von did not know was that Rewi already had his earthwork fortification established with trenches and bunkers as defence against British artillery. A broad ditch surrounded the fort with a wide fighting parapet. The trenches were designed in a way that the Maori could create an enfilading fire against attackers and the deadly cross-fire system from the trenches was akin to an ambush. The earthworks were cleverly camouflaged using sticks and ferns, and the hidden trenches could not be seen until it was too late for the attacking force. Instead of the high wooden wall, he had low picket fences designed to slow down the assaulting force, and also partially covered with ferns to conceal it until the last moment. Rewi Maniapoto would stand and fight, knowing that his smaller force would inflict terrible casualties against the British.

Rewi could see the British artillery being brought up for the battle and knew that only sheer courage and his tactics gave them any chance of winning. His fighting force was poorly armed. Most had double-barrelled shotguns or the old-style muskets while there were a few Enfields, captured from previous successful skirmishes. Those who did not have firearms were armed with tomahawks and other traditional weapons for hand-to-hand combat in the trenches. The stage had been set to defend the confiscation of traditional lands.

First contact for von Tempsky's rangers came when they passed by an old *pa* site in the advance in the early hours of the morning. The skirmish resulted in the death of a Maori warrior before the rangers advanced towards Rewi's *pa*. Just before dawn, the skirmishing proper began.

The Maoris had been at prayer when they first saw their enemy advancing in line towards them and quickly took up arms to defend their *pa*. The rangers and other British forces advanced four abreast towards a paling fence to be met with a ferocious and well-disciplined volley of shots. Men fell, including a British officer from a regular unit. The shotguns had the advantage of two shots to the attacking force of single shots from their Enfields. Such was the fire from the *pa* that the attackers faltered, and then retreated. Von Tempsky could see the confusion caused by the disciplined Maori defence and noted an old stockyard fence before his men, confused as to its purpose.

The retreating British forces immediately sought cover, many using their bayonets to scrape out hollows at the edge of the cultivated land. A rippling fire had poured into the advancing British troops and many had fallen dead or wounded. The first encounter had gone to Rewi and his warriors. But it was far from over.

*

Charles Forbes had come to despise the location of his exile. The town was just as filthy as the slums of London and the locals appeared to be former convicts from the Australian colonies who had come seeking gold or a new life. Charles considered the New Zealand settlers to be uncouth and too independently minded, and although the people still professed their loyalty to the Queen in England, he sometimes wondered if he was actually in a British colony.

His accommodation was little better than a village inn would provide. It was time to move on to somewhere civilised. He had unlimited wealth to go anywhere and considered that Canada might be a better choice.

Charles carefully picked his way across the muddy road outside his accommodation to walk to the docks, where he would enquire as to the next ship travelling across the Pacific to the British colony of Canada. Drays with their cargoes rumbled by, and men in uniforms of many types lounged in the street in front of the places where alcohol was served.

Charles reached a wooden sidewalk in front of a cluster of shops when his attention was drawn to a couple of red-coated soldiers strolling along the timber sidewalk on the opposite side of the street. The distance was not far and Charles had keen eyesight. He gasped when he looked upon the face of the British captain.

'Good Lord!' he muttered, continuing to fix the face of the captain, who was joking with the big NCO wearing the distinctive medal of the Victoria Cross. It was that alone that convinced Charles he had been right in his first sighting of the man he was totally convinced was impersonating his half-brother, Samuel.

Charles turned away, lest he also be identified by the hated man calling himself Samuel Forbes. He stepped inside a shop that sold clothing until the two soldiers disappeared into a hotel not far from his own.

Had the devil sent him this opportunity to kill the man he most hated in the world? Charles had the advantage of surprise. Of all the places and times, destiny had fated Charles to be in this place with the last remaining obstacle to him inheriting all of the Forbes estate for himself. Charles had come to learn from experience that killing another human was not that hard. It was just a matter of doing it discreetly.

TWENTY-SEVEN

Charles met with Phineas Smith in his room at the hotel. Auckland was a small town compared to those cities he knew in England and he could not afford to be seen accidentally by the man who was impersonating his half-brother. Charles had already been warned that the overcrowding by men in uniform had attracted crime, prostitution and drunkenness and that he needed to be wary on the streets, especially at night. At least the criminal reputation for this English outpost was useful for what Charles had in mind when he met his Pacific agent.

'There is a British officer in the town who is accompanied by a sergeant major with a thick beard. The sergeant major wears the Victoria Cross.'

'You mean Sergeant Major Curry,' Smith said. 'An acquaintance of mine who deals in gold and precious stones told me about him when Curry and a Captain Forbes attempted to sell him two rubies. My friend said he did not have enough money to proceed with the purchase.'

'Interesting,' Charles said. 'Your information confirms my suspicions.'

'What interest do you have in them?' Smith asked. 'Is this Captain Forbes a relative of yours?'

'Not that man,' Charles replied. 'He is an imposter and worse, he is the man responsible for murdering a woman who was once dear to me.'

At first, Smith was at a loss for words, but quickly recovered. 'So, is he some kind of threat to you?'

Charles looked Smith directly in the eye. 'I need to see him dead.'

'That is a rather drastic statement, Mr Forbes,' Smith said. 'Murder gets you hanged in New Zealand.'

'I am sure on this rude frontier people can have accidents. With the trouble south of here, not much heed is paid to such misadventures, such as a man drowning in the bay.'

Smith's eyes narrowed. 'I might know of some men capable of carrying out such a nefarious deed,' he said. 'I am always happy to provide extra services.'

Charles took the hint and walked over to the bed, slipping a money belt out from beneath the mattress. From it, he withdrew a wad of English pounds, peeling off a few and handing them to Smith.

'There is enough there for you and whatever you pay the scoundrels you hire,' Charles said. He could see the expression of surprise and greed in the shadowy agent's eyes as he quickly calculated what lay in his hands.

'We would need a good plan to get the captain somewhere isolated in the night,' Smith said, already working out who he could trust to carry out the murder plot. Smith

271

knew of two men who had travelled from Singapore on the same ship that had brought him to New Zealand – just ahead of British justice. He also knew where they were and how badly they needed money to survive.

'I leave the details to you, Mr Smith. I trust that I can count on your discretion.'

'You can,' Smith replied, clutching the wad of British notes. 'Is there anything else I can do?'

Charles pondered a moment before producing more notes from the money belt. 'Yes. I would like you to purchase me a revolver that I can easily conceal. One does not know what kind of ruffians I might meet when I am in possession of such a large amount of cash.'

'I can do that and promise to have what you require before the sun goes down today,' Smith said, pocketing all the money.

Satisfied all was under control, Charles dismissed Smith and sat down on a chair in the relatively sparse hotel room. Even though Charles knew the British captain to be an imposter, his death did not automatically mean that Charles could lay claim to the fortune that was his right to possess. The real Samuel Forbes was serving with the Northern army in America, but it would be very awkward for Samuel to lay claim to his rightful inheritance when it would prove he had swapped places with an imposter to defraud his own family. Charles would deal with that problem when it arose.

For now, he would have the satisfaction of killing the man who had taken Jane Wilberforce from him almost a decade ago. He stared at the wall and felt his hatred rise. He had been forced to slay Jane when he had learned she was pregnant to the imposter. Charles touched a hand to the scars on his face from the beating the imposter had given him in Kent, so many years ago. The man would now pay with his life.

★

Smith found the two men living rough down at the docks. He explained what he wanted and showed them the money. Neither man hesitated. They were tough and dangerous men who had killed before.

Smith devised a plan to have this man known as Captain Forbes lured into the dark and dangerous world of the Auckland docks at night. He remembered how his friend in the gold trade had mentioned that both the captain and his offsider were attempting to sell precious stones. All Smith had to do was bring his friend into the plot with an offer of English pounds, and the two assassins would do the rest. It would be an easy way of making money.

★

Ian was in a deep sleep in his hotel room when the knock at the door brought him instantly awake. Years of living dangerously had honed his instincts to the point that an alien sound would bring him alert.

'Captain Forbes, it is Mr Markes . . . we met when you wanted to sell me the ruby.'

Ian shook the sleep from his body, groped for his pistol on the table beside him and sat up. He recognised the voice on the other side of the locked door.

'What do you want, Mr Markes?' Ian asked irritably. He resented being wrenched out of his slumbers after a night drinking with Conan in the bar below.

'I am sorry to disturb you, but something has come up of a nature that you may find fortuitous to you,' Markes said. 'A wealthy Yankee has arrived in Auckland on his yacht and in a conversation with him I mentioned that you had a ruby for sale. I am sure he has the cash to pay you the price you ask, but the deal has to be done before he sails to Sydney Town at first light. I can take you to him now. He assures me that he will pay in sterling.'

Ian guessed it was the early hours of the morning, and he was aware that he and Conan were to report to the army HQ later that morning. Conan was inebriated and Ian thought it best that he be allowed to sleep it off. Ian would split the proceeds of the sale with Conan and they could do the same for the sale of the second ruby in Sydney Town. He thought for a moment and considered how convenient it would be to have a large amount of English pounds at hand while he and Conan were in New Zealand.

'I will be with you in a moment,' Ian replied, quickly pulling on a pair of civilian-style pants and a jacket he had purchased that day so that he and Conan could drink together without arousing any talk of he, as an officer, drinking with a non-commissioned officer. Such an occasion was frowned upon by the rules of the British army.

Ian slipped his revolver under the belt of his trousers at his back and covered it with his jacket. He put the ruby in his pocket and stepped into the darkened hallway where the precious metals dealer waited for him.

'We must hurry, Captain Forbes,' Markes said. 'I must emphasise that time is not on our side at this moment.'

Ian had not completely shaken off the effects of sleep and his mind not fully functioning. 'Very well, Mr Markes. Take me to the Yankee buyer but be aware that if there is any attempt at robbery, you will be the first to pay for treachery.'

Markes shifted nervously. Maybe he would be able to take possession of the stone when the unlucky man was dead, but he did not doubt that the infantry captain was capable of carrying out his threat.

For a fleeting moment, Ian thought to wake Conan but was confident in being able to protect himself. Ian followed Markes from the hotel, through dark and muddy streets until they came to the docks where Ian could see the many different ships at anchor in the bay with their lanterns lit. There were very few people to be seen at this time of night and the only sounds were of raucous drunken men in the nearby taverns that catered to sailors and soldiers on leave.

Markes led Ian down a dark slope where Ian could see a sloop at anchor a short distance away. Its decks were lit and all seemed normal, but in a split-second, Ian's finely honed instincts for survival warned him that this smelled of an ambush. Before he could react, he saw from the corner of his eye a figure looming out of the night. Ian swung to face the threat, grasping for the revolver in his belt, but had hardly touched it when he felt his arms firmly gripped by a second figure he had not seen approach in the dark from behind. Already Ian could see Markes scuttling to a safe distance and knew there was no sense in calling to him for help. Ian struggled to free himself but the man who held him was big and strong. It was then that Ian saw the long blade in the hand of the man he had first attempted to confront.

'Kill him!' a voice hissed out of the dark from the bank above. Ian well knew the voice and could not believe that it could be so.

*

It was late evening when the Duffy clan gathered in the kitchen of the Erin Hotel. Kate, Bridget, Francis and Max sat around the table with a glowing lantern between them.

'I have met with Mrs O'Grady and she has agreed to care for Josiah. Bernard and she are taking their family to the colony of Queensland in a month to take up land there. Mary feels that Josiah would be a welcome part of the family as he would be the young man amongst her five daughters. I am sure the girls will welcome him as a little brother and Mary has told me that she will treat the boy as her own. Bernard is in agreement, as he has always wanted a son. Mary has promised that Josiah will go to school and get a good education from the nuns up there.'

'The O'Grady family are good people,' Francis said. 'I feel that you have made the right choice for the boy's future.'

'We do not know if the boy is a Catholic,' Max interjected. 'What if he was raised in the Church of England? Is it right he become one of your faith?'

Bridget turned to Max, who she knew was a Lutheran at birth. 'It is only right that Josiah be brought up a Christian,' she said. 'No matter what the fanatics say, I doubt God discriminates against His children.'

Max reluctantly nodded his grudging agreement. No one really knew about the boy's past and all they could agree on was that because he came from England and had a biblical name, he must be a Christian.

'Has anyone spoken to Josiah about your decision, Aunt Bridget?' Kate asked.

'I think it best you tell him, Kate,' Bridget said. 'You will be travelling to Queensland with Kevin once you wed, and Josiah will not be far from you. He will take comfort in that.'

Kate considered her aunt's plan and knew it was the best of all options they had considered. The O'Grady family were God-fearing, hard-working immigrants who had accumulated some wealth. No doubt the girls would spoil Josiah as their little brother. 'I suppose you have a point.' Kate sighed and the matter was settled as Josiah slept soundly in his bed upstairs. Within a month, Josiah would set out on another adventure to the wild frontier of the Queensland colony.

★

Ian struggled to free himself but the huge man behind him, wrapping Ian in a bone-crunching grip, lifted him from the ground as the man's companion brought the long blade to waist level, preparing to plunge it into Ian.

'I'm goin' to gut ya, soldier boy,' the smaller man growled as he moved in. Ian could smell the foul breath of rotted teeth and could see the man on the ground above clamber down the muddy slope. Charles Forbes was recognisable even in the dimness of the docks.

'I had not intended to be here, whoever you really are,' Charles said, stepping closer so that he was now within a couple of paces. 'But the thought of actually seeing you die was just too much for me to get a good night's sleep.'

'You want to do 'im, mister?' the man with the knife asked.

For a moment, Charles pondered the question. 'No, but I would like to see if you can slit his belly so that his guts fall out before he dies,' Charles calmly said.

'Ironic,' Ian gasped. 'You are the gutless one here. How about you and I square off?'

'No, I do not get my hands dirty,' Charles said with a grim smile. 'Of course, that is if you don't count your beloved Jane all those years ago . . . and one or two since. When the men here have finished with you, they will take you out in a boat and dump your body in the harbour. I have been told by the locals that this part of the world is well-known for its sharks.'

'I think that we should get it over with, Mr Forbes,' Markes said nervously. He knew that he was about to become party to murder and did not really want to be present. The sun would rise and no doubt blood would be left on the rocks to mark the murderous deed.

Charles turned to him. 'I think that you are right, Mr Markes,' he said.

'But before you do him, could I search his pockets?' Markes asked, knowing that Ian had the precious stone on him for the supposed sale.

'Any valuables 'e might 'ave on 'im are ours,' the man with the knife snarled. 'You back orf, mister.' Markes obliged, knowing that he could share the same fate as the man he had lured to his imminent death.

Charles turned to the knife man. 'Do it now, and make it painful,' he said and waited with trembling excitement to see this man posing as his brother die a slow and agonising death.

The executioner stepped forward, turning the blade upside down so he could insert its sharp point and use the razor edge to slit Ian's stomach up to the sternum. He had done this before in Singapore to great effect on a man who had failed to pay a gambling debt.

TWENTY-EIGHT

A gunshot in the dark brought immediate attention to the men at the waterside holding Ian.

'Drop the knife or I will drop you.' Ian well knew the voice and immediately kicked backwards at the hulking man who held him in a bear hug. The startled man released his vice-like grip with a grunt of pain as Ian's heel caught him in the leg below the knee. Immediately, Ian reeled away, drawing his revolver.

Both would-be assassins backed off, leaving Conan and Ian holding guns on the four-man party. When Ian glanced at Charles in the murky light, he could see that he also held a pistol in his hand, pointed at Ian.

'You killed Jane, you murderous bastard,' Ian snarled, raising his own revolver at Charles. It was a stand-off between the two supposed brothers. 'I always knew it was you.'

'I had no choice,' Charles replied, his voice shaking. 'I know that you are not my half-brother, Samuel.'

Ian reached into his pocket and retrieved the ruby. He held it out so that the two ruffians could see it. 'You can still have this,' he said, grimly addressing the two men. 'All you have to do is gut the bastard with the gun pointed at me and throw his body in the harbour.'

Conan had carefully made his way down the muddy slope to take up a position only paces away. He had his big Colt revolver on the two men sent to kill Ian, who were shifting uneasily from side to side. Charles was very aware that even if he fired at the imposter, the big man with the beard would shoot him.

'You cannot kill me,' Charles said with a voice cracking with fear. 'You are an officer of the Queen!'

'Not here, I'm not,' Ian said. 'Jane was carrying my child. You killed two people I loved, and I know in my gut that you killed poor Harry the stableboy.'

'If you are so sure, spare me and place me in the hands of the law,' Charles pleaded. 'Let the law of England take its course. I will surrender my pistol if you promise to do that.'

'You are lower than a red-bellied black snake,' Ian growled, his fury rising. 'I have no doubt that if I spare your life and hand you over to the traps, you will just slither out of any charge for murder. You have confessed in the court of natural justice and you will pay for your crimes here.'

Before Charles could react, Ian raised his pistol and fired. The bullet tore through Charles' throat, causing him to drop his revolver and clutch at the deadly wound. He slumped to his knees, attempting to gasp for breath as the blood welled from the wound and filled his lungs. Death did not come quickly before Charles pitched forward into the mud.

Ian turned to the pair of assassins, now attempting to

back away. Ian still held the ruby in his hand. 'If you want this ruby, all you have to do is inform the authorities that you found this man's body here, slain by a person unknown. If you attempt to betray me, I promise you both that you will not live long.'

The two men looked to Markes, who was attempting to make himself as inconspicuous as possible. He nodded vigorously and the smaller of the men who still had his knife agreed to the deal. Ian knew it was time to depart as the sun would reveal the body of Charles, now lying face-down in the mud.

'You,' Ian said, gesturing to Markes. 'I expect that you have been paid for your treachery and I should mete out punishment, but I am sure that we can make a deal for your silence.'

'Yes, Captain.' Markes hesitated. The man with the gun pointed at him was obviously not Samuel Forbes from what he had overheard in the last few deadly minutes.

'It is Captain Forbes,' Ian said. 'I want to know if Charles organised with you this attempt on my life?'

'A Mr Phineas Smith approached me to set up this deal,' Markes answered with a gulp of terror, eyeing the pistol levelled at him. 'He's an agent for the Forbes enterprises in Asia and the Pacific.'

'Where do we find this Mr Smith?' Ian asked, and Markes named his hotel.

'Remember this, Mr Markes. You lured me to this place to have me killed. I was forced to shoot in self-defence and I am sure that any court of law would take the word of a gentleman officer of the Queen over any story you might attempt to use, so it is not in your interest to tell the traps what happened here this morning. Do we understand each other?'

'Yes, Captain . . . Forbes. You have my word I was not here – nor were you.'

'Good,' Ian said, lowering his pistol and turning to the two criminal flotsam of the Pacific who were even now rifling through the clothing of Charles for any valuables. Ian handed the ruby to the knife man, who snatched it, fearing he would be shot and Ian retain the precious stone. But Ian reached down and recovered the pistol from Charles' dead hand.

'Report finding the body to the police when the sun rises,' Ian said to the two men.

Ian joined Conan and they made their way up the slippery bank.

'Do you trust those murdering bastards to keep their deal?' Conan asked.

'They have what they want,' Ian replied as the two men walked through the darkened streets of Auckland to return to their hotel. 'Conan, how is it that you followed me?'

'I heard you talking to Markes and decided that you just might need a bit of protection. So I got up and quickly dressed to follow you to the harbour,' Conan explained. 'I heard that there is a bit of crime here and besides, I figured I might be able to sell my ruby as well.'

'I am sorry that I did not include you in what I thought was a deal with some fictitious Yankee,' Ian said. 'I intended to split those proceeds, then sell your ruby in Sydney Town.'

Conan slapped him on the shoulder. 'It is your luck that kept us both alive this morning,' Conan said. 'If you had included me, then we both might have ended up in the harbour as fish bait. Fate and luck are a queer thing. But why not just have those two thugs simply dispose of the body in the harbour? There would hardly be much interest in another dead man found here.'

'The New Zealand police need to identify that the dead man is, in fact, the honourable Charles Forbes, and have that information relayed to London,' Ian said. 'That will mean only Samuel Forbes and Alice Campbell are the remaining heirs to the Forbes estates. It will mean that Samuel and Alice will not have Charles standing in their way when Sir Archibald finally dies and they inherit the estates between them.' He did not add that the report would also no doubt be welcome news to Lady Rebecca Montegue-Jenkins, Jane's twin sister.

'Bloody smart,' Conan said with a smile. 'I can see why you are the officer and I am the non-commissioned officer.'

'Before we return to our warm beds, we need to make one more visit to tidy up any loose ends,' Ian said, and Conan knew what he meant.

★

Phineas Smith was annoyed at the cold thing on his cheek, but he came conscious almost immediately when a distant voice commanded him to wake up. In the darkness of the hotel room, he realised the cold thing touching his cheek was the barrel of a gun, behind which he could see two shadowy figures looming over him.

'Don't bother to get out of bed as this is just a courtesy visit,' the man said, pushing the barrel of his revolver harder into Smith's face. 'You will leave New Zealand on the first ship out of here and never return. It would not do your health well if you suffered a violent crime one night in the town. But before you depart, you are to report to the police that your employer, Mr Charles Forbes, has gone missing. You will describe him and, if necessary, identify his body. Then you will ensure that his father, Sir Archibald, receives news of his son's unfortunate demise. Is that clear?'

Smith could hear the icy threat behind the outline of the man holding the gun into his face and, in his fear, wet his bed. Smith had no doubt the man meant every word and attempted to nod his head in understanding. Then he saw a shower of stars as the pistol was reversed and slammed down on his head.

When he regained consciousness some hours later, Smith wondered through his splitting headache if it had been a hideous dream. The he saw the blood stain forming a halo around his head on the pillow, and knew he had to report a missing person.

That afternoon Phineas Smith identified the body of his former employer, which had been discovered at the edge of the harbour.

'A couple of ruffians found his body and reported the matter to us early this morning. We were fortunate that you came in to report Mr Forbes missing,' a police sergeant said, standing beside the body on the morgue slab.

'What has happened to Mr Forbes?' Smith asked.

'It appears that he was either shot or stabbed in the throat,' the sergeant replied. 'The doctor who will do the post-mortem will have a clearer idea when he submits his report to us. You don't have any idea who might want to harm Mr Forbes?'

Smith had a terrifying recollection of the man standing over him that early morning. Although he could not clearly distinguish who he was, he had a good idea that the tables had been turned on Charles Forbes. 'I am afraid that I cannot help,' he replied.

'The ruffians who found the body said that they think it was done by some Chinese sailors they saw that evening loitering in the area,' the sergeant said. 'Probably never find them as we know a ship with a Chinese crew sailed this morning.'

'A pity,' Smith said, guessing that the two ruffians were the men he had hired to kill Samuel Forbes. If they had turned on Charles Forbes, it had something to do with the man who had threatened him. He had to be formidable to get the two dangerous killers on his side. Smith shuddered. It was time to return to Singapore.

★

The sun rose on the second day of the siege of Rewi's *pa* at Orakau. Rewi knew he was low on everything from water to ammunition, food and fighting men, and could see that his defensive works had been completely surrounded.

On the third day, Lieutenant General Cameron had arrived with fresh reinforcements for the besiegers, who were extremely reluctant to assault the fortified position of trenches and bunkers. An obvious conclusion to the military action was for the defenders to surrender. An offer was made for the women to leave unharmed, but they chose to stay with their men to the bitter end rather than seek a promise to be spared.

If the men die, the women and children must die also. From within the walls of the *pa* an equal answer was given to the surrender offer, *Friend, I will fight you forever, forever!*

Two Armstrong breech-loading rifled artillery guns were wheeled to within 350 yards of the *pa* and commenced firing into the fortifications. Explosions erupted within the earthen defences, but the Maori warriors were protected from the flying shrapnel by the arrangement of trenches. It was suggested by an engineer officer that a sap be dug towards the centre of the Maori defences so that the attacking force would have cover in the final assault.

Von Tempsky and his rangers were appointed to cover the east side of the *pa* and took cover in a hollow with a swamp to their rear. They lay for a couple of hours under well-directed fire from the embrasures in the *pa*. The ranger commander respected the accuracy of the Enfield rifles in the hands of the Maoris and kept his men in the hollow to avoid the Maori sharpshooters. While he and his men kept watch from their position, the sap was commenced, aimed at the north-west corner of the *pa*. Eventually, when the number two detachment of the Forest Rangers arrived, the Von's men were pulled back to a position out of the line of fire.

At midday, observing from their new position, von Tempsky noticed a column of Maori reinforcements arriving to assist the besieged defenders. He quickly redeployed his men to counter the threat, noting at least three hundred armed warriors moving in the forest. Von Tempsky forced-marched his men across a swamp and up an adjoining ridge covered in manuka scrub. He and his men could hear the reinforcing Maoris calling in high-pitched voices to the defenders. The sound of a *haka* – a Maori war chant – erupted and very soon, a contingent of the warriors broke from cover to fire upon the Forest Rangers, who returned fire with their carbines. The Maoris wisely fell back and eventually von Tempsky was joined by a detachment of Forest Rangers under the command of his colleague, Captain Jackson.

For three days and two nights, the defenders held out, but the situation was critical. Outnumbered, outgunned and lacking supplies, Rewi had to make a choice. He split his people into small groups and broke through a part of the cordon, fleeing across open land to the Puniu River. Immediately, they were pursued by a detachment of cavalry and Forest Rangers and it was then that under a storm of bullets most of the Maori casualties occurred. The pursuing

British had seventeen killed and fifty wounded during the battle for the *pa* and took out their anger on the helpless men and women they pursued. Many of the British would feel the shame of their barbarity on the helpless women, bayoneted where they fell. With the *pa* captured, many felt that the final defiance had been subdued by force of Imperial arms.

They were wrong.

TWENTY-NINE

Ian realised that he and Conan were basically a nuisance to the military command in New Zealand. They were like orphans, and it was up to Ian to find a home while they waited to fulfill their duties as recognised observers acting on behalf of the British army. He and Conan did not object to remaining in their hotel accommodation as it kept them away from the often meaningless duties of military administration.

Ian would report in to the military HQ each morning to be told that he and Conan were not as yet required for duties, so both men exchanged their military uniforms for civilian garb which allowed them to mix socially with the local population of Auckland. They blended well with the many Australian colonial immigrants in search of enlistment into one of the British irregular regiments or settlement on land seized from the Maori people. Ian was able to read in the local paper that a British aristocrat had been discovered shot to death on the Auckland docks some days earlier and the suspected killers were probably Chinese sailors. The police stated that the chances of finding Charles Forbes' murderers were extremely remote.

Ian folded the paper as he and Conan sat at a table in the bar of a hotel. They were drinking bottles of imported English beer and smoking American cigars.

'Do you think those in charge will ever have us go about our duties here?' Conan asked, looking around the bar at the handful of rough-looking men hunched over their drinks.

'When July arrives, I will no longer be an officer of the Queen, and will travel to Sydney to find my son,' Ian replied. 'That is all I care about now.'

'I have written to Molly and promised her that I will also finish my time with the regiment and return to her as a civilian, never again to roam in the red coat of a soldier.'

'I suppose that you will settle by the fireside as a married man, smoking your pipe and telling stories of our life in foreign lands fighting for the Queen,' Ian said with the hint of a smile.

Conan looked at Ian. 'I am hoping to convince Molly that she should travel with me to dear old Ireland and set up a shop in Dublin to cater to the sweet tooths of the gentry there,' Conan said, surprising Ian.

'Do you think that Molly will agree to your proposal?' Ian asked.

'I don't know,' Conan replied gloomily. 'I don't think I can live in London. I miss the fresh smell of the earth in the shadow of the hills and even the smell of burning gum trees. I was born to the soil of the colony, where the air is clean. We are both rich men and able to start a new life, but mine will not be back in New South Wales.'

'Why not?' Ian asked.

Conan hesitated before saying, 'Those are reasons I would rather not discuss.' Ian could see that he should not ask why at this moment.

Instead, he changed the mood of the conversation. 'Sarn't Major, I never took you for a sentimental philosopher.' Ian grinned, taking a gulp of his beer. 'I think I should order another round before we go in search of our midday meal,' he added and was about to rise from the table when a man entered the bar wearing the strange, dull uniform of a bushman. He cast about until his eyes rested on the two men in civilian clothes. He immediately walked over to them.

'Captain Forbes?' he asked tentatively.

Ian glanced up at the man, who was wearing a revolver and had a wicked-looking knife in his belt. 'I am he,' Ian answered.

'Compliments of the Von, sir, he would like to finally make your acquaintance. I can take you and Sergeant Major Curry to him if that is convenient? I will escort you to Drury tomorrow. I will bring horses for the journey down the Great South Road at eight in the morning.'

'It is convenient,' Ian said as Conan swallowed the last of his beer. 'We will be ready for the journey.'

The man left and Ian realised that he had not even identified himself, and Ian wondered what kind of military unit he and Conan were about to meet with.

★

The following morning, Ian and Conan met the same man, this time leading three saddled horses outside to their hotel.

'I am Corporal Todd, sir,' the man said without saluting Ian, who was dressed in his uniform of a British captain. The corporal now had a strange-looking carbine strapped over his back.

'I have a feeling that you are an Australian colonial,' Ian said.

'I am, sir,' the corporal answered. 'I'm from Goulburn in New South Wales.'

Ian looked at Conan, and the two men exchanged knowing glances. For the first time in almost ten years, they were possibly serving alongside fellow colonials.

'There are a lot of us colonials from Australia serving with the Forest Rangers,' Corporal Todd continued as he swung himself into the saddle. 'The Von prefers to enlist men who have experience living off the land.'

'What is that carbine you have?' Conan asked.

'It's a Calisher and Terry capping breech-loading percussion carbine, sir,' the corporal dutifully answered. 'The Von recognised that it was ideal for the dense bush we work in.'

'I believe that it was meant for the cavalry,' Conan continued. 'You can't attach a bayonet to it.'

'True,' the corporal admitted. 'We have our pistols and knives for any close-quarter fighting.'

Ian was impressed at the equipment of the Forest Rangers. After his experiences with the regiment in the special operations he had led over the years in the Crimea and India, he approved of their leader's choice of weapons.

The three horsemen set off and travelled down the Great South Road, hewn out of earth, rock and forest by the New Zealand military for the logistics of waging war in the Waikato district and beyond. By late afternoon, the three horsemen reached the small village of Drury and Ian could see a large military encampment of tents not far away. They came to a halt outside a hotel.

'This is the Von's HQ,' Todd said, dismounting.

Ian and Conan also dismounted and stretched their bodies, feeling the curious eyes of the half a dozen tough-looking men upon them. Each man was heavily armed with the carbine, revolver and long knife. Ian guessed that they were members of the irregular Ranger company. None saluted the senior officer in his red coat, and Ian guessed they were probably colonial-born men with little respect for English formality.

The corporal led them inside the hotel where they saw an aristocratic-looking man poring through papers on a table. He glanced up and stood with a smile, advancing with his hand out.

'You must be Captain Forbes,' he said, gripping Ian's hand firmly. 'I am Captain von Tempsky.'

'My sergeant major, Curry,' Ian said, nodding towards Conan who was glancing around the bar.

'I see that you have earned the honour of the Victoria Cross,' von Tempsky said to Conan.

'Yes, sir,' Conan replied, not impressed with the lack of discipline amongst the Forest Rangers he had encountered outside the hotel.

'Take a seat, gentlemen,' the Von said, gesturing to his table. 'What would you like to drink?' Both Ian and Conan said that an English beer would be fine and von Tempsky turned to Corporal Todd to fill the order.

'I have read a report from the army files of your military exploits, Captain Forbes,' the Von said. 'You would have made a fine Ranger officer.'

'The missions called for the unusual tactics I employed,' Ian answered. 'I think the nature of modern war relies on the British army recognising the importance of highly trained small forces, well-armed with the appropriate weapons to engage in operations such as I have read you are conducting against the Maoris.'

'Do you know, Captain Forbes, that my adversaries amongst the Maori warriors have given me a special name?

They refer to me as *manu-rau* which means "many birds". It is a grudging respect for my men and I to be in the forest and use surprise to attack them. Although the British army uses us as deep-ranging reconnaissance to locate the Maori positions, from time to time we are forced to defend ourselves, or conduct ambushes when the opportunity arises.'

'I can see that your choice of weapons suits the dense scrub I have seen since arriving,' Ian said. 'The selection of your men is interesting.'

The Von looked pleased at Ian's observations. 'We recruit men from across the Tasman who are prepared to live under the harsh conditions of the bush. One of my small parties of men carries an Enfield that you are used to for long-range shots, while the rest are armed with both a revolver and Terry breech loader. I also attempt to have a Maori speaker in each party. My men are paid at a higher rate than their militia comrades and receive a double ration of rum at the end of a mission. But it is not the higher pay or rum that tends to bring recruits but a chance to actually get into the fight. They may appear to lack discipline but have proved to be first-class soldiers in the role they have been assigned. I even have a couple of muscular Negroes from Jamaica in my service who have proved themselves as fine fighting men. You should be able to see my men in training in the next few days, although I have heard a rumour from General Cameron's HQ that trouble may have flared up on the coast. We may be back in action before we know it.'

'What kind of trouble?' Ian asked, disappointed that he and Conan had missed the action at Orakau.

'From what I know,' von Tempsky said, 'there is a rather formidable *pa* near Tauranga Harbour. I suspect that

General Cameron will not be able to resist bringing up his artillery to bombard the fortifications, and finally bring the resistance by the Maoris to an end. At least with the new Armstrongs he may be able to avoid a direct assault on the earthwork trenches, which we have found to be a death trap to men in the open.'

Although Ian had a dim view of some British tactics employed in the past, he also gave credit to this new enemy as being courageous and intelligent. This was their land of birth, and they were not about to hand it over to Queen Victoria without a fight.

'Will your rangers be employed in any action on the coast?' Ian asked

Captain von Tempsky frowned. 'I am not sure. I've heard rumours my company may be utilised elsewhere.'

'If that occurs, I pray that you will not be insulted if my sergeant major and I request an attachment to General Cameron's staff to observe any actions on the coast,' Ian said, and von Tempsky shrugged.

'I would not be insulted, Captain Forbes,' he said. 'In your shoes – with the freedom you have been granted by the English authorities – I might make the same request. No doubt we will meet again in the near future. In the meantime, accommodation has been arranged for you in the camp you rode past. Corporal Todd will escort you to meet with the camp commandant and have you quartered.'

Ian thanked the former Prussian army officer, and he and Conan reported to the military HQ at Drury, where Ian was happy to run into a captain he had met years earlier in London at his club. Fortune was doubly on his side when his friend said that he could have Ian and Conan transferred to the coast to observe the upcoming action.

★

As Ella's ship steamed into the great harbour at Sydney Town and docked at Circular Quay, the young Englishwoman was surprised by how pretty the natural environment was. Ella had organised from London to have a house purchased for her on the edge of the harbour and had been assured that the cottage came with a maid and footman, having belonged to a very wealthy member of the Sydney community who had once known her father. Levi Goldberg was at the wharf when the ship docked to meet Ella, a man in his late fifties with a crop of grey hair, spectacles and a portly build. He had many friends in Sydney society, and had made his small fortune importing and exporting goods from New South Wales to England.

'Oy, Miss Ella,' Levi had said as he had walked towards Ella with his arms outstretched. 'I would recognise you anywhere. You were always a beautiful young woman, even when you were a child.'

Ella did not remember Levi but was pleased to receive his warm welcome and pleased that he instantly recognised her. 'Mr Goldberg, I must thank you for all that we discussed in our correspondence,' Ella said a warm smile.

'It is the least I could do for the daughter of Ikey Solomon, may God rest his soul. Come,' Levi said. 'I have a carriage to convey us to your new home and I have organised for your luggage to follow us. Welcome to Sydney Town. I think you will find it is not as uncivilised as you might have been led to believe. The people here are different from those I remember from my days in England. They do not seem to care that we are Jews. All they care about is making money. But let us get you to the house and settled in.'

Ella was escorted to a fine carriage drawn by two thoroughbred horses and a driver wearing an expensive uniform and top hat. Levi assisted Ella into the open carriage as a balmy breeze and blue skies dominated the day. They travelled for a short time until they came to a flower-adorned cottage built of sandstone that overlooked the sparkling waters of the great harbour. Ella was impressed by her new colonial residence, noting the small, well-kept front garden.

'You are home,' Levi said.

'It is home until I find my son,' Ella said. 'Then I shall return to London with him. I have purchased this house because I wish my son to be in a place that I call home as soon as I find him. He has been far from his home for too long.'

'A pity, but your choice to purchase will pay dividends when you eventually sell this house,' Levi said. 'There are fortunes to be made here by enterprising people, and from what I have heard over the years, your father certainly did well to amass the fortune he did. I know that you must miss your father's guiding hand but you are, after all, your father's daughter.'

Ella was not sure how she should accept the compliment. After all, her father had founded his fortune on crime. She didn't respond, entering the cottage instead where she was introduced to her footman and maid. The girl, around fourteen years old, curtsied and the footman bowed his head. Some things did not change from London society, Ella thought.

Tea and cucumber sandwiches were offered on a small patio at the rear of the two-storeyed cottage, where Levi sat with Ella. It was time to discuss Ella's mission to the colonies.

'I have friends within the Sydney constabulary,' Levi said, sipping from the fine china cup. 'They will be of great assistance in finding your son.'

'This situation must appear strange, Mr Goldberg,' Ella said, gazing across the waters of the harbour. 'I have a birth certificate in my possession that names my son's father as Captain Ian Steele who, ironically, was born in this colony.'

'I do not judge,' Levi said. 'Love is a powerful force none of us are immune from.'

With a sense of relief, Ella appreciated Levi's non-judgemental comment. 'Indeed,' she said, relieved to have dealt with the matter.

However, Levi asked, 'Where is your son's father now?'

Ella pursed her lips. 'The last I was able to ascertain, Captain Steele is with his regiment in India.' She pointedly changed the subject. 'The man who took custody of Josiah should be relatively easy to locate: Professor Shortland. I am sure the colony is not big enough to have many learned academics of that name.'

'I have some bad news,' Levi said, placing his cup of tea on the patio table. 'As per your request, I made some inquiries about Professor Shortland and his wife. It appears that the professor was killed in an accident and his wife immediately organised to return to England after his funeral.'

'Did she have Josiah with her?' Ella asked, her heart thumping with disappointment. She had travelled halfway across the world and now was learning that Josiah could be on his way back to England.

'The good news is that it looks like she did not. It appears she just left him like an orphan to struggle on his own.'

Ella felt a flash of hatred for a woman who could simply dump a child to the mercy of a land that would be alien to him. And yet if she had not, Josiah would be at sea by now. 'Do we have any idea where he might be?'

'There is more good news,' Levi said with a smile. 'It appears he was befriended by an Irish family who own the

Erin Hotel near the centre of Sydney Town. I thought that you might wish to join me to visit them. They are by all accounts an honest family and will be able to help us find Josiah. I have made arrangements for us to be taken first thing tomorrow, although I can see in your face that you would like to visit them now.'

'I understand that you have done more than I could have ever expected and I thank you from the bottom of my heart,' Ella said, hope brimming. 'I will respect your advice and we will go together tomorrow to this Erin Hotel.'

'Good,' Levi said, rising from his chair. 'You can use this time to make your new house a place fit for the return of Josiah. I am sure you will have much to discuss when you are both finally together.'

Levi departed and Ella stared across the harbour. Her son was so close, and she knew she would not sleep this coming night.

THIRTY

Ian and Conan gazed at the two formidable redoubts of earthworks and timber palings across the plain. Already Cameron had moved his troops up from the nearby British encampment of Te Papa and concentrated his big artillery guns in a bombardment on the Maori defences.

When Cameron observed a breach had been made in the main redoubt, the British general ordered an attack on the opening. The artillery bombardment had been ferocious and to the observers, it was impossible that any living creature could have survived. At around 4 pm an infantry regiment and naval brigade assembled into a column for the assault, advancing with fixed bayonets on the smoking ruins of the trenches.

'Good to see the Enfield being used,' Conan said as he watched one of the elite British units march smartly forward. Ian removed his pipe, lit it and watched the smoke curl away on a gentle breeze, feeling some pity for his enemy. Never before had he seen such a heavy bombardment on such a small area. Ian had come to admire the Maori warriors and remembered how the real Samuel Forbes had mentioned their bravery when he had encountered the warriors on the battlefield.

'Poor sods,' Conan said beside Ian. 'I wonder if there are any left alive to resist.'

The British troops disappeared from sight, clambering down into the deep entrenchments and the shots and shouts of men engaged in hand–to–hand combat drifted across the plain. Conan glanced at Ian in surprise; obviously, some Maori warriors had survived the shelling.

Then, ten minutes later, both men observed a stream of British troops scrambling back to their assembly point in total panic. Many were running without their weapons, and Ian could see the shock and fear in their expressions from where he and Conan stood.

'God almighty!' Conan swore, and Ian instinctively reached for his revolver, as if expecting a sea of Maori warriors to follow in hot pursuit. 'I think we should withdraw to the main body,' Ian said, his revolver in hand. 'It seems that the big guns were useless.'

But the retreating troops were not followed, leaving over a hundred of their comrades dead and wounded in the trenches, with few casualties on the defenders' side. Those who had been able to report had been debriefed and the picture emerged of a total defeat. Seventeen hundred well–trained British troops had been defeated by a fraction of their number.

When Ian caught up with the captain he had known from his club in London, he could see absolute consternation written in his face.

'What happened?' Ian asked the shaken officer.

'From a few reports by those who got back, they said the Maori let them enter the trenches and came out from underground tunnels to engage us at close quarters with shotguns and axes. Our troops had trouble wielding their bayonet-attached Enfields in the confinement of the earth-works. I heard that we lost nine out of ten officers in the trench fighting. How do these savages know so much about warfare?' the captain said, trembling with frustration. 'How are we ever going to defeat them?'

That night, the warriors in the *pa* quietly slipped out to assemble at another point in their well-disciplined withdrawal. The following day, it was announced that the British army had secured a victory as they took the *pa*.

On the same evening, Ian and Conan sat around a camp-fire, sharing a bottle of rum. The rest of the army camped at Te Papa and no one in the military hierarchy paid them much attention.

'It is not going to look good for Cameron,' Ian said, staring at the glowing coals of the fire. 'I don't think that they build their fortifications as a last resort. I get the feeling that they are simply well-designed killing fields. Maybe we could learn something from the Maori about entrenchment. I have a feeling it will be the future of warfare in the years to come.'

'I think that the Forest Rangers might be the answer to subduing the Maori,' Conan said, poking at the glowing embers with a stick and watching the sparks drift up into a starry night. 'This is one of those guerrilla wars we were talking about. A handful of men can hold off the might of an army with hit-and-run tactics.'

Ian grinned, taking a swig from his canteen and letting the rum warm his body in the chill of the New Zealand night. Soon, winter would come to the land, with sleet, rain and biting cold. 'Conan, I don't think those in the hierarchy of the British army are interested in our views on the nature of warfare. Let's raise our mugs to the good men on both sides who will not be able to stand a round of drinks for ever more.'

Conan raised his mug and both men reflected on the many battles they had fought, and the friends they had lost. Ian knew he was very close to leaving death and destruction behind him. His yearnings for Ella came to mind as the muted sounds of an army at rest drifted to them in the dark. He wondered what she would be doing at this moment. Had she received his letter, and was her reply somewhere in a mail sack at sea on its way to the southern hemisphere? And what of their son, somewhere in Sydney Town?

The fire burned away, and the two soldiers sat watching the flames, locked in their thoughts of those they loved.

★

Major Samuel Forbes rode at the head of his regiment along the dusty dirt roads outside Chancellorsville. They had marched past the reminders of the disastrous defeat of the Union forces a year earlier, where bleaching bones of the dead still littered the fields.

Samuel had personally begged General Ulysses Simpson Grant, the newly appointed commander of all Union forces, for the posting. The general had known of the former British officer's award of America's highest honour.

'Major Forbes,' he had said. 'I am aware that you have a wooden leg and sympathise that this will hinder you to an extent leading soldiers in battle.'

'Sir, with all due respect, there are many men in service who have similar injuries to mine who still fight on the frontlines.'

'Yes, but they are on the Reb side,' Grant had replied with a slight smile. 'I suppose if you are mounted, your leg should not be a hindrance. It might do the men good to know that their commander is prepared to face the rebels with his wound rather than remain safe in Washington. I will give you your regiment, Major Forbes, and hope that I do not live to regret my decision.'

Samuel remembered feeling his hopes soar. He had always been against war, but now he felt there was little else in his life after the death of James. Was it that he had an unconscious desire to die and possibly join his beloved partner in the arms of death? Or was it that he felt that the great crusade of Abraham Lincoln was worth the sacrifice? Samuel had no illusions that the primary reason for the civil war was not the humanitarian freedom of slaves, but the political reunification of the American states, but Samuel also knew victory would mean the enforcement of the law to free all men of colour and that had been the driving force behind James' enlistment. Samuel would carry on James' burning crusade to see that dream come true, no matter what.

So the Northern Army of the Potomac marched ever south, with the aim of capturing the Confederate capital of Richmond. Grant knew that the enemy ahead was still a formidable force, despite lacking manpower and basic supplies. The army's baggage train spread for sixty-one miles along the country roads, and one hundred and eighteen thousand well-armed, well-fed and well-equipped Northern soldiers marched those same roads, heading south to attempt to crush Lee's retreating Confederate forces.

Samuel marvelled at the stands of green pines and flowering dogwood trees they passed on the march. It was spring and a time for birth and renewal of the land. His leg still ached constantly when he trudged with the aid of a walking stick and he had a good supply of laudanum, which helped to ease the throbbing pain. As he rode at the head of his regiment, Samuel reflected on Ian Steele in the British army. They had been in sporadic correspondence over the years, and Samuel wondered if Ian was still alive. He had read about the British battles on the North West Frontier of India and only hoped Ian, who was born to be a soldier, was safe and well.

A horseman galloped up and Samuel could see that he was a captain from General Grant's staff.

'Sir, we are going to bivouac here tonight,' he said.

Samuel gazed at a sprawling horizon of densely packed trees and secondary growth ahead of them. The captain saw Samuel staring at the forest.

'I heard it's called the Wilderness,' he said as if anticipating Samuel's question. 'The general don't want to get entangled in there because we won't be able to use our cavalry and artillery to any effect. But we have reports from our scouts that Bobby Lee has sent in some of his troops. I was here last year, and we left a lot of good boys in there.'

Samuel fully agreed with the captain's assessment. The Wilderness looked like some monster growling a dare to enter the thick scrub.

*

Ella alighted from her carriage outside the Erin Hotel, wrinkling her nose at the stench of spilled ale. Levi escorted her inside the bar, where only a few hardcore drinkers sat around tables, nursing spirit and beer glasses before them. The sight of the finely dressed pretty lady caused them to glance in her direction.

Levi and Ella saw a heavily muscled man polishing glasses behind a bar top and approached him.

'Sir,' Levi said. 'My name is Levi Goldberg and this is Miss Solomon, formerly of London. We wish to ask if you are familiar with a young boy around six years old by the name of Josiah? From my enquiries, you may have befriended him at your establishment.'

Max ceased polishing a glass with a clean rag. 'Vhy do you vant to know about the boy?' he asked suspiciously.

'He is Miss Solomon's son and was taken without her knowledge or permission from London to Sydney Town,' Levi answered. 'As you can appreciate, Miss Solomon is rather distraught over the matter, and wishes to be reunited with her son.'

'The boy never mentioned to us that he vas taken against his vill to be here,' Max countered. 'How do I know that you are not lying?'

Ella reached into her bag and produced the birth certificate, handing it to the tough German.

'I don't read English,' Max grunted, eyeing the paper. 'I vill get Mr Duffy, he owns The Erin.'

Levi and Ella waited a moment before a man in his fifties appeared, following Max to the front bar.

'I am Frank Duffy, publican of these licensed premises,' he said, holding the birth certificate. 'According to what I can read here, it says that the mother of Josiah is one Ella Solomon, and a man with the name of Ian Steele is his father. How do I know this document is not a forgery?'

'I can assure you, Mr Duffy, that any court in this land can verify that the document you hold is genuine,' Levi said with a touch of anger in his statement. 'We just wish to know where Miss Solomon's son is.'

Frank frowned. 'I wish I could help you, but Josiah is somewhere north of us on his way to the colony of Queensland with a good Christian family.'

Ella and Levi exchanged concerned glances and Levi spoke. 'We would be grateful for a more detailed explanation,' he said.

'If what you are saying is true, I will assist you in any way I can,' Frank said. 'The boy deserves a mother.' Frank then gave all the information about the family that had adopted Josiah and their eventual destination.

'Queensland,' Levi said. 'It would have been better if he had travelled to Victoria.'

'Why is that?' Ella queried, concern in her question.

Levi turned to Ella. 'Queensland is a place of savage natives and rough frontiersmen. They are not as civilised as we who live in the southern colonies.'

'Then I must travel to Queensland,' Ella said without hesitation, and now the three men stared at her with pity. Colonial Queensland was a wild frontier, where explorers journeyed, many never to return.

THIRTY-ONE

It was a desolate place several feet above the main supply route between the Cambridge redoubt and Te Awamutu, with the bush only about two hundred yards to their rear. Although a redoubt had been built by an infantry regiment, the men occupying the high ground slept with their arms close at hand.

Von Tempsky and his rangers were posted to carry out scouting of the bush and protecting travel on the road where the redoubt had been built as a base of operations. Ian and Conan joined the ranger detachment at the permanent redoubt, observing and recording what they saw of the Forest Ranger operations. Previous to the establishment of the fortification, Colonel MacNeil, aide-de-camp to General Cameron, had been ambushed on the stretch of track, highlighting the necessity of putting out patrols.

Conan joined a small group of rangers who had been stood down from patrolling operations in the thick scrub, while Ian located their commander in his tent, poring over paperwork.

'Ah, Captain Forbes,' von Tempsky said when he saw Ian at the entrance to his HQ. 'You have arrived in time to join me in a small celebration. Enter and find a camp stool.'

'What are we celebrating?' Ian asked, sitting himself down on a camp stool as von Tempsky produced a very valuable bottle of rum from a small chest by his camp stretcher.

'I have just been notified that I have received my majority,' von Tempsky said, pouring a shot of rum into battered tin mugs.

'Well, may I be one of the first to congratulate you, Major von Tempsky.' Ian raised his mug and took a swallow.

'Thank you, Captain Forbes,' the Von responded. 'I must say that the promotion pleases me well. The higher rank will enable me to have the authority to pursue better conditions for my men.'

They were interrupted when a staff sergeant arrived at the tent flap to announce he had been able to obtain a loaf of fresh bread for the Von and his two junior officers while the rest of the rangers would receive hard tack biscuits.

'Send back the bread to the bakers. My officers and I will have hard tack if that is all the army can offer.'

'Yes, sir,' the staff sergeant replied, and left with the prized loaf of fresh bread.

'I admire your dedication to the needs of your men,' Ian said. 'I doubt that many of my brother officers in British regiments would do the same.'

'The men need to know that those who command them share their hardships,' von Tempsky said with a shrug. 'So, how are your observations proceeding on the role of rangers in modern warfare?'

'I can say that I have somewhat of a bias towards your ranger companies,' Ian replied, taking another swig of the dark rum. 'Inadvertently, I have found myself carrying out similar operations in India and feel that there is a place in the army in the years ahead for small, well-armed and well-trained soldiers with a proven ability to withstand the harshest conditions in the forests. I have noted that each of your men must be able to swim and you also ensure one of your soldiers is able to speak the dialect of the Maori. This is all rather unconventional to the British army.'

'We often have a need to cross waterways,' the Von said. 'That is why I insist each man is able to swim. And from time to time, we need to listen in to warrior encampments.'

'I doubt that rule would go well with the British regiments. Swimming is not something that our soldiers have had a chance to practise when you consider where they are recruited from in the slums of towns and cities in England.'

'Most of the men I recruit are from the Australian colonies,' von Tempsky said. 'They are well adapted to living in the bush, and swimming is something they like to do in the warmer months. I have read your sergeant major's record of service, which is very impressive. I noted that he is considered one of the best marksmen with the Enfield in your regiment. I have tasked Sergeant Duffy to conduct a small range practice this afternoon for the men in my detachments who are armed with the Enfield. Possibly your man could provide a few ideas on how to be even more accurate with the rifled muskets?'

'I am sure Sarn't Major Curry would be pleased to assist where he can,' Ian said with a smile, finishing his tot of rum and placing the tin mug at his feet. 'It would be advantageous to my report if we can carry out a patrol with one of your detachments to observe your bushcraft.'

'I can arrange that,' the Von said. 'I try to keep away from the regiment posted with us as they insist that my rangers carry out navvy work on the fortifications. My men are above those menial duties and if the colonel commands me to supply my men for digging duties, I will have to tell him that they are out in the bush, and then brief my rangers to disappear. They can have a picnic away from the prying eyes of the infantrymen here.'

The more Ian learned of the leadership of the newly appointed major, the more he liked and admired him. Ian had read reports by British officers of how undisciplined they were, and how they lacked respect for officers of the British army, but there was also a grudging respect for the men who they criticised, that they were highly effective in locating the enemy and fighting this bush war.

Ian excused himself and sought out Conan, who was chatting to a small party of rough-looking rangers. It was apparent that he had ingratiated himself with them when they learned that the British senior non-commissioned officer who had earned the Victoria Cross was in fact a colonial-born man. When Ian approached the group, one of the rangers saluted him and Ian, surprised, returned the salute.

'I've been telling the boys about some of our missions,' Conan said, and Ian now knew where the new-found respect had come from. 'I was telling them how you are known as the Colonial amongst the men of our regiment. Sergeant Duffy here is from Sydney Town, and he's recognised as the best shot in the Von's company. He and I are going to have a little bet.'

Ian looked at the broad-shouldered man in his twenties

with a broken nose, and Ian sensed that a fighter lay behind the grey eyes. 'Sergeant Duffy, you feel that you can out-shoot Sarn't Major Curry?' Ian asked.

A broad smile warmed the ranger's expression. 'I will give it a try,' he replied, hefting the Enfield in his big hand. A murmur of voices drifted from the dozen or so rangers standing around. Ian could hear bets being laid on the outcome of the shooting match between the British army officer and the colonial ranger. From what Ian could hear, the ranger sergeant was the favoured winner.

Ian reached into his pocket and produced a shilling coin. 'I will back Sarn't Major Curry,' Ian said with a grin and one of the rangers, obviously self-appointed as the holder of bets, accepted the coin.

'You will be sorry, sir,' he said with a smile. 'We hate taking money from a Queen's captain.' Laughter followed the ranger's statement.

Narrow wooden palings were set up at fifty paces, one hundred paces and three hundred paces. It would be the best of three shots to decide the winner. An Enfield was handed to Conan and the rule was for them to take their shots from a standing pose for the first near target, then they could either choose to sit or kneel for the second and third shots. A crowd gathered as the word got around concerning the shooting match.

'To make it interesting, I will also present the winner with a bottle of rum,' Ian declared as the two competi-tors took their positions on the improvised range. Ian's announcement raised a cheer from the rangers.

'Yer goin' to share the bottle with the boys when you win, Michael,' a sergeant called to the big ranger.

Ian called the men to face their targets and fire in their own time. The Enfields banged a second apart, and the near palings both splintered under the impact of the heavy-calibre Minie bullets. All cheered.

Now it was time to select the next closest targets and Conan assumed a kneeling position whilst Michael chose to sit. Both shooters took more time aiming, controlling their breathing and observing the drift of the wind across the range. Conan fired first and his target fell over. Michael fired a couple of seconds later and also secured a bullseye, his paling splintering. Again, a cheer erupted, recognising the skills of the two men, before a nervous silence fell as the final targets were engaged. Both men retained their shooting poses. Michael fired first, and it was obvious that he had missed. A groan swept over the rangers. Then Conan fired with the same result. A cheer went up from the crowd.

'What happens now, sir?' the bookmaker asked.

'I say they continue firing until one emerges as the victor,' Ian replied and felt a little like a cricket umpire at an English county match.

Conan and Michael reloaded their rifled muskets. Duffy turned to Conan, extending his hand. 'Good luck, sir,' he said, and Conan returned the good wishes. Silence fell, killing the babble of men laying more bets on the outcome. This time, not all bets were on their own marksman. Conan adopted a sitting position like his opponent. The usual hush fell as the two men levelled the long barrels at the distant targets. Ian noticed how Conan very carefully checked the wind drift by tossing some dried grass in the air and observing its fall.

It was Michael who fired first again and a great groan went up when the shot missed. Conan took his time before squeezing the trigger. The butt bit into his shoulder and all saw the paling splinter at the end of the range. The watching rangers gave a cheer for Conan's deadly accuracy with the

Enfield, and the bookmaker began paying out coins won in the betting.

Conan rose and walked over to Duffy. 'I feel that you have earned the bottle of rum,' he said.

Michael extended his hand to congratulate Conan. 'It's no dishonour being beaten by a fellow Irishman,' the sergeant said. 'We could do with you in the rangers.'

'Well shot, Sergeant Duffy,' Ian said. 'Sarn't Major Curry has had a lot of practice in the past, and that was probably his advantage.'

'Sir, if I may say so, you're not like any other British officer I have met. You are more like our own officers,' Duffy said with a frown. 'I hear that you are called the Colonial. It suits you, sir.'

Ian smiled. 'Sergeant, if you only knew.'

★

The ship that had left Circular Quay in Sydney had sailed north to the outpost of Townsville in the newly established colony of Queensland. Since they had disembarked, Josiah had walked along winding, rough tracks beside the big wheels of the bullock-drawn dray as they left the relative civilisation of Townsville. At the end of the day, he was exhausted and looked forward to sleeping at night by the campfire.

The O'Grady family had taken Josiah into their fold as if he was born to them, and Bernard was already teaching the young boy skills such as handling the four bullocks hauling the dray and maintaining the dray with all the goods needed by isolated property owners to trek west. Bernard was a kind man and patient with Josiah, while his wife also doted on the newest member of the O'Grady brood. But the girls fussed over him so much that it was annoying.

The five daughters of Bernard and Mary O'Grady ranged from six to fourteen years old, and to Josiah, they were strange creatures.

Josiah did not know where he was but found the bush around him strange. He marvelled at the kangaroos hopping across the rough track before them, and even strange furry creatures in the limbs of trees bordering the road north. Bernard told him they were called monkeys, but was corrected by his eldest daughter, Caroline, that they were in fact known as koalas.

The three eldest daughters also walked beside the dray and when Josiah flagged, Caroline would take his hand, speaking encouraging words to him to keep going. The dray groaned under the mountain of goods it carried and, at the end of the day, a large canvas sheet was attached to the side of the dray to make a shelter for the women against any rain, while Bernard and Josiah slept under a blanket. Josiah noticed how Bernard slept with a shotgun by his side and wondered why. He did not know of the evil men who preyed upon travellers in the lonely stretches of the great Australian forests, and had not heard the term 'bushranger'.

On this night, it was cool but not cold by the camp-fire, and Josiah fell asleep almost immediately following a hearty meal of lamb stew and potatoes. But, as he slept, dreams came to him of the face of his Aunt Ella. He could feel her arms embrace him and sensed her overwhelming love. Despite the kindness of the O'Gradys, Josiah cried in his sleep for the loss of the love he had known and was in despair that he would never see her again.

*

Sir Archibald Forbes' health had deteriorated further since the departure of his son, Charles. The gout crippled his portly body, and he wheezed whenever he stood up. Too many cigars and too much port were taking a toll on his health, and now that he never left the manor, his only real pleasure was reading his morning newspaper. He was irritable and short with the servants who tiptoed around him, who were only pleased he still lived to provide them with employment.

His valet came to the billiard room with a letter on a sterling silver tray. He bowed, as Sir Archibald liked his lessers to do, and Sir Archibald slit open the sealed letter with a brass opener shaped like a scimitar. The servant hovered nearby, awaiting further instructions as his master read the letter.

'Oh God!' Sir Archibald gasped, dropping the letter to the floor, his face turning purple as he pitched forward from his great leather chair. The startled servant was rooted to the carpet, dropping the silver platter and watching in horror as Sir Archibald's body went through a short struggle to stay alive. Before the servant could react, Sir Archibald was dead from a massive heart attack.

With tentative steps, the servant stepped forward, uttering 'Sir Archibald?' He knelt down to see the staring eyes bulging from his dead master's purple face, gazing in horror at nothing. The servant scooped up the letter and read that Sir Archibald's son, Charles, had been murdered in a most foul manner in the distant colony of New Zealand.

It was then that the servant snapped from his shock to call for the head butler.

THIRTY-TWO

Lady Rebecca Montegue-Jenkins welcomed the detective sergeant's unexpected visit to her townhouse in London. He was ushered into a drawing room by a servant.

'Sergeant, calling on me at this time of day is somewhat of a surprise,' the lady said, settling down on a divan as Robert stood respectfully at the centre of the room, his hat in his hands. 'Would you care for tea?'

'My apologies, Lady Montegue-Jenkins, but I have come into receipt of some news that I know you should be privy to,' Robert replied. 'It has been reported to us that our suspect in the murder of Jane Wilberforce was himself slain in the colony of New Zealand some weeks ago.' Robert could see the expression of absolute surprise on the woman's face.

'How was he killed?' she asked.

'It appears that he was shot through the throat and bled

to death,' Robert answered. 'I am afraid his death means closing the case on him being the killer of Miss Wilberforce.'

Lady Montegue-Jenkins rose from the divan, brushing down her elegant dress. 'Your news calls for something stronger than tea and cakes,' she said, crossing the floor to a liquor cabinet and retrieving a crystal decanter of sherry. 'Will you join me?'

'My thanks, Lady Montegue-Jenkins, but I must return to my station. My visit is not official. I wanted you to be the first to know, considering our efforts late last year to bring the man to justice.'

'Thank you, Detective Sergeant,' she said, pouring herself a small glass of the sweet fortified wine.

'If you will excuse me, your ladyship, I will take my leave.'

Rebecca nodded gracefully at the detective sergeant, who was shown to the main entrance by a servant. She sat down on the divan with her mind racing. So, the monster was finally dead. She wondered if he'd been murdered by cut-throats or if justice had been truly served.

She had been able to keep track of Ian Steele's movements and knew that he was currently in New Zealand. Was it a coincidence that Charles would be killed in New Zealand at the same time Ian was stationed there? Was it the guiding hand of her twin sister reaching out from the grave to lead the man she had loved more than life to the place and time of the fatal meeting?

Rebecca swallowed the contents of the sherry glass and stared at the sun shining through a tall window. She fancied that she could see the smiling face of her twin Jane in the shadows.

Rebecca recalled reading an article in a newspaper about a former British officer caught up in the American civil war. The article had given details and the name of

Samuel Forbes. Rebecca had felt her heart skip a beat when she had read the report and gazed at the woodcut portrait of the real Samuel Forbes. The likeness was uncanny with that of Ian Steele, the colonial-born imposter. Now, with Charles dead and news that Sir Archibald had died in his manor in Kent, Rebecca knew that the vast Forbes empire of wealth would be solely inherited by the real Samuel Forbes. But what of Ian Steele? What was his destiny when Samuel returned to London to settle the will?

Rebecca poured herself another sherry and sat down on the divan with a sigh. Samuel Forbes was in America, Ian Steele was in New Zealand, and her dear friend Ella was in New South Wales. How complicated life was, she mused.

★

The sun beat down on Samuel's regiment, causing men to collapse. It was an unseasonal heat, Samuel's second-in-command Captain Clarke commented as Samuel led his infantry along a primitive road no better than a track, cleared through the dense forest of green pines and flowering dogwood trees. He could see that the sun had dried the undergrowth and that visibility in the bush either side was very limited. His orders to form a line to sweep the adjoining forest of any rebel forces had appeared simple in the explanation at Grant's HQ. Samuel's regiment was tasked with capturing the junction on Brock Road in an undulating terrain covered in a sea of trees. The whole Wilderness was crisscrossed with tracks, and these would become vital in moving the large forces of both sides around the battlefield contested between General Robert E. Lee and General Ulysses S. Grant.

Samuel cared little for strategy but more for the survival of the men of his regiment, who had been entrusted to his leadership. He eased himself from his horse and handed the reins to a soldier standing nearby. He slid his walking stick from a scabbard on his horse as Samuel knew that this would be a war on foot in the forest his regiment had been tasked to clear. He called in his company commanders for a briefing, after which he turned to Lieutenant Davidson. 'I will be establishing my headquarters with your company, Mr Davidson,' Samuel said. 'Make sure that your men have a plentiful supply of water in their canteens, and at least a day's rations. We will establish a skirmish line and sweep forward to make contact with the enemy. Are there any questions, gentlemen?'

When Samuel scanned his four officers' faces he could see natural concern, but also an expression of confidence – despite the fact they were denied their artillery support due to the nature of the Wilderness.

Then the regiment stepped into the gloom of the trees with bayonets fixed. Before them were the unseen, well-concealed enemy infantry waiting to wreak hell on Samuel's men. It did not take long before the regiment's well-planned line of advance was broken into small parties by the nature of the thick scrub and trees. Visibility from one end of the skirmish line to the other was impossible. Samuel limped alongside Lieutenant Davidson at the centre of his line of march. Within the hour, sporadic shots became full-fledged volleys and the sound and smell of battle took on an even more ominous sign. Thick smoke billowed from amongst the trees where spent wadding had set the dry undergrowth alight. The smoke drifted through the gaps in the forest, leaving men coughing. It had become an unexpected new factor in staying alive and the primitive fear of being burned alive caused Samuel to shiver as he gripped his walking stick and revolver.

A volley of shots erupted from the scrub ahead and two men near Samuel fell. Lieutenant Davidson roared orders to take cover and return fire. One of his men shouted back that they could not see the detachment of Johnny Rebs who had fired on them. Then Samuel heard the terrible sound of men stabbing with bayonets, firing point-blank and clubbing with rifle butts as another section of the company had stumbled on the party of Confederate soldiers. He could not see the vicious hand-to-hand fight and knew that now he had little control over the outcome of his advance into the Wilderness. It had come down to sergeants and corporals in charge of their sections to continue the battle against a determined and dangerous enemy.

Samuel stumbled forward. He was not a religious man but found himself praying that if there was a God that He would protect the men in his command. But Samuel knew that the rebels were also praying to the same Christian God. God had not stayed the hand of the soldier who had killed the only man Samuel truly loved above his own life. Whose side was God really on?

'Look out, sir!' a soldier cried out and Samuel realised that he was failing to concentrate on the immediate situation. In a second, he saw a shabbily dressed, bearded rebel soldier loom from the cover of a thicket with his bayonet-tipped rifle, lunging at Samuel. Before Samuel could react, a bullet from an unknown source smashed into the body of the Confederate soldier, causing him to drop to the thick mat of leaves on the forest floor. Samuel was shaken but paused to look down on the man at his feet. He was not dead and had rolled over on his back to stare up at Samuel, who could see that he was a man probably in his sixties. His face was wrinkled and tanned as if he had once been a farmer exposed to the weather. Samuel could see blood pooling around the dirty, tattered shirtfront, and trickling from the dying man's mouth. For a moment, his eyes closed, but then opened to stare back at Samuel standing over him. Then the old soldier attempted to put his hand in his trouser pocket. Samuel knelt down beside the dying man and reached inside the pocket that the rebel had not had the strength to reach. He retrieved a photograph of a woman about the same age as the dying man with two fine-looking boys in the uniforms of the Confederacy. Samuel guessed these must be the man's wife and sons. Samuel placed the photograph in the hand of the soldier, placing his hand on the man's blood-stained chest. When he looked at the man's face, he knew that he was already dead, and Samuel wondered as to the fate of the two young men in the photograph. For a moment, Samuel was oblivious to the battle raging around him as small detachments of men from both sides shot, stabbed and beat each other to death in the thick undergrowth of the Wilderness forest.

Samuel was hardly aware that tears streaked his grimy face. For a moment, he was alone with a man who should have been home with his family but now lay dead at Samuel's feet. Samuel stood to scan for his regiment's whereabouts. Oddly, it had taken an ordinary man from the other side dying at Samuel's feet to remind him why he had hated war so much and now, here he was, commanding a Union regiment in a land far from his own. He hated war but knew he had the skills to lead men in combat. If only his grandfather could see him now, Samuel thought bitterly.

THIRTY-THREE

The light produced by the fires burning in the tinder-dry undergrowth threw garish shadows on the taller trees. From the improvised log-and-earth fortification, the soldiers of Samuel's regiment could hear the pitiful cries of dying men calling for help, water and their mothers. Occasionally, the scream of a soldier too wounded to crawl away from the encroaching flames split the air.

Samuel sat with his back against a log, closing his eyes as if that would block out the terrible situation.

'Poor goddamn boys,' Lieutenant Davidson muttered. 'Getting burned to death is not right – even for a Reb.'

'Let us hope that we fight our way out of this hellhole,' Samuel said.

'It's worse than Gettysburg,' Davidson said. 'At least there we didn't have to worry about being burned alive.'

'You were at Gettysburg?' Samuel asked.

'I was with the sharpshooters when we held up the Rebs,' Davidson replied. 'I got promoted to lieutenant after Gettysburg. I suppose that was because my regiment had very little left to promote.'

'So, you volunteered for the war,' Samuel said.

'I got paid by a rich man's son in New York to take his place in the ballot,' Davidson said. 'You know what they say, rich man's war, poor man's fight. I needed the three hundred dollars to provide for my wife and five children. I was desperate and here I am.'

Samuel guessed that his junior officer was a man of experience and moral fortitude to have remained when many who had accepted the rich men's sons' payments had enlisted and then deserted. But not Lieutenant Davidson.

'The men know how you won your medal,' Davidson said. 'They have great faith in their Limey Officer.'

'I was in the wrong place at the wrong time,' Samuel sighed. 'And it cost me my leg. I would rather have my leg back.'

Both men fell silent as the cries of the wounded drifted against the background of undergrowth crackling in the warm night. Wildfire had not been in the planning of the close-quarter fighting of the Wilderness campaign.

*

Captain Ian Steele was preparing his kit for a patrol with one of the Von's small detachments when a ranger corporal arrived at his tent.

'Sir, I have a message for you from HQ,' the corporal said, handing Ian the folded paper.

'Thank you, Corporal,' Ian said, unfolding the sheet of paper. For a second his heart skipped a beat. The message read that he was to take a ship and cross the Tasman Sea to Sydney Town, where he was to submit his report on his observations of the operations of the Company of Forest Rangers. It was signed by a senior officer at army HQ in Auckland. Ian was to sail on the first ship out of Auckland, within the week. Ian folded the paper and his first stop was to find Conan, who he located smoking his pipe and staring down the road that the rangers patrolled against the ambush of supply wagons.

Ian hurried to him. 'Hurrah! Conan, we're going home,' Ian said by way of greeting, waving the orders from Auckland.

Conan frowned. 'I can't go home,' he said. 'I learned from one of the boys in the rangers that there is an open case on the death of your mother. If I go home, they will arrest me, and I will surely swing on the gallows. I have already requested a passage back to India to rejoin the regiment before it ships out to England.'

Ian knew that it had been Conan's brother who had brutally killed his mother and that Conan had tried to stop him. Conan lived with that shame every day of his life.

'I can see what you mean and understand why you must avoid returning to New South Wales. But you could go to another colony and the traps would never catch you,' Ian said with sadness. Now he realised that Conan's name had not been mentioned in the movement order.

'I would not want Molly to live always wondering if the law would catch up one day,' Conan said, removing his pipe to plug it with tobacco. 'Molly has waited for almost ten years for me to be at her side. I think it is time for me to be with her. But I will always miss the time we shared. You and I should have been dead a thousand times over but have been spared to find what is truly important in this life, and it is not war.'

Ian placed his hand on his friend's shoulder and could have sworn he saw a tear forming at the corner of the tough sergeant major's eye. Ian knew that this could not be true for the recipient of the Victoria Cross. 'I truly understand, old friend,' Ian said.

'You have a son to find across the Tasman,' Conan said. 'And we both have the fortunes to ensure that we protect and provide for those we love. It is time to be born again into a life away from the death we have lived with.'

'Sarn't Major, you are getting to sound like an old woman.' Ian laughed softly. 'But a wise one.'

He extended his hand and Conan accepted it with a crushing grip. Both knew that they were closer than brothers and would always remain so beyond even the veil of death.

'When do you leave?' Conan asked.

'I have to pack and leave this afternoon to be able to board the ship from Auckland to Sydney,' Ian replied. 'There will not be time to make my farewells.'

'I will do that,' Conan said. 'The rangers have taken a liking to the Colonial.'

Ian walked away but paused to look back at Conan standing alone on the road, staring at the slope below as he puffed his pipe. It was permitted for an officer to cry, so long as he was not seen by a soldier doing so. Tears rolled down Ian's cheeks as he knew he would probably not see his friend and comrade again.

Within an hour, Ian was on a horse riding north to Auckland, leaving behind ten years of his life. As a boy in his village at the foothills of the soaring sandstone cliffs of the mountain range, he had dreamed of serving in the British army of the Queen. Now, he had achieved the dream but had often found it more of a nightmare in the sounds, smells and fear of combat. As he rode, he wondered if he would find his son and when he did, what would be the outcome. The thought was as frightening as facing battle.

★

The sun blazed down and Bernard O'Grady stared at the slope of crumbling rocks that blocked his path. The water supply for his family and Josiah was almost gone and his dream of claiming the acreage of land he had purchased in Sydney Town was turning into a pipedream. He looked back at the dray loaded with supplies, surrounded by the women in his life. Mary sat on a rock, listless and exhausted from the trek west. Bernard knew he must stay strong for his family, stroking his long beard and mulling over the very few options he had left. To persist in pushing forward over the low, rocky hills covered in dry scrub could mean finding better land beyond and a supply of water. But it could also mean his family dying a slow, agonising death from thirst. He knew that three days before, they had passed a waterhole. It had had little in it but at least some water remained in the riverbed. He knew turning back was at least a chance to survive.

Then Bernard saw something at the top of the ridge that chilled him with fear. Out of the shimmering heat, he saw a party of a dozen Aboriginal warriors armed with long spears silently gazing down on his bullock dray.

'Fetch the gun!' Bernard barked to Josiah, standing only feet behind him. Josiah ran back to the dray, pulled out the double-barrelled shotgun and stumbled back to Bernard. He, too, saw the Aboriginal warriors. Bernard had been warned before leaving Townsville that the tribes west of the port town could be dangerous as they resisted the Europeans encroaching on their tribal lands.

Bernard was terrified. He was outnumbered and had read in southern newspapers of how the Indigenous people had learned from bitter experience that the white man's guns took time to reload and used this knowledge to frighten them into firing at long range before mounting a fast and ferocious attack.

Bernard realised that he was trembling as Josiah stood by his side. 'Go back to the dray,' he said quietly. 'Protect the women.' Bernard well knew his request was futile as he was asking a boy to do a man's job, but it was all he could think to say.

Reluctantly, Josiah walked back to the terrified women gathered around the dray. Mary O'Grady was already praying, her fingers running through her rosary beads, while the girls stood ashen-faced, staring up at the ridge.

'Are we going to die?' the second oldest of the five girls asked, reaching out to grip Josiah's hand. Josiah did not answer but wondered at the scene of the silent warriors simply watching them. Then, without a word, the Aboriginal party turned their backs on the terrified Europeans below the high ground, disappearing off the rocky ridge like a shimmering mirage.

Bernard did not move for some minutes before returning to the dray. 'We are returning to Townsville,' he said in a flat voice. He still had funds to establish a business in the frontier town and realised that he had never been born to conquer the vast colony's frontier. He was city-born and admitted that this was a land in which only the toughest would survive.

The sun set at their backs as they made their return trek to the coast and relative civilisation.

★

During the day, reinforcements had been brought forward to add numbers to Samuel's regiment, fortified behind their logs and earthworks. News of the separate clashes in and around the Wilderness were confused and Samuel hardly cared as his only concern was for the immediate ground around him and keeping as many of his men alive as possible. Samuel had ensured his men took time to eat their rations and prime their Springfield rifled muskets during the day.

It was around late afternoon when the enemy came crashing at them through the tangle of undergrowth, whooping their rebel yells meant to instil fear in the Union ranks. The rebels were concealed by the forest until they were almost on Samuel's line and the fighting came down to bloody hand-to-hand clashes, volleys of point-blank fire and the mingling of blue and grey. Such was the ferocity of the desperate enemy assault that Samuel's section of the line was forced to break, and Samuel found himself yelling orders to stand firm, but to no avail. As he quickly assessed their situation, he could see that some of the men of his regiment had not panicked but would stop to reload the cumbersome rifled muskets, fire and retreat to reload and fire again.

Samuel suddenly found himself alone, cut off from his regiment, slashing his walking cane at the thicket he was entangled in. He could hear the isolated battles being fought all around him in the falling gloom of evening, but it had become a blur of sounds, smells and sights. Samuel did not know where the shot came from that flung him off his feet. He only knew that he had been hit in the stomach as he lay on the dry, matted covering of leaves and fir tree needles. The pain was now overwhelming him, and Samuel knew there was little hope of crawling to a place of safety. There was no safety anywhere in this hell of tangled trees and thick forest.

'Water.' The gasping request from only feet away surprised Samuel as he lay on his back. He turned his head to see the figure of a Confederate soldier lying on his stomach almost within arm's reach. Without thinking, Samuel reached for his canteen and stretched it over to the wounded enemy.

'Can't move,' the rebel soldier groaned. 'Damn Yankee shot me in the back.' Samuel could now see that the man was around his own age and had a long beard shot with grey. Samuel dragged himself a few feet towards the rebel soldier, whose expression of surprise was obvious when he recognised that Samuel was from the enemy. Despite the recognition, the rebel soldier reached out to take the canteen and swallowed the tepid water in gulps. When he had finished, he passed back the almost empty canteen.

'I see you got gut shot,' the rebel soldier said without animosity. 'Me, I think I got my backbone shot. Looks like we go to the pearly gates together.'

'It is possible that either your side or mine might find us soon, and get us medical help,' Samuel said, knowing there was little chance of that happening in the swirling battle around them.

'You don't sound like a Yankee,' the critically wounded Confederate soldier observed. 'I've heard enough of them on the battlefield. Are you a Dutchman?'

'English,' Samuel replied.

'We always thought that you English would come and fight on our side,' the rebel said. 'Like the Frenchies did for us when my great-granddaddy fought with Washington against the Limeys.'

'Not while you retain slaves,' Samuel replied, forcing off a wave of pain with a grimace.

'I ain't got no slaves,' the Confederate said. 'I ain't even got a mule. All the slaves belong to the rich plantation folks who got exemption from the fighting.'

Samuel found it strange to be on this tiny section of the battlefield, having a discussion with a fellow wounded soldier from the other side. The Americans never failed to intrigue him. He sensed no real animosity from the rebel soldier, and they could have been in a tavern sharing a drink. It was true for the other side as well; a rich man's war fought by the poor. Maybe only officers from rich families should face each other on the battlefield and sort it out, leaving the poor to eke out their living and feed their families. It was a stupid thought, but Samuel already knew how stupid he was for being propped up against a tree, dying for a cause that wasn't his.

Thick smoke curled across the earth towards them, the sound of crackling timber and the glow of fire in the late-afternoon gloom of the Wilderness followed the acrid smoke.

'It's coming for us!' the rebel soldier said with rising terror. 'I can't move!'

Samuel realised that his chance of escaping the approaching fire was also virtually nil. Now he could see a low wall of flames dancing from thicket to thicket with searing fingers of fire. They both lay in its path, and even now Samuel could feel the radiant heat burning his exposed flesh.

'Shoot me!' the rebel soldier screamed as the fire wrapped itself around his body, burning through the tattered uniform. Samuel did not hesitate. He raised his pistol, levelled it and pointed it at the agonised eyes of the soldier being burned alive. The bullet exploded between the eyes begging mercy, and the man was no longer in pain.

Samuel glanced down and could see the fire reaching for his legs. He turned the heavy revolver to the side of his head and, with a final thought of James, fired. The real heir to the vast Forbes fortune was dead.

THIRTY-FOUR

Captain Ian Steele passed through the gates of Sydney's military headquarters of Victoria Barracks. The great sandstone set of two-storeyed buildings facing him were impressive and the guard at the main entrance saluted him. Ian returned the salute and located a duty officer, who directed him to the office of a colonel who had received Ian's initial report on the operations of the Companies of Forest Rangers in the wars of New Zealand.

The duty officer came out of the colonel's office and ushered Ian in. A smartly uniformed officer sat behind a large, wooden desk with a portrait of a young Queen Victoria dominant on the wall behind him, and there were also maps of New Zealand on an adjoining wall. Ian snapped off a smart salute.

'Take a seat, Captain Forbes,' the colonel said, gesturing to a chair just off to the side of the colonel's desk. Ian noted from the colonel's uniform adornments that he was from an old British regiment of some renown. 'I have read your report on what you have observed of these ranger companies,' he said. 'It is an impressive report and very persuasive but, after consultation with others of the committee, we have come to the conclusion they have no place in future conflicts the British army may face. We have our cavalry scouts who are more than capable of carrying out reconnaissance missions.'

Ian was not surprised by the British officer's conclusion and felt his anger flare but refrained from displaying his bitter disappointment at the conclusion made by the military committee. 'Sir, the facts and figures demonstrate the rangers' effectiveness in fighting the type of guerrilla warfare the Maori use against the army,' Ian defended. 'They are small in number but have been instrumental in disrupting the activities of the enemy in the bush.'

'Ah, but that is it,' the British colonel replied. 'We do not envisage such operations against primitive tribesmen as much as we do a possible war in Europe against the rising Prussian or Russian threat. The same kind of operations as used by the rangers can be supplemented by our militias in Africa or elsewhere. Besides, from what my colleagues inform me, the rangers are little better than soldiers of fortune – undisciplined – and even carry barbaric weapons such as hatchets for close-quarter fighting! Damned uncivilised, if you ask me.'

Ian realised that the recommendations of his report would be filed and forgotten.

'I have heard that you will no longer be with us after this week,' the colonel said. 'It is a pity to see an officer with your considerable experience leave the service of the Queen.'

'I will truly miss the men of my regiment and my fellow

officers,' Ian replied. 'But I have plans for the future in the Australian colonies. There appear to be unlimited opportunities for advancement here.'

'I was conversing with a friend in the mess who told me that you were always known to your men as the Queen's Colonial because of your previous service back in the forties on garrison duties before being sent to fight the Maori. It also seems that your soldiers felt that you treated them with respect and compassion.' Ian felt a swell of pride until the colonel continued. 'Not a good trait in a British officer. The men must be aware of the class difference between themselves and their betters who lead them. With more time in Her Majesty's service, you would have come to understand that soldiers require the strictest of discipline.'

Ian listened, angry at the way this senior British officer belittled his service.

'I don't think there is anything else to discuss, Captain Forbes, and I wish you well for the future,' the British colonel said. 'Will you be dining in the mess for lunch today?'

'No, sir, I have an important mission to undertake,' Ian replied. 'If there is nothing else, may I depart?'

'You are dismissed, Captain Forbes, and good luck in whatever your future may be.'

Ian saluted, turned on his heel and marched out of the office.

He took a carriage to Macquarie Street in the heart of the city to his accommodation at the prestigious Australian Club. He had been able to easily attain membership because of his membership to a certain British gentlemen's club in London. Ian had chosen the club to be his base of operations in search of his son as he knew that at the club he would be rubbing shoulders with the most influential people in Sydney society.

Ushered to his room, Ian changed into a civilian suit, hanging his uniform on a rack. He stared at it for a moment and remembered that it represented a decade of his life but snapped himself out of those memories – good and bad – to concentrate on finding his son.

All he had to go on was the scant information Nikolai had given him just before his death in the hills of northern India. Ian took a hired hackney to Sydney University where he was informed by an administrator that Professor Shortland had been killed in a road accident many months before. Ian was also able to glean that the academic's wife had returned to England, and the little boy they knew as Josiah had disappeared.

Ian returned to the horse-drawn carriage where he was met by the driver, sitting high behind the partially covered cabin for the passenger. 'From your look, sir, I would say that you have had no luck in whatever you were trying to find out,' the driver said. He was a man in his sixties and his back was bent from a life of hard labour.

Ian looked up at him. 'As a man who has, no doubt, great knowledge of Sydney Town, who would you recommend I speak with if I was looking for a lost person?'

The driver removed his cap and scratched his head. 'I know a trap not far from here who might know something,' he said. 'A big Irish constable who knows this area. I can take you to him.'

'I will pay extra,' Ian said. 'And a bonus if he is of any assistance in my search.'

*

He was certainly big. Constable Farrell had a long-time broken nose and, in some ways, reminded Ian of Conan Curry – except Conan would not have wanted to be introduced to the nemesis of those avoiding prosecution.

'You say you are lookin' for a boy about six years old with the moniker Josiah,' Constable Farrell said with a frown. 'It happens that I know of a boy who might match what you are sayin'.'

Ian felt a surge of hope. 'I would be very grateful if you could assist me,' Ian said.

'What is this boy to you, Mr Steele?' Farrell asked suspiciously, and Ian decided that he should be truthful.

'He is my long-lost son, Constable. I have been soldiering for the Queen for the past years and the boy's mother informed me he had been snatched away from London to be transported to Sydney Town. Now that I am no longer a soldier of the Queen, I wish to find my son and return him to his mother.' It was not the complete truth, but Ian felt it might reassure the Irish policeman.

'You look like a gentleman,' Farrell said. 'I will need just a little money for my time if I am to take you to people who may be able to help.' Ian slipped a pound note from the currency he carried, and the policeman's eyes lit up. It was a sizeable fee.

'Come with me,' he said, pocketing the note and leading Ian away from the carriage and driver. Before he left, Ian passed the driver a pound note and also asked him to wait. Ian's heart was pounding as they walked a short distance to stop in front of a public house with a sign above the door reading, *The Erin*. What if his son was here? The thought flashed through Ian's mind and he felt his hands tremble. The policeman strode inside to be greeted by a thick-set man mopping the floor before the first customers arrived.

'Max, is young Josiah here?' Farrell asked.

'*Nein*,' Max answered. 'He vent to Queensland *mit* ze O'Gradys.'

'When?' Ian asked, stepping forward to be eyed suspiciously by the tough German.

'Vot is it to you?' Max asked, pushing aside the mop.

'Mr Steele says he is the boy's father,' Farrell said.

Max paused, looking Ian up and down and seemingly satisfied with what he saw. 'Mr Duffy knows more about the boy,' Max replied. 'I vill fetch him.'

Max disappeared into a back room and returned seconds later with a dignified and intelligent-looking man. The policeman introduced Ian, and the two men shook hands.

'Max told me that you are looking for Josiah,' Frank said. 'We were able to get him a good family, the O'Gradys, who have departed for Queensland some weeks ago. They were travelling to the port of Townsville where Mr O'Grady was to set out for the interior to take up land. I would suppose by now the family is somewhere west of Townsville on the track.'

Ian's heart sank. He had only been weeks away from possibly meeting his son.

Duffy regarded Ian shrewdly. 'I saw your name on the birth certificate Miss Solomon showed me to prove her story. That was days ago, just after the O'Gradys left.'

'Miss Solomon!' Ian gasped. 'She was here?'

'Yes, she left her address in case we had any news of Josiah. If you wait a moment, I will fetch it.'

Ella was in Sydney! Ian felt his head swimming. Duffy returned in a short moment with a slip of paper in his hand which he passed to Ian. 'I pray that you are reunited with Josiah, Mr Steele. Miss Solomon explained the circumstances that brought Josiah to our shores. The boy is a wonderful child, smart and independent, and deserves a good mother and father.'

Ian thanked Frank Duffy for all that he had done to

assist in the search for his son and left the hotel with the burly Irish constable.

'I hope that helped, Mr Steele,' Farrell said when they returned to the carriage driver waiting patiently. Ian thanked Farrell and turned to the driver, informing him of the address, and the driver said he knew where the street was. Ian took his seat and the carriage set off.

Had fate been kind to him? Ian asked himself, and then felt a deep darkness when he considered his meeting with the woman he loved since they'd first met so long ago. Would she still hold any feelings for him? Ian hardly noticed the busy streets of the city as they travelled east towards the harbour. Would she even recognise him? So many questions without answers.

At first the rain began to spatter as Ian was driven to the harbour. Then it became a downpour and both Ian and the driver were soaked to the skin. But the cottage was located, and Ian hurried to the house on the edge of the harbour, where he rapped on the door. It was opened by a young maid.

'Is this the residence of Miss Solomon?' Ian asked and the maid looked alarmed at the figure in the rain.

'Missus, there is a man who has come visiting,' she called back over her shoulder.

Then he saw her.

For a moment, she simply stared, as if attempting to focus a ghost from her past, and threw her hands up to her mouth.

'Ian!'

Ian noticed that she had used his real name and stepped past the confused maid.

'Ella!'

For a moment, they stared at each other in the hallway, only a couple of paces apart. Ella broke first, tears streaming down her face, as she flung herself into Ian's arms.

The maid appeared even more confused. 'Should I fetch the police?' she asked, and Ella shook her head.

'No, Annie, this is a dear friend I have not seen in many years,' Ella replied through her sobs, and the maid was smart enough to realise that her presence was no longer required and disappeared into the kitchen.

Ian held Ella as if never to let her go and they stood in the hallway for some time, holding each other close.

'I have caused you to become as wet as I,' Ian said, gently disengaging the embrace and gazing down at Ella's tear-streaked face. 'You are still as beautiful as the day I first laid my eyes on you. It has taken years and I do not expect you to forgive me for the lie I was forced to tell you about my real identity, but the man standing before you *is* Ian Steele, formerly an officer in the Queen's service. Now, I am just Ian Steele who has returned home, and found the reason for surviving the battles I have fought. I love you, Ella Solomon. If you will allow me, I will never again be apart from you for the rest of our lives.' Ian poured out his feelings but was not sure of the response he would receive to his awkward statement of love.

'That is my wish also,' Ella said immediately. 'But first, I must find our son. I was never able to tell you that I gave birth after you had gone away.'

'I only recently learned of our son, when I was in India,' Ian replied. 'My reason for being in Sydney Town is to find him, but it appears he has travelled to Townsville in Queensland. It was because of my enquiries with the Duffy family that I was able to locate you. We have so much to talk about.'

'I have organised to travel by a coastal ship to Townsville in three days' time. It was the only one I could find steaming for the far north. You must come with me,' Ella said, and Ian once again embraced her.

'We will be together when Josiah will finally learn who he really is,' he promised.

Ella stepped back. 'You must dry your wet clothes or you will catch a fever,' she said. 'I think it would be wise if you stayed here, out of the storm for the night. I will have Annie make up a bed for you in the spare bedroom.'

Ian agreed as it gave him an excuse to be with Ella this night. He went to his driver and paid him a generous fare for his assistance. The driver looked at the five pounds in his hand, and felt getting soaked was worth it.

That evening after a light supper, the two retired to the living room where a small log fire burned in a hearth. Annie had been granted the night off and they were alone. It felt to Ian as though no time had passed between them and the years of separation did not exist.

Later that night, when they had eventually retired to sleep, Ian turned down the lantern beside his bed and listened to the rain beating on the tiled roof.

He could not sleep for the thoughts and emotions whirling through his head, and was considering the possibility of rising when the door to his room opened, and Ella stepped inside. Ian pulled back the blankets and Ella slipped in beside him.

Perhaps he would stay in bed after all.

THIRTY-FIVE

I an knew there was one important task he must complete before he travelled north with Ella, and explained his mission to Ella who expressed her understanding that he do so alone. The hours together had cemented their love for each other and there would be many other matters to discuss between them about the future. All that could be done when Ian returned from his visit west of Sydney.

Ian obtained a good horse and rode out towards his home village at the foot of the Blue Mountains. But it was not the place of his birth he was seeking but the grand property of Sir George Forbes located a few miles from Ian's old blacksmith's forge.

Ian arrived just after dusk to be met by barking dogs and the candle-lit sandstone house of Samuel's actual father. He was met by a young man, who took the reins of Ian's mount. Ian explained that he was a friend of the landed aristocrat and was shown to the house. Within moments, Ian was taken to the living room of Sir George, where he was shocked to see how much the old man had aged. Sir George did not attempt to rise from the leather armchair, and in the flicker of the dim candlelight Ian could see that Sir George was afflicted by some kind of illness.

'Sir George, it is Ian Steele,' Ian said, approaching the man in the leather chair.

Sir George squinted, focusing on Ian, and a slow smile of recognition came to his face. 'Mr Steele, come closer. It has been many years since I sent you to London on our mission.'

Ian pulled up a fine wooden chair to sit almost directly in front of the old man.

'I am afraid my time on this earth is limited,' Sir George said sadly. 'But I shall soon be reunited with my beloved Samuel, my dear son.'

'What do you mean, Sir George?' Ian asked with some alarm. He couldn't mean . . .

'You possibly do not know that my Samuel was killed fighting for the Union army in America,' Sir George replied. 'I have a friend in New York who wrote to me of his death on a campaign with General Grant. It seems that Samuel brought great honour to the Forbes name in his own right after all, but God knows why he should volunteer to fight for Abraham Lincoln. He could have remained with his grandfather's regiment instead of requesting that you take his place. I have contacts in England and they have kept me abreast of your own sterling career with the regiment. How ironic that you should survive and my son die doing something he always detested.'

'I am truly saddened to hear of Samuel's death,' Ian said. 'The little time we spent together, I found that we had much in common, and I considered him as a brother.'

Sir George reached out feebly with his hand to touch Ian on the forearm. 'Now that my son has passed, his share of the Forbes inheritance will go to Charles, that wretched excuse for a human being.'

'Charles is dead,' Ian said. 'He was slain in New Zealand.'

Sir George almost sat up straight at hearing of the death of his detested nephew. 'When my brother finally passes, that means you will be able to return and claim all the property of the Forbes family.'

'I do not intend to return to London, Sir George,' Ian said. 'My home is here now. I am once again known to the world as Ian Steele. I would hope that if it is known that Samuel is no longer with us, the Forbes inheritance will be left to you and Alice.'

A weak smile appeared on Sir George's haggard face. 'Your magnanimous offer to leave all to Alice only increases my esteem of you, Mr Steele. As far as I am concerned, all my colonial property will be willed to you from me, and Alice will obtain legal right over all Forbes estates and enterprises. This house and estate will be yours.'

Ian tried to protest the offer but was waved off by Sir George. 'My solicitor is visiting tomorrow to finalise my will, and I will be ensuring that you will be the sole beneficiary. It is the least I can do for your sacrifices over the past decade. I will hear no more protests, Mr Steele. It is your duty to accede to the wishes of a dying man. Now, call my valet and we will share a sherry before you retire for the night. There is much to discuss.'

Ian remained for the night and took breakfast with Sir George in the morning. Ian was genuinely fond of the brother of Sir Archibald; the two brothers were as different as their sons. When Ian mounted his horse to leave, he looked back over his shoulder to see the old man sitting in a wheelchair on his spacious veranda. Ian waved and Sir George waved back. It was the last time Ian saw the old man alive. Within a month, he would be dead from the cancer that riddled his body.

★

Josiah was looking forward to returning to the bark hut that had now become his new home on the outskirts of Townsville. Upon his return to the port town, Bernard O'Grady had been able to use the last of his savings to set up a transport business with his dray, conveying goods to the far-flung, isolated properties in the district. Bernard's eldest daughter, Caroline, secured a position as a governess on one of the more affluent stations near their new home, while his wife, Mary, remained in Townsville working as a seam-stress. The O'Gradys had been able to send the youngest girls to a school in the bush, but Bernard had come to rely on Josiah to accompany him with the great bullock-drawn dray.

Josiah's face had tanned under the Queensland sun, and his young muscles developed from the hard physical work trudging beside the great wagon filled with supplies. At night, he slept under the stars, marvelling at their vast expanse across the southern sky. Bernard had pointed out the constellation of the Southern Cross and told Josiah how he had stood under the flag of that cluster of stars at some place called the Eureka Stockade a decade earlier. Josiah did not understand what he meant about a rebellion but enjoyed the Irishman's company. He was kind but tough, always prompting the young boy to achieve even more in the arduous work of a bullocky. Josiah had come to learn about the care of their bullocks and how to chock the wheels of the cart when they had to ascend slopes.

He was also taught how to use a new rifle Mr O'Grady had purchased in Townsville. It was a Snider and when fired, it bit hard into Josiah's shoulder, bruising him. Mr O'Grady said that between his shotgun and Josiah's rifle they could hold off any who might attempt to rob them on the lonely tracks.

It was a lonely life under the blazing sun of the Queensland frontier, and the young boy would remember the kind face of Aunt Ella before he drifted off to sleep. She was never forgotten but lately, he had trouble remembering what she looked like.

A few scattered bark huts heralded their return to Townsville and very soon, their home came into view, nestled amongst a stand of gum trees where noisy cockatoos rose from the branches, screeching their calls.

'Look, young Josiah. We seem to have visitors,' Mr O'Grady said, peering through a shimmering heat haze. 'Fancy visitors, by the look of their carriage. Maybe wealthy customers, eh?'

The bullocks plodded forward until they saw Mary O'Grady appear from the hut with a strange man and woman standing beside her. She waved, and both Mr O'Grady and Josiah waved back.

Within minutes, the bullock dray was brought to a halt beside the bark hut. Josiah's eye was caught by the face of the pretty woman who stood beside the strange man. He tried to search his young memories as the face was vaguely familiar.

'Aunt Ella!' he exclaimed as it came to him, and she smiled widely and rushed forward to embrace him.

'Oh, Josiah, my love. I have found you at last.' Josiah was aware that she was weeping and he could not understand why this should be. Crying was for when you were hurt or very sad. When Josiah glanced at the strange man, he could see that he was deep in conversation with Mr and Mrs O'Grady, who did not look like she was very happy.

Josiah experienced the crushing embrace of his Aunt Ella from which he feared he might never be released. Eventually, she did let him go only to kneel in the dust, stroking his face with her gloved hand. 'You have grown up so strong,' she said between her tears. 'I have come such a long way to take you home.'

The strange man strode over to he and Aunt Ella, and for a moment he simply stared at Josiah. 'It is time to take you home, son,' he said. Josiah looked to Mr O'Grady, who grudgingly nodded his head.

The man extended his hand to Josiah, and the boy wondered whether he should accept the gesture.

'Go with Mr Steele, Josiah,' Mr O'Grady said solemnly. 'He is your father.'

Josiah heard the words but couldn't quite understand what they meant. He could see tears streaming down Mrs O'Grady's face. She rushed to Josiah and hugged him to her ample bosom. 'The girls and me will miss you, Josiah,' she said. 'Don't forget to write to us when you go with this gentleman and lady.'

'Why do I have to go with them, Mrs O'Grady?' Josiah countered.

'Because they are your mother and father,' she replied, patting Josiah on the cheek.

The statement made little sense to the confused boy. It would take patient love and time to sort that matter out.

EPILOGUE

Christmas 1864

The snow was falling gently in the Canadian province of Vancouver. In the picturesque village, Dr Peter Campbell had his medical practice and was well respected by all those living in the district. So, too, was his wife Alice and their three children. It was a mere two days before Christmas Day and Alice stood in her kitchen, gazing across an open field covered in a soft white blanket. A log fire in their well-established house warmed the rooms and her children begged to go outside to play, but Alice stood her ground and assured them that they were to finish decorating the fir tree their father had dragged into the house the previous day.

Alice loved her life in Canada, so far from the smog and congestion of London. The air was fresh with the scent of pine and she had already begun feeding a herd of deer in their backyard whenever they drifted in at night. Alice turned away from the kitchen window when she saw her husband riding up to the house. He preferred to use a horse in winter as it did not get stuck in snow drifts. She hurried to the door to welcome the former army surgeon, take his wet coat and usher him to the big log fireplace where his children would assault him with shrill cries of welcome.

Alice kissed Peter when he closed the door behind him, and he handed her a letter.

'Very rare for us to have a letter sent from London,' Peter said, taking off his heavy coat. 'It is addressed to you, my tiger lady.' It was an old joke between them, referring to the time Alice had taken on and killed a tiger in India and lived to tell the tale. The skin now took centre place in the living room.

Alice puzzled at the letterhead and then remembered that the name was that of the Forbes family solicitors. She carefully opened the letter and began to read the many pages while Peter stood near her. Alice gasped.

'What is it?' her husband asked, seeing the stricken expression on his wife's face.

'It's Samuel. He's dead!' Alice exclaimed.

'Good God!' Peter exclaimed, stepping forward to hold his wife. 'Where? India?'

'No, in America,' Alice said, looking up at her husband with a confused expression. 'But that is impossible. Sam was with the army in India, not the army of Mr Lincoln in America. The solicitors have written his death was confirmed from letters and documents recovered from his New York apartment, but his body is missing in a place they call the Wilderness. They inform me that my brother was also awarded America's highest medal for courage. It has to be a terrible mistake.'

Alice stood trembling and then broke into a deep sobbing, dropping the remaining pages of the letter on the floor. Peter bent down and continued reading the letter.

'It appears that your father and brother Charles are also deceased, and that you are now the sole beneficiary of the Forbes inheritance. My God!' Peter said. 'If Samuel was killed serving with the Union army in America, who was the man we both knew as Samuel? As you know, my brother sent me a letter from India before he was killed to say he was serving alongside Samuel. Samuel could not be in two places at once . . .'

Alice looked at her husband with shock. 'Is it possible that the Samuel we knew was in fact an imposter?'

Peter shook his head. 'I don't know what to think anymore.'

No matter the mystery, it was clear Alice alone would inherit a vast fortune. Three weeks later, a letter arrived from the colony of New South Wales. It was signed by one Ian Steele, who apologised for deceiving Peter and Alice for a decade but also had an explanation as to why. Alice could not condemn the man who had also been a brother to her, and Peter only knew Ian as one of his best friends in war and peace.

★

The honourable member for his electorate, Mr Clive Jenkins, was sitting in the dining room of his gentlemen's club, consuming a delicious meal of fish while recounting his heroic days as an officer fighting in the Crimea. The other members of parliament sitting around the table, smoking cigars and drinking port wine, would mutter, 'Hear, hear.' Jenkins was a rising star in the party and tipped to be the next prime minister. Although many did not speak it aloud, they knew his rise to prominence was influenced by his beautiful wife's contacts in the drawing rooms of fashionable London society.

'By Jove, I had this incompetent officer, Captain Samuel Forbes, who I was forced at gunpoint to prevent running when the Muscovites were on us outside Sebastopol. You might remember his family, his father Sir Archibald . . .' Jenkins raised his fork to his open mouth loaded with fish pieces before ending his sentence and, suddenly, he attempted to gasp, dropping the fork with a clatter on the table. He thrashed about, startling the members sitting around him.

'Good heavens!' one of the men sitting next to him exclaimed. 'I think poor old Clive has a fishbone stuck in his throat. His only hope is to cough it up. Someone fetch a doctor!'

Death came slowly and agonisingly to the honourable member just before a doctor arrived. His body lay on the floor of the dining room, surrounded by his fellow members, who muttered how terrible it was for a hero of the Crimean War to die in such a meaningless manner. But very few mourned the passing of the pompous jackass. Even his wife, Lady Rebecca, hardly shed a tear at his funeral and if she did, some said quietly in the church, it was only because all her work to make her husband the first man in Britain had been wasted.

★

There were many in Ian's village who welcomed him home with his new bride, Ella, and their young son, Josiah. They knew that Ian had left for England to make his fortune, and had returned after doing so. None knew that he had fought his way through many campaigns for the Queen in distant and exotic lands. Some queried why Sir George Forbes would leave his well-earning sheep farm of merinos to the former blacksmith, but rumours circulated it had been because of a business connection with the Forbes family in England that he'd earned the generous gift. All who came into contact with Ian admired him and were taken by Josiah as a gentle and intelligent young lad.

Ian had declared an open Christmas Day at his newly acquired property, where there would be a lamb on the spit and a lot of alcohol, with presents for the children of the village. Under a blazing Australian sun, there would also be roast duck, fish and baked vegetables, followed by fruit puddings and custard. Ian's gift to his former apprentice, Francis Sweeney, was the title deeds to the blacksmith shop and house that had once been the home of Ian's mother. Francis had openly wept at Ian's generosity.

On Boxing Day, Ella and Ian sat on the wide veranda of Sir George's former house, gazing out at the fields under a haze of smoke from a bushfire many miles away. They held hands and Ella sipped a glass of lemonade while Ian puffed on his pipe.

'Do you ever wish to return to London?' Ian asked quietly.

'Only to tidy affairs there,' Ella said, placing her head on Ian's shoulder. 'This is a new world for me to start a new life with you and Josiah.' Ian nodded and they continued to share the soft breeze from the small valley below, bordered by the giant gum trees. To have his wife and son with him had been worth the struggle of the last decade. He was rich in financial wealth, but richer still for having both of them in his life. Only Ella knew how much it had cost Captain Ian Steele in his body and soul to be with her, and none other in the colony would know of his military past.

Ian occasionally visited the graves of his mother and father, buried alongside each other in the little graveyard at the village. He would place wildflowers on the graves and stand in silence, speaking to them both. In his thoughts he explained to his father how he now understood why he had never spoken of his time on the battlefields of the Napoleonic Wars. Nor would he ever tell his own son what it was like to face the reality of a painful death from bullet, bayonet or bomb on the battlefield. That was only something soldiers talked about with their own.

A letter arrived from London early the following year, and Ian smiled as he read it on the veranda of his home. It was an invitation from former Sergeant Major Conan Curry VC to his wedding to Miss Molly Williams. Ian broke into a wide smile. From the date on the letter, they'd been married a month before it arrived. Maybe Ian would travel just one more time to London, with Ella and their son.

There were still some alive who knew of the deeds of the legendary Captain Ian Steele – the Queen's Colonial – but very few.

AUTHOR NOTES

In the first part of this novel I have used the geographic term 'the North West Frontier'. It was not until 1901 that the area covering the Umbeyla Pass would be known by this name, but many readers would be familiar with it from their interest in Anglo-Indian history, so I have used it to open the story. I have also referred to the local warriors as Pashtuns, as basically they were the enemy the British army confronted in the rugged and craggy hill region. Of the approximately 6000 British troops who fought, one in six would be either killed or wounded in that battle, which was an extremely high figure for any campaign the British army fought in the Victorian era. It should be noted that the British prevailed in that campaign, defeating the Pashtun warriors, but at a heavy cost. The scenes portrayed in the novel are from the memoirs of the men who fought that campaign.

In the second part of the novel, set amongst the Waikato campaign in New Zealand, we meet Major Gustavus Ferdinand von Tempsky. He was real, and the canvas on which I have portrayed the fighting is very much based on his own memoirs, penned before he was eventually killed in action. Von Tempsky was a man bigger than anything Hollywood could portray, whose extraordinary life can be found in research.

It is interesting to note that the British General Duncan Cameron, mentioned in this novel, would eventually tender his resignation in protest against what he called an inappropriate war against the Maori people. He left New Zealand in 1865. He was considered by many of his time as one of the best high-ranking officers ever to serve in Queen Victoria's army.

The long story of the British and Maori conflict can be found in many books. They highlight the courage of a valiant people forced to fight for their land against an overwhelming Imperial force. Of the many indigenous peoples the British Empire attempted to subdue, the Maori warriors proved to be amongst the most courageous and intelligent foe. In later years they would prove their outstanding bravery on the battlefields of Europe as part of the Allied forces in two world wars and in later conflicts – and, of course, on the rugby field.

ACKNOWLEDGEMENTS

Special thanks to Brianne Collins and Libby Turner for their editing work on this project. As always, my thanks to my publisher, Cate Paterson. I would also like to express my thanks to Tracey Cheetham, Charlotte Howells and to Milly Ivanovic for her patient, continuing contact.

I would like to acknowledge the following people whose friendship has assisted me in my writing year: John and June Riggall, Kevin Jones OAM and Family, John Wong, Dr Louis and Christine Trichard, Rod Henshaw, Betty Irons OAM, Bob Mansfield, Larry Gilles, Nerida Marshall, Mick and Andrea Prowse, Rea Francis, John Carroll, Chuck and Jan Digney, Dan Frogan, Ty Mckee, Kaz and family. Rod and Brett Hardy, Peter and Kaye Lowe, Kristie Hildebrand, Rod Pratt and all at my Gulmarrad Rural Fire Service Brigade. To Ken and Barb at *The Outback City Express* for years of support and also Lynne Mowbray in our local media.

I also extend thanks to all members of the NSW RFS who I had the honour of serving beside for the seven months we were active in the fire season of 2019/20.

This is also a chance to recognise my contact with my mates in the Northern Rivers Retired Police Association and the 1/19 Royal New South Wales Regimental Association.

A recognition of the bond between authors extends to my mates, Dave Sabben MG, Greg Barron, Simon Higgins and my old cobber, Tony Park.

Not least to my family of Tom Watt, Tim Payne, Virginia Wolfe and the Duffy Clan. Also my sister, Lindy, and brother-in-law, Jock.

Last but not least, I want to acknowledge the important role that my Aunt Joan Payne has played in my life. My Aunt Joan is a veteran of WWII who served with the Women's Royal Australian Auxiliary Air Force – the last of her generation in my family.

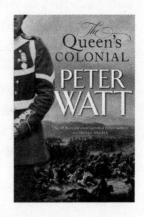

The Queen's Tiger
Peter Watt

Peter Watt brings to the fore all the passion, adventure and white-knuckle battle scenes that made his beloved Duffy and Macintosh novels so popular.

It is 1857. Colonial India is a simmering volcano of nationalism about to erupt. Army surgeon Peter Campbell and his wife Alice, in India on their honeymoon, have no idea that they are about to be swept up in the chaos.

Ian Steele, known to all as Captain Samuel Forbes, is fighting for Queen and country in Persia. A world away, the real Samuel Forbes is planning to return to London – with potentially disastrous consequences for Samuel and Ian both.

Then Ian is posted to India, but not before a brief return to England and a reunion with the woman he loves. In India he renews his friendship with Peter Campbell, and discovers that Alice has taken on a most unlikely role. Together they face the enemy and the terrible deprivations and savagery of war – and then Ian receives news from London that crushes all his hopes . . .

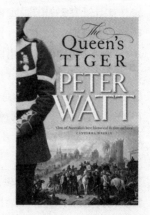

'**Watt has a true knack for producing captivating historical adventures filled with action, intrigue and family drama**'
Canberra Weekly